Nora Roberts & J. D. Robb

Remember When

J. D. Robb

Anthologies

FROM THE HEART
A LITTLE MAGIC
A LITTLE FATE

MOON SHADOWS
(with Jill Gregory, Ruth Ryan Langan, and Marianne Willman)

The Once Upon Series
(with Jill Gregory, Ruth Ryan Langan, and Marianne Willman)
ONCE UPON A CASTLE
ONCE UPON A STAR
ONCE UPON A DREAM
ONCE UPON A ROSE
ONCE UPON A KISS
ONCE UPON A MIDNIGHT

* * *

SILENT NIGHT
(with Susan Plunkett, Dee Holmes, and Claire Cross)

OUT OF THIS WORLD
(with Laurell K. Hamilton, Susan Krinard, and Maggie Shayne)

BUMP IN THE NIGHT
(with Mary Blayney, Ruth Ryan Langan, and Mary Kay McComas)

DEAD OF NIGHT
(with Mary Blayney, Ruth Ryan Langan, and Mary Kay McComas)

THREE IN DEATH

SUITE 606
(with Mary Blayney, Ruth Ryan Langan, and Mary Kay McComas)

Also available . . .

THE OFFICIAL NORA ROBERTS COMPANION
(edited by Denise Little and Laura Hayden)

#1 *New York Times* bestselling author
Nora Roberts
returns to Chesapeake Bay
and her beloved Quinn family for the story of
Seth Quinn, the long-awaited conclusion
to the breathtaking saga . . .

CHESAPEAKE BLUE

"After a five-year absence, Seth Quinn has returned home from Europe a world-renowned artist. He's ready to settle down in the same picturesque town on the Bay where the three stepbrothers who raised him now live. Soon, Seth meets beautiful, independent Drusilla Whitcomb Banks and falls in love with her almost immediately. Life takes on an idyllic glow—until someone from his past begins blackmailing him . . . A poignant and often humorous tale . . . guaranteed to please the many fans who were waiting for Seth's story . . . Excellent."   —*Library Journal*

"Roberts, a huge name in the romance genre, delivers . . . luscious prose . . . a touch of the supernatural, and plenty of toe-curling sex."   —*The Boston Globe*

"Thank you, thank you, thank you, Ms. Roberts. Four years after Nora Roberts introduced her fans to the Quinns in one of her many and much-loved trilogies, she treats us to another visit to St. Christopher . . . Roberts gives her fans what she does best, reviving old characters and blending in new. This is a wonderful gift."   —*The Columbia State* (SC)

"A welcome crescendo to the story-symphony that is the family Quinn in all its boisterous, loving resonance."
—*BookPage*

Turn the page for a complete list of titles by
Nora Roberts and J. D. Robb
from The Berkley Publishing Group . . .

NORA ROBERTS

CHESAPEAKE BLUE

JOVE BOOKS, NEW YORK

THE BERKLEY PUBLISHING GROUP
Published by the Penguin Group
Penguin Group (USA) Inc.
375 Hudson Street, New York, New York 10014, USA
Penguin Group (Canada), 90 Eglinton Avenue East, Suite 700, Toronto, Ontario M4P 2Y3, Canada
(a division of Pearson Penguin Canada Inc.)
Penguin Books Ltd., 80 Strand, London WC2R 0RL, England
Penguin Group Ireland, 25 St. Stephen's Green, Dublin 2, Ireland (a division of Penguin Books Ltd.)
Penguin Group (Australia), 250 Camberwell Road, Camberwell, Victoria 3124, Australia
(a division of Pearson Australia Group Pty. Ltd.)
Penguin Books India Pvt. Ltd., 11 Community Centre, Panchsheel Park, New Delhi—110 017, India
Penguin Group (NZ), Cnr. Airborne and Rosedale Roads, Albany, Auckland 1310, New Zealand
(a division of Pearson New Zealand Ltd.)
Penguin Books (South Africa) (Pty.) Ltd., 24 Sturdee Avenue, Rosebank, Johannesburg 2196,
South Africa

Penguin Books Ltd., Registered Offices: 80 Strand, London WC2R 0RL, England

This is a work of fiction. Names, characters, places, and incidents either are the product of the author's imagination or are used fictitiously, and any resemblance to actual persons, living or dead, business establishments, events, or locales is entirely coincidental. The publisher does not have any control over and does not assume any responsibility for author or third-party websites or their content.

CHESAPEAKE BLUE

A Jove Book / published by arrangement with the author

PRINTING HISTORY
G. P. Putnam's Sons hardcover edition / December 2002
Jove international edition / June 2003
Jove mass-market edition / February 2004

Copyright © 2002 by Nora Roberts.
Excerpt from *Naked in Death* by J. D. Robb copyright © 1995 by Nora Roberts.
Cover design and imaging by Honi Werner.
Stepback art by Steve Ferlauto.

ISBN: 978-0-515-13626-5

JOVE®
Jove Books are published by The Berkley Publishing Group,
a division of Penguin Group (USA) Inc.,
375 Hudson Street, New York, New York 10014.
JOVE and the "J" design are trademarks belonging to Penguin Group (USA) Inc.

PRINTED IN THE UNITED STATES OF AMERICA

11 10 9 8 7 6 5

TO EVERY READER WHO EVER ASKED

When are you going to
tell Seth's story?

There is a destiny that makes us brothers;
None goes his way alone:
All that we send into the lives of others
Comes back into our own.

EDWIN MARKHAM

Art is the accomplice of love.

RÉMY DE GOURMONT

ONE

⌐──⌐

H E WAS COMING home.
Maryland's Eastern Shore was a world of marshes
and mudflats, of wide fields with row crops straight as sol-
diers. It was flatland rivers with sharp shoulders, and secret
tidal creeks where the heron fed.

It was blue crab and the Bay, and the watermen who har-
vested them.

No matter where he'd lived, in the first miserable decade
of his life, or in the last few years as he approached the end
of his third decade, only the Shore had ever meant home.

There were countless aspects, countless memories of that
home, and every one was as bright and brilliant in his mind
as the sun that sparkled off the water of the Chesapeake.

As he drove across the bridge, his artist's eye wanted to
capture that moment—the rich blue water and the boats
that skimmed its surface, the quick white waves and the
swoop of greedy gulls. The way the land skimmed its edge,
and spilled back with its browns and greens. All the thick-

ening leaves of the gum and oak trees, with those flashes of color that were flowers basking in the warmth of spring.

He wanted to remember this moment just as he remembered the first time he'd crossed the Bay to the Eastern Shore, a surly, frightened boy beside a man who'd promised him a life.

HE'D sat in the passenger seat of the car, with the man he hardly knew at the wheel. He had the clothes on his back, and a few meager possessions in a paper sack.

His stomach had been tight with nerves, but he'd fixed what he thought was a bored look on his face and had stared out the window.

If he was with the old guy, he wasn't with *her*. That was as good a deal as he could get.

Besides, the old guy was pretty cool.

He didn't stink of booze or of the mints some of the assholes Gloria brought up to the dump they were living in used to cover it up. And the couple of times they'd been together, the old guy, Ray, had bought him a burger or pizza.

And he'd talked to him.

Adults, in his experience, didn't talk to kids. At them, around them, over them. But not to them.

Ray did. Listened, too. And when he'd asked, straight out, if he—just a kid—wanted to live with him, he hadn't felt that strangling fear or hot panic. He'd felt like maybe, just maybe, he was catching a break.

Away from her. That was the best part. The longer they drove, the farther away from her.

If things got sticky, he could run. The guy was really old. Big, he was sure as shit big, but old. All that white hair, and that wide, wrinkled face.

He took quick, sidelong glances at it, began to draw the face in his mind.

His eyes were really blue, and that was kind of weird because so were his own.

He had a big voice, too, but when he talked it wasn't like yelling. It was kind of calm, even a little tired, maybe.

He sure looked tired now.

"Almost home," Ray said as they approached the bridge. "Hungry?"

"I dunno. Yeah, I guess."

"My experience, boys are always hungry. Raised three bottomless pits."

There was cheer in the big voice, but it was forced. The child might have been barely ten, but he knew the tone of falsehood.

Far enough away now, he thought. If he had to run. So he'd put the cards on the table and see what the fuck was what.

"How come you're taking me to your place?"

"Because you need a place."

"Get real. People don't do shit like that."

"Some do. Stella and I, my wife, we did shit like that."

"You tell her you're bringing me around?"

Ray smiled, but there was a sadness in it. "In my way. She died some time back. You'd've liked her. And she'd have taken one look at you and rolled up her sleeves."

He didn't know what to say about that. "What am I supposed to do when we get where we're going?"

"Live," Ray told him. "Be a boy. Go to school, get in trouble. I'll teach you to sail."

"On a boat?"

Now Ray laughed, a big booming sound that filled the car and for reasons the boy couldn't understand, untied the nerves in his belly. "Yeah, on a boat. Got a brainless puppy—I always get the brainless ones—I'm trying to housebreak. You can help me with that. You're gonna have chores, we'll figure that out. We'll lay down the rules, and you'll follow them. Don't think because I'm an old man I'm a pushover."

"You gave her money."

Ray glanced away from the road briefly and looked into eyes the same color as his own. "That's right. That's what she understands, from what I can see. She never understood you, did she, boy?"

Something was gathering inside him, a storm he didn't recognize as hope. "If you get pissed off at me, or tired of having me around, or just change your mind, you'll send me back. I won't go back."

They were over the bridge now, and Ray pulled the car to the shoulder of the road, shifted his bulk in the seat so they were face-to-face. "I'll get pissed off at you, and at my age I'm bound to get tired from time to time. But I'm making you a promise here and now, I'm giving you my word. I won't send you back."

"If she—"

"I won't let her take you back," Ray said, anticipating him. "No matter what I have to do. You're mine now. You're my family now. And you'll stay with me as long as that's what you want. A Quinn makes a promise," he added, and held out a hand, "he keeps it."

Seth looked at the offered hand, and his own sprang damp. "I don't like being touched."

Ray nodded. "Okay. But you've still got my word on it." He pulled back onto the road again, gave the boy one last glance. "Almost home," he said again.

Within months, Ray Quinn had died, but he'd kept his

word. He'd kept it through the three men he'd made his sons. Those men had given the scrawny, suspicious and scarred young boy a life.

They had given him a home, and made him a man.

Cameron, the edgy, quick-tempered gypsy; Ethan, the patient, steady waterman; Phillip, the elegant, sharp-minded executive. They had stood for him, fought for him. They had saved him.

His brothers.

THE gilded light of the late-afternoon sun sheened the marsh grass, the mudflats, the flat fields of row crops. With the windows down he caught the scent of water as he by-passed the little town of St. Christopher.

He'd considered swinging into town, heading first to the old brick boatyard. Boats by Quinn still custom made wooden boats, and in the eighteen years since the enter-prise had started—on a dream, on guile, on sweat—it had earned its reputation for quality and craftsmanship.

They were probably there, even now. Cam cursing as he finished up some fancywork in a cabin. Ethan quietly lap-ping boards. Phil, up in the office conjuring up some snazzy ad campaign.

He could go by Crawford's, pick up a six-pack. Maybe they'd have a cold one, or more likely Cam would toss him a hammer and tell him to get his ass back to work.

He'd enjoy that, but it wasn't what was drawing him now. It wasn't what was pulling him down the narrow country road where the marsh still crept out of the shadows and the trees with their gnarled trunks spread leaves glossy with May.

Of all the places he'd seen—the great domes and spires

of Florence, the florid beauty of Paris, the stunning green hills of Ireland—nothing ever caught at his throat, filled up his heart, like the old white house with its soft and faded blue trim that sat on a bumpy lawn that slid back into quiet water.

He pulled in the drive, behind the old white 'Vette that had been Ray and Stella Quinn's. The car looked as pristine as the day it had rolled off the showroom floor. Cam's doing, he thought. Cam would say it was a matter of showing proper respect for an exceptional machine. But it was all about Ray and Stella, all about family. All about love.

The lilac in the front yard was smothered with blooms. That was a matter of love, too, he reflected. He'd given Anna the little bush for Mother's Day when he was twelve.

She'd cried, he remembered. Big, beautiful brown eyes flooded with tears, laughing and swiping at them the whole time he and Cam planted it for her.

She was Cam's wife, and so that made Anna his sister. But inside, he thought now, where it counted, she was his mother.

The Quinns knew all about what was inside.

He got out of the car, into the lovely stillness. He was no longer a scrawny boy with oversized feet and a suspicious eye.

He'd grown into those feet. He was six-one with a wiry build. One that could go gawky if he neglected it. His hair had darkened and was more a bronzed brown than the sandy mop of his youth. He tended to neglect that as well and, running a hand through it now, winced as he recalled his intention to have it trimmed before leaving Rome.

The guys were going to rag on him about the little ponytail, which meant he'd have to keep it for a while, out of principle.

He shrugged and, dipping his hands into the pockets of his worn jeans, began to walk, scanning the surroundings. Anna's flowers, the rockers on the front porch, the woods that haunted the side of the house and where he'd run wild as a boy.

The old dock swaying over the water, and the white sailing sloop moored to it.

He stood looking out, his face, hollow-cheeked and tanned, turned toward the water.

His lips, firm and full, began to curve. The weight he hadn't realized was hanging from his heart began to lift.

At the sound of a rustle in the woods, he turned, enough of the wary boy still in the man to make the move swift and defensive. Out of the trees shot a black bullet.

"Witless!" His voice had both the ring of authority and easy humor. The combination had the dog skidding to a halt, all flopping ears and lolling tongue as it studied the man.

"Come on, it hasn't been that long." He crouched, held out a hand. "Remember me?"

Witless grinned the dopey grin that had named him, instantly flopped down and rolled to expose his belly for a rub.

"There you go. That's the way."

There had always been a dog for this house. Always a boat at the dock, a rocker on the porch and a dog in the yard.

"Yeah, you remember me." As he stroked Witless, he looked over to the far end of the yard where Anna had planted a hydrangea over the grave of his own dog. The loyal and much-loved Foolish.

"I'm Seth," he murmured. "I've been away too long."

He caught the sound of an engine, the sassy squeal of

tires from a turn taken just a hair faster than the law allowed. Even as he straightened, the dog leaped up, streaked away toward the front of the house.

Wanting to savor the moment, Seth followed more slowly. He listened to the car door slam, then to the lift and lilt of her voice as she spoke to the dog.

Then he just looked at her, Anna Spinelli Quinn, with the curling mass of dark hair windblown from the drive, her arms full of the bags she'd hefted out of the car.

His grin spread as she tried to ward off the desperate affection from the dog.

"How many times do we have to go over this one, simple rule?" she demanded. "You do not jump on people, especially me. Especially me when I'm wearing a suit."

"Great suit," Seth called out. "Better legs."

Her head whipped up, those deep brown eyes widened and showed him the shock, the pleasure, the welcome all in one glance.

"Oh my God!" Heedless of the contents, she tossed the bags through the open car door. And ran.

He caught her, lifted her six inches off the ground and spun her around before setting her on her feet again. Still he didn't let go. Instead, he just buried his face in her hair.

"Hi."

"Seth. Seth." She clung, ignoring the dog that leaped and yipped and did his best to shove his muzzle between them. "I can't believe it. You're here."

"Don't cry."

"Just a little. I have to look at you." She had his face framed in her hands as she eased back. So handsome, she thought. So grown-up. "Look at all this," she murmured and brushed a hand at his hair.

"I meant to get some of it whacked off."

"I like it." Tears still trickled even as she grinned. "Very bohemian. You look wonderful. Absolutely wonderful."

"You're the most beautiful woman in the world."

"Oh boy." She sniffled, shook her head. "That's no way to get me to stop all this." She swiped at tears. "When did you get here? I thought you were in Rome."

"I was. I wanted to be here."

"If you'd called, we would've met you."

"I wanted to surprise you." He walked to the car to pull the bags out for her. "Cam at the boatyard?"

"Should be. Here, I'll get those. You need to get your things."

"I'll get them later. Where's Kevin and Jake?"

She started up the walk with him, glanced at her watch as she thought about her sons. "What day is this? My mind's still spinning."

"Thursday."

"Ah, Kevin has rehearsal, school play, and Jake's got softball practice. Kevin's got his driver's license, God help us, and is scooping up his brother on his way home." She unlocked the front door. "They should be along in an hour, then peace will no longer lie across the land."

It was the same, Seth thought. It didn't matter what color the walls were painted or if the old sofa had been replaced, if a new lamp stood on the table. It was the same because it *felt* the same.

The dog snaked around his legs and made a beeline for the kitchen.

"I want you to sit down." She nodded to the kitchen table, under which Witless was sprawled, happily gnawing on a hunk of rope. "And tell me everything. You want some wine?"

"Sure, after I help you put this stuff away." When her

eyebrows shot up, he paused with a gallon of milk in his hand. "What?"

"I was just remembering the way everyone, including you, disappeared whenever it was time to put groceries away."

"Because you always said we put things in the wrong place."

"You always did, on purpose so I'd kick you out of the kitchen."

"You copped to that, huh?"

"I cop to everything when it comes to my guys. Nothing gets by me, pal. Did something happen in Rome?"

"No." He continued to unpack the bags. He knew where everything went, where everything had always gone in Anna's kitchen. "I'm not in trouble, Anna."

But you are troubled, she thought, and let it go for now. "I'm going to open a nice Italian white. We'll have a glass and you can tell me all the wonderful things you've been doing. It seems like years since we've talked face-to-face."

He shut the refrigerator and turned to her. "I'm sorry I didn't get home for Christmas."

"Honey, we understood. You had a showing in January. We're all so proud of you, Seth. Cam must've bought a hundred copies of the issue of the *Smithsonian* magazine when they did the article on you. The young American artist who's seduced Europe."

He shrugged a shoulder, such an innately Quinn gesture, she grinned. "So sit," she ordered.

"I'll sit, but I'd rather you caught me up. How the hell is everyone? What're they doing? You first."

"All right." She finished opening the bottle, got out two glasses. "I'm doing more administrative work these days than casework. Social work involves a lot of paperwork, but it's not as satisfying. Between that and having two teenagers in the house, there's no time to be bored. The boat business is thriving."

She sat, passed Seth his glass. "Aubrey's working there."

"No kidding?" The thought of her, the girl who was more sister to him than any blood kin, made him smile. "How's she doing?"

"Terrific. She's beautiful, smart, stubborn and, according to Cam, a genius with wood. I think Grace was a little disappointed when Aubrey didn't want to pursue dancing, but it's hard to argue when you see your child so happy. And Grace and Ethan's Emily followed in her mother's toe shoes."

"She still heading to New York end of August?"

"A chance to dance with the American Ballet Company doesn't come along every day. She's grabbing it, and she swears she'll be principal before she's twenty. Deke's his father's son—quiet, clever and happiest when he's out on the water. Sweetie, do you want a snack?"

"No." He reached out, laid a hand over hers. "Keep going."

"Okay, then. Phillip remains the business's marketing and promotion guru. I don't think any of us, including Phil, ever thought he'd leave the ad firm in Baltimore, give up urban living and dig down in Saint Chris. But it's been, what, fourteen years, so I don't suppose we can call it a whim. Of course he and Sybill keep the apartment in New York. She's working on a new book."

"Yeah, I talked to her." He rubbed the dog's head with his foot. "Something about the evolution of community in cyberspace. She's something. How are the kids?"

"Insane, as any self-respecting teenager should be. Bram was madly in love with a girl named Cloe last week.

That could be over by now. Fiona's interests are torn between boys and shopping. But, well, she's fourteen, so that's natural."

"Fourteen. Jesus. She hadn't had her tenth birthday when I left for Europe. Even seeing them on and off over the last few years, it doesn't seem . . . it doesn't seem possible that Kevin's driving, and Aub's building boats. Bram's sniffing after girls. I remember—" He cut himself off, shook his head.

"What?"

"I remember when Grace was pregnant with Emily. It was the first time I was around someone who was having a baby—well, someone who wanted to. It seems like five minutes ago, and now Emily's going to New York. How can eighteen years go by, Anna, and you not look any older?"

"Oh, I've missed you." She laughed and squeezed his hand.

"I've missed you, too. All of you."

"We'll fix that. We'll round everybody up and have a big, noisy Quinn welcome-home on Sunday. How does that sound?"

"About as perfect as it gets."

The dog yipped, then scrambled out from under the table to run toward the front door.

"Cameron," Anna said. "Go on out and meet him."

He walked through the house, as he had so often. Opened the screen door, as he had so often. And looked at the man standing on the front lawn, playing tug-of-war with the dog over a hunk of rope.

He was still tall, still built like a sprinter. There were glints of silver in his hair now. He had the sleeves of his work shirt rolled up to the elbows, and his jeans were white at the stress points. He wore sunglasses and badly beaten Nikes.

At fifty, Cameron Quinn still looked like a badass.

In lieu of greeting, Seth let the screen door slam behind him. Cameron glanced over, and the only sign of surprise was his fingers sliding off the rope.

A thousand words passed between them without a sound. A million feelings, and countless memories. Saying nothing, Seth came down the steps as Cameron crossed the lawn. Then they stood, face-to-face.

"I hope that piece of shit in the driveway's a rental," Cameron began.

"Yeah, it is. Best I could do on short notice. Figured I'd turn it in tomorrow, then use the 'Vette for a while."

Cameron's smile was sharp as a blade. "In your dreams, pal. In your wildest dreams."

"No point in it sitting there going to waste."

"Less of one to let some half-assed painter with delusions of grandeur behind its classic wheel."

"Hey, you're the one who taught me to drive."

"Tried to. A ninety-year-old woman with a broken arm could handle a five-speed better than you." He jerked his head toward Seth's rental. "That embarrassment in my driveway doesn't inspire the confidence in me that you've improved in that area."

Smug now, Seth rocked back on his heels. "Test-drove a Maserati a couple of months ago."

Cam's eyebrows winged up. "Get out of here."

"Had her up to a hundred and ten. Scared the living shit out of me."

Cam laughed, gave Seth an affectionate punch on the

arm. Then he sighed. "Son of a bitch. Son of a bitch," he said again as he dragged Seth into a fierce hug. "Why the hell didn't you let us know you were coming home?"

"It was sort of spur-of-the-moment," Seth began. "I wanted to be here. I just needed to be here."

"Okay. Anna burning up the phone lines letting everybody know we're serving fatted calf?"

"Probably. She said we'd have the calf on Sunday."

"That'll work. You settled in yet?"

"No. I got stuff in the car."

"Don't call that butt-ugly thing a car. Let's get your gear."

"Cam." Seth reached out, touched Cam's arm. "I want to come home. Not just for a few days or a couple weeks. I want to stay. Can I stay?"

Cam drew off his sunglasses, and his eyes, smoke-gray, met Seth's. "What the hell's the matter with you that you think you have to ask? You trying to piss me off?"

"I never had to try, nobody does with you. Anyway, I'll pull my weight."

"You always pulled your weight. And we missed seeing your ugly face around here."

And that, Seth thought as they walked to the car, was all the welcome he needed from Cameron Quinn.

THEY'D kept his room. It had changed over the years, different paint for the walls, a new rug for the floor. But the bed was the same one he'd slept in, dreamed in, waked in.

The same bed he'd sneaked Foolish into when he'd been a child.

And the one he'd sneaked Alice Albert into when he'd thought he was a man.

He figured Cam knew about Foolish, and had often wondered if he'd known about Alice.

He tossed his suitcases carelessly on the bed and laid his battered paint kit—one Sybill had given him for his eleventh birthday—on the worktable Ethan had built.

He'd need to find studio space, he thought. Eventually. As long as the weather held, he could work outdoors. He preferred that anyway. But he'd need somewhere to store his canvases, his equipment. Maybe there was room in the old barn of a boatyard, but that wouldn't suit on a permanent basis.

And he meant to make this permanent.

He'd had enough of traveling for now, enough of living among strangers to last him a lifetime.

He'd needed to go, to stand on his own. He'd needed to learn. And God, he'd needed to paint.

So he'd studied in Florence, and worked in Paris. He'd wandered the hills of Ireland and Scotland and had stood on the cliffs in Cornwall.

He'd lived cheap and rough most of the time. When there'd been a choice between buying a meal or paint, he'd gone hungry.

He'd been hungry before. It had done him good, he hoped, to remember what it was like not to have someone making sure you were fed and safe and warm.

It was the Quinn in him, he supposed, that made him hell-bent to beat his own path.

He laid out his sketch pad, put away his charcoal, his pencils. He would spend time getting back to basics with his work before he picked up a brush again.

The walls of his room held some of his early drawings. Cam had taught him how to make the frames on an old miter box at the boatyard. Seth took one from the wall to study it. It showed promise, he thought, in the rough, undisciplined lines.

But more, much more, it showed the promise of a life.

He'd caught them well enough, he decided. Cam, with his thumbs tucked in his pockets, stance confrontational. Then Phillip, slick, edging toward an elegance that nearly disguised the street smarts. Ethan, patient, steady as a redwood in his work clothes.

He'd drawn himself with them. Seth at ten, he thought. Thin, narrow shoulders and big feet, with a lift to his chin to mask something more painful than fear.

Something that was hope.

A life moment, Seth thought now, captured with a graphite pencil. Drawing it, he'd begun to believe, in-the-gut believe, that he was one of them.

A Quinn.

"You mess with one Quinn," he murmured as he hung the drawing on the wall again, "you mess with them all."

He turned, glanced at the suitcases and wondered if he could sweet-talk Anna into unpacking for him.

Not a chance.

"Hey."

He looked toward the doorway and brightened when he saw Kevin. If he had to fiddle with clothes, as least he'd have company. "Hey, Kev."

"So, you really hanging this time? For good?"

"Looks like."

"Cool." Kevin sauntered in, plopped on the bed and propped his feet on one of the suitcases. "Mom's really jazzed about it. Around here, if Mom's happy, everybody's happy. She could be soft enough to let me use her car this weekend."

"Glad I can help." He shoved Kevin's feet off the suitcase, then unzipped it.

He had the look of his mother, Seth thought. Dark, curling hair, big Italian eyes. Seth imagined the girls were already tumbling for him like bowling pins.

"How's the play?"

"It rocks. Totally rocks. *West Side Story.* I'm Tony. When you're a Jet, man."

"You stay a Jet." Seth dumped shirts haphazardly in a drawer. "You get killed, right?"

"Yeah." Kevin clutched his heart, shuddered with his face filled with pain and rapture. Then slumped. "It's great, and before I do the death thing, we've got this kick-ass fight scene. Show's next week. You're gonna come, right?"

"Front row center, pal."

"Check out Lisa Maxdon, she plays Maria. Total babe. We've got a couple of love scenes together. We've been doing a lot of practicing," he added and winked.

"Anything for art."

"Yeah." Kevin scooted up a little. "Okay, so tell me about all the Euro chicks. Pretty hot, huh?"

"The only way to get burned. There was this girl in Rome. Anna-Theresa."

"A two-named girl." Kevin shook his fingers as if he'd gotten them too close to a flame. "Two-named girls are way sexy."

"Tell me. She worked in this little trattoria. And the way she served pasta al pomodoro was just amazing."

"So? Did you score?"

Seth sent Kevin a pitying look. "Please, who're you talking to here?" He dumped jeans in another drawer. "She had hair all the way down to her ass, and a very fine ass it was.

Eyes like melted chocolate and a mouth that wouldn't quit."

"Did you draw her naked?"

"I did about a dozen figure studies. She was a natural. Totally relaxed, completely uninhibited."

"Man, you're killing me."

"And she had the most amazing . . ." Seth paused, his hands up to chest level to demonstrate. "Personality," he said, dropping his hands. "Hi, Anna."

"Discussing art?" she said dryly. "It's so nice of you to share some of your cultural experiences with Kevin."

"Um. Well." The killing smile she was aiming in his direction had always made Seth's tongue wither. Instead of trying to use it, he fell back on an innocent grin.

"But tonight's session on art and culture is now over. Kevin, I believe you have homework."

"Right. I'll get right to it." Seeing his history assignment as an escape hatch, Kevin bolted.

Anna stepped into the room. "Do you think," she asked Seth pleasantly, "that the young woman in question would appreciate being whittled down to a pair of breasts?"

"Ah . . . I also mentioned her eyes. They were nearly as fabulous as yours."

Anna took a shirt out of the open drawer, folded it neatly. "Do you think that's going to work with me?"

"No. Begging might. Please don't hurt me. I just got home."

She took out another shirt, folded it. "Kevin's sixteen, and I'm perfectly aware his major interest at this time is naked breasts and his fervent desire to get his hands on as many as possible."

Seth winced. "Jeez, Anna."

"I am also aware," she continued without breaking

stride, "that this predilection—while hopefully becoming more civilized and controlled—remains deep-seated in the male species throughout its natural life."

"Hey, you want to see some of my landscape sketches from Tuscany?"

"I am surrounded by you." Sighing a little, she took out yet another shirt. "Outnumbered, and have been since I walked into this house. That doesn't mean I can't knock every one of your stupid heads together when necessary. Understood?"

"Yes, ma'am."

"Good. Show me your landscapes."

LATER, when the house was quiet and the moon rode over the water, she found Cam on the back porch. She stepped out, and into him.

He wrapped an arm around her, rubbing her shoulder against the night's chill. "Settle everyone down?"

"That's what I do. Chilly tonight." She glanced up at the sky, at the ice points of stars. "I hope it stays clear for Sunday." Then she simply turned her face into his chest. "Oh, Cam."

"I know." He stroked a hand over her hair, rubbed his cheek against it.

"To see him sitting at the kitchen table. Watching him wrestling with Jake and that idiot dog. Even hearing him talking about naked women with Kevin—"

"What naked women?"

She laughed, shook back her hair as she looked at him. "No one you know. It's so good to have him home."

"I told you he'd come back. Quinns always come back to the roost."

"I guess you're right." She kissed him, one long, warm meeting of lips. "Why don't we go upstairs?" She slid her hands down, gave his butt a suggestive squeeze. "And I'll settle you down, too."

TWO

⁓

R ISE AND SHINE, pal. This ain't no flophouse."
The voice, and the gleeful sadism behind it, had
Seth groaning. He flopped onto his stomach, dragged the
pillow over his head. "Go away. Go far, far away."

"If you think you're going to spend your days around
here sleeping till the crack of noon, think again." With rel-
ish, Cam yanked the pillow away. "Up."

Seth opened one eye, rolled it until he focused on the
bedside clock. It wasn't yet seven. He turned his face back
into the mattress and mumbled a rude suggestion in Italian.

"If you think I've lived with Spinelli all these years and
don't know that means 'kiss my ass,' you're stupid as well
as lazy."

To solve the problem, Cam ripped the sheets away,
snagged Seth's ankles and dragged him to the floor.

"Shit. *Shit!*" Naked, his elbow singing where it had
cracked the table, Seth glared up at his persecutor. "What

the hell's with you? This is my room, my bed, and I'm trying to sleep in it."

"Put some clothes on. I've got something for you to do out back."

"Goddamn it, you could give a guy twenty-four hours before you start on him."

"Kid, I started on you when you were ten, and I'm not close to being finished. I've got work, so let's get moving."

"Cam." Anna strode to the doorway, hands on hips. "I told you to wake him up, not knock him down."

"Jesus." Mortified, Seth tore the sheet out of Cam's hands and clutched it around his waist. "Jesus, Anna, I'm naked here."

"Then get dressed," she suggested, and walked away.

"Out back," Cam told him as he strode from the room. "Five minutes."

"Yeah, yeah, yeah."

Some things never changed, Seth thought as he yanked on jeans. He could be sixty living in this house, and Cam would still roust him out of bed like he was twelve.

He snagged what was left of a University of Maryland sweatshirt and dragged it over his head as he stalked from the room.

If there wasn't coffee, hot and fresh, somebody was going to get their ass seriously kicked.

"Mom! I can't find my shoes!"

Seth glanced toward Jake's room as he headed for the stairs.

"They're down here," Anna called back. "In the middle of my kitchen floor, where they don't belong."

"Not *those* shoes. Jeez, Mom. The *other* shoes."

"Try looking up your butt," came the carefully modulated suggestion from Kevin's room. "Your head's already up there."

"No problem finding your butt," was the hissed response. "Since you wear it right on your shoulders."

Such familiar family dynamics would have made Seth smile—if it hadn't been shy of seven A.M. If his elbow hadn't been throbbing like a bitch. If he had had a hit of caffeine.

"Neither one of you could find your butts with your own hands," he grumbled as he sulked down the steps.

"What the hell's up with Cam?" he demanded of Anna when he stalked into the kitchen. "Is there any coffee? Why does everybody wake up yelling around here?"

"Cam needs to see you outside. Yes, there's a half pot left, and everyone wakes up yelling because it's how we like to greet the day." She poured coffee into a thick white mug. "You're on your own for breakfast. I have an early meeting. Don't pout, Seth. I'll bring home ice cream."

The day began to look marginally brighter. "Rocky Road?"

"Rocky Road. Jake! Get these shoes out of my kitchen before I feed them to the dog. Go outside, Seth, or you'll spoil Cam's sunny mood."

"Yeah, he looked real chipper when he yanked me out of bed." Stewing over it, Seth walked out the kitchen door.

There they were, almost as Seth had drawn them so many years before. Cam, thumbs in pockets, Phillip, slicked up in a suit, Ethan, with a faded gimme cap over his windblown hair.

Seth swallowed coffee, and the heart that had lodged in his throat. "This is what you dragged me out of bed for?"

"Same smart mouth." Phillip caught him in a hug. His

eyes, nearly the same tawny gold as his hair, skimmed over Seth's ragged shirt and jeans. "Christ, kid, didn't I teach you anything?" With a shake of his head, he fingered the dull-gray sleeve. "Italy was obviously wasted on you."

"They're just clothes, Phil. You put them on so you don't get cold or arrested."

With a pained wince, Phillip stepped back. "Where did I go wrong?"

"Looks okay to me. Still a little scrawny. What's this?" Ethan tugged on Seth's hair. "Long as a girl's."

"He had it in a pretty little ponytail last night," Cam told him. "He looked real sweet."

"Up yours," Seth said, laughing.

"We'll get you a nice pink ribbon," Ethan said with a chuckle and grabbed Seth in a bear hug.

Phillip nipped the mug out of Seth's hand, took a sip. "We figured we'd come by and get a look at you before Sunday."

"It's good to see you. Really good to see you." Seth flicked a glance at Cam. "You could've said everyone was here instead of dumping me out of bed."

"More fun that way. Well." Cam rocked back on his heels.

"Well," Phillip agreed, and set the mug on the porch rail.

"Well." Ethan gave Seth's hair another tug. Then got an iron grip on his arm.

"What?"

Cam only grinned and locked a hold on his other arm. Seth didn't need the gleam in their eyes to understand.

"Come on. You're kidding, right?"

"It's got to be done." Before Seth could begin to struggle, Phillip scooped his legs out from under him. "It's not like you've got to worry about getting that snazzy outfit wet."

"Cut it out." Seth bucked, tried to kick as he was carried off the porch. "I mean it. That water's fucking cold."

"Probably sink like a stone," Ethan said mildly as they muscled Seth toward the dock. "Looks like living in Europe turned him into a wimp."

"Wimp, my ass." He fought against their hold, fought not to laugh. "Takes three of you to take me out. Bunch of feeble old men," he snarled. With grips, he thought, like steel.

That had Phillip's brow quirking. "How far do you think we can throw him?"

"Let's find out. One," Cam announced as they stood swinging him between them on the dock.

"I'll kill you." Swearing, laughing, Seth wiggled like a fish.

"Two," Phillip said with a grin. "Better save your breath, kid."

"Three. Welcome home, Seth," Ethan said as the three of them hurled him in the air.

He was right. The water was freezing. It stole the breath he hadn't bothered to save, chilled him right down to the bone. When he surfaced, spitting it out, shoving at his hair, he heard his brothers howling with delight, saw them ranged together on the dock with the early sun showering down and the old white house behind them.

I'm Seth Quinn, he thought. And I'm home.

THE early-morning dip went a long way toward purging any jet lag. Since he was up, Seth decided he might as well get things done. He drove back to Baltimore, turned in the rental, and after some wheeling and dealing at a dealership, drove toward the Shore the proud owner of a muscular Jaguar convertible in saber silver.

He knew it shouted: Officer, may I have a speeding ticket please! But he couldn't resist.

Selling his art was a two-edged sword. It sliced at his heart each time he parted with a painting. But he was selling very well and might as well reap some of the benefits.

His brothers, he thought smugly, were going to be green when they got a load of his new ride.

He cut back on his speed as he cruised into St. Chris. The little water town with its busy docks and quiet streets was another painting to him, one he'd re-created countless times, from countless angles.

Market Street with its shops and restaurants ran parallel to the dock, where crab pickers still set up tables on weekends to perform for the tourists. Watermen like Ethan would bring the day's catch there.

The town spread back with its old Victorian houses, its saltboxes and clapboards shaded by leafy trees. Lawns would be tidy. Neat, quaint, historic drew in the tourists, who would browse in the shops, eat in the restaurants, cozy up in one of the B and B's for a relaxing weekend at the Shore.

Locals learned to live with them, just as they learned to live with the gales that blew in from the Atlantic, and the droughts that sizzled their soybean fields. As they learned to live with the capricious Bay and her dwindling bounty.

He passed Crawford's and thought of sloppy submarine sandwiches, dripping ice cream cones and town gossip.

He'd ridden his bike on these streets, racing with Danny and Will McLean. He'd cruised with them in the second-hand Chevy he and Cam had fixed up the summer he turned sixteen.

And he'd sat—man and boy—at one of the umbrella tables while the town bustled by, trying to capture what it was about this single spot on the planet that shone so bright for him.

He wasn't sure he ever had, or ever would.

He eased into a parking space so he could walk down to the dock. He wanted to study the light, the shadows, the colors and shapes, and was already wishing he'd thought to bring a sketch pad.

It amazed him, constantly, how much beauty there was in the world. How it changed and it shifted even as he watched. The way the sun struck the water at one exact instant, how it spread or winked away behind a cloud.

Or there, he thought, the curve of that little girl's cheek when she lifted her face to look at a gull. The way her laugh shaped her mouth, or the way her fingers threaded through her mother's in absolute trust.

There was power in that.

He stood watching a white boat heel to in blue water, its sails snap full as they caught the wind.

He wanted to be out on the water again, he realized. Be part of it. Maybe he'd shanghai Aubrey for a few hours. He'd make a couple more stops, then swing by the boatyard and see if he could steal her.

Scanning the street, he started back for his car. A sign painted on a storefront caught his attention. *Bud and Bloom,* he read. Flower shop. That was new. He strolled closer, noting the festive pots hanging on either side of the glass.

The window itself was filled with plants and what he thought of as whatnots. Clever ones, though, Seth thought, finding himself amused by the spotted black-and-white cow with pansies flowing over its back.

In the lower right-hand corner of the window, written in the same ornate script, was: *Drusilla Whitcomb Banks, Proprietor.*

It wasn't a name he recognized, and since the painted script informed him the shop had been established in September of the previous year, he imagined some fussy widow, on the elderly side. White hair, he decided, starched dress with a prim floral print to go with sensible shoes and the half-glasses she wore on a gold chain around her neck.

She and her husband had come to St. Chris for long weekends, and when he'd died, she'd had too much money and time on her hands. So she'd moved here and opened her little flower shop so that she could be somewhere they'd been carefree together while doing something she'd secretly longed to do for years.

The story line made him like Mrs. Whitcomb Banks and her snobby cat—she'd *have* to have a cat—named Ernestine.

He decided to make her, and the many women in his life, happy. With flowers on his mind, Seth opened the door to the musical tinkle of bells.

The proprietor, he thought, had an artistic eye. It wasn't just the flowers—they were, after all, just the paint. She had daubed, splashed and streamed her paints very well. Flows of colors, a mix of shapes, a contrast of textures covered the canvas of her shop. It was tidy, just as he'd expected, but not regimented or formal.

He knew enough of flowers from the years of living with Anna to recognize how cleverly she'd paired hot-pink gerbera with rich blue delphiniums, snowy-white lilies with the elegance of red roses. Mixed in with those sweeps of color were the fans and spikes and tongues of green.

And the whimsy again, he noted, charmed. Cast-iron pigs, flute-playing frogs, wicked-faced gargoyles.

There were pots and vases, ribbons and lace, shallow dishes of herbs and thriving houseplants. He got the impression of cannily arranged clutter in a limited and well-used space.

Over it all were the fairy-tale notes of "Afternoon of a Faun."

Nice going, Mrs. Whitcomb Banks, he decided and prepared to spend lavishly.

The woman who stepped out of the rear door behind the long service counter wasn't Seth's image of the talented widow, but she sure as hell belonged in a fanciful garden.

He gave his widow extra points for hiring help who brought faeries and spellbound princesses to a man's mind.

"May I help you?"

"Oh yeah." Seth crossed to the counter and just looked at her.

Long, slim and tidy as a rose, he thought. Her hair was true black, cut close to follow the lovely shape of her head while leaving the elegant stem of her neck exposed. It was a look, he thought, that took considerable female guts and self-confidence.

It left her face completely unframed so that the delicate ivory of her skin formed a perfect oval canvas. The gods had been in a fine mood the day they'd created her, and had drawn her a pair of long, almond-shaped eyes of moss green, then added a nimbus of amber around her pupils.

Her nose was small and straight, her mouth wide to go

with the eyes, and very full. She'd tinted it a deep, seductive rose.

Her chin had the faintest cleft, as if her maker had given it a light finger brush of approval.

He would paint that face; there was no question about it. And the rest of her as well. He saw her lying on a bed of red rose petals, those faerie eyes glowing with sleepy power, those lips slightly curved, as if she'd just wakened from dreaming of a lover.

Her smile didn't waver as he studied her, but the dark wings of her eyebrows lifted. "And just what can I help you with?"

The voice was good, he mused. Strong and smooth. Not a local, he decided.

"We can start with flowers," he told her. "It's a great shop."

"Thanks. What sort of flowers did you have in mind today?"

"We'll get to that." He leaned on the counter. In St. Chris, there was always time for a little conversation. "Have you worked here long?"

"From the beginning. If you're thinking ahead to Mother's Day, I have some lovely—"

"No, I've got Mother's Day handled. You're not from around here. The accent," he explained when those brows lifted again. "Not Shore. A little north, maybe."

"Very good. D.C."

"So, the name of the shop. Bud and Bloom. Is that from Whistler?"

Surprise, and speculation, flickered over her face. "As a matter of fact, it is. You're the first to tag it."

"One of my brothers is big on stuff like that. I can't remember the quote exactly. Something about perfect in its bud as in its bloom."

" 'The masterpiece should appear as the flower to the painter—perfect in its bud as in its bloom.' "

"Yeah, that's it. I probably recognized it because that's what I do. I paint."

"Really?" She reminded herself to be patient, to relax into the rhythm. Part of the package in the little town was slow, winding conversations with strangers. She'd already sized him up. His face was vaguely familiar, and his eyes, a very striking blue, were frank and direct in their interest. She wouldn't stoop to flirtation, certainly not to make a sale, but she could be friendly.

She'd come to St. Chris to be friendly.

Because she imagined he painted houses, she sorted through her mind for an arrangement that would suit his budget. "Do you work locally?"

"I do now. I've been away. Do you work here alone?" He glanced around, calculating the amount of work that went into maintaining the garden she'd created. "Does the proprietor come in?"

"I work alone, for now. And I am the proprietor."

He looked back at her and began to laugh. "Boy, I wasn't even close. Nice to meet you, Drusilla Whitcomb Banks." He held out a hand. "I'm Seth Quinn."

Seth Quinn. She laid her hand in his automatically and did her own rapid readjustment. Not a face she'd seen around town, she realized, but one she'd seen in a magazine. No housepainter, despite the old jeans and faded shirt, but an artist. The local boy who'd become the toast of Europe.

"I admire your work," she told him.

"Thanks. I admire yours. And I'm probably keeping you from it. I'm going to make it worth your while. I've got some ladies to impress. You can help me out."

"Ladies? Plural?"

"Yeah. Three, no four," he corrected, thinking of Aubrey.

"It's a wonder you have time to paint, Mr. Quinn."

"Seth. I manage."

"I bet you do." Certain types of men always managed. "Cut flowers, arrangements or plants?"

"Ah . . . cut flowers, in a nice box. More romantic, right? Let me think." He calculated route and time, and decided he'd drop by to see Sybill first. "Number one is sophisticated, chic, intellectual and practical-minded, with a softgooey center. Roses, I guess."

"If you want to be predictable."

He looked back at Dru. "Let's be unpredictable."

"Just a moment. I have something in the back you should like."

Something out here I like, he thought as she turned toward the rear door. He gave his heart a little pat.

Phillip, Seth thought as he wandered the shop, would approve of the classic, clean lines of that ripening, peach-colored suit she wore. Ethan, he imagined, would wonder how to give her a hand with all the work that must go into running the place. And Cam . . . well, Cam would take one long look at her and grin.

Seth supposed he had bits of all three of them inside him.

She came back carrying an armload of streamlined and exotic flowers with waxy blooms the color of eggplant.

"Calla lilies," she told him. "Elegant, simple, classy and in this color spectacular."

"You nailed her."

She set them in a cone-shaped holding vase. "Next?"

"Warm, old-fashioned in the best possible way." Just thinking of Grace made him smile. "Simple in the same way. Sweet but not sappy, and with a spine of steel."

"Tulips," she said and walked to a clear-fronted, refrigerated cabinet. "In this rather tender pink. A quiet flower that's sturdier than it looks," she added as she brought them over for him to see.

"Bingo. You're good."

"Yes, I am." She was enjoying herself now—not just for the sale, but for the game of it. This was the reason she'd opened the shop. "Number three?"

Aubrey, he thought. How to describe Aubrey. "Young, fresh, fun. Tough and unstintingly loyal."

"Hold on." With the image in mind, Dru breezed into the back again. And came out with a clutch of sunflowers with faces as wide as a dessert plate.

"Jesus, they're perfect. You're in the right business, Drusilla."

It was, she thought, the finest of compliments. "No point in being in the wrong one. And since you're about to break my record for single walk-in sales, it's Dru."

"Nice."

"And the fourth lucky woman?"

"Bold, beautiful, smart and sexy. With a heart like . . ." Anna's heart, he thought. "With a heart beyond description. The most amazing woman I've ever known."

"And apparently you know quite a few. One minute." Again, she went into the back. He was admiring the sunflowers when Dru came back with Asiatic lilies in triumphant scarlet.

"Oh man. They're so Anna." He reached out to touch one of the vivid red petals. "So completely Anna. You've just made me a hero."

"Happy to oblige. I'll box them, and tie ribbons on each that coordinate with the color of the flowers inside. Can you keep them straight?"

"I think I can handle it."

"Cards are included. You can pick what you like from the rack on the counter."

"I won't need cards." He watched her fit water-filled nipples on the end of the stems. No wedding ring, he noted. He'd have painted her regardless, but if she'd been married it would have put an end to the rest of his plans.

"What flower are you?"

She flicked him a glance as she arranged the first flowers in a tissue-lined white box. "All of them. I like variety." She tied a deep purple ribbon around the first box. "As it appears you do."

"I kind of hate to shatter the illusion that I've got a harem going here. Sisters," he said, gesturing toward the flowers. "Though the sunflowers are niece, cousin, sister. The exact relationship's a little murky."

"Um-hm."

"My brothers' wives," he explained. "And one of my brothers' oldest daughter. I figured I should clear that up since I'm going to paint you."

"Are you?" She tied the second box with pink ribbon edged with white lace. "Are you really?"

He took out his credit card, laid it on the counter while she went to work on the sunflowers. "You're thinking I'm just looking to get you naked, and I wouldn't have any objection to that."

She drew gold ribbon from its loop. "Why would you?"

"Exactly. But why don't we start with your face? It's a good face. I really like the shape of your head."

For the first time, her fingers fumbled a bit. With a half laugh, she stopped and really looked at him again. "The shape of my head?"

"Sure. You like it, too, or you wouldn't wear your hair that way. Makes a powerful statement with a minimum of fuss."

She tied off the bow. "You're clever at defining a woman with a few pithy phrases."

"I like women."

"I figured that out." As she finished up the red lilies, a pair of customers came in and began to browse.

A good thing, Dru thought. It was time to move the artistic Mr. Quinn along.

"I'm flattered you admire the shape of my head." She picked up his credit card to ring up the sale. "And that someone of your talent and reputation would like to paint me. But the business keeps me very busy, and without a great deal of free time. What free time I do have, I'm extremely selfish with."

She gave him his total, slid the sales slip over for his signature.

"You close at six daily and don't open on Sundays."

She should've been annoyed, she thought, but instead she was intrigued. "You don't miss much, do you?"

"Every detail matters." After signing the receipt, he plucked out one of her gift cards, turned it over to the blank back.

He drew a quick study of her face as the blossom of a long-stemmed flower, then added the phone number at home before he signed it. "In case you change your mind," he said, offering it.

She studied the card, found her lips quirking. "I could probably sell this on eBay for a tidy little sum."

"You've got too much class for that." He piled up the boxes, hefted them. "Thanks for the flowers."

"You're welcome." She came around the counter to open the door for him. "I hope your . . . sisters enjoy them."

"They will." He shot her a last look over his shoulder. "I'll be back."

"I'll be here." Tucking the sketch into her pocket, she closed the door.

IT had been great to see Sybill, to spend an hour alone with her. And to see the pleasure she got from arranging the flowers in a tall, clear vase.

They were perfect for her, he concluded, just as the house she and Phillip had bought and furnished, the massive old Victorian with all the stylized details, was perfect for her.

She'd changed her hairstyle over the years, but now it was back to the way he liked it best, swinging sleek nearly to her shoulders with all that richness of color of a pricey mink coat.

She hadn't bothered with lipstick for the day of working at home, and wore a simple and crisp white shirt with pegged black trousers, what he supposed she thought of as casual wear.

She was the mother of two active children, as well as being a trained sociologist and successful author. And looked, Seth thought, utterly serene.

He had reason to know that that serenity had been hard-won.

She'd grown up in the same household as his mother. Half sisters who were like opposite sides of a coin.

Since even the thought of Gloria DeLauter clenched his stomach muscles, Seth pushed it aside and concentrated on Sybill.

"When you, Phil and the kids came over to Rome a few months ago, I didn't think the next time I'd see you would be here."

"I wanted you to come back." She poured them each a glass of iced tea. "Totally selfish of me, but I wanted you back. Sometimes in the middle of whatever was going on, I'd stop and think: Something's missing. What's missing? Then, oh yes, Seth. Seth's missing. Silly."

"Sweet." He gave her hand a squeeze before picking up the glass she set down for him. "Thanks."

"Tell me everything," she demanded.

They talked of his work and hers. Of the children. Of what had changed and what had stayed the same.

When he got up to leave, she wrapped her arms around him and held on just a minute longer. "Thanks for the flowers. They're wonderful."

"Nice new shop on Market. The woman who owns it seems to know her stuff." He walked with Sybill, hand in hand, toward the door. "Have you been in there?"

"Once or twice." Because she knew him, very well, Sybill smiled. "She's very lovely, isn't she?"

"Who's that?" But when Sybill merely tipped her head, he grinned. "Caught me. Yeah, she's got some face. What do you know about her?"

"Nothing, really. She moved here late last summer, I think, and had the store open by fall. I believe she's from the D.C. area. It seems to me my parents know some Whitcombs, and some Bankses from around there. Might be relatives." She shrugged. "I can't say for certain, and my parents and I don't . . . communicate very often these days."

He touched her cheek. "I'm sorry."

"Don't be. They have two spectacular grandchildren whom they largely ignore." As they've ignored you, she thought. "It's their loss."

"Your mother's never forgiven you for standing up for me."

"Her loss." Sybill spoke very precisely as she caught his face in her hands. "My gain. And I didn't stand alone. No one ever does in this family."

She was right about that, Seth thought as he drove toward the boatyard. No Quinn stood alone.

But he wasn't sure he could stand pulling them into the trouble he was very much afraid was going to find him, even back home.

THREE

~⁀~

ONCE DRU HAD rung up the next sale and was alone in the shop again, she took the sketch out of her pocket.

Seth Quinn. Seth Quinn wanted to paint her. It was fascinating. And as intriguing, she admitted, as the artist himself. A woman could be intrigued without being actively interested.

Which she wasn't.

She had no desire to pose, to be scrutinized, to be immortalized. Even by such talented hands. But she was curious, about the concept of it, just as she was curious about Seth Quinn.

The article she'd read had included some details on his personal life. She knew he'd come to the Eastern Shore as a child, taken in by Ray Quinn before Ray died in a single-car accident. Some of the story was a little nebulous. There'd been no mention of parents, and Seth had been very closed-mouthed in the interview in that area. The facts given were that Ray Quinn had been his grandfather, and on his death, Seth had been raised by Quinn's three adopted sons. And their wives as they had come along.

Sisters, he'd said, thinking of the flowers he'd bought. Perhaps they had been for the women he considered his sisters.

It hardly mattered to her.

She'd been more interested in what the article had said about his work, and how his family had encouraged his early talent. How they had supported his desire to study in Europe.

It was a fortunate child, in Dru's opinion, who had a family who loved him enough to let him go—to let him discover, to fail or succeed on his own. And, she thought, who apparently welcomed him back just as unselfishly.

Still, it was difficult to imagine the man the Italians had dubbed *il maestro giovane*—the young master—settling down in St. Christopher to paint seascapes.

Just as she assumed it was difficult for many of her acquaintances to imagine Drusilla Whitcomb Banks, young socialite, contentedly selling flowers in a small waterfront shop.

It didn't matter to her what people thought or what they said—any more than she supposed such things mattered to Seth Quinn. She'd come here to get away from the demands and expectations, the sticky grip of family, and the unrelenting upheaval of being used as the fraying rope in the endless game of tug-of-war her parents played.

She'd come to St. Chris for peace, the peace that she'd yearned for most of her life.

She was finding it.

Though her mother would be thrilled—perhaps, stubbornly, *because* her mother would be thrilled at the prospect of her precious daughter capturing the interest of Seth Quinn—Dru had no intention of cultivating that interest. Neither the artistic interest, nor the more elemental and frankly sexual interest she'd seen in his eyes when he'd looked at her.

Or, if she was being honest, the frankly sexual interest she'd felt for him.

The Quinns were, by all reports, a large, complex and unwieldy family. God knew she'd had her fill of family.

A pity, she admitted, tapping the card on her palm before dropping it into a drawer. The young master was attractive, amusing and appealing. And any man who took the time to buy flowers for his sisters, and wanted to make sure each purchase suited the individual style of the recipient, earned major points.

"Too bad for both of us," she murmured, and shut the drawer with a final little snap.

HE was thinking of Dru as she was thinking of him, and pondering just what angles, just what tones would work best on a portrait. He liked the idea of a three-quarter view of her face, with her head turned to the left, but her eyes looking back, out of the canvas.

That would suit the contrast of her cool attitude and sexy chic.

He never doubted she'd consent to pose. He had an entire arsenal of weapons to battle a model's reluctance. All he had to do was decide which one would work best on Drusilla.

Tapping his fingers on the wheel to the outlaw beat of Aerosmith that blasted out of his stereo, Seth considered her.

There was money in her background, he decided. Seth recognized designer cut and good fabric even if he was more interested in the form beneath the fashion. Then there was the cadence of her voice. It said high-class private school to him.

She'd tagged James McNeill Whistler for the name of her shop. Which meant, he thought, she'd had a very tony education, or someone pounding poetry and literature into her head as Phil had done with him.

Probably both.

She was comfortable with her looks and didn't fluster when a man made it clear she attracted him.

She wasn't married, and instinct told him she wasn't attached. A woman like Dru didn't relocate to tag along after a boyfriend or lover. She'd moved from Washington, started a business and run it solo because that's just the way she wanted it.

Then he remembered just how far off the mark he'd been regarding the fictional Widow Whitcomb Banks, and decided to hedge his bets by doing a little research before approaching her again.

Seth pulled into the parking lot of the old brick barn the Quinns had bought from Nancy Claremont when the woman's tight-fisted, tight-assed husband had keeled over dead of a heart attack while arguing with Cy Crawford over the price of a meatball sub.

Initially they'd rented the massive building, one that had been a tobacco warehouse in the 1700s, a packinghouse in the 1800s and a glorified storage shed for much of the 1900s.

Then it had been a boatyard, transformed and outfitted by the brothers Quinn. For the last eight years, it had belonged to them.

Seth looked up at the roof as he climbed out of the car. He'd helped reshingle that roof, he remembered, and had nearly broken his neck doing it.

He'd smeared the hot fifty-fifty mix on seams, and burned his fingers. He'd learned to lap boards in the bottomless well of Ethan's patience. He'd sweated like a pig along with Cam repairing the dock. And had escaped by whatever means presented themselves every time Phil had tried to shoehorn him into learning to keep the books.

He walked to the front, stood with his hands on his hips studying the weathered sign. BOATS BY QUINN. And noted that another name had been added to the four that had been there since the beginning.

Aubrey Quinn.

Even as he grinned, she shoved out of the front door.

She had a tool belt slung at her hips and an Orioles fielder's cap low over her forehead. Her hair, the color of burnt honey, was pulled through the back loop to swing at her back.

Her scarred and stained work boots looked like a doll's.

She had such little feet.

And a very big voice, he thought when she let out a roaring whoop as she charged him.

She leaped, boosted herself with a bounce of her hands off his shoulders and wrapped her legs around his waist. The bill of her cap rapped him in the forehead when she pressed her mouth to his in a long, smacking kiss.

"My Seth." With a loud hooting laugh, she chained her arms around his neck. "Don't go away again. Damn it, don't you dare go away again."

"I can't. Too much happens around here when I'm gone. Tip back," he ordered, and dipped her away far enough to study her face.

At two, she'd been a tiny princess to him. At twenty, she was an athletic, appealing handful.

"Jeez, you got pretty," he said.

"Yeah? You too."

"Why aren't you in college?"

"Don't start." She rolled her bright green eyes and hopped down. "I did two years, and I'd've been happier on a chain gang. This is what I want to do." She jerked a thumb toward the sign. "My name's up there to prove it."

"You always could wrap Ethan around your finger."

"Maybe. But I didn't have to. Dad got it, and after some initial fretting, so did Mom. I was never the student you were, Seth, and you were never the boatbuilder I am."

"Shit. I leave you alone for a few years, and you get delusions of grandeur. If you're going to insult me, I'm not going to give you your present."

"Where is it? What is it?" She attacked by poking her fingers in his ribs where she knew him to be the most vulnerable. "Gimme."

"Cut it out. Okay, okay. Man, you don't change."

"Why mess with perfection? Hand over the loot and nobody gets hurt."

"It's in the car." He pointed toward the lot and had the satisfaction of seeing her mouth drop open.

"A Jag? Oh baby." She darted over the stubble of lawn to the lot to run her fingers reverently over the shining silver hood. "Cam's going to cry when he sees this. He's just going to break down and cry. Let me have the keys so I can test her out."

"Sure, when we're slurping on Sno Kones in hell."

"Don't be mean. You can come with me. We'll buzz up to Crawford's and get some . . ." She trailed off as he got the long white box out of the trunk. She blinked at the box, blinked at him before her eyes went soft and dewy.

"You bought me flowers. You got me a girl present. Oh, let me see! What kind are they?" She pulled a work knife out of her belt, sliced the ribbon, then yanked up the lid. "Sunflowers. Look how happy they are."

"Reminded me of you."

"I really love you." She stared hard at the flowers. "I've been so mad at you for leaving." When her voice broke, he gave her an awkward pat on the shoulder. "I'm not going to cry," she muttered and sucked it in. "What am I, a sissy?"

"Never."

"Okay, well, anyway, you're back." She turned to hug him again. "I really love the flowers."

"Good." He slapped a hand on the one that was trying to sneak into his pocket. "You're not getting the keys. I've got to take off anyway. I've got flowers for Grace. I want to swing by and see her on my way home."

"She's not there. This is her afternoon for running errands, then she'll pick Deke up from school and drop him off for his piano lesson and so on and so on. I don't know how she does it all. I'll take them to her," Aubrey added. "Flowers will take some of the sting out of missing you today."

"Tell her I'll try to get by tomorrow, otherwise I'll see her Sunday." He carted the box from his trunk to the snappy little blue pickup.

Aubrey laid her flowers in the cab with her mother's. "You've got some time now. Let's go get Cam and show off your car. I tell you, he's going to break down and sob like a baby. I can't wait."

"You've got a mean streak, Aub." Seth slung his arm

around her shoulders. "I like that about you. Now, tell me what you know about the flower lady. Drusilla."

"Aha." Aubrey leered up at him as they walked toward the building. "So that's the way the garden grows."

"Might."

"Tell you what. Meet me at Shiney's after dinner. Say about eight. Buy me a drink and I'll spill everything I know."

"You're underage."

"Yeah, like I've never sipped a beer before," she retorted. "A soft drink, Daddy. And remember, I'll be legal in less than six months."

"Until then, when I'm buying, you drink Coke." He tipped down the bill of her cap, then dragged open the door to the noise of power tools.

CAM didn't break down and weep, Seth thought later, but he had drooled a little. Nearly genuflected. Right before, Seth mused as he parked in front of Shiney's Pub, Cam—being bigger and meaner than Aubrey—snagged the keys and peeled off to take it for a spin.

Then, of course, they spent a very satisfying hour standing around admiring the engine.

Seth glanced at the pickup beside his car. One thing about Aubrey, she was always prompt.

He opened the door to Shiney's and felt yet one more homecoming. Another constant of St. Chris, he thought. Shiney's Pub would always look as if it needed to be hosed down, the waitresses would always be leggy, and it would offer the very worst live bands to be found in the entire state of Maryland.

While the lead singer massacred Barenaked Ladies,

Seth scanned the tables and bar for a little blonde in a fielder's cap.

His eyes actually passed over her, then arrowed back.

She was indeed at the bar, urbane and curvy in unrelieved black, her burnt-honey hair spiraling down her back as she carried on a heated conversation with a guy who looked like Joe College.

Mouth grim, body poised for a confrontation, Seth headed over to show College Boy just what happened when a guy hit on his sister.

"You're full of it." Aubrey's voice snapped like a whip and had Seth's mouth moving into a snarl. "You are so absolutely full of it. The pitching rotation is solid, the infield's got good gloves. The bats are coming around. By the All-Star Game, the Birds will be playing better than five-hundred ball."

"They won't see five hundred all season," her opponent shot back. "And they're going to be digging another level down in the basement by the All-Star Game."

"Bet." Aubrey dug a twenty out of her pocket, slapped it on the bar.

And Seth sighed. She might've looked like a tasty morsel, but nobody nibbled on his Aubrey.

"Seth." Spotting him, Aubrey reached out, hooked his arm and yanked him to the bar. "Sam Jacoby," she said with a nod toward the man sitting beside her. "Thinks because he plays a little softball he knows something about the Bigs."

"Heard a lot about you." Sam held out a hand. "From this sentimental slob here who thinks the Orioles have a shot at climbing their pitiful way up to mediocre this season."

Seth shook hands. "If you want to commit suicide, Sam, get a gun. It's got to be less painful than inciting this one to peel every inch of skin slowly off your body with a putty knife."

"I like to live dangerously," he said and slid off the stool. "Take a seat. I was holding it for you. Gotta split. See you around, Aub."

"You're going to owe me twenty bucks in July," she called out, then shifted her attention to Seth. "Sam's a nice enough guy, except for the fatal flaw that encourages him to root for the Mariners."

"I thought he was hitting on you."

"Sam?" Aubrey gazed back toward the tables with a smug and female look in her eye that made Seth want to squirm. "Sure he was. I'm holding him in reserve. I'm sort of seeing Will McLean right now."

"Will?" Seth nearly choked. "Will McLean?" The idea of Aubrey and one of his boyhood pals together—that way—had Seth signaling the bartender. "I really need a beer. Rolling Rock."

"Not that we get to see each other that often." Knowing she was turning the screw, Aubrey continued gleefully. "He's an intern at Saint Chris General. Rotations at the hospital are a bitch. But when we do manage the time, it's worth it."

"Shut up. He's too old for you."

"I've always gone for older men." Deliberately, she pinched his cheek. "Cutie pie. Plus there's only, like, five years' difference. Still, if you want to talk about my love life—"

"I don't." Seth reached for the bottle the bartender set in front of him, drank deep. "I really don't."

"Okay, enough about me then, let's talk about you. How many languages did you score in when you were plundering Europe?"

"Now you sound like Kevin." And it wasn't nearly as comfortable a topic to explore with Aubrey. "I wasn't on a sexual marathon. I was working."

"Some chicks really fall for the artistic type. Maybe your flower lady's one of them, and you'll get lucky."

"Obviously you've been hanging around with my brothers too much. Turned you into a gutter brain. Just tell me what you know about her?"

"Okay." She grabbed a bowl of pretzels off the bar and began to munch. "So, she first showed up about a year ago. Spent a week hanging around. Checking out retail space," she said with a nod. "I got that from Doug Motts. Remember Dougie—roly-poly little kid? Couple years behind you in school."

"Vaguely."

"Anyway, he lost the baby fat. He's working at Shore Realtors now. According to Doug, she knew just what she was looking for, and told them to contact her in D.C. when and if anything that came close opened up. Now, Doug . . ." She pointed toward her empty glass when the bartender swung by. "He'd pretty much just started at the Realtor's and was hoping to hook this one. So he poked around some, trying to dig up information on his prospective client. She'd told him she'd visited Saint Chris a couple times when she was a kid, so that gave Doug his starting point."

"Ma Crawford," Seth said with a laugh.

"You got it. What Ma Crawford doesn't know ain't worth knowing. And the woman's got a memory like a herd of elephants. She recalled the Whitcomb Bankses. Name like that, who wouldn't? But they stuck out more because she remembered Mrs. WB from when *she* was a girl visiting here with her family. Her really seriously kick-your-butt-to-Tuesday rich family. Whitcomb Technologies. As in we make everything. As in Fortune Five Hundred. As in Senator James P. Whitcomb, the gentleman from Maryland."

"Ah. *Those* Whitcombs."

"You bet. The senator, who would be the flower lady's grandfather, had an affection for the Eastern Shore. And his daughter, the current Mrs. WB, married Proctor Banks—what kind of name is Proctor, anyway?—of Banks and Shelby Communication. We're talking mega family dough with this combo. Like a fricking empire."

"And young, nubile and extremely wealthy Drusilla rents a storefront in Saint Chris and sells flowers."

"Buys a building in Saint Chris," Aubrey corrected. "She bought the place, prime retail space for our little kingdom. A few months after Doug had the good fortune to be manning the desk at Shore Realtors when she walked in, that place went on the market. Previous owners live in PA, rented it to various merchants who had their ups and downs there. Remember the New Age shop—rocks, crystals, ritual candles and meditation tapes?"

"Yeah. Guy who ran it had a tattoo of a dragon on the back of his right hand."

"That place lasted longer than anybody figured it would, but when the lease came up for renewal last year, it went bye-bye. Doug, smelling commission, gives the young WB a call to tell her a rental just opened up on Market, and she makes him salivate when she asks if the owners are interested in selling. When they were, and a deal was struck, he sang the 'Hallelujah Chorus.' Then she makes him the happiest man in Saint Chris when she tells him to find her a house, too. She comes down, takes a look at the three he shows her, takes a liking to this ramshackle old Victorian on Oyster Inlet. Prime real estate again," Aubrey added. "No flies on flower lady."

"That old blue house?" Seth asked. "Looked like a half-eaten gingerbread house? She bought *that*?"

"Lock and stock." Aubrey nodded as she crunched pretzels. "Guy bought it about three years ago, snazzed it up, wanted to turn it."

"Nothing much around there but marsh grass and thickets." But it rose over a curve of the flatland river, he remembered. That tobacco-colored water that could gleam like amber when the sun beamed through the oak and gum trees.

"Your girl likes her privacy," Aubrey told him. "Keeps to herself. Courteous and helpful to her customers, polite, even friendly, but carefully so. She blows cool."

"She's new here." God knew he understood what it was like to find yourself in a place, one that had just exactly what you wanted, and not be sure if you'd find your slot.

"She's an outlander." Aubrey jerked a shoulder in a typical Quinn shrug. "She'll be new here for the next twenty years."

"She could probably use a friend."

"Looking to make new friends, Seth? Somebody to go chicken necking with?"

He gestured for another beer, then leaned in until his nose bumped hers. "Maybe. Is that what you and Will do in your spare time?"

"We skip the chicken, and just neck. But I'll take you out in the pram if you've got a hankering. I'll captain. It's been so long since you manned a sail, you'd probably capsize her."

"Like hell. We'll go out tomorrow."

"That's a date. And speaking of dates, your new friend just came in."

"Who?" But he knew, even before he swiveled around on the stool. Before he scanned the evening crowd and spotted her.

She looked sublimely out of place among the watermen with their wind-scored faces and scarred hands and the university students with their trendy shoes and baggy shirts.

Her suit was still crisp and perfect, her face an oval of alabaster in the dull light.

She had to know heads turned as she walked in, he thought. Women always knew. But she moved with purpose and easy grace around the stained tables and rickety chairs.

"Classy" was Aubrey's one-word summation.

"Oh yeah." Seth dug out money for the drinks, tossed it on the bar. "I'm ditching you, kid."

Aubrey widened her eyes in exaggerated shock. "Color me amazed."

"Tomorrow," he said, then leaned down to give her a quick kiss before strolling off to intercept Dru.

She stopped by a table and began speaking to a waitress. Seth's attention was so focused on Dru it took him a moment to recognize the other woman.

Terri Hardgrove. Blond, sulky and built. They'd dated for a couple of memorable months during his junior year of high school. It had not ended well, Seth recalled and nearly detoured just to avoid the confrontation.

Instead he tried an easy smile and kept going until he caught some of their conversation.

"I'm not going to take the place after all," Terri said as she balanced her tray on the shelf of one hip. "J.J. and me worked things out."

"J.J." Dru angled her head. "That would be the lowlife,

lying scum you never wanted to see again even if he was gasping his last, dying breath?"

"Well." Terri shifted her feet, fluttered her lashes. "We hadn't worked things out when I said that. And I thought, you know, screw him, I'll just get me a place of my own and get back in the game. It was just that I saw your For Rent sign when I was so mad at him and all. But we worked things out."

"So you said. Congratulations. It might've been helpful if you'd come by this afternoon as we'd agreed and let me know."

"I'm really sorry, but that's when . . ."

"You were working things out," Dru finished.

"Hey, Terri."

She squealed. It came flooding back to Seth that she'd always been a squealer. Apparently, she hadn't grown out of it.

"Seth! Seth Quinn! Just look at you."

"How's it going?"

"It's going just fine. I heard you were back, but now here you are. Big as life and twice as handsome, and famous, too. It's sure been some while since Saint Chris High."

"Some time," he agreed and looked at Dru.

"Y'all know each other?" Terri asked.

"We've met," Dru said. "I'll leave you to catch up on old times. I hope you and J.J. are very happy."

"You and J.J. Wyatt?"

Terri preened. "That's right. We're practically engaged."

"We'll catch up later. You can tell me all about it." He took off, leaving Terri pouting at his back as he caught up with Dru.

"J.J. Wyatt," Seth began as he stepped beside Dru. "Offensive tackle on the Saint Chris High Sharks. Went on to crush as many heads as he could manage at the local university before even his bulldog skill on the football field couldn't keep him from flunking out."

"Thank you for that fascinating slice of local history."

"You're pissed. Why don't I buy you a drink and you can tell me all about it?"

"I don't want a drink, thank you, and I'm getting out of here before my eardrums are permanently damaged by that amazingly loud and untalented band's horrendous version of 'Jack and Diane.'"

He decided it was a point in her favor that she could recognize the mangled song, and pulled open the door for her.

"The flowers were a hit."

"I'm glad to hear it." She took her keys out of a streamlined, buff-colored purse.

He started to suggest they go somewhere else for a drink, but could see by the irritated line between her eyebrows that she'd just shut him down.

"So, you've got a space to rent?"

"Apparently." She moved, dismissively, to the driver's side of a black Mercedes SUV.

Seth got his hand on the handle before she did, then just leaned companionably against the door. "Where?"

"Above the shop."

"And you want to rent it?"

"It's empty. It seems like a waste of space. I can't drive my car unless I'm inside of it," she pointed out.

"Above the shop," he repeated, and brought the building back into his mind. Two stories, yeah, that was right. "Bank of three windows, front and back," he said aloud. "Should be good light. How big is it?"

"Nine hundred square feet, including a small galley-style kitchen."

"Big enough. Let's take a look."

"Excuse me?"

"Show me the space. I might be interested."

She gave the keys in her hand an impatient jiggle. "You want me to show you the apartment now?"

"You don't want to waste space, why waste time?" He opened her car door. "I'll follow you back. It won't take long," he said with that slow, easy grin. "I make up my mind pretty quick."

FOUR

SHE MADE UP her mind quickly as well, Dru thought as she backed out of the pub's lot. And she had Seth Quinn pegged.

A confident man, and a talented one. Each aspect probably fed into the other. The fact that his rough edges managed to have a sheen of polish was intriguing, something she was certain he knew very well.

And used very well.

He was attractive. The lean, lanky build that looked as though it had been designed to wear those worn-out jeans. All that burnished blond hair, straight as a pin and never quite styled. The hollowed cheeks, the vivid blue eyes. Not just vivid in color, she thought now. In intensity. The way he looked at you, as if he saw something no one else could see. Something you couldn't see yourself.

It managed to be flattering, jolting and just a bit off-putting all at once.

It made you wonder about him. And if you were wondering about a man, you were thinking about him.

Women, she concluded, were like paints on a palette to him. He could dab into any one of them at his whim. The way he'd been snuggled up with the blonde in the bar—a little play she'd noted the instant she herself had walked in—was a case in point.

Then there'd been the way he'd smiled at the waitress, the terminally foolish Terri. Wide, warm and friendly, with just a hint of intimacy. Very potent, that smile, Dru mused, but it wasn't going to work on her.

Men who bounced from woman to woman because they could were entirely too ordinary for her tastes.

Yet here she was, she admitted, driving back to the shop to show him the second-floor apartment when what she really wanted to do was go home to her lovely, quiet house.

It was the sensible thing to do, of course. There was no point in the space staying empty. But it galled that he'd assumed she'd take the time and trouble simply because he wanted her to.

There was no problem finding a parking space now. It was barely nine on a cool spring evening, but the waterfront was all but deserted. A few boats moored, swaying in the current, a scatter of people, most likely tourists, strolling under the light of a quarter moon.

Oh, how she loved the waterfront. She'd nearly howled with glee when she'd been able to snag the building for her shop, knowing she'd be able to step outside any time of the day and see the water, the crabbers, the tourists. To feel that moist air on her skin.

Even more, to feel part of it all, on her own merits, her own terms.

It would have been smarter, more sensible again, to have taken the room above for her own living quarters. But she'd made the conscious and deliberate decision not to live where she worked. Which, Dru admitted as she swung away from Market to drive to the rear of her building, had been a handy excuse to find a place out of the town bustle, someplace on the water again. An indulgent space all her own.

The house in Georgetown had never felt all her own.

She killed the lights, the engine, then gathered her purse. Seth was there, opening her door, before she could do it for herself.

"It's pretty dark. Watch your step." He took her arm, started to steer her to the wooden staircase that led to the second level.

"I can see fine, thanks." She eased away from him, then opened her bag for the keys. "There's parking," she began. "And a private entrance, as you see."

"Yeah, I see fine, too. Listen." Halfway up the stairs, he laid a hand on her arm to stop her. "Just listen," he said again and looked out over the houses that lined the road behind them. "It's great, isn't it?"

She couldn't stop the smile. She understood him perfectly. And it was great, that silence.

"It won't be this quiet in a few weeks." He scanned the dark, the houses, the lawns. And again she thought he saw what others didn't. "Starting with Memorial Day the tourists and the summer people pour in. Nights get longer, warmer, and people hang out. That can be great, too, all that noise. Holiday noise. The kind you hear when you've got an ice cream cone in your hand and no time clock ticking away in your head."

He turned, aimed those strong blue eyes at her. She could have sworn she felt a jolt from them that was elementally physical.

"You like ice cream cones?" he asked her.

"There'd be something wrong with me if I didn't." She moved quickly up the rest of the steps.

"Nothing wrong with you," he murmured, and stood with his thumbs tucked in his front pockets while she unlocked the door.

She flicked a switch on the wall to turn on the lights, then deliberately left the door open at his back when he stepped in.

She saw immediately she needn't have bothered. He wasn't giving her a thought now.

He crossed to the front windows first, stood there looking out in that hip-shot stance that managed to be both relaxed and attentive. And sexy, she decided.

He wore a pair of ragged jeans with more style than a great many men managed to achieve in a five-thousand-dollar suit.

There were paint flecks on his shoes.

She blinked, tuning back in to the moment when he began to mutter.

"Excuse me?"

"What? Oh, just calculating the light—sun, angles. Stuff." He crossed back to the rear windows, stood as he had at the front. Muttered as he had at the front.

Talked to himself, Dru noted. Well, it wasn't so odd, really. She held entire conversations with herself in her head.

"The kitchen—" Dru began.

"Doesn't matter." Frowning, he stared up at the ceiling,

his gaze so intense and focused she found herself staring up with him.

After a few seconds of standing there, silent, staring up, she felt ridiculous. "Is there a problem with the ceiling? I was assured the roof was sound, and I know it doesn't leak."

"Uh-huh. Any objection to skylights—put in at my expense?"

"I . . . well, I don't know. I suppose—"

"It would work."

He wandered the room again, placing his canvases, his paints, his easel, a worktable for sketching, shelves for supplies and equipment. Have to put in a sofa, or a bed, he thought. Better a bed in case he worked late enough to just flop down for the night.

"It's a good space," he said at length. "With the skylights, it'll work. I'll take it."

She reminded herself that she hadn't actually agreed to the skylights. But then again, she couldn't find any reason to object to them. "That was quick, as advertised. Don't you want to see the kitchen, the bathroom?"

"They got everything kitchens and bathrooms are supposed to have?"

"Yes. No tub, just a shower stall."

"I'm not planning on taking too many bubble baths." He moved back to the front windows again. "Prime view."

"Yes, it's very nice. Not that it's any of my business, but I assume you have any number of places you can stay while you're here. Why do you need an apartment?"

"I don't want to live here, I want to work here. I need studio space." He turned back. "I'm bunking at Cam and Anna's, and that suits me. I'll get a place of my own eventually, but not until I find exactly what I want. Because I'm not visiting Saint Chris. I'm back for good."

"I see. Well, studio space then. Which explains the sky-lights."

"I'm a better bet than Terri," he said because he felt her hesitation. "No loud parties or shouting matches, which she's famous for. And I'm handy."

"Are you?"

"Hauling, lifting, basic maintenance. I won't come crying to you every time the faucet drips."

"Points for you," she murmured.

"How many do I need? I really want the space. I need to get back to work. What do you say to a six-month lease?"

"Six months. I'd planned on a full year at a time."

"Six months gives us both an early out if it's not jelling."

She pursed her lips in consideration. "There is that."

"How much are you asking?"

She gave him the monthly rate she'd settled on. "I'll want first and last month's rent when you sign the lease. And another month's rent as security deposit."

"Ouch. Very strict."

Now she smiled. "Terri annoyed me. You get to pay the price."

"Won't be the first time she's cost me. I'll have it for you tomorrow. I've got a family thing on Sunday, and I have to order the skylights, but I'd like to start moving things in right away."

"That's fine." She liked the idea of him painting over her shop, of knowing the building that was hers was fulfilling its potential. "Congratulations," she said and offered a hand. "You've got yourself a studio."

"Thanks." He took her hand, held it. Ringless, he thought again. Long, faerie fingers and unpainted nails. "Given any thought to posing for me?"

"No."

His grin flashed at her flat, precise answer. "I'll talk you into it."

"I'm not easily swayed. Let's clear this all up before we start on what should be a mutually satisfying business relationship."

"Okay, let's. You have a strong, beautiful face. As an artist, as a man, I'm drawn to the qualities of strength and beauty. The artist wants to translate them. The man wants to enjoy them. So, I'd like to paint you, and I'd like to spend time with you."

Despite the breeze that danced through the open door, she felt entirely too alone with him. Alone, and boxed in by the way he held her hand, held her gaze.

"I'm sure you've had your quota of women to translate and enjoy. Such as the buxom blonde in black you were co-zied up with at the bar."

"Who . . . ?"

Humor exploded on his face. It was, Dru thought, like light bursting through shadows.

"Buxom Blonde in Black," he repeated, seeing it as a ti-tle. "Jesus, she'll *love* that. There'll be no living with her. That was Aubrey. Aubrey Quinn. My brother Ethan's old-est daughter."

"I see." And it made her feel like an idiot. "It didn't seem to be a particularly avuncular relationship."

"I don't feel like her uncle. It's more a big-brother thing. She was two when I came to Saint Chris. We fell for each other. Aubrey's the first person I ever loved, absolutely.

She's got strength and beauty, too, and I've certainly trans-
lated and enjoyed them. But not in quite the same way I'd
like to do with yours."

"Then you're going to be disappointed. Even if I were
interested, I don't have the time to pose, and I don't have
the inclination to be enjoyed. You're very attractive, Seth,
and if I were going to be shallow—"

"Yeah." Another brilliant, flashing grin. "Let's be shallow."

"Sorry." But he'd teased a smile out of her again. "I gave
it up. If I were going to be, *I* might enjoy *you*. But as it
stands, we're going to settle for the practical."

"We can start there. Now, since you asked me a question
earlier, I get to ask you one."

"All right, what?"

He saw by the way her face turned closed-in and wary
that she was braced for something personal she wouldn't
care to answer. So he shifted gears. "Do you like steamed
crabs?"

She stared at him for nearly ten seconds and gave him
the pleasure of watching her face relax. "Yes, I like
steamed crabs."

"Good. We'll have some on our first date. I'll be by in
the morning to sign the lease," he added as he walked to
the open door.

"The morning's fine."

He looked down as she leaned over to lock the door behind them. Her neck was long, elegant. The contrast between it and the severe cut of the dark hair was sharp and
dramatic. Without thinking, he skimmed a finger along the
curve, just to sample the texture.

She froze, so that for one instant they made a portrait of

themselves. The woman in the rich-colored suit, slightly bent toward a closed door, and the man in rough clothes with a fingertip at the nape of her neck.

She straightened with a quick jerk of movement, and Seth let his hand drop away. "Sorry, irritating habit of mine."

"Do you have many?"

"Yeah, afraid so. That one wasn't anything personal. You've got a really nice line back there." He stuck his hands in his pockets so it wouldn't become personal. Not yet.

"I'm an expert on lines, nice or otherwise." She breezed by him and down the steps.

"Hey." He jogged after her. "I've got better lines than that one."

"I'll just bet you do."

"I'll try some out on you. But in the meantime . . ." He opened her car door. "Is there any storage space?"

"Utility room. There." She gestured toward a door under the steps. "Furnace and water heater, that sort of thing. And some storage."

"If I need to, can I stick some stuff in there until I get the space worked out? I've got some things coming in from Rome. They'll probably be here Monday."

"I don't have a problem with that. The key's inside the shop. Remind me to give it to you tomorrow."

"Appreciate it." He closed the door for her when she'd climbed in, then he knocked on the window. "You know," he said when she rolled down the window, "I like spending time with a smart, self-confident woman who knows what she wants and goes out and gets it. Like you got this place. Very sexy, that kind of direction and dedication."

He waited a beat. "That was a line."

She kept her eyes on his as she rolled the glass up between their faces again.

And she didn't let herself chuckle until she'd driven away.

THE best thing about Sundays, in Dru's opinion, was waking up slowly, then clinging to that half-dream state while the sunlight shivered through the trees, slid through the windows and danced on her closed lids.

Sundays were knowing absolutely nothing had to be done, and countless things could be.

She'd make coffee and toast a bagel in her own kitchen, then have her breakfast in the little dining room while she leafed through catalogues for business.

She'd putter around the garden she'd planted—with her own hands, thank you—while listening to music.

There was no charity luncheon, no community drive, no obligatory family dinner or tennis match at the club cluttering up her Sundays now.

There was no marital spat between her parents to referee, and no hurt feelings and sorrowful looks because each felt she'd taken the side of the other.

All there was, was Sunday and her lazy enjoyment of it.

In all the months she'd lived here, she'd never once taken that for granted. Nor had she lost a drop of the flood of pleasure it gave her to stand and look out her own windows.

She did so now, opening the window to the cool morning. From there she could admire her own private curve of the river. There were no houses to get in the way and make her think of people when she only wanted to be.

There was the speckled leaves of the liverwort she'd

planted under the shade of oaks, its buds a cheery pink. And lily of the valley, with its bells already dancing. And there, the marsh grass and rushes with the little clearing she'd made for the golden-yellow iris that liked their feet wet.

She could hear the birds, the breeze, the occasional plop of a fish or a frog.

Forgetting breakfast, she wandered through the house to the front door so she could stand on the veranda and just look. She wore the boxers and tank she'd slept in, and there was no one to comment on the senator's granddaughter's dishabille. No reporter or photographer looking for a squib for the society page.

There was only lovely, lovely peace.

She picked up her watering can and carried it inside to fill while she started the coffee.

Seth Quinn had been right about one thing, she thought. She was a woman who knew what she wanted and went out and got it. Perhaps it had taken her some time to realize what that thing was, but when she had, she'd done what needed to be done.

She'd wanted to run a business where she could feel creative and happy. And she'd been determined to be successful, in her own right. She'd toyed with the idea of a small nursery or gardening service.

But she wasn't fully confident in her skills there. Her gardening ventures had been largely confined to her little courtyard in Georgetown, and potted plants. And while she'd been very proud of her efforts there and delighted with the results, it hardly qualified her as an expert.

But she knew flowers.

She'd wanted a small town, where the pace was easy and the demands few. And she'd wanted the water. She'd always been pulled to the water.

She loved the look of St. Christopher, the cheerful tidiness of it, and the ever changing tones and moods of the Bay. She liked listening to the clang from the channel markers, and the throaty call of a foghorn when the mists rolled in.

She'd grown accustomed to and nearly comfortable with the casual friendliness of the locals. And the good-heartedness that had sent Ethan Quinn over to check on her during a storm the previous winter.

No, she'd never live in the city again.

Her parents would have to continue to adjust to the distance she'd put between them. Geographically and emotionally. In the end, she was certain it was best for everyone involved.

And just now, however selfish it might be, she was more concerned with what was best for Drusilla.

She turned off the tap and, after sampling the coffee, carried it and the watering can outside to tend to her pots.

Eventually, she thought, she would add a greenhouse so that she could experiment with growing her own flowers to sell. But she'd have to be convinced she could add the structure without spoiling the fanciful lines of her home.

She loved its peaks and foolishly ornate gingerbread trim. Most would consider it a kind of folly, with its fancy-work and deep blue color out here among the thickets and marsh. But to her it was a statement.

Home could be exactly where you needed, exactly what you needed it to be, if you wanted it enough.

She set her coffee down on a table and drenched a jardiniere bursting with verbena and heliotrope.

At a rustle, she looked over. And watched a heron rise like a king over the high grass, over the brown water.

"I'm happy," she said out loud. "I'm happier than I've ever been in my life."

She decided to forgo the bagel and catalogues and changed into gardening clothes instead.

For an hour she worked on the sunny side of the house where she was determined to establish a combination of shrubbery and flower bed. The bloodred blooms of the rhododendrons she'd planted the week before would be a strong contrast to the blue of the house once they burst free. She'd spent every evening for a month over the winter planning her flowers. She wanted to keep it simple and a little wild, like a mad cottage garden with columbine and delphiniums and sweet-faced wallflowers all tumbled together.

There were all kinds of art, she thought smugly as she planted fragrant stock. She imagined Seth would approve of her choices of tone and texture here.

Not that it mattered, of course. The garden was to please herself. But it was satisfying to think an artist might find her efforts creative.

He certainly hadn't had much to say for himself the day before, she remembered. He'd whipped in just after she opened the doors, handed over the agreed amount, looped his signature on the lease, snatched up the keys, then bolted.

No flirtation, no persuasive smile.

Which was all for the best, she reminded herself. She didn't want flirtations and persuasions right at the moment.

Still, it would have been nice, on some level, to imagine holding the option for them in reserve.

He'd probably had a Saturday-morning date with one of the women who'd pined for him while he'd been gone. He looked like the type women might pine for. All that scruffy hair, the lanky build.

And the hands. How could you not notice his hands—wide of palm, long of finger. With a rough elegance to them that made a woman—some women, she corrected—fantasize about being stroked by them.

Dru sat back on her heels with a sigh because she knew she'd given just that scenario more than one passing thought. Only because it's the first man you've been attracted to in . . . God, who knew how long?

She hadn't so much as had a date in nearly a year.

Her choice, she reminded herself. And she wasn't going to change her mind and end up with Seth Quinn and steamed crabs.

She would just go on as she was, making her home, running her business while he went about his and painted over her head every day.

She'd get used to him being up there, then she'd stop noticing he was up there. When the lease was up, they'd see if . . .

"Damn it. The key to the utility room."

She'd forgotten to give it to him. Well, he'd forgotten to remind her to give it to him.

Not my problem, she thought and yanked at a stray weed. He's the one who wanted to use the storage, and if he hadn't been in such a hurry to go, she would've remembered to give him the key.

She planted cranesbill, added some larkspur. Then, cursing, pushed to her feet.

It would nag at her all day. She'd obsess, she admitted as she stalked around the house. She'd worry and wonder about whatever it was he had coming in from Rome the next day. Easier by far to take the duplicate she had here at home, drive over to Anna Quinn's and drop it off.

It wouldn't take more than twenty minutes, and she could go by the nursery while she was out.

She left her gardening gloves and tools in a basket on the veranda.

SETH grabbed the line Ethan tossed him and secured the wooden boat to the dock. The kids leaped out first. Emily with her long dancer's body and sunflower hair, and Deke, gangly as a puppy at fourteen.

Seth caught Deke in a headlock and looked at Emily. "You weren't supposed to grow up while I was gone."

"Couldn't help it." She laid her cheek on his, rubbed it there. "Welcome home."

"When do we eat?" Deke wanted to know.

"Guy's got a tapeworm." Aubrey leaped nimbly onto the dock. "He ate damn near half a loaf of French bread five minutes ago."

"I'm a growing boy," he said with a chuckle. "I'm going to charm Anna out of something."

"He actually thinks he's charming," Emily said with a shake of her head. "It's a mystery."

The Chesapeake Bay retriever Ethan called Nigel landed in the water with a happy splash, then bounded up onshore to run after Deke.

"Give me a hand with this, Em, since the jerk's off and running." Aubrey grabbed one end of the cooler Ethan had set on the dock. "Mom may water up," she said to Seth under her breath. "She's really anxious to see you."

Seth stepped to the boat, held out his hand and closed it around Grace's. If Aubrey had been the first person he'd loved, Grace had been the first woman he'd both loved *and* trusted.

Her arms slid around him as she stepped on the dock, and her cheek rubbed his with that same female sweetness as Emily's had. "There now," she said quietly, on a laughing sigh. "There now, that feels just exactly right. Now everything's where it belongs."

She leaned back, smiled up at him. "Thank you for the tulips. They're beautiful. I'm sorry I wasn't home."

"So was I. I figured I'd trade them for some of your homemade fries. You still make the best."

"Come to dinner tomorrow. I'll fix some for you."

"With sloppy joes?"

She laughed again, reached back with one hand to take Ethan's. "Well, that hasn't changed, has it? With sloppy joes. Deke will be thrilled."

"And chocolate cake?"

"Guy expects a lot for a bunch of flowers," Ethan commented.

"At least I didn't swipe them from Anna's garden, then try to blame it on innocent deer and bunny rabbits."

Ethan winced, sent a wary look toward the house to make certain Anna wasn't within hearing distance. "Let's not bring that up again. Damn near twenty years ago, and she'd still scalp me for it."

"I heard you got them from the very pretty florist on Market Street." Grace tucked her arm around Seth's waist as they walked toward the house. "And that you've rented the place above the shop for a studio."

"Word travels."

"Fast and wide," Grace agreed. "Why don't you tell me all about it?"

"Nothing to tell, yet. But I'm working on it."

●

* * *

SHE was running behind now, and it was her own fault. There was no reason, no *sane* reason she'd felt compelled to shower, to change out of her grubby gardening clothes. Certainly no reason, she thought, irritated with herself, to have spent time on her precious Sunday fussing with makeup.

Now it was past noon.

Didn't matter, she told herself. It was a lovely day for a drive. She'd spend two minutes on Seth Quinn and the key, then indulge herself at the nursery.

Of course now she'd have to change *back* into her gardening clothes, but that was neither here nor there. She'd plant, then make fresh lemonade and sit and bask in the glow of a job well done.

Feel the air! Brisk with spring, moist from the water. The fields on either side of the road were tilled and planted, and already running green in the rows. She could smell the sharp edge of fertilizer, the richer tones of earth that meant spring in the country.

She made the turn, caught the glint of the sun off the mudflats before the trees took over with their deep shadows.

The old white house was perfect for its setting. Edged by woods, with water hemming its back, and the tidy, flower-decked lawn skirting its front. She'd admired it before, the way it sat there, so cozy and comfortable with its front porch rockers and faded blue shutters.

While she felt the whimsy and the privacy of her own home suited her perfectly, she could admire the character of the Quinn place. It gave a sense of order without regimentation. The kind of home, she reflected, where feet were allowed to prop on coffee tables.

No one would have dreamed to rest a heel on her mother's Louis XIV. Not even her father.

The number of cars in the drive made her frown. A white Corvette—vintage, she assumed—a sturdy SUV of some sort that appeared to have some hard miles on it. A snappy little convertible, a dented, disreputable-looking hatchback that had to be twenty years old, a manly pickup truck and a sleek and muscular Jaguar.

She hesitated, then mentally assigned the vehicles. The SUV was the family car. The 'Vette was undoubtedly former race-car driver Cameron Quinn's—as would be the truck as work vehicle, giving Anna the convertible and the old hand-me-down to the oldest boy, who must be old enough to drive.

The Jag was Seth's. She'd noticed it, with some admiration, the night before. And if she hadn't, she'd heard all about his recent acquisition from chatting customers in her shop.

She nosed up behind it.

Two minutes, she reminded herself, and grabbed her purse as she turned off the engine.

Instantly, she heard the blast of music. The teenagers, she figured as she started toward the front door, her steps unconsciously timed to the beat of Matchbox 20.

She admired the pots and tubs of flowers on the porch. Anna, she knew, had a clever hand for mixing flowers. She knocked briskly, then bumped it up to a pound before she sighed.

No one was going to hear her over the music, even if she used a battering ram.

Resigned, she stepped off the porch and started toward the side of the house. She heard more than music now. There were shouts, squeals and what she could only describe as maniacal laughter.

The kids must be having a party. She'd just go back, pass off the key to one of Anna's boys and be on her way.

The dog came first, a cannonball of black fur with a lolling tongue. He had a bark like a machine gun, and though she was very fond of dogs, Dru stopped on a dime.

"Hi there. Ah, nice dog."

He seemed to take that as an invitation to race two wild circles around her, then press his nose to her crotch.

"Okay." She put a firm hand under his jaw, lifted it. "That's just a little too friendly." She gave him a quick rub, then a nudge, and managed one more step before the boy streaked screaming around the side of the house. Though he held a large plastic weapon in his hand, he was in full retreat.

He managed to veer around her. "Better run," he puffed out, an instant before she saw a flash of movement out of the corner of her eye.

An instant before she was shot dead in the heart, by a stream of cold water.

The shock was so great that her mouth dropped open but she couldn't manage a sound. Just behind her the boy murmured, "Uh-oh."

And deserted the field.

Seth, the water rifle in his hand, his hair dripping from the previous attack, took one look at Dru. "Oh, shit."

Helpless, Dru looked down. Her crisp red shirt and navy pants were soaked. The splatter had managed to reach her face, making the time she'd spent fiddling with it a complete waste.

She lifted her gaze, one that turned from stunned to searing when she noted that Seth looked very much like a man struggling not to laugh.

"Are you *crazy*?"

"Sorry. Really." He swallowed hard, knowing the laugh fighting to burst out of his throat would damn him. "Sorry," he managed as he walked to her. "I was after Jake—little bastard nailed me. You got caught in the cross fire." He tried a charming smile, dug a bandanna out of the back pocket of his jeans. "Which proves there are no innocent bystanders in war."

"Which proves," she said between her teeth, "that some men are idiots who can't be trusted with a child's toy."

"Hey, hey, this is a Super Soaker 5000." He lifted the water gun but, catching the gleam in her eyes, hastily lowered it again. "Anyway, I'm really sorry. How about a beer?"

"You can take your beer and your Super Soaker 5000 and—"

"Seth!" Anna rushed around the house, then let out a huge sigh. "You moron."

"Jake," he said under his breath and vowed revenge. "Anna, we were just—"

"Quiet." She jabbed a finger at him, then draped an arm around Dru's shoulder. "I apologize for the idiot children. You poor thing. We'll get you inside and into some dry clothes."

"No, really, I'll just—"

"I insist," Anna interrupted, herding her toward the front of the house. "What a greeting. I'd say things aren't usually so crazy around here, but I'd be lying."

Keeping a firm hand on Dru—Anna knew when someone was poised for escape—she guided her into the house and up the stairs.

"It's a little crazier today as the whole gang's here. A welcome-home for Seth. The guys are about to boil up some crabs. You'll stay."

"I couldn't intrude." Her temper was rapidly sliding toward embarrassment. "I just stopped by to drop off the utility-room key for Seth. I really should—"

"Have some dry clothes, some food, some wine," Anna said warmly. "Kevin's jeans ought to work." She pulled a blue cotton shirt out of her own closet. "I'll just see if I can find a pair in the black hole of his room."

"It's just a little water. You should be down with your family. I should go."

"Honey, you're soaked and you're shivering. Now get out of those wet things. We'll toss them in the dryer while we eat. I'll just be a minute."

With this, she strode out and left Dru alone in the bedroom.

The woman hadn't seemed so . . . formidable, Dru decided, on her visits to the flower shop. She wondered if anyone ever won an argument with her.

But the truth was, she was chilled. Giving up, she stripped off the wet shirt, gave a little sigh and took off the equally wet bra. She was just buttoning up when Anna came back in.

"Success." She offered Dru a pair of Levi's. "Shirt okay?"

"Yes, it's fine. Thank you."

"Just bring your wet things down to the kitchen when you're ready." She started out again, then turned back. "And, Dru? Welcome to bedlam."

Close enough, Dru thought. She could hear the shouts and laughter, the blast of music through the open window.

It seemed to her half of St. Christopher must be partying in the Quinns' backyard.

But when she snuck a peek out, she realized the noise was generated by the Quinns all by themselves. There were teenagers of varying sizes and sexes running around, and two, no three dogs. Make that four, she noted as an enormous retriever bounded out of the water and raced over the lawn to shake drops on as many people as possible.

The young boy Seth had been chasing was doing precisely the same thing. Obviously, Seth had managed to catch up with him.

Boats were tied to the dock—which explained, she supposed, why the number of cars in the drive didn't match the number of picnickers.

The Quinns sailed.

They were also loud, wet and messy. The scene below was nothing like any of her parents' outdoor social events or family gatherings. The music would have been classical, and muted. The conversations would have been calm and ordered. And the tables would have been meticulously set with some sort of clever theme.

Her mother was brilliant with themes, and dictated her precise wishes to the caterer, who knew how to deliver.

She wasn't certain she knew how to socialize, even briefly, in the middle of this sort of chaos. But she could hardly do otherwise without being rude.

She changed into the Levi's. The boy—Kevin, she thought Anna had said—was tall. She had to roll up the legs a couple of times into frayed cuffs.

She glanced in the pretty wood-framed mirror over the bureau and, sighing, took a tissue to deal with the mascara smudges under her eyes caused by her unexpected shower.

She gathered the rest of her wet things and started downstairs.

There was a piano in the living room. It looked ancient and well used. The red lilies she'd sold Seth stood in a cut-crystal vase atop it, and spilled their fragrance into the air.

The sofa appeared new, the rug old. It was, Dru thought, very much a family room, with cheerful colors, cozy cushions, a few stray dog hairs and the female touches of the flowers and candles. Snapshots were scattered here and there, all in different frames. There had been no attempt at coordination, and that was the charm of it, she decided.

There were paintings—waterscapes, cityscapes, still lifes—that she was certain were Seth's. But it was a lovely little pencil sketch that drew her over.

It was the rambling white house, flanked by woods, trimmed by water. It said, with absolute simplicity: This is home. And it touched a chord in her that made her yearn.

Stepping closer, she studied the careful signature in the bottom corner. Such a careful signature, she recognized it as a child's even before she read the date printed beneath.

He'd drawn it when he was a child, she realized. Just a little boy making a picture of his home—and already recognizing its value, already talented and insightful enough to translate that value, that warmth and stability with his pencil.

Helplessly, her heart softened toward him. He might be an idiot with an oversized water pistol, but he was a good man. If art reflected the artist, he was a very special man.

She followed the sound of voices back into the kitchen. This, she recognized immediately, was another family center, one captained by a female who took cooking seriously. The long counters were a pristine white making a bright, happy contrast to the candy-apple-red trim. They were covered with platters and bowls of food.

Seth stood with his arm around Anna's shoulders. Their heads were close together, and though she continued to unwrap a bowl, there was a unity in their stance.

Love. Dru could feel the flow of it from across the room, the simple, strong, steady flow of it. The din might have continued from outside, people might have winged in and out the back door, but the two of them made a little island of affection.

She'd always been attracted to that kind of connection, and found herself smiling at them before the woman—that would be Grace—backed out of the enormous refrigerator with yet another platter in hand.

"Oh, Dru. Here, let me take those."

Grace set the bowl aside; Anna and Seth turned. And Dru's smile dimmed into politeness.

Her heart might have softened toward the artist, but she wasn't about to let the idiot off the hook too easily.

"Thanks. They're only damp really. The shirt got the worst of it."

"I got the worst of it." Seth tipped his head toward Anna before he stepped forward. "Sorry. Really. I don't know how I mistook you for a thirteen-year-old boy."

The stare she aimed at him could have frozen a pond at ten paces. "Why don't we just say I was in the wrong place at the wrong time and leave it at that."

"No, this is the right place." He took her hand, lifted it to his lips in what she imagined he thought of as a charming gesture. And damn it, it was. "And it's always the right time."

"Gack," was Jake's opinion as he swung through the

back door. "Crabs are going in," he told Seth. "Dad says for you to get your ass out there."

"Jake!"

Jake sent his mother an innocent look. "I'm just the messenger. We're *starving*."

"Here." Anna stuffed a deviled egg in his mouth. "Now carry this outside. Then come back, without slamming the door, and apologize to Dru."

Jake made mumbling noises around the egg and carried the platter outside.

"It really wasn't his fault," Dru began.

"If this wasn't, something else was. Something always is. Can I get you some wine?"

"Yes, thanks." Obviously, she wasn't going to be able to escape. And the fact was, she was curious about the family that lived in a young artist's pencil sketch. "Ah, is there something I can do to help?"

"Grab whatever, take it out. We'll be feeding the masses shortly."

Anna lifted her eyebrows as Seth grabbed a platter, then pushed the door open for Dru and her bowl of coleslaw. Then Anna wiggled those eyebrows at Grace. "They look cute together."

"They do," Grace agreed. "I like her." She wandered to the door to spy out with Anna. "She's always a little cool at first, then she warms up—or relaxes, I guess. She's awfully pretty, isn't she? And so . . . polished."

"Money usually puts a gleam on you. She's a bit stiff yet, but if this group can't loosen her up, nothing can. Seth's very attracted."

"So I noticed." Grace turned her head toward Anna. "I guess we'd better find out more about her."

"My thoughts exactly." She went back to fetch the wine.

* * *

THE Quinn brothers were impressive examples of the species individually. As a group, Dru decided, they were staggering. They might not have shared blood, but they were so obviously fraternal—tall, lanky, handsome and most of all male.

The quartet around the huge steaming pot simply exuded manhood like other men might a distinctive aftershave. She didn't doubt for a moment that they knew it.

They were what they were, she thought, and were pretty damned pleased about it.

As a woman she found that sort of innate self-satisfaction attractive. She respected confidence and a good, healthy ego. When she wandered around to the brick pit where they steamed the crabs to deliver, at Anna's request, a foursome of cold beer, she caught the end of a conversation.

"Asshole thinks he's Horatio fucking Hornblower." From Cam.

"More like Captain fucking Queed." Muttered by Ethan.

"He can be anybody he wants, as long as his money's green." Delivered with a shrug by Phillip. "We've built boats for assholes before, and will again."

"One fuckhead's the same as—" Seth broke off when he spotted Dru.

"Gentlemen." She never batted an eyelash. "Cold beer for hot work."

"Thanks." Phillip took them from her. "Heard you've already cooled off once today."

"Unexpectedly." Relieved of the bottles, she lifted her wineglass to her lips, sipped. "But I prefer this method to the Super Soaker 5000." Ignoring Seth, she looked at

Ethan. "Did you catch them?" she asked, gesturing to the pot.

"Deke and I, yeah." He grinned when Seth cleared his throat. "We took him along for ballast," he told Dru. "Got blisters on his city hands."

"Couple days in the boatyard might toughen him up," Cam speculated. "Always was puny though."

"You're just trying to insult me so I'll come in and do the hot fifty-fifty work." Seth tipped back his beer. "Keep dreaming."

"Puny," Phillip said, "but smart. Always was smart."

"I wonder if I could come in sometime, take a look around at your work."

Cam tilted his head toward Dru. "Like boats, do you?"

"Yes, I do."

"Why don't we go for a sail," Seth asked her.

She spared him a glance that was on the edge of withering. "Keep dreaming," she suggested and strolled away.

"Classy," was Phillip's opinion.

"She's a nice girl," Ethan said as he checked the pot.

"Hot," Cam commented. "Very, very hot."

"You want to cool off, I'll be happy to stick the Super Soaker 5000 up your ass," Seth told him.

"Got a bead on her?" Cam shook his head as if in pity. "She looks out of your league to me, kid."

"Yeah." Seth gulped more beer. "I'm a big fan of interleague play."

Phillip watched Seth wander off, then chuckled. "Our boy's going to be spending a hell of a lot of money on flowers for the next little while."

"That particular bloom's got some long stems on her," Cam remarked.

"Got careful eyes." Ethan gave the traditional Quinn

shoulder jerk when Cam frowned at him. "Watches everything, including Seth, but it's all one step back, you know. Not because she's shy—the girl isn't shy. She's careful."

"She comes from big money and politics." Phillip considered his beer. "Bound to make you careful."

"Saint Chris is a funny place for her to end up, isn't it?" To Cam's mind, family forged you—the family you were born to or the family you made. He wondered how Dru's had forged her.

SHE'D intended to stay no more than an hour. A polite hour while her clothes dried. But somehow she was drawn into a conversation with Emily about New York. And one with Anna about gardening. Then there were the mutual acquaintances with Sybill and Phillip from D.C.

The food was wonderful. When she complimented the potato salad, Grace offered her the recipe. Dru wasn't quite sure how to announce that she didn't cook.

There were arguments—over baseball, clothes, video games. It didn't take her long to realize it was just another kind of interaction.

Dogs sidled up to the table and were ordered firmly away—usually after someone snuck food into a canine mouth. The breeze blew in cool over the water while as many as six conversations went on at the same time.

She kept up. Early training had honed her ability to have something to say to everyone and anyone in social situations. She could comment about boats and baseball, food and music, art and travel even when the talk of them and more leaped and swirled around her.

She nursed a second glass of wine and stayed far longer than she'd intended. Not just because she couldn't find a polite way to leave. Because she liked them. She was amused by and envious of the intimacy of the family. Despite their numbers and the obvious differences—could sisters be less alike than the sharp-tongued, sports-loving Aubrey and Emily, the waiflike ballerina?—they were all so firmly interlinked.

Like individual pieces of one big, bold puzzle, Dru decided. The puzzle of family always fascinated her. Certainly her own continued to remain a mystery to her.

However colorful and cheerful they seemed on the surface, Dru imagined the Quinn puzzle had its share of shadows and complications.

Families always did.

As did men, she thought, turning her head deliberately to meet Seth's dead-on stare. She was perfectly aware that he'd watched her almost continuously since they'd sat down to eat. Oh, he was good at the conversation juggling, too; she'd give him that. And from time to time he'd tune his attention fully on someone else. But his gaze, that straight-on and vivid blue gaze, would always swing back to her.

She could feel it, a kind of heat along her skin.

She refused to let it intrigue her. And she certainly wasn't going to let it fluster her.

"The afternoon light's good here." His eyes still on Dru, he scooped up a forkful of pasta salad. "Maybe we'll do some outdoor work. You got anything with a long, full skirt? Strapless or sleeveless to show off your shoulders. Good strong shoulders," he added with another scoop of pasta. "They go with the face."

"That's lucky for me, isn't it?" She dismissed him with a slight wave of her hand and turned to Sybill. "I enjoyed your last documentary very much, the studies and examples of blended family dynamics. I suppose you based some of your findings on your own experiences."

"Hard to get away from it. I could study this bunch for the next couple of decades and never run out of material."

"We're all Mom's guinea pigs," Fiona stated as she handily picked out another crab. "Better watch out. You hang out around here, Seth'll have you naked on a canvas and Mom'll have you analyzed in a book."

"Oh, I don't know." Aubrey gestured with her drink. "Annie Crawford hung around here for months, and Seth never did paint her—naked or otherwise. I don't think Sybill ever wrote about her either, unless I missed the one about societal placement of brainless bimbos."

"She wasn't brainless," Seth put in.

"She called you Sethie. As in, 'Oh, Sethie, you're a regular Michael Dee Angelo.' "

"Want me to start trotting out some of the guys you hung with a few years back? Matt Fisher, for instance?"

"I was young and shallow."

"Yeah, you're old and deep now. Anyway"—he shifted that direct gaze to Dru again—"you got a long, flowy thing? Little top?"

"No."

"We'll get something."

Dru sipped the last of her wine, tilted her head slightly to indicate interest. "Has anyone ever declined to be painted by you?"

"No, not really."

"Let me be the first."

"He'll do it anyway," Cam told her. "Kid's got a head like a brick."

"And that comes from the most flexible, most reasonable, most accommodating of men," Anna declared as she rose. "Anybody got room for dessert?"

They did, though Dru didn't see how. She declined offers of cakes, pies, but lost the battle of wills over a double fudge brownie that she nibbled on before changing back into her own clothes.

She folded the borrowed shirt and jeans, set them on the bed, took one last look around the cozy bedroom, then started down.

Dru stopped short in the kitchen doorway when she spotted Anna and Cam in front of the sink in an embrace a great deal more torrid than she expected from parents of teenagers.

"Let's go upstairs and lock the door," Dru heard him say—and wasn't sure where to look when she noted Cam's hands slide around possessively to squeeze his wife's butt. "No one will miss us."

"That's what you said after dinner last Thanksgiving." There was both warmth and fun in her voice when Anna linked her arms around Cam's neck. "You were wrong."

"Phil was just jealous because he didn't think of it first."

"Later, Quinn. If you behave, I might just let you . . . Oh, Dru."

From the easy grins on their faces, Dru concluded she was the only one of the trio who was the least bit embarrassed. "I'm sorry. I wanted to thank you for the hospitality. I really enjoyed the afternoon."

"Good. Then you'll come again. Cam, let Seth know Dru's leaving, will you?" And damned if she didn't give his butt a squeeze before easing out of his arms.

"Don't bother. You have a wonderful family, a beautiful home. I appreciate your letting me share them today."

"I'm glad you dropped by," Anna said, giving Cam a silent signal as she laid an arm over Dru's shoulder to walk her to the front door.

"The key." Shaking her head, Dru dug into her purse. "I completely forgot the reason I came by in the first place. Would you give this to Seth? He can store whatever he needs to in there for the time being. We'll work out the details later."

Anna heard the kitchen door slam. "You might as well give it to him yourself. Come back," she said, then gave Dru a quick, casual kiss on the cheek.

"Taking off?" A little winded, Seth hurried up to catch Dru on the front porch. "Why don't you stay? Aubrey's getting a softball game together."

"I have to get home. The key." She held it out while he only stood looking at her. "Utility room? Storage?"

"Yeah, yeah." He took it, stuffed it in his pocket. "Listen, it's early, but if you want to split, we can go somewhere. A drive or something."

"I have things to do." She walked toward her car.

"We'll have to try for less of a crowd on our second date."

She paused, looked back at him over her shoulder. "We haven't had a first date yet."

"Sure we did. Steamed crabs, just as predicted. You get to pick the menu and venue for date number two."

Jiggling the car keys in her hand, she turned to face him. "I came by to give you the key, got blasted with a water gun and had a crab feast with your large, extended family. That doesn't make this a date."

"This will."

He had a smooth move—so smooth she never saw it coming. Maybe if she had, she'd have evaded. Or maybe not. But that wasn't the issue as his hands were cupped on her shoulders and his mouth was warm and firm on hers.

He lifted her, just slightly. He tilted his head, just a little. So his lips rubbed hers—a seductive tease—and his hands cruised down her body to add an unexpected punch of heat.

She felt the breeze flutter against her cheeks, and heard the blast of music as someone turned the stereo up to scream again. And when the hard line of him pressed against her, she realized she'd been the one to move in.

The long, liquid tugs deep in her belly warned her, but still she shot her fingers through that thick, sun-streaked hair and let his hands roam.

He'd meant to *suggest* with a kiss, to tease a smile or a frown out of her so he could have the pleasure of watching either expression move over her face.

He'd only intended to skim the surface, perhaps to show them both hints of what could lie beneath. But when she'd leaned into him, locked around him, he sank.

Women were a dazzling array of colors for him. Mother, sister, lover, friend. But he'd never had another woman strike him with such brilliance. He wanted to steep in it, in her until they were both drenched.

"Let me come home with you, Drusilla." He skimmed his lips over her cheek, down to her throat, back up and along the finger-brush indentation in her chin, and to her mouth. "Let me lie down with you. Be with you. Let me touch you."

She shook her head. She didn't like speed, she reminded herself. A smart woman never turned a corner until she'd looked at the map for the entire route—and even then, she went forward only with caution.

"I'm not impulsive, Seth. I'm not rash." She put her hands on his shoulders to nudge him away, but her gaze was direct. "I don't share myself with a man just because there's heat."

"Okay." He pressed his lips to her forehead before he stepped back. "Stay. We'll play some ball, maybe go for a sail. We'll keep it simple today."

With some men, the suggestion would have been just another ploy to persuade her into bed. But she didn't sense that with him. He meant what he said, she decided. "I might actually like you after a while."

"Counting on it."

"But I can't stay. I left a number of things undone to come by, and I've stayed much longer than I intended."

"Didn't you ever ditch school?"

"No."

He braced a hand on the car door before she could open it, and his face was sincerely shocked. "Not once?"

"Afraid not."

"A rule player," he considered. "Sexy."

She had to laugh. "If I said I'd skipped school once a week, you'd have called me a rebel and said *that* was sexy."

"Got me. How about dinner tomorrow night?"

"No." She waved him away from the car door. "I need to think about this. I don't want to be interested in you."

"Which means you are."

She slid behind the wheel. "Which means I don't want to be. I'll let you know if I change my mind. Go back to your family. You're lucky to have them," she said, then closed the car door.

He watched her back out, then drive away. His blood was still warm from the kiss, and his mind too full of her and the possibilities for him to take notice of the car that eased from the shoulder of the road by the trees, then followed after Dru's.

FIVE

⌒

SHE KNEW HE'D moved in. Now and again when Dru went into the back room of the shop, she could hear music through the vents. It didn't surprise her that he played it loud, or that his choices varied from head-banging rock to mellow blues and into passionate opera.

Nothing about Seth Quinn surprised her.

He came and went during the first week of his lease without any rhyme or reason she could see. Occasionally he breezed in and out of the shop, to ask if she needed anything, to let her know he'd be starting on the skylights, to tell her he'd moved some things into the storage space and made a copy of the key.

He was always friendly, never seemed particularly rushed. And never once attempted to follow up on the steamy afternoon kiss.

It irked her, for a number of reasons. First, she'd been set to deflect any follow-up, at least for the time being. She had no intention of Seth, or any man, taking her availability for granted.

That was simply principle.

And, of course, it was expected that he *would* follow up. A man didn't ask to take you to bed one day, then treat you like a casual neighbor the next.

So perhaps he had surprised her after all. Which only irritated her more.

Just as well, she told herself as she worked on the small tabletop arrangements she sold to one of the waterfront's upscale restaurants. She was settling into St. Chris, into her business, into the kind of life she'd always wanted—without knowing she wanted it. A relationship, whether it was an affair, a romance or just no-strings sex, would change the balance.

And she was so enjoying the balance.

The only person who needed anything from her, demanded anything from her, expected anything from her these days was herself. That, in itself, was like a gift from God.

Pleased with the combination of narcissus and sprekelia, she loaded the arrangements into refrigeration. Her part-time delivery man would pick them up, along with the iris and tulips and showy white lilies ordered by a couple of the local B and B's.

She heard Seth arrive—the sound of the car door slamming, the crunch of footsteps over gravel, then the quick slap of them up the back steps.

Moments later came the music. Rock today, she noted with a glance at the overhead vent. Which probably meant he'd be up on the roof shortly, working on the skylights.

She went back into the shop, picked up the plant she'd

earmarked, then headed out the back and up the steps. A polite knock wouldn't do, not with the music blaring, so she used the side of her fist to pound.

"Yeah, yeah, it's open. Since when do you guys knock?"

He turned, in the act of strapping on a tool belt, as she opened the door. "Hey." His smile came quick and easy. "I thought you were one of my brothers, but you're a lot better-looking."

"I heard you come in." She would not be a cliché, she promised herself. She would *not* entertain ridiculous fantasies because she'd come upon a long, lanky male wearing a tool belt. "I thought you might like these."

"What? Wait." Amused at himself, he walked into the tiny kitchen where he'd set a tabletop stereo and turned down the volume. "Sorry."

His hammer bounced against his hip. He was wearing jeans that were equal parts holes and denim. His T-shirt was faded gray and splotched with paint and what was probably some sort of engine grease. He hadn't shaved.

She was not, absolutely not, attracted to rough, untidy men.

Usually.

"I brought you a plant." Her tone was sharper, more impatient than she intended. Her own words came back to haunt her. No, she didn't want to be interested in Seth Quinn.

"Yeah?" Despite her tone, he looked very pleased as he crossed over and took the pot from her. "Thanks," he said as he studied the green leaves and little white blossoms.

"It's a shamrock," she told him. "Quinn. It seemed to fit."

"Guess it does." Then those blue eyes lifted, locked on hers. "I appreciate it."

"Don't let it dry out." She glanced up. Two skylights were already installed. And he was right, she mused, they made all the difference. "You've been busy."

"Hmm. Traded some time at the boatyard for some labor here. Cam's going to give me a hand today, so we should finish up."

"Well then." She glanced around. After all, she reminded herself, she owned the place. She could take some interest in what went on there.

He had canvases stacked against two of the walls. An easel with a blank canvas was already set up in front of the windows. She wasn't sure how he'd managed to muscle the enormous worktable up the stairs and through the rather narrow door, but it was plopped in the center of the room and already covered with the detritus of the artist: brushes, paints, a mason jar of turpentine, rags, pencils, chalks.

There were a couple of stools, an old wooden chair, an even older table topped by a particularly ugly lamp.

Shelves, again wood, held more painting supplies.

He'd hung nothing on the walls, she noted. There was nothing but space, tools and light.

"You seem to be settling in. I'll let you get back to it." But one of the propped canvases drew her. It was a wash of purple over green. A riot of wild foxglove under pearly light pulled her in so that she could almost feel the brush of leaves and petals on her skin.

"A roadside in Ireland," he said. "County Clare. I spent a few weeks there once. Everywhere you look it's a painting. You can never really translate it on canvas."

"I think you have. It's wonderful. Simple and strong. I've never seen foxglove growing wild on a roadside in Ireland. But now I feel I have. Isn't that the point?"

He stared at her a moment. The morning sun speared through the skylight and streamed over her, accented the line of jaw and cheek. "Just stand there. Just stand right there," he repeated as he swung to his worktable. "Ten minutes. Okay, I lied. Twenty tops."

"Excuse me?"

"Just stand there. Damn it, where's my—ah." He scooped up a hunk of charcoal, then dragged his easel around. "No, don't look at me. Look over there. Wait."

He moved quickly, snatching up the painting of fox-gloves, pulling out a nail from his pouch, then pounding it into the wall. "Just look at the painting."

"I don't have time to—"

"At the painting." This time his voice snapped, so full of authority and impatience, she obeyed before she thought it through. "I'll pay you for the time."

"I don't want your money."

"In trade." He was already stroking the charcoal over the canvas. "You've got that house by the river. You probably need things done off and on."

"I can take care of—"

"Uh-huh, uh-huh. Tilt your chin up a little, to the right. Jesus, Jesus, this light. Relax your jaw. Be pissed off later, just let me get this."

Who the hell was he? she wondered. He stood there, legs apart, body set like a man poised to fight. He had a tool belt slung at his hips and was sketching in charcoal as if his life depended on it.

His eyes were narrowed, so intense, so *focused*, that her heart jumped a little each time they whipped up and over her face.

On the stereo AC/DC was on the highway to hell. Through the open window came the cry of gulls as they swooped over the bay. Not entirely sure why she'd allowed herself to be ordered around, she stood and studied the foxgloves.

She began to see it gracing her bedroom wall.

"How much do you want for it?"

His eyebrows remained knit. "I'll let you know when I've finished it."

"No, the painting I'm staring at while I'm trying not to be annoyed with you. I'd like to buy it. You have an agent, I imagine. Should I contact him or her?"

He only grunted, not the least interested in business at the moment, and continued to work. "Don't move your head, just your eyes. And look at me. That's some face, all right."

"Yes, and I'm certainly all aflutter by your interest in it, but I have to go down and open for the day."

"Couple more minutes."

"Would you like to hear my opinion of people who can't take no for an answer?"

"Not right now." Keep her occupied, keep her talking, he thought quickly. Oh Jesus, it was perfect—the light, the face, that cool stare out of mossy green eyes. "I hear you've got old Mr. Gimball doing deliveries for you. How's that working out?"

"Perfectly fine, and as he's going to be pulling up in back very shortly—"

"He'll wait. Mr. Gimball used to teach history when I was in middle school. He seemed ancient then, as creaky as the dead presidents he lectured about. Once some of us found this big snake skin. We brought it in and curled it up on Mr. G's desk chair before third period."

"I'm sure you thought that was hysterically funny."

"Are you kidding? I was eleven. I nearly cracked a rib

laughing. Didn't you ever pull stunts like that on teachers in your private school for girls?"

"No, and why do you assume I went to a private school for girls?"

"Oh, sugar, it's all over you." He stepped back, nodded at the canvas. "Yeah, and it looks good on you." He reached forward, softened a line of charcoal with his thumb before he looked over at her. "You want to call this a sitting or our second date?"

"Neither." It took every ounce of will, but she didn't cross over to look at what he'd drawn.

"Second date," he decided, as he tossed the charcoal aside, absently picked up a rag to clean it off his hands. "After all, you brought me flowers."

"A plant," she corrected.

"Semantics. You really want the painting?"

"That would depend on how much really wanting it jacks up the price."

"You're pretty cynical."

"Cynicism is underrated. Why don't you give me your representative's name? Then we'll see."

He loved the way that short, sleek hair followed the shape of her head. He wanted to do more than sketch it. He needed to paint it.

And to touch it. To run his hands over that silky, dense black until he'd know its texture in his sleep.

"Let's do a friendly trade instead. Pose for me, and it's yours."

"I believe I just did."

"No. I want you in oil." And in watercolors. In pastels. In bed.

He'd spent a great deal of time thinking about her over the last few days. Enough time to have concluded that a woman like her—with her looks, her background—would be used to men in active pursuit.

So he'd slowed things down, deliberately, and had waited for her to take the next step. To his way of thinking, she had. In the form of a houseplant.

He wanted her personally as much as he wanted her professionally. It didn't matter which came first, as long as he got both.

She shifted her gaze to the painting again. It was always a pleasure, and a bit of a shock, when he saw desire in someone's eyes when they looked at his work. Seeing it in Dru's he knew he'd scored, professionally.

"I have a business to run," she began.

"I'll work around your schedule. Give me an hour in the mornings before you open when you can manage it. Four hours on Sundays."

She frowned. It didn't seem like so very much, when he put it like that. And oh, the painting was gorgeous. "For how long?"

"I don't know yet." He felt a little ripple of irritation. "It's art, not accounting."

"Here?"

"To start, anyway."

She debated, argued with herself. Wished she'd never seen the damn painting. Then because it was a foolish woman who made any agreement without looking at all the terms, she walked to the easel, around the canvas. And studied her own face.

She'd expected something rough and, well, sketchy, as he'd taken no more than fifteen minutes to produce it. Instead, it was detailed and stunning—the angles, the shadows, the curves.

She looked very cool, she decided. A bit aloof and so

very, very serious. Cynical? she thought and gave in to the smile that tugged at her mouth.

"I don't look particularly friendly," she said.

"You weren't feeling particularly friendly."

"Can't argue with that. Or with the fact that you have an amazing gift." She sighed. "I don't have a dress with a long, full skirt and a sleeveless top."

And he grinned. "We'll improvise."

"I'll give you an hour tomorrow. Seven-thirty to eight-thirty."

"Ouch. Okay." He walked over, took the painting from the wall, held it out to her.

"You're trusting."

"Trust is underrated."

When her hands were full, he took her arms. He gave her that slight lift again, brought her to her toes. And the door swung open.

"Nope," Seth muttered as Cam strode in. "They never knock."

"Hi, Dru. Kiss the girl on your own time, kid. I don't smell any coffee." Obviously at home, he went toward the kitchen, then spotted the canvas. His face lit with pure delight. "Easiest fifty I ever made. I bet Phil Seth here would talk you into posing before the week was up."

"Oh, really?"

"No offense. Rembrandt here wants to paint something, he finds a way. He'd be a fool to pass up the chance to do that," he added, and the look on his face when he studied the canvas again was so filled with pride, she softened. "He's a pain in the ass half the time, but he's no fool."

"I'm aware of the pain-in-the-ass factor. I'll reserve judgment on whether or not he's a fool until I get to know him better. Seven-thirty," she said to Seth on her way out. "That's A.M."

Cam said nothing, just laid a beat with an open hand on his heart.

"Kiss ass."

"So, are you going to paint her, or poke at her?" Cam hooted out a laugh at Seth's vicious snarl. "What goes around comes around, kid. You spent a lot of time being disgusted at the idea of us poking at girls—as you put it— not so long ago."

"Since it is more than fifteen years that's not so long ago in your mind, it proves you're really getting old. Sure you should go up on the roof? Might have a spell up there and fall off."

"I can still kick your ass, kid."

"Sure. With Ethan and Phil holding me down, you might have a shot at taking me." He laughed when Cam caught him in a headlock. "Oh man, now I'm scared."

But they both remembered a time he would have been, when a skinny, smart-mouthed young boy would have frozen with terror at a touch, rough or gentle.

Knowing it, remembering it, Seth nearly blurted out the trouble he was keeping so tightly locked in the far corner of his mind.

No, he'd handled it, he told himself. And would handle it again, if and when.

HE was a man of his word. When the last of the skylights was in place, he followed Cam to the boatyard to put in a few hours.

Once, he'd thought he'd make his living here, working

side by side with his brothers building wooden sailing vessels. The fact was, some of his best memories were tucked inside the old brick building, flavored with his sweat, a little blood and the thrill of learning to be a part of something.

It had changed over the years. Refined, as Phillip would say. The walls were no longer bare and patched drywall, but painted a simple, workingman's white.

They'd fashioned a sort of entryway that opened to the stairs leading to Phillip's office and the second-story loft. It separated, in theory, the main work area.

Lining the walls were rough-framed sketches of various boats built by Quinn over the years. They depicted the progress of the business, and the growth of the artist.

He knew, because Aubrey had told him, that an art collector had come in two years before and offered his brothers a quarter million for the fifty sketches currently on display.

They'd turned him down flat, but had offered to build him a boat based on any sketch he liked.

It had never been about money, he thought now, though there had been some lean times during those first couple years. It had always been about the unit. And a promise made to Ray Quinn.

The work area itself hadn't changed very much. It was still a big, echoing, brightly lit space. There were pulleys and winches hanging from the ceiling. Saws, benches, stacks of lumber, the smell of freshly sawn wood, linseed oil, sweat, coffee, the boom of rock and roll, the buzz of power saws, the lingering scent of onions from someone's lunchtime sub.

It was all as familiar to him as his own face.

Yes, once he'd thought he'd spend his life working there, listening to Phillip bitch about unpaid invoices, watching Ethan's patient hands lapping wood, sweating with Cam as they turned a hull.

But art had consumed it. The love of it had taken him away from boyhood ambitions. And had, for a time, taken him from his family.

He was a man now, he reminded himself. A man who would stand on his own ground, fight his own battles and be what it was he was meant to be.

Nothing, no one, was going to stop him.

"You plan on standing there with your thumb up your ass much longer?" Cam asked him. "Or are we going to get some work out of you this afternoon?"

Seth shook himself back to the present. "Doesn't look like you need me," he pointed out.

He spotted Aubrey working on the deck planking of a skiff, her electric screwdriver whirling. She wore an Orioles fielder's cap with her long tail of hair pulled through the back. Ethan was at the lathe, turning a mast with his faithful dog sprawled at his feet.

"Hull of that skiff needs to be caulked and filled."

Grunt work, Seth thought and sighed. "And what are you going to be doing?"

"Basking in the glory of my little empire."

The basking included detailing the bulkhead for the cockpit, the sort of carpentry Cam turned into an art.

Seth did the grunt work; it was hardly the first time. He knew how to plank, he thought, a bit resentfully as Aubrey's drill continued its bump and grind over his head.

"Hey." She bent down to talk to him. "Will's got the night off. We're going to get some pizza, catch a flick after. You want in?"

It was tempting. He wanted to connect with Will again, not only because they'd been friends, but because he wanted to check out any guy who was sniffing around Aubrey.

He weighed that against spending the evening as a fifth wheel.

"Village Pizza?"

"Still the best in Saint Chris."

"Maybe I'll swing in," Seth decided. "Say hi to Will. I'll pass on the flick. I've got to get started early tomorrow."

"I thought you artistic types called your own hours."

Seth worked oakum into a seam of beveled planking on the hull. "Subject's calling these."

"What subject?" She sat back on her heels, then suddenly understood when she noted the expression on his face. "Ooooh, fancy flower lady's going to pose for the famous artist. I got more juice on her."

"I'm not interested in gossip." He managed to hold firm on that for nearly ten seconds. "What kind of juice?"

"Juicy juice, sweetheart. I got it from Jamie Styles, who got it from her cousin who was a Senate page a few years ago. Dru and a certain high-level White House aide were a very hot item back then."

"How hot?"

"Hot enough to burn up the society columns in the *Post* for nearly a year. And to warrant what Jamie's cousin describes as an engagement ring with a diamond the size of a doorknob. Then the diamond disappears, hot goes cold, and the high-level aide starts burning up the newsprint with a blonde."

"She was engaged?"

"Yeah. Briefly, according to my source. It came out that the blonde was a factor *before* the broken engagement. If you get my drift."

"He was cheating on Dru with the bimbo?"

"It so happens that this blonde was—is—a hotshot lawyer, assistant White House counsel or something."

"Must've been tough on Dru, having all that personal business splashed around in the press."

"She strikes me as someone who'd stand up to it pretty well. She's nobody's doormat. And I bet you a month's pay she busted that cheating bastard's balls before she stuffed the ring down his throat."

"You would," Seth said with approval and pride. "Right before you mopped the floor with his lying tongue. But Dru doesn't come off as the violent type. More like she froze him to death with one chilly look and a few icy words."

Aubrey snorted. "A lot you know about women. Still waters, pal of mine. They not only run deep, you bet your ass they can run hot, too."

MAYBE, Seth thought as he dropped his filthy, aching body back behind the wheel of his car. But he'd lay money Dru had sliced the guy in two without spilling a single drop of blood.

He knew what it was to have little personal details of your life—embarrassing, intimate details—nibbled on by the press.

It could be she'd come here to get away from all that. He knew just how she felt.

He glanced at the time as he pulled out. He could use that pizza Aubrey had mentioned, and it seemed a waste of effort to drive all the way home to shower off the day's work, then head right back into town.

So he'd just swing by and clean up at the studio. He'd brought over some towels and soap. He even remembered to toss a spare pair of jeans and a shirt into the closet.

He might just find Dru still at the shop and talk her into a friendly pizza. Which would, he thought, pleased with the idea, constitute date number three.

She'd get that cool, I-am-not-amused expression on her face when he called it that, he thought. And that quick light in her eyes that gave her humor away.

He was crazy about that contrast.

He could spend hours—days—contemplating the varieties of shadow and light in her.

But her car was gone from the little lot behind her building. He considered calling her, persuading her to come back into town, before he remembered he didn't have a phone.

He'd have to take care of that, he mused. But since he couldn't call from there, he'd clean up, buzz over to Village Pizza and call her from a pay phone.

Somebody was bound to have her number.

Better, he decided as he started up the steps, he'd get a pizza to go and stop by her house on the way home. With a bottle of Merlot.

What kind of woman would turn a guy away when he had pizza and wine?

Satisfied with the plan, he stepped inside, and felt something skid under his foot. Frowning, he reached down and picked up the folded note that had been slipped under his door.

His stomach pitched as the bottom fell out of his world.

Ten thousand should hold me. I'll be in touch.

Seth simply sat on the floor just inside the studio door and crumpled the paper into a tiny, mean ball.

Gloria DeLauter was back. He hadn't expected her to find or follow him so quickly. He hadn't been prepared, he admitted, to find her nipping at his heels barely two weeks after he'd left Rome.

He'd wanted time to think, to decide. He flipped the little wad of paper across the room. Well, ten thousand would buy him time, if he wanted to piss the money away.

He'd done it before.

When it came to his mother, there was no price he wouldn't pay to be free of her. And more, to keep his family free of her.

It was, of course, exactly what she counted on.

Six

⌢

HE WAS SITTING on the dock, pole fishing with a smear of Anna's Brie for bait. The sun was summer-hot on his back, with an August weight to it that drenched the skin and set the brain to dreaming.

He wore nothing but cut-off jeans and a pair of wire-rim sunglasses.

He liked looking through them at the way the light beat down from a hazy blue sky and smacked the water. And he thought, idly, that he might just set the pole aside in a bit and slide right in to cool off.

The water lapped lazily against the hull of the little pram with blue sails tied to the dock. A jay was bitching in the trees, and when a stingy little breeze passed by, it carried a hint of roses from a bush that had lived there longer than he.

The house was quiet. The lawn leading to it was lush and freshly mown. He could smell that, too. Newly cut grass, roses, lazy water. Summer smells.

It didn't strike him as odd, though it was still spring.

Something had to be done, and he wished to God he knew what, to keep that house quiet, the air summer-peaceful. And his family safe.

He heard the yip of a dog, then the scrambling of canine feet on the dock. Seth didn't look up, even when the cold nose nudged at his cheek. He simply lifted an arm so the dog could wriggle against his side.

It was always comforting, somehow, to have a dog at your side when your thoughts were heavy.

But that wasn't enough for the dog, whose tail pounded a drumbeat on the dock as its tongue slathered over Seth's cheek.

"Okay, okay, cool it. Thinking here," he began, then felt his heart jump into his throat as he shifted to nudge the dog down.

Not Cam's dog, but his own. Foolish, who'd died in Seth's arms five years before. Speechless, Seth stared as those familiar doggie eyes seemed to laugh into his at the world's best joke.

"Wait a minute, wait a minute." Joy and shock tangled inside him as he grabbed the dog's muzzle. Warm fur, cold nose, wet tongue. "What the hell is this?"

Foolish gave another cheerful bark then flopped adoringly across Seth's lap.

"There you are, you stupid idiot," Seth murmured, as unspeakable love gushed inside him. "There you are, you idiot. Christ, oh Christ, I've missed you." He bobbled the pole, let go of it as he grabbed for his dog.

A hand reached out, snagged the pole before it dropped into the water.

"Wouldn't want to waste that fancy cheese." The woman who sat beside him, legs dangling over the dock, took charge of the pole. "We figured Foolish would cheer you up. Nothing like a dog, is there? For companionship, love, comfort and pure entertainment. Nothing biting today?"

"No, not . . ."

The words slipped back down his throat as he looked at her. He knew that face; he'd seen it in pictures. Long and thin, scattershot freckles over the nose and cheeks. She had a shapeless khaki hat over messy red curls that were streaked with silver. And her dark green eyes were unmistakable.

"You're Stella. Stella Quinn." Stella Quinn, he thought as he tried to make sense of it, who'd been dead more than twenty years.

"You turned out handsome, didn't you? Always thought you would." She gave the stubby ponytail a friendly tug. "Need a haircut, boy."

"I guess I'm dreaming."

"I guess you are," she said easily, but her hand moved from his hair to his cheek and gave it a rub before she tipped down his dark glasses. "You've got Ray's eyes. I fell for his eyes first, you know."

"I always wanted to meet you." You got your wishes in dreams, Seth decided.

"Well, here we are." With a chuckle, she tapped his sunglasses back in place. "Never too late, is it? Never cared much for fishing myself. Like the water—to look at, to swim in. Still, fishing's good for thinking, or not thinking at all. If you're going to brood, might as well have a line in the water. You never know what you'll pull up."

"I never dreamed about you before. Not like this."

The fact was, he'd never dreamed with this kind of clarity. He could feel the warm fur under his hand, and the steady beat of heart as Foolish panted in the heat.

He felt the strength of the sun on his bare back, and could hear, in the distance, the putt and purr of a workboat. The jay never stopped its piercing song.

"We figured it was time I got to play Grandma." She gave Seth an affectionate pat on the knee. "I missed that while I was here. Getting to fuss and coo over the babies when they came, spoiling you and the others. Dying's damn inconvenient, let me tell you."

When he simply stared at her, she let out a long, clear laugh. "It's natural enough to be a little spooked. It's not every day you sit around talking to a ghost."

"I don't believe in ghosts."

"Hard to blame you." She looked out over the water, and something in her face spoke of absolute contentment. "I'd've baked cookies for you, though I was never much of a cook. But you can't have everything, so you take what you can get. You're Ray's grandson, so that makes you mine."

His head was reeling, but he didn't feel dizzy. His pulse was galloping, but he didn't feel fear. "He was good to me. I only had him for a little while, but he was . . ."

"Decent." She nodded as she said it. "That's what you told Cam when he asked you. Ray was decent, you said, and you sure as hell hadn't had much decent up till then, poor little guy."

"He changed everything for me."

"He gave you a chance to change everything. You've done a pretty good job of it, so far. Can't choose where you come from, Seth. My boys and you know that better than anyone. But you can choose where you end up, and how you get there."

"Ray took me in, and it killed him."

"You say something like that and mean it, you're not as

smart as everyone thinks. Ray'd be disappointed to hear you say it."

"He wouldn't have been on that road if it hadn't been for me."

"How do you know that?" She poked him again. "If not that road that day, another road another day. Damn fool always drove too fast. Things happen, and that's that. They happen a different way, we'd sit around complaining about it just the same. Waste a lot of living on the ifs and ors, if you ask me."

"But—"

"But hell. George Bailey learned his lesson, didn't he?"

Baffled, fascinated, Seth shifted. "Who?"

Stella rolled her eyes toward heaven. "*It's a Wonderful Life*. Jimmy Stewart as George Bailey. Decides it would be better for everyone if he'd never been born, so an angel shows him the way things would've worked out if he hadn't."

"And you're going to show me?"

"Do I look like an angel to you?" she asked, amused.

"No. But I'm not thinking it'd be better if I'd never been born either."

"Change one thing, change everything. That's the lesson. What if Ray hadn't brought you here, if he hadn't run into that damn telephone pole? Maybe Cam and Anna wouldn't have met. Then Kevin and Jake wouldn't have been born. You wishing them away?"

"No, Jesus, of course not. But if Gloria—"

"Ah." With a satisfied nod, Stella lifted a finger. "There's the nub, isn't it? No point in saying 'if Gloria,' or 'but Gloria.' Gloria DeLauter is reality."

"She's back."

Her face softened, her voice gentled. "Yes, honey, I know. And it weighs on you."

"I won't let her touch their lives again. I won't let her fuck up my family. She only wants money. It's all she's ever wanted."

"You think?" Stella sighed. "Well, if you do, I suppose you'll give it to her. Again."

"What else can I do?"

"You'll figure it out." She handed him the pole.

He woke sitting on the side of the bed, his hand loosely fisted as if it held a fishing pole.

And when he opened those fingers, they shook a little. When he drew one careful breath, he'd have sworn he smelled the faint drift of summer grass.

Weird, he thought and raked his fingers through his hair. Very weird dream. And he could swear he felt the lingering warmth from his dog stretched across his lap.

THE first ten years of his life had been a prison of fear, abuse and neglect. It had made him stronger than most ten-year-old boys. And a great deal more wary.

Ray Quinn's pre-Stella affair with a woman named Barbara Harrow had been brief. He'd put it so completely behind him that his three adopted sons had been totally unaware of it. Just as Ray had been unaware of the product of that affair.

Gloria DeLauter.

But Gloria had known about Ray, and had tracked him down. In her usual style she'd used extortion and blackmail to bleed Ray for money. And had, in essence, sold her son to her father. But Ray had died suddenly, before he found the way to tell his sons, and his grandchild, of the connection.

To the Quinn brothers, Seth had simply been another of Ray Quinn's strays. They'd been bound to him by no more than a promise to a dying man. But that had been enough.

They'd changed their lives for him. They'd given him a home, stood up for him, shown him what it was to be part of a family. And they'd fought to keep him.

Anna had been his caseworker. Grace his first surrogate mother. And Sybill, Gloria's half sister, had brought back the only soft memories of his childhood.

He knew how much they'd sacrificed to give him a life. A life as decent as Ray Quinn. By the time Gloria had stepped back into the picture, hoping to bleed them for more money, he'd been one of them.

One of the brothers Quinn.

This wasn't the first time Gloria had approached him for money. He'd had three years to forget her, to feel safe after his new family had circled around him. Then she'd slith-ered back to St. Chris and had extorted money from a fourteen-year-old boy.

He'd never told them of it.

A few hundred that first time, he remembered. It was all he could manage without his family finding out—and had satisfied her. For a little while.

He'd paid her off each time she'd come back, until he'd fled to Europe. His time there hadn't been only to work and to study, but to escape.

She couldn't hurt his family if he wasn't with them, and she couldn't follow him across the Atlantic.

Or so he'd thought.

His success as an artist, the resulting publicity, had given Gloria big ideas. And bigger demands.

He wondered now if it had been a mistake to come home, as much as he'd needed to. He knew it was a mistake to continue to pay her. But the money meant nothing. His family meant everything.

He imagined Ray had felt the same.

In the clear light of day, he knew the sensible thing, the *sane* thing would be to tell her to get lost, to ignore her. To call her bluff.

But then he'd get one of her notes, or come face-to-face with her, and he'd clutch. He found himself strangled between his helpless childhood and the desperate need to shield the people he loved.

So he paid, with a great deal more than money.

He knew how she worked. She wouldn't pop up on his doorstep right away. She'd let him stew and worry and wonder, until ten thousand seemed like a bargain for a little peace of mind. She wouldn't be staying in St. Chris, wouldn't risk being seen and recognized by his brothers or sisters. But she'd be close.

However dramatic, however paranoid it was, he'd swear he could all but feel her—the hate and the greed—breathing down his neck.

He wasn't running again. She wouldn't make him deprive himself of home and family a second time. He would, as he had before, lose himself in his work and live his life. Until she came.

He'd wheedled a second morning session out of Dru. From the sitting the previous week he knew she expected him to be prepared when she arrived, precisely at seven-thirty, and for him to be ready to start. And to stop exactly sixty minutes later.

And to ensure he did, she'd brought a kitchen timer with her.

The woman had no tolerance for artistic temperament. That was all right with Seth. In his opinion, he didn't have an artistic temperament.

He was using pastels, just a basic study for now. It was an extension of the charcoal sketch. A way for him to learn her face, her moods, her body language before he roped her into the more intense portraits he'd already planned in his mind.

When he looked at her, he felt all the models he'd used throughout his career had been simply precursors to Drusilla.

She knocked. He'd told her it wasn't necessary, but she kept that formal distance between them. That, he thought as he walked to the door, would have to be breached.

There could be no formality, and no distance, between them if he was to paint her as he needed to paint her.

"Right on time. Big surprise. Want coffee?"

He'd had his hair cut. It was still long enough to lay over the collar of the torn T-shirt that seemed to be his uniform, but the ponytail was gone. It surprised her that she missed it. She'd always felt that sort of thing was an affectation on a man.

He'd shaved, too, and could almost be deemed tidy if you ignored the holes in the knees of his jeans and the paint splatters on his shoes.

"No, thanks. I've had a cup already this morning."

"One?" He closed the door behind her. "I can barely form a simple declarative sentence on one hit of coffee. How do you do it?"

"Willpower."

"Got a lot of that, do you?"

"As a matter of fact."

To his amusement, she set the timer on his workbench,

set at sixty. Then went directly to the stool he'd set out for her, slid onto it.

She noticed the change immediately.

He'd bought a bed.

The frame was old—a simple black iron head—and the footboard showed some dings. The mattress was bare and still had the tags.

"Moving in after all?"

He glanced over. "No. But it's better than the floor if I end up working late and bunking here. Plus it's a good prop."

Her brow lifted. "Oh, really?"

"Are you usually so preoccupied with sex, or is it just around me?" It made him laugh when her mouth dropped open. "A prop," he continued as he moved to his easel, "like that chair over there, those old bottles." He gestured toward the bottles stacked in a corner. "The urn and this cracked blue bowl I've got in the kitchen. I pick up things as they catch my eye."

He studied his pastels, and his mouth curved. "Including women."

She relaxed her shoulders. He'd notice if they were stiff, and it would make her feel even more foolish. "That's quite a speech for one 'oh, really.' "

"Sugar, you pack a lot of punch into an 'oh, really.' Do you remember the pose?"

"Yes." Obediently she propped her foot on the rung of the stool, laced her hands around her knee, then looked over her left shoulder as if someone had just spoken to her.

"That's perfect. You're really good at this."

"I sat like this for an hour just a few days ago."

"An hour," he repeated as he began to work. "Before the wild debauchery of the weekend."

"I'm so used to wild debauchery it doesn't have a partic-ular impact on my life."

It was his turn. "Oh, really?"

He mimicked her tone so perfectly, she broke the pose to look toward him, laughing. He always managed to make her laugh. "I minored in WD in college."

"Oh, if only." His fingers hurried to capture the bright, beautiful laughter. "I know your type, baby. You walk around being beautiful, smart, sexy and unapproachable so we guys just suffer and dream."

It was, obviously, the wrong thing to say as the humor on her face died instantly—like flipping a switch. "You don't know anything about me, or my type."

"I didn't say that to hurt your feelings. I'm sorry."

She shrugged. "I don't know you well enough for you to hurt my feelings. I know you just well enough to have you annoy me."

"Then I'm sorry for that. I was joking. I like hearing you laugh. I like seeing it."

"Unapproachable." She heard herself mutter it before she could bite down on the urge. Just as her head jerked around before she could pull back the temper. "Did you think I was so damned unapproachable when you grabbed me and kissed me?"

"I'd say the act speaks for itself. Look. A lot of times when a guy sees a woman—a beautiful one he's attracted to—he gets clumsy. It's easier to figure she's out of reach than to analyze his own clumsiness. Women . . ."

If furious was what he was going to get out of her, then he'd capture fury in pastels. "They're a mystery to us. We want them. We can't help it. That doesn't mean you don't scare the hell out of us, one way or the other, more than half the time."

She would have sniffed if he wouldn't have made such a predictable response. "Do you honestly expect me to believe you're afraid of women?"

"Well, I had some advantage, with all those sisters." He was working now, but she'd forgotten he was working. Sometimes, that was only better. So he continued to talk while she frowned at him. "But the first girl I was ever serious about? It took me two weeks to get up the nerve to call her on the phone. Your kind doesn't know what my kind go through."

"How old were you?"

"Fifteen. Marilyn Pomeroy, a giddy little brunette."

"And how long were you serious about Marilyn?"

"About as long as it took me to work up the nerve to call her. Two weeks, give or take. What can I say? Men are no damn good."

Her lips twitched and curved. "That goes without saying. I was serious about a boy when I was fifteen. Wilson Bufferton Lawrence. The Fourth. Buff to his friends."

"Jesus, where do you guys come up with these names? What do you do with somebody named Buff? Play polo or squash?"

He'd leveled her temper, she realized. It was something else he was good at. Since he didn't appear to mind her being mad, it often seemed a waste of time to *be* mad.

"Tennis, actually. On what you'd call our first official date, we played tennis at the club. I beat him in straight sets, and that was the end of our tender romance."

"You'd have to expect someone who answers to Buff to be an asshole."

"I was crushed, then I was mad. I liked being mad better."

"Me too. What became of Buff?"

"Hmmm. As I was informed by my mother over the weekend, he's going to be married for the second time this fall. His first marriage lasted slightly longer than our long-ago tennis match."

"Better luck next time."

"Naturally," she said, very soberly, "he's in finance, as is expected of a fourth-generation Lawrence, and the happy couple is house hunting for their little fifty-room love nest as we speak."

"It's nice to know you're not still bitter."

"I was reminded, a total of five times, I believe, that I've yet to afford my parents the pleasure of spending lavish amounts of money on a wedding that would show the Lawrences, among others, a thing or two."

"So . . . you and your mother had a nice visit on Mother's Day." Though her expression now all but radiated irritation, he kept working. "Careful, you could spill blood with that sneer."

She took a deep breath, angled her head properly again. "My visits with my mother can rarely be defined as 'nice.' I suspect you spent this past Sunday going to see each one of your mothers—sisters."

"It's hard to pin down just what they are. Yeah, I spent some time with each of them. Took them their presents. And since each one of them cried, I figure they were a big hit."

"What did you get them?"

"I did small family portraits. Anna and Cam and the boys, and so on, for each one."

"That's nice. That's lovely," she said softly. "I got my mother a Baccarat vase and a dozen red roses. She was very pleased."

He set down his pastels, dusted his hands on his jeans as he crossed to her. And took her face in his hands. "Then why do you look so sad?"

"I'm not sad."

In response, he simply pressed his lips to her forehead, keeping them there as he felt her tense, then relax.

She couldn't remember ever having a conversation like this with anyone before. And she couldn't fathom why it seemed perfectly natural to have it with him. "It would be difficult for you to understand a conflicted family when yours is so united."

"We have plenty of conflicts," he corrected.

"No. Not at the core, you don't. I need to get downstairs."

"I still have some time left," he said, holding her in place when she started to slide off the stool.

"You've stopped working."

"I still have some time left," he repeated, and gestured to her timer. "If there's one thing I know about, it's family conflict, and what it does to you inside. I spent the first third of my life in a constant state of conflict."

"You're speaking of before you came to live with your grandfather? I've read stories about you, but you don't discuss that aspect," she said when his head came up.

"Yeah." He waited for the constriction in his chest to ease. "Before. When I lived with my biological mother."

"I see."

"No, sugar, you don't. She was a whore and a drunk and a junkie, and she made the first few years of my life a nightmare."

"I'm sorry." He was right, she supposed, it was something she couldn't see clearly. But she touched his hand, then took his hand, in an instinctive gesture of comfort. "It must have been horrible for you. Still, it's obvious she's nothing to you."

"That's what you got out of one statement from me and a handful of articles?"

"No. That's what I got after eating crab and potato salad with you and your family. Now you look sad," she murmured, and shook her head. "I don't know why we're talking about these things."

He wasn't sure why he'd brought up Gloria himself. Maybe it was as simple as speaking out loud to chase away ghosts. Or as complex as needing Dru to know who he was, all the way through.

"That's what people do, people who are interested in each other. They talk about who they are and where they've come from."

"I told you—"

"Yeah, you don't want to be interested. But you are." He traced a finger over her hair, from the short, spiky bangs to the tender nape. "And since we've been dating for several weeks—"

"We haven't dated at all."

He leaned down and caught her up in a kiss as hot as it was brief. "See?" Before she could comment, his mouth took hers again. Softer now, slower, deeper, with those wonderful hands skimming over her face, along her throat and shoulders.

Every muscle in her body went loose. Every vow she'd made about men and relationships crumbled.

When he eased back, she took a careful breath. And changed her line in the sand. "I may end up sleeping with you, but I'm not dating you."

"So, I'm good enough to have sex with, but I don't get a candlelit dinner? I feel so cheap."

Damn it. *Damn* it. She liked him. "Dating's a circular, often tortuous route to sex. I choose to skip it. But I said I might sleep with you, not that I would."

"Maybe we should play tennis first."

"Okay. You're funny. That's appealing. I admire your work, and I like your family. All completely superfluous to a physical relationship, but a nice bonus all in all. I'll think about it."

Saved by the bell, she thought when the timer buzzed. She got off the stool, then wandered to the easel. She saw her face a half dozen times. Different angles, different expressions. "I don't understand this."

"What?" He joined her at the easel. *"Bella donna,"* he murmured, and surprised a shiver out of her.

"I thought you were doing a study of me sitting on the stool. You started it, but you've got all these other sketches scattered around it."

"You weren't in the mood to pose today. You had things on your mind. They showed. So I worked with them. It gives me some insight, and some ideas about what I want in a more formal portrait."

He watched her brow knit. "You said I could have four hours on Sunday," he reminded her. "I'd like to work outside, weather permitting. I've been by your house. It's terrific. Any objection to working there?"

"At my house?"

"It's a great spot. You know that or you wouldn't be there. You're too particular to settle. Besides, it'll be simpler for you. Ten o'clock okay?"

"I suppose."

"Oh, and about the foxgloves? How many more sittings can I get if I frame it for you?"

"I don't—"

"If you bring it back to me, I'll frame it, then you can decide what it's worth in trade. Fair enough?"

"It's down in the shop. I was going to take it to a framer this week."

"I'll stop down and get it before I leave today." He walked his fingers up her arm. "I guess there's no point in asking you to have dinner with me tonight."

"None at all."

"I could just stop by your place later for some quick, cheap sex."

"That's awfully tempting, but I don't think so." She strolled to the door, then glanced back at him. "If and when we go there, Seth, I can promise it won't be cheap. And it won't be quick."

When the door closed, he rubbed his belly that had tightened at that last provocative look she'd sent him.

He glanced back at the canvas. She was, he decided, quite a number of women rolled up in one fascinating package. Every single one of them appealed to him.

"SOMETHING'S troubling him." Anna boxed Cam into the bathroom—one place almost guaranteed to provide space for an uninterrupted conversation in her personal madhouse. She paced the confined area and talked to his silhouette on the shower curtain.

"He's okay. He's just getting his rhythm back."

"He's not sleeping well. I can tell. And I swear I heard him talking to himself the other night."

"You do plenty of solo babbling when you're pissed off," Cam mumbled.

"What did you say?"

"Nothing. Just talking to myself."

With an expression between smug and grim—because she'd heard him perfectly—Anna flushed the toilet. Then smiled in cool satisfaction as he cursed at the sudden blast of hot water. "Goddamn it, why do you *do* that?"

"Because it irritates you and gets your attention. Now about Seth—"

"He's painting," Cam said in exasperation. "He's working at the boatyard, he's catching up with the family. Give him some time, Anna."

"Have you noticed what he's not doing? He's not going out with his friends. He's not dating Dru, or anyone else. Though it's clear from the way he looks at her there isn't going to *be* anyone else for the time being."

Or ever, she concluded.

"He's downstairs playing video games with Jake," she continued. "On a Friday night. Aubrey told me he's only hung out with her once since he got back home. How many weekends did you hang around the house when you were his age?"

"This is Saint Chris, not Monte Carlo. All right, all right," he said quickly, before she flushed on him again. The woman could be vicious. He loved that about her. "So he's preoccupied, I'm not blind. I got pretty preoccupied myself when I got tangled up with you."

"If I thought it was infatuation, or interest or just healthy lust where Dru's considered, I wouldn't be worried. And I am worried. I can't put my finger on it, but when I'm worried about one of my men, there's a reason."

"Fine. So go hound him."

"No. I want you to go hound him."

"Me?" Cam whisked back the curtain enough to stare at her. "Why me?"

"Because. Mmm, you sure are cute when you're wet and annoyed."

"That's not going to work."

"Maybe I should come in there and wash your back," she said and began to unbutton her blouse.

"Okay, that's going to work."

SEVEN

CAM JOGGED DOWNSTAIRS. There was nothing like a spin in the shower with Anna to brighten his mood. He poked a head in the den where his youngest son and Seth were waged in deadly, bloody battle. There were curses, grunts, shouts.

Some of them were from the animation on-screen.

As usual, Cam found himself drawn into the war. Axes swung, blood flew, swords clashed. And he lost track of reality until Jake let out a triumphant cry.

"I kicked your ass."

"Shit, you got lucky."

Jake pumped his joystick in the air. "I *rule*, baby. Bow to the king of Mortal Kombat."

"In your dreams. Let's go again."

"Bow to the king," Jake repeated joyously. "Worship me, lesser mortal."

"I'll worship you."

Seth made his grab. Cam watched them wrestle for a

moment. More grunts, impossible threats, a young boy's dopey giggles. Seth and Jake, he thought, weren't so different in age than he and Seth.

But Jake had an innocence Seth had never been allowed. Jake had never had to question who he was, or if the hands reaching for him meant him harm.

Thank God for it.

Cam leaned lazily against the doorjamb and yelled, "Come on, Anna, they're just fooling around."

At the mention of her name, Seth and Jake rolled apart and shot twin looks of panic and guilt toward the doorway.

"Got you," Cam barked with amusement.

"That was cold, Dad."

"That's how to win a battle without a single blow. You." He pointed at Seth. "Let's go."

"Where ya going?" Jake demanded, scrambling up. "Can I go?"

"Have you cleaned your room, done your homework, found the cure for cancer and changed the oil in my car?"

"Come on, Dad," Jake whined.

"Seth, grab some beer and head outside. I'll be right along."

"Sure. Later, kid"—Seth tapped a fist in his palm—"I'm taking you out."

"You couldn't take me out if you brought me flowers and a box of chocolate."

"Good one," Cam commented as Seth snorted out a laugh and left the room.

"I've been saving it," Jake told him. "How come I can't go with you guys?"

"I need to talk to Seth."

"Are you mad at him?"

"Do I look mad at him?"

"No," Jake said after a careful study of his father's face. "But you can be sneaky about that stuff."

"I just need to talk to him."

Jake jerked a shoulder, but Cam saw the disappointment in his eyes—Anna's Italian eyes—before he plopped back on the floor and reached for his joystick.

Cam squatted. "Jake." He caught the scent of bubble gum and youthful sweat. There were grass stains on the knees of Jake's jeans. His shoes were untied.

It struck him unexpectedly, as it often did, that staggering slap of emotion that was love and pride and puzzlement rolled into one strong fist against his heart.

"Jake," he said again and ran his hand over his son's hair. "I love you."

"Jeez." Jake hunched his shoulders and, with his chin tucked, shifted his gaze up to meet his father's. "I know, and stuff."

"I love you," Cam repeated. "But when I get back, there's going to be a bloody coup, and a new king in Quinnland. And believe what I'm saying, you will bow to me."

"You wish."

Cam rose, pleased with the cocky expression on Jake's face. "Your days of rule are numbered. Start praying, pal."

"I'll pray that you don't slobber on me when you're begging for mercy."

He had to admit, Cam decided as he walked toward the back door, he'd raised a bunch of wiseasses. It did a man proud.

"What's up?" Seth asked, tossing Cam a beer as he swung out the back door.

"Gonna take a little sail."

"Now?" Automatically, Seth looked up at the sky. "It'll be dark in an hour."

"Afraid of the dark, Mary?" Cam sauntered to the dock, stepped nimbly into the day sailer. He set the beer aside while Seth cast off.

As he had countless times in the past, Seth lifted the oar to push away from the dock. He hoisted the main, and the sound of the canvas rising was sweet as music. Cam manned the rudder, finessing the wind so they glided, smooth and nearly silent, away from shore.

The sun was low, its beams striking the water, sheening the marsh grass, dying in the narrow channels where the shadows went deep and the water went dark and secret.

They motored through, maneuvering between markers, down the river, through the sound. And into the Bay. Balanced to the sway, Seth hoisted the jib, trimmed the sails.

And Cam caught the wind.

They flew in the wooden boat with its bright work glinting and its sails white as dove's wings. There was salt in the air, and the thrilling roll, that rise and fall of waves as deeply blue as the sky.

The speed, the freedom, the absolute joy of skating over the water while the sun went soft toward twilight drained every worry, every doubt, every sorrow from Seth's heart.

"Coming about," Cam called out, setting to tack to steal more wind, steal more speed.

For the next fifteen minutes, they barely spoke.

When they slowed, Cam stretched out his legs and popped the top on his beer. "So, what's going on with you?"

"Going on?"

"Anna's radar tells her something's up with you, and she nagged me into finding out what it is."

Seth bought some time by opening his own beer, taking

the first cold sip. "I've just been back a couple weeks, so I've got a lot on my mind, that's all. Figuring things out, settling in, that kind of thing. She doesn't have to worry."

"I'm supposed to go back and tell her she doesn't have to worry? Oh yeah, that'll go down real smooth." He took another drink. "Look, we don't have to go through all that you-know-you-can-talk-to-me-about-anything crap, do we? Going that route's only going to make us both feel like morons."

"No." But it worked a smile out of Seth. "Just tell her I'm thinking about what happens next. I've got to get a place of my own sooner or later. My rep's bugging me about putting together another showing, and I'm not sure what direction I want to take there. I haven't even finished putting the studio together yet."

"Uh-huh." Cam glanced toward shore, and the pretty old house tucked back on the banks of the river.

When Seth followed the look, he shifted in the bow. He'd been so wrapped up in the sail, he hadn't noticed the direction.

"Sexy flower queen's not home yet," Cam commented. "Maybe she's got a date."

"She doesn't date."

"Is that why you haven't moved on her yet?"

"Who says I haven't?"

Cam only laughed, sipped beer. "If you had, kid, you'd look a hell of a lot more relaxed."

Got me there, Seth thought, but shrugged.

"In fact, I can drop you off here. You can try the 'I was just in the neighborhood so can I come in and get you naked' gambit."

"That one ever work for you?"

"Ah." Cam let out a long, wistful sigh, stared up at the

sky as if into deep, dreamy memories. "The stories I could tell. The way I figure it, the more a guy gets sex, the more he thinks about it. And the less a guy gets sex, the more he thinks about it. But at least when he's getting it, he sleeps better."

Seth patted his pockets. "Got a pen? I want to write that one down."

"She's a very tasty morsel."

Amusement fled. "She's not a fucking snack."

"Okay." Having nailed the answer he wanted, Cam nodded. "I wondered if you were really tangled up about her."

Seth hissed out a breath, looked back toward the fanciful blue house tucked among the trees until it was out of sight. "I don't know what I am. I've got to get my life settled, and until I do, I don't have time for . . . tangles. But I look at her and . . ." He shrugged. "I can't figure it out. I like being around her. Not that she's easy. Half the time it's like dealing with a porcupine. One in a tiara."

"Women without spines are fine for a one-nighter, or a good time. But when you're looking for the long haul . . ."

Shock and panic erupted on Seth's face. "I didn't say that. I just said I liked being around her."

"And you got puppy eyes when you said it."

"Bullshit." And the fact that he could feel the heat of a flush working up his neck mortified him. He could only hope the light was too dim for Cam to spot it.

"Another minute, you'd've whimpered. You going to trim that jib, or just let her reef?"

Muttering to himself, Seth adjusted the lines. "Look, I want to paint her, I want to spend some time with her. And I want to get her into bed. I can manage all three on my own, thanks."

"If you do, maybe you'll start sleeping better."

"Dru doesn't have anything to do with how I'm sleeping. Or not much anyway."

Cam came about again and headed toward home. Twilight was falling. "So are you going to tell me what's keeping you up at night, or do I have to pry that out of you, too? You don't tell me, Anna's going to make both of our lives hell until you spill it."

He thought of Gloria, and the words crammed in his throat. If he let the first one out, the rest wouldn't just spill. It would be an avalanche. All he could see was his family buried under it.

He could tell Cam anything. Anything but that.

But maybe it was time to unload something else. "I had this really weird dream."

"Are we going back to sex?" Cam asked. "Because if we are we should've brought more beer along."

"I dreamed about Stella."

The wicked humor on Cam's face drained, leaving it naked and vulnerable. "Mom? You dreamed about Mom?"

"I know it's weird. I never even met her."

"What was she . . ." It was strange how grief could hide inside you. Like a virus, lying low for months, even years, only to spring out and leave you weak and helpless again. "What were you doing?"

"Sitting on the dock in back of the house. It was summer. Hot, sweaty, close. I was fishing, just a pole and a line and some of Anna's Brie."

"You'd better've been dreaming," Cam managed. "Or you're a dead man."

"See, that's the thing. The line's in the water, but I *knew* I'd copped the cheese for bait. And I could smell roses, feel the heat of the sun. Then Foolish plops down next to me. I know he's gone—I mean in the dream I know—so I'm pretty damn surprised to see him. Next thing I know Stella's sitting on the dock beside me."

"How did she look?"

It didn't seem like an odd question while they were gliding along on quiet water in the dimming light. It seemed perfectly rational. "She looked terrific. She had on this old khaki hat, no brim. The kind you just yank down over your head, and her hair was falling all out of it."

"Jesus." Cam remembered the old hat, and the way she'd stuffed her unmanageable hair under it. Did they have a picture of her in that ugly cap? He couldn't recall.

"I don't want to mess you up with this."

Cam only shook his head. "What happened in the dream?"

"Not a whole lot. We just sat there and talked. About you guys, and Ray and . . ."

"What?"

"How they figured it was time she got to play Grandma, since she'd missed out on that before. It wasn't what we said so much as how real it seemed. Even when I woke up sitting on the side of the bed, it seemed real. I don't know how to explain it."

"No, I get you." Hadn't he had a number of conversations with his father, after Ray had died? And hadn't his brothers both had similar experiences?

But it had been so long now. Longer yet since they'd lost their mother. And none of them had ever had that wrenching chance to talk to her again. Even in dreams.

"I always wanted to meet her," Seth continued. "It feels like I have."

"How long ago was this?"

"Last week, I guess. And before you start, I didn't say anything at the time because I figured you might freak. You gotta admit, it's a little spooky."

You ain't seen nothing yet, Cam thought. But that was one of the aspects of being a Quinn Seth would have to find out on his own.

"If you dream about her again, ask her if she remembers the zucchini bread."

"The what?"

"Just ask her," Cam said as they drifted home.

WHEN they got home, dinner was cooking. And Dan McLean was standing by the stove, holding a beer and leaning in for Anna to feed him a spoonful of red sauce.

"What the hell's he doing here?" Cam demanded, and fixed a scowl on his face because Dan would expect it.

"Mooching. That's terrific, Miz Q. Nobody makes it like you. It makes having to see his face again easier," he added, and nodded toward Seth.

"Weren't you mooching here two weeks ago?" Cam asked him.

"Nah. I mooched at Ethan's two weeks ago. I like to spread myself around."

"More of you to spread around than there was last time I saw you." Seth hooked his thumbs in his pockets and took a long look at his childhood friend. Dan had filled out in a way that indicated solid gym time.

"Can't men just say, 'Hi, it's good to see you again'?" Anna wondered.

"Hi," Seth echoed. "It's good to see you again."

They moved together in the one-armed hold that constitutes a male hug.

Cam sniffed at the simmering pots. "Christ, I'm tearing up. This is so touching."

"Why don't you set the table," Anna suggested to Cam. "Before you make a sentimental fool of yourself."

"Let the moocher set it. He knows where everything is. I've got to go dethrone and execute our youngest child."

"Make sure you do it within twenty minutes. We're eating in twenty-one."

"I'll set the table, Miz Q."

"No, get out of my kitchen. Take your beer and manly ways outside. I don't know why I couldn't have had just one girl. I don't know why that was too much to ask."

"Next time this one comes over to eat our food, make him put on a dress," Cam called over his shoulder as he headed for the den and his son's date with destiny.

"Cam loves me like a brother," Dan said and, at home, opened the refrigerator to get Seth a beer. "Let us go and sit outside like men, scratching and telling sexual lies."

They sat on the steps. Each took a pull from his beer. "Aub says you're digging in this time. Got yourself a studio over the florist."

"That's right. Aub says? My information is your little brother's after her."

"When he gets the chance. I see more of her than I see of Will. They've got him doing so many double shifts at the hospital he calls out 'stat!' and other sexy medical terms in his sleep."

"You guys still bunking together?"

"Yeah, for now. Mostly I've got the apartment to myself. He lives and breathes the hospital. Will McLean, M.D. Ain't that some shit?"

"He really got off dissecting frogs in biology. You wimped out."

Even from this distance, the thought made Dan grimace. "It was, and continues to be, a disgusting rite of passage. No frog's ever caused me harm. Now that you're back, it screws my plans to visit you in Italy, have the two of us sit at some sidewalk cafe—"

"Trattoria."

"Whatever, and ogle sexy women. Figured we'd catch a lot of action, with you being all artistic and me being so damn handsome."

"What happened to that teacher you were seeing? Shelly?"

"Shelby. Yeah, well, that's another thing that put my little fantasy in the dust." Dan dug in his pocket, pulled out a jeweler's box and flipped the top with his thumb.

"Holy hell, McLean," Seth managed as he blinked at the diamond ring.

"Got big plans tomorrow night. Dinner, candlelight, music, get down on one knee. The whole package." Dan blew out a shaky breath. "I'm scared shitless."

"You're getting married?"

"Man, I hope so, because I love her to pieces. You think she'll go for this?"

"How do I know?"

"You're the artist," Dan said and shoved the ring under Seth's nose. "How's it look to you?"

It looked like a fancy gold band with a diamond in the center. But friendship demanded more than that. "It looks great. Elegant, classic."

"Yeah, yeah." Obviously pleased, Dan studied it again. "That's her, man. That's Shelby. Okay." Breathing out, he put the box back in his pocket. "Okay then. She really wants to meet you. She's into that art crap. That's how I hit on her the first time. Aubrey dragged me to this art show at the university because Will was tied up. And there's Shelby standing in front of this painting that looked like maybe a chimp had done. I mean, what is with that shit that's just streaks and splatters of paint? It's a scam, if you ask me."

"I'm sure Pollock died in shame."

"Yeah, right, whatever. Anyhow, I went up to her and pulled that 'what does it say to you?' kind of line. And you know what she says?"

Enjoying seeing his friend so besotted, Seth leaned back against the step. "What did she say?"

"She said the five-year-olds in her kindergarten class do better work with fingerpaints. Man oh man, it was love. So that's when I pulled out the big guns and told her I had this friend who was an artist, but he painted real pictures. Then I drop your name and she nearly fainted. I guess that's when it really hit me you'd become a BFD."

"You still have that sketch I did of you and Will hanging over your toilet?"

"It's in a place of honor. So, how about you meet Shelby and me some night next week? For a drink, maybe something to eat."

"I can do that, but she may fall for me and leave you brokenhearted."

"Yeah, that'll happen. But just in case, she's got this friend—"

"No." The horror of it had Seth throwing up a blocking hand. "No fix-ups. You'll just have to take your chances on your girl falling under the spell of my fatal charm."

* * *

AFTER the meal, and the noise, Seth let Dan drag him off for a night at Shiney's. It turned into a marathon of reminiscence and bad music.

They'd left the porch and living room lamp on for him, so he made it all the way upstairs before he tripped over the dog sprawled across the bathroom doorway.

He cursed under his breath, limped off to his room and stripped down to the skin where he stood. His ears were still ringing from the last horrendous set when he flopped facedown on the bed.

It was good to be home, was his last thought, and he fell dreamlessly into sleep.

"MOM?" In the office of the boatyard, Phillip sat heavily in his chair. "He dreamed about Mom?"

"Maybe it was a dream, maybe it wasn't."

Ethan rubbed his chin. "He said she was wearing that old cap?"

"That's right."

"She wore it often enough," Phillip pointed out. "He's probably seen a picture of her wearing it."

"She's not wearing it in any of the pictures we've got sitting around our place." Cam had looked. "I'm not saying he hasn't seen a picture, and I'm not saying it wasn't just a dream. But it's odd. She used to come down and sit on the dock with us like that. She didn't care much for fishing, but if one of us was sitting out there brooding over something, she'd come out and sit until we started talking about whatever it was we had in our craw."

"She was good at it," Ethan agreed. "Good at getting down to the meat of it."

"It doesn't mean this is anything like what happened with us after Dad died."

"You didn't want to believe that either," Ethan pointed out as he hunted up a bottle of water from Phillip's office refrigerator.

"I know this. Something's bothering the kid and he doesn't want to talk about it. Not to me anyway." It stung a little, Cam admitted. "If anybody can get it out of him, it's Mom. Even in a dream. In the meantime, I guess we just watch him. I'm going down before he figures out we're up here talking about him."

Cam started out, then stopped and turned back. "I told him if he dreams about her again to ask her about the zucchini bread."

Both his brothers looked blank. Ethan remembered first and laughed so hard he had to sit on the edge of the desk.

"Christ." Phillip eased back in his chair. "I'd forgotten all about that."

"We'll see if she remembers," Cam said, then started down into the din of the work area. He'd gotten to the last step when the outer door opened, spilling in sunshine just ahead of Dru.

"Well, hello, gorgeous. Looking for my idiot brother?"

"Which idiot brother?"

His grin was pure appreciation. "You catch on. Seth's earning his keep."

"Actually, I wasn't—" But Cam already had her hand and was leading her along.

Legs spread, his back to her, Seth stood on the decking of the boat, stripped to the waist. His back and arms showed considerably more muscle than might be expected from a man who wielded a paintbrush for a living. He guzzled from a bottle of water like a man who hadn't had a drink in a week.

Her own mouth went dry watching him.

Shallow, Dru told herself. Shallow, shallow, shallow, to be interested in a man simply because he looked hot and hard and handsome. She appreciated intellect and strength of character and personality and . . . a really excellent butt, she admitted.

Sue her.

She managed to avoid licking her lips before he turned. He reached up to swipe at his brow with his forearm, then spotted her.

Now, in addition to the long male body clad only in jeans and work boots, her senses were assaulted by the lethal power of his smile.

She saw his mouth move—it was, like his butt, excellent. But the words he spoke were drowned out by the music.

Willing to assist, Cam walked over and turned the stereo down to merely loud.

"Hey!" Aubrey's head popped up from under the deck. "What gives?"

"We've got company."

Dru watched, with some interest, as Seth ran a hand over Aubrey's shoulder as he jumped down from the deck. "We're on for tomorrow, right?" he asked her as he walked over, pulling a bandanna out of his pocket to wipe his hands and face.

"Yes." Dru noted that Aubrey continued to watch, with considerable interest of her own. "I didn't mean to interrupt your work. I was running some errands while Mr. G watches the shop, and I thought I'd come in and have a look at the operation here."

"I'll show you around."

"You're busy." And your blond companion is watching me like your guard dog, Dru decided. "In any case, I'm told it's probably you I want to see," she said to Cam.

Cam gestured at Seth. "I told you that's what all the pretty ladies say. What can I do for you?"

"I want to buy a boat."

"Is that so?" Cam draped an arm around her shoulders and turned to lead her toward the stairs. "Well, sugar, you've come to the right place."

"Hey!" Seth called out. "I can talk about boats."

"Junior partner. We try to humor him. So, what kind of boat are you interested in?"

"Sloop. Eighteen feet. Arc bottom, cedar hull. Probably a spoon bow, though I'd be flexible if the designer has another idea. I want something with good balance, reliable stability, but when I want to move, I want to move."

She turned to study the gallery of sketches and told herself she'd admire the art of them later. For now, she wanted to make her point.

"This hull, this bow," she said, gesturing to two sketches. "I want something dependable, quick to the wind, and I want a boat that lasts."

She obviously knew her boats. "A custom job like that's going to cost you."

"I don't expect it comes free, but I don't discuss terms with you, do I? I believe that's your brother Phillip's area—and if there are any other specific design details, that would be Ethan's."

"Done your homework."

"I like to know who I'm dealing with, and I prefer dealing with the best. That, by all accounts, is Quinn Brothers. How soon can you work up a design?"

Man, oh man, Cam thought, you're going to drive the kid crazy. And it's going to be fun to watch. "Let's go upstairs and we'll figure it out."

IT was Ethan who walked her down and out thirty minutes later. The lady, he'd discovered, knew port from starboard, had very specific ideas about what she wanted, and held her own against a group of men who'd never had their rough edges quite smoothed off.

"We'll have a draft of the design drawn up by the end of next week," he told her. "Sooner if we can browbeat Seth into doing most of it."

"Oh?" She sent what she hoped was a casual glance toward the work area. "Does he do some of the designing?"

"When we can pin him down. Always had a knack. Pretty obvious he draws better than the three of us put together, and then some."

She followed his gaze and looked at the gallery of boats. "It's a wonderful collection, and retrospective, I suppose. You can see his artistic progress very clearly."

"This one here." He tapped his finger against the sketch of a skipjack. "He did this drawing when he was ten."

"Ten?" Fascinated, she moved closer, studying it now as a student might study the early works of a master in a museum. "I can't imagine what it would be like to be born with that kind of gift. It would be a burden for some, wouldn't it?"

In his way, Ethan took his time considering, following the lines of his old skipjack as seen through the eyes and talent of a child. "I guess it would. Not for Seth. It's a joy for him, and what you'd call a channel. Always has been. Well."

He was never long on conversation, so offered her a quiet smile and his hand. "It's going to be a pleasure doing business with you."

"Likewise. Thanks for making time for me today."

"We always got time."

He showed her out, then wandered into the driving beat of Sugar Ray and power sanders. He was halfway to the lathe when Seth shut off his tool.

"Dru up with the guys?"

"Nope. She went on."

"Went on? Well, damn it, you could've said something." He vaulted down from the boat and sprinted for the door.

Aubrey frowned after him. "He's half stuck on her already."

"Seems like." Ethan tilted his head at the look on her face. "Problem?"

"I don't know." She shrugged. "I don't know. She's just not what I pictured for him, that's all. She's all kind of stiff and fancy, with a high snoot factor, if you ask me."

"She's alone," Ethan corrected. "Not everybody's as easy with people as you are, Aubrey. Besides the fact, it's what Seth pictures that matters."

"Yeah." But she was far from sold on Drusilla.

EIGHT

$\sim$

SINCE HE HADN'T told her what to wear for the sitting, Dru settled on the simple, with blue cotton pants and a white camp shirt. She watered her gardens, changed her earrings twice, then made a fresh pot of coffee.

Maybe the hoops had been a better choice, she thought, fingering the little lapis balls dangling from her ear. Men liked women in hoop earrings. Probably had some strange sultry gypsy fetish.

And what the hell did she care?

She wasn't sure she wanted him to make another move on her. One move, after all, invariably led to another, and she wasn't interested in the chessboard of relationships just now.

Or hadn't been.

Jonah had certainly checkmated her, she thought, and enjoyed the little flash of anger. The problem had been she'd believed she was in control of the board there, that all the game pieces were in correct positions.

She'd been completely oblivious to the fact that he'd been playing on another board simultaneously.

His disloyalty and deception had damaged her heart and her pride. While her heart had healed, perhaps too easily, she admitted, her pride remained bruised.

She would never be made a fool of again.

If she was going to develop a relationship with Seth— and the jury was still out on that one—it would be on her terms.

She'd proven to herself that she was more than an ornament for a man's arm, a notch in his bedpost or a rung in the ladder of his career advancement.

Jonah had miscalculated on that score.

More important, she'd proven that she could stand on her own and make a very contented life.

Which didn't mean, she admitted, that she didn't miss a certain amount of companionship, or sexual heat, or the heady challenge of the mating dance with an interesting, attractive man.

She heard his tires crunch on her gravel drive. One step at a time, she told herself, and waited for him to knock.

All right, she thought, so she did feel a rush of heat the minute she opened the door and looked at him. It only proved that she was human, and she was healthy.

"Good morning," she said, as manners had her stepping back to let him inside.

"Morning. I love this place. I just realized that if you hadn't snapped it up before I got back home, I would have."

"Lucky for me."

"I'll say." He scanned the living area as he wandered. Strong colors, good fabrics, he mused. It could've used a little more clutter for his taste, but it suited her with its good, carefully selected pieces, the fresh flowers and the tidy air of it all.

"You said you wanted to work outside."

"Yeah. Oh, hey, your painting." He shifted the package wrapped in brown paper under his arm and handed it to her. "I'll hang it for you if you've picked your spot."

"That was quick." And because she couldn't resist, she sat on the sofa and ripped off the wrapping.

He'd chosen thin strips of wood stained a dull gold that complemented the rich tones of the flowers and foliage so that the frame was as simple and strong as the painting.

"It's perfect. Thank you. It's a wonderful start to my Seth Quinn collection."

"Planning on a collection?"

She ran a finger over the top of the frame as she looked up at him. "Maybe. And I'd take you up on hanging it for me because I'm dying to see how it looks, but I don't have the proper hanger."

"Like this?" He dug the one he'd brought with him out of his pocket.

"Like that." She angled her head, considered. "You're very handy, aren't you?"

"Damn near indispensable. Got a hammer, and a tape measure, or should I get mine out of my car?"

"I happen to have a hammer and other assorted household tools." She rose, went into the kitchen and came back with a hammer so new it gleamed.

"Where do you want it?"

"Upstairs. My bedroom." She turned to lead the way. "What's in the bag?"

"Stuff. The guy who rehabbed this place knew what he

was doing." Seth examined the satin finish on the banister as they climbed to the second floor. "I wonder how he could stand to let it go."

"He likes the work itself—and the profit. Once he's finished, he's bored and wants to move on. Or so he told me when I asked just that."

"How many bedrooms? Three?"

"Four, though one's quite small, more suited to a home office or a little library."

"Third floor?"

"A finished attic, which has potential for a small apartment. Or," she said with a glance at him, "an artist's garret."

She turned into a room, and Seth saw immediately she'd selected what suited her best here as well. The windows gave her a view of the river, a sweep of trees and shady garden. The window trim was just fussy enough to be charming, and she'd chosen to drape filmy white gauze in a kind of long swag around them in lieu of formal curtains. It diffused the sunlight and still left the view and the craftsmanship of the trim.

She'd gone for cerulean blue on the walls, scattered a couple of floral rugs on the pine floor, and had stuck with antiques for the furnishings.

The bed was tidily made, as he'd expected, and covered with a white quilt with intricate interlocking rings and rosebuds that seemed to have been crafted specifically for the sleigh bed.

"Great piece." He leaned down to get a closer look at the workmanship of the quilt. "Heirloom?"

"No. I found it at an arts-and-crafts fair in Pennsylvania last year. I thought the wall between these windows. It'll be good light without direct sun."

"Good choice." He held the painting up. "And it'll be

like another window, so you'll have flowers during the winter."

Her thoughts, Dru admitted, exactly.

"About here?"

She stepped back, checked the position from several different angles—resisting, only because it was a bit too suggestive, lying down on the bed to see how it would look to her when she woke in the mornings.

"That's perfect."

He reached behind the painting, scraped a vague mark on the wall with his thumbnail, then set it aside to measure.

It was odd, she thought, having a man in her bedroom again. And far from unpleasant to watch him with his tools and his painting, his rough clothes and his beautiful hands.

Far from unpleasant, she admitted, to imagine those beautiful hands on her skin.

"See what you think about what's in the bag," he said without looking around.

She picked it up, opened it. And her eyebrows lifted high as she took out the long, filmy skirt—purple pansies rioting against a cool blue background—and the thin-strapped, narrow top in that same shade of blue.

"You're a determined man, aren't you?"

"It'll look good on you, and it's the look I'm after."

"And you get what you're after."

He glanced back now, his expression both relaxed and cocky. "So far. You got any of those . . ." He made a circle with his finger in the air. "Hoop ear things. They'd work with that."

I should've known, Dru thought, but only said, "Hmm."

She laid the skirt and top on the bed, then stepped back as he fixed the painting on its hook. "Left bottom needs to come up a little—too much. There. That's perfect. Painted, framed and hung by Quinn. Not a bad deal on my side."

"It looks good from my end, too," he said, staring at her.

When he took a step toward her, she considered taking one toward him. Before the phone rang.

"Excuse me." For the best, she assured herself as she picked up the bedside phone. "Hello."

"Hello, princess."

"Dad." Pleasure, distress and, shamefully, a thread of annoyance knotted inside her. "Why aren't you on the seventh green by this time on a Sunday morning?"

"I've got some difficult news." Proctor let out a long sigh. "Sweetheart, your mother and I are getting divorced."

"I see." The pulse in her temple began to throb. "I need you to wait just a minute." She pushed the hold button, turned to Seth. "I'm sorry, I need to take this. There's coffee in the kitchen. I shouldn't be long."

"Okay." Her face had gone blank on him. It was very still and very empty. "I'll grab a cup before I go out to set up. Take your time."

She waited until she heard him start down the steps, then sat on the side of the bed and reconnected with her father. "I'm sorry, Dad. What happened?" And bit her tongue before she could finish the question with: this time.

"I'm afraid your mother and I haven't been getting along for quite a while. I've tried to shield you from our problems. I have no doubt we'd have taken this step years ago if it hadn't been for you. But, well, these things happen, princess."

"I'm very sorry." She knew her job well and finished with, "Is there anything I can do to help?"

"Ah well. I'm sure I'd feel better if I could explain things to you, so I'm sure you're not upset by all this. It's too complicated to discuss on the phone. Why don't you come up this afternoon? We'll have lunch, just you and me. Nothing would brighten my day more than spending it with my little girl."

"I'm sorry. I've got a commitment today."

"Surely, under the circumstances, this is more important."

Her temple throbbed, and guilt began to roil in her stomach. "I can't break this engagement. In fact, I was just about to—"

"All right. That's all right," he said in a voice that managed to be both long-suffering and brisk. "I'd hoped you'd have some time for me. Thirty years. Thirty, and it comes down to this."

Dru rubbed at the tension banding the back of her neck. "I'm sorry, Dad."

She lost track of the times she echoed that phrase during the rest of the conversation. But she knew when she hung up she was exhausted from repeating it.

No sooner had she set the phone down, than it rang again.

Thirty years, Dru thought, might account for the sixth sense her parents had in regard to each other. Resigned, she picked up the phone.

"Hello, Mom."

HE'D spread a red blanket on the grass near the bank of the river where there were both beams of sunlight and dappled shade. He added a wicker picnic basket, propping an open bottle of wine and a stemmed glass against it. A slim book with a ragged white cover lay beside it.

She'd changed into the clothes he'd brought, put on the

hoop earrings as he'd requested. And had used the time to steady herself.

His table was up, his sketch pad on it. At the foot was a portable stereo, but instead of the driving rock, it was Mozart. And that surprised her.

"Sorry I held you up," she said as she stepped off the porch.

"No problem." One look at her face had him crossing to her. He put his arms around her and, ignoring her flinch, held her gently.

A part of her wanted to burrow straight into that unquestioning offer of comfort. "Do I look that bad?"

"You look that sad." He brushed his lips over her hair. "You want to do this some other time?"

"No. It's nothing, really. Just habitual family insanity."

"I'm good at that." He tipped her head back with his fingers. "An expert on family insanity."

"Not this kind." She eased back. "My parents are getting divorced."

"Oh baby." He touched her cheek. "I'm sorry."

"No, no, no." To his bafflement, she laughed and pressed the heels of her hands to her temples. "You don't get it. They whack the *D* word around like a Ping-Pong ball. Every couple of years I get the call. 'Dru, I have difficult news.' Or 'Dru, I'm not sure how to tell you.' Once, when I was sixteen, they actually separated for nearly two months. Being careful to time it during my summer break so my mother could flee to Europe with me for a week, then my father could drag me off with him to Bar Harbor to sail."

"Sounds more like you've been the Ping-Pong ball."

"Yes, it does. They wear me out, which is why I ran away before . . . before I started to despise them. And still,

I wish to God they'd just go through with it. That sounds cold and selfish and horrible."

"No, it doesn't. Not when you've got tears in your eyes."

"They love me too much," she said quietly. "Or not enough. I've never been able to figure it out. I don't suppose they have either. I can't be with them, standing in as their crutch or their referee the rest of my life."

"Have you told them?"

"Tried. They don't hear." She rubbed her arms as if smoothing ruffled feathers. "And I have absolutely no business dumping my mess in your lap."

"Why not? We're practically going steady."

She let out a half laugh. "You're awfully good at that."

"I'm good at so many things. Which one is this?"

"At listening, for one." She leaned forward, kissed his cheek. "I've never been particularly good at asking anyone to listen. I don't seem to have to with you. And for two"— she kissed his other cheek—"you're good at making me laugh, even when I'm annoyed."

"I'll listen some more—and make you laugh—if you kiss me again. And aim for here this time," he added, tapping a finger to his lips.

"Thanks, but that's about it. Let's put it away. There's nothing I can do about them." She eased away from him. "I assume you want me on the blanket."

"Why don't we toss this for today and go for a sail? It always clears my head."

"No, you're already set up, and it'll take my mind off things. But thanks, really, Seth."

Satisfied that the sadness on her face had lifted, he nodded. "Okay. If you decide you want to stop after all, just say so. First, lose the shoes."

She stepped out of the canvas slides. "A barefoot picnic."

"There you go. Lie down on the blanket."

She'd assumed she'd be sitting on it, skirts spread as she read the book. But she stepped onto the blanket. "Face up or down?"

"On your back. Scoot down a little more," he suggested as he walked around her. "Let's have the right arm over your head. Bend your elbow, relax the hand."

"I feel silly. I didn't feel silly in the studio."

"Don't think about it. Bring your left knee up." She did, and when the skirt came with it, smoothed it back down over her legs.

"Oh, come on." He knelt down and had her eyes going to slits when he pulled up the hem of the skirt so it exposed her left leg to mid-thigh.

"Aren't you supposed to say something about how you're not hitting on me, but that this is all for the sake of art?"

"It is for the sake of art." The back of his fingers skimmed her thigh as he fussed with the lie of the material. "But I'm hitting on you, too." He slid the strap of her top off her shoulder, studied the result, nodded.

"Relax. Start with your toes." He rubbed a hand over her bare foot. "And work your way up." Watching her, he ran his hand up her calf, over her knee. "Turn your head toward me."

She did, and glanced over the paint supplies he'd set up by his easel. "Aren't those watercolors? I thought you said you wanted oil."

"This one's for watercolors. I've got something else in mind for oils."

"So you keep saying. Just how many times do you think you can persuade me to do this?"

"As many as it takes. You're having a quiet afternoon by the water," he told her as he began sketching lightly on the paper. "A little sleepy from wine and reading."

"Am I alone?"

"For the moment. You're just daydreaming now. Go wherever you want."

"If it were warmer, I'd slide into the river."

"It's as warm as you want it to be. Close your eyes, Dru. Dream a little."

She did as he asked. The music, soft, romantic, was a caress on the air.

"What do you think of when you paint?" she asked him.

"Think?" At the question his mind went completely blank. "I don't know. Ah . . . shape, I guess. Light, shadow. Jeez. Mood. I don't have an answer."

"You just answered the question I didn't ask. It's instinct. Your talent is instinctive. It has to be, really, as you were so clever at drawing so young."

"What did you want to do when you were a kid?" Her body was a long, slim flow to him. Shape.

"Lots of things. A ballerina, a movie star, an explorer. A missionary."

"Wow, a missionary. Really?" The sun slid through the leaves and lay softly on her skin. Light and shadow.

"It was a brief ambition, but a profound one. What I didn't think I'd be was a businesswoman. Surprise."

"But you like it."

"I love it. I love being able to take what I once assumed was a personal passion and a small talent for flowers and do something with it." Her mind began to drift, like the river that flowed beside her. "I've never been able to talk to anyone the way I seem to be able to talk to you."

"No kidding?" She looked like a faerie queen—the exotic shape of her eyes, the sexy pixie cap of dark hair. The utter female confidence of the pose. A faerie queen drowsing alone in her private glade. Mood.

"Why do you think that is?" he wondered.

"I haven't a clue." And with a sigh, she fell asleep.

THE music had changed. A woman with a voice like heartbreak was singing about love. Still half dreaming, Dru shifted. "Who is that singing?" she murmured.

"Darcy Gallagher. Some pipes there. I caught a show she did with her two brothers a couple years ago in County Waterford. Little place called Ardmore. It was amazing."

"Mmm. I think I've heard—" She broke off when she opened her eyes and found Seth sitting beside the blanket with a sketchbook instead of standing behind the table. "What're you doing?"

"Waiting for you to wake up."

"I fell asleep." Embarrassed, she rose on one elbow. "I'm sorry. How long was I out?"

"Dunno. Don't have a watch." He set the book aside. "No need to be sorry. You gave me just what I was after."

Trying to clear her head, she looked over at the table. The watercolor paper was, frustratingly, out of her line of sight. "You finished?"

"No, but I got a hell of a start. Watch or no watch, my stomach's telling me it's lunchtime." He flipped the lid on a cooler.

"You brought a real picnic."

"Hamper was for art, cooler's for practicality. We've got bread, cheese, grapes, some of this pâté Phil swears by." He pulled out plates as he spoke. "And though I had to debase myself and beg, some of Anna's pasta salad. And this terrific wine I discovered in Venice. It's called Dreams. Seemed to fit."

"You're trying to make this a date," she said warily.

"Too late." He poured the first glass, handed it to her. "It already is a date. I wanted to ask why you took off so fast yesterday, when you came by the boatyard."

"I'd finished my business." She chose a chilled grape, bit through its tart skin. "And I had to get back to work."

"So you want a boat?"

"Yes, I do. I like to sail."

"Come sailing with me. That way you can check out how seaworthy a boat by Quinn is."

"I'll think about it." She sampled the pâté, made a sexy little sound of pleasure. "Your brother Phillip has excellent taste. They're very different, your brothers. Yet they hang together like a single unit."

"That's family."

"Is it? No, not always, not even usually, at least in my experience. Yours is unique, in a number of ways. Why aren't you scarred?"

He looked up from scooping out pasta salad. "Sorry?"

"There's been enough information dribbled through the stories I've read about you, and what I've heard just living in Saint Chris, to tell me you had a very hard childhood. You told me so yourself. How do you get through that without being damaged?"

The press articles had barely skimmed the surface, Seth thought. They knew nothing of the young boy who had hidden from or fought off more than once the slick, groping hands of the drunks or druggies Gloria had brought home.

They didn't know about the beatings or the blackmail, or the fear that remained a hard kernel lodged in his heart.

"They saved me." He said it with a simple honesty that made her throat burn. "It's not an exaggeration to say that they saved my life. Ray Quinn, then Cam and Ethan and Phil. They turned their world around for me, and because of it, turned mine around with it. Anna and Grace and Sybill, Aubrey, too. They made a home for me, and nothing that happened before matters nearly as much as everything that came after."

Unspeakably moved, she leaned forward and touched her lips to his. "That's for three. For making me like you. You're a good man. I don't know just what to do with you."

"You could start by trusting me."

"No." She eased back again, broke off a small hunk of bread. "Nothing starts with trust. Trust develops. And with me, that can take considerable time."

"I can probably guarantee I'm nothing like the guy you were engaged to." When her body went rigid, he shrugged. "I'm not the only one who gets written about or talked about."

And when she'd touched on a personal area, she reminded herself, he hadn't frozen up. "No, you're nothing like Jonah. We never had a picnic with his sister's pasta salad."

"Dinner at Jean-Louis at the Watergate or whatever tony French place is currently in fashion. Openings at the Kennedy Center. Clever cocktail parties inside the Beltway, and the occasional Sunday afternoon brunch with copacetic friends." He waited a beat. "How'd I do?"

"Close enough." Dead on target.

"You're way outside the Beltway now. His loss."

"He seems to be bearing up."

"Did you love him?"

She opened her mouth, then found herself answering with complete honesty. "I don't know anymore. I certainly believed I did or I'd never have planned to marry him. He was attractive, brilliant, had a deadly sarcasm that often posed for witty—and sometimes was. And, as it turned out, the fidelity of an alley cat. Better I found that out before we were married than after. But I learned something valuable about myself due to the experience. No one cheats on me without serious consequences."

"Bruised his balls, did you?"

"Oh, worse." She nibbled delicately on pâté. "He left his cashmere coat, among other items, at my place. While I was coldly packing up his things, I took it back out of the packing box, cut off the sleeves, the collar, the buttons. And since that was so satisfying, I put, one by one, all his Melissa Etheridge CDs in the microwave. She's a wonderful artist, but I can't listen to her today without feeling destructive urges. Then I put his Ferragamo loafers in the washing machine. These acts were hard on my appliances, but good for my soul. Since I was on a roll, I started to flush my three-carat, square-cut Russian white diamond engagement ring down the toilet, but sanity prevailed."

"What did you do with it?"

"I put it in an envelope, wrote 'For His Sins' on the front, then dropped it into the collection box at a little church in Georgetown. Overdramatic, but again, satisfying."

This time Seth leaned over, touched his lips to hers. "Nice job, champ."

"Yes, I thought so." She brought her knees up, sipped her wine while she looked out over the water. "A number of my acquaintances think I left D.C. and moved here because of Jonah. They're wrong. I've loved it here since that first time we came with my grandfather. When I knew I had to make the break, start fresh, I tried to imagine myself living in different places, even different countries. But I always came back here in my head. It wasn't impulsive, though again, a lot of people think so. I planned it for years. That's how I do things, plan them out. Step by step."

She paused, rested her chin on her knees as she studied him. "Obviously, I've missed a step somewhere with you or I wouldn't be sitting here on the grass drinking wine on a Sunday afternoon and telling you things I had no intention of talking about."

She lifted her head again, sipped wine. "You listen. That's a gift. And a weapon."

"I'm not going to hurt you."

"Healthy people don't step toward a relationship with the intention of hurting each other. Still, they do. Maybe it'll be me who ends up hurting you."

"Let's see." He cupped a hand at the back of her neck, rubbing lightly as he bent down to lay his lips on hers. "No," he said after a moment. "No bruises yet."

Then shifting, he framed her face with his hands to lift it until their lips met again.

Very soft, suddenly deep and wrenchingly gentle, his mouth moved on hers. With silky glides he teased her tongue into a dance as his fingers trailed down the line of her throat, over the curve of her shoulders.

She tasted of the wine that spilled unnoticed when her hand went limp on the glass. He found the quick catch and release of her breath when she drew him closer as arousing as a moan.

He laid her back on the blanket, sliding down with her as her arms linked around his neck.

She wanted his weight. She wanted his hands. She wanted his mouth to go on and on taking from hers. She felt the brush of his fingers on her collarbone, and shivered. They skimmed over the thin material of her top, then slipped down to dance over her breast.

He murmured her name before he grazed his teeth over her jaw. And his hand, so beautifully formed, so rough from work, molded her.

Heat flashed through her, urging her to give and to take. Instead, she pressed a hand to his shoulder. "Wait. Seth."

His mouth came back to hers, hungrier now, and with the dangerous flavor of urgency. "Let me touch you. I have to touch you."

"Wait."

He bit off an oath, rested his forehead on hers while his blood raged. He could feel her body vibrating under his, and knew she was just as needy. "Okay. Okay," he managed. "Why?"

"I'm not ready."

"Oh, sugar. Any more ready, you'd be past me."

"Wanting you isn't the same as being ready." But she was afraid he was right. "I didn't intend for this to happen, not like this. I'm not going to make love with a man who appears to be involved with someone else."

"Involved with who? Jesus, Dru, I just got back home, and I haven't looked at another woman since the first time I saw you."

"You've been involved with this one long before you saw me." He looked so blank, so disheveled, so frustrated she wanted to giggle. But she stayed firm. "Aubrey."

"What about Aubrey?" It took him several jolting seconds to understand her meaning. "*Aubrey?* Me and . . .

Christ on a crutch, are you kidding?" He'd have laughed if the idea hadn't left him so shocked. "Where do you get that?"

"I'm not blind." Irritated, she shoved at him. "Move, will you?"

"I'm not involved with . . ." He couldn't even say it, but he sat back. "It's not like that. Jesus, Dru, she's my sister."

"No, she isn't."

"Niece."

"Nor is she that. And maybe you are oblivious to what's between you—though you don't strike me as a dolt—but I doubt very much she is."

"I don't think about her that way."

"Maybe you haven't, on a conscious level."

"At all." The very idea had panic dancing in his throat. "None of the levels. Neither does she."

Dru smoothed down her skirt. "Are you certain?"

"Yeah." But the seed had been planted. "Yes. And if you've got some insane notion that me being with you is somehow cheating on Aubrey, you can forget it."

"What I think," Dru said calmly, "is that I'm not going to have an affair with a man who I suspect is attracted to someone else. Maybe you should work this out with Aubrey before anything goes any further between us. But for now I think we'd better call it a day. Do you mind if I take a look at the painting?"

"Yes." He snapped it out. "I mind. You can see it when it's finished."

"All right." Well, well, she mused, artistic temperament rears its head. "I'll just pack up the food for you. I assume you want at least one more sitting," she said as she began to pack the cooler. "I should be able to give you some time next Sunday."

He stood, stared down at her. "You're a case. Some ass-hole cheats on you so that means we're all cheats?"

"No." She understood his temper, and since it seemed a reasonable conclusion for him to make, she didn't lose hers. "Not at all. In fact, I think you're as honest as they come. I couldn't consider being with you if I thought otherwise. But as I said, I'm not ready to take this step with you, and I have reservations over your feelings toward someone else—and hers toward you."

She looked up then. "I've been the clichéd victim of the other woman, Seth. I won't do that to anyone else."

"Sounds like instead of you asking me about scars, I should've asked you."

She rose now, nodded. "Yes, maybe you should have. Since you're going to sulk, I'll leave you to it."

He caught her arm before she could breeze by, whipped her around so fast she felt fear burst like a bomb in her throat. "You keep taking those steps one at a time, sugar. It might take you longer to fall on your face, but you'll fall just as hard."

"Let me go now."

He released her, turned his back on her to pack up his gear. More shaken than she wanted to admit, Dru made herself walk slowly into the house.

It was, she admitted, still a retreat.

NINE

WOMEN. SETH TOSSED the cooler into the trunk of the car, heaved the hamper in behind it. Just when you thought you understood them, they turned into aliens. And those aliens had the power to change a normal, reasonable man into a blithering idiot.

There was nothing a man could do to keep up with them.

He tossed in the blanket, kicked the tire, then yanked the blanket back out again. He stared over at her house and gave it a satisfactory snarl.

His mutters were a combination of curses, pithy remarks and considerable blithering as he stomped back for his folding table and watercolor paper.

And there she was, sleeping on the red blanket in the dappled sunlight. All long limbs and color, with the face of a sleeping faerie queen.

"I ought to know who I'm attracted to," he told her as he carefully lifted the painting-in-progress and carried it to the car. "One guy turns out to be a putz, and damns us all?"

He laid the paper on the blanket, scowled at it. "Well, that's your problem, sister."

Sister, he thought and felt an uneasy jittering in his gut. Why the hell had she put that in his head about Aubrey? It was off, that's all. It was way, way off.

It had to be.

He loved Aubrey. Of course he did. But he'd never thought about . . . Had he?

"You see, you *see*?" He jabbed a finger at the painting. "That's what your kind does to us. You confuse everything until we start questioning our own brains. Well, it's not going to work with me."

Because it was more comfortable, he switched back to temper as he finished loading his car. He had nearly made the turn for home when he swung the car around, punched the gas.

"We'll just settle this thing." He spoke aloud and nodded at the painting. "Once and for all. And we'll see who's the idiot."

He pulled up in the drive at Aubrey's house, leaped out of the car and strode to the door with his outrage and temper still leading the way. He didn't knock. No one would have expected him to.

The living room, like the rest of the house, was picture-pretty, cluttered just enough to be comfortable, and ruthlessly clean. Grace had a knack for such things.

Once she'd made her living as a single parent cleaning other people's homes. Now she ran her own business, a cleaning service with more than twenty employees who handled homes and businesses on the Shore.

Her own home was one of her best advertisements—and at the moment it was also entirely too quiet.

"Aubrey?" he shouted up the stairs. "Anyone home?"

"Seth?" Grace hurried in from the kitchen. In her bare feet and cropped pants, her hair pulled carelessly back from her face, she looked entirely too young to have a daughter some wrong-headed woman thought he was attracted to.

Jesus, he'd *baby-sat* for Aubrey.

"Come on back," she told him with a quick kiss. "Ethan and Deke are out back fixing the lawn mower. I was just making some lemonade."

"I just dropped by to see Aubrey about . . ." Oh no, he thought, he couldn't go there with Grace. "Is she around?"

"She plays softball Sunday afternoons."

"Right." Seth jammed his hands in his pockets and scowled. "Right."

"Honey, is something wrong? Did you and Aubrey have a fight?"

"No. No, I just need to . . . talk to her about something."

"She should be back in an hour or so. Emily, too. Em's off with her boyfriend. Why don't you go on out with Ethan and Deke, stay for dinner? We're cooking out later."

"Thanks, but . . . I've got some things . . ." It felt weird, too weird, looking at Grace's face, seeing Aubrey in it and thinking what he was thinking. "I gotta go."

"But—" She was talking to his back as he rushed out the door. Anna was right, Grace thought with a sigh. Something was troubling their boy.

I T was the bottom of the sixth, with two on, two out when Seth arrived at the park. Aubrey's team, the Blue Crabs, was down by a run to their longtime nemesis, the Rockfish.

Spectators munched on hot dogs, slurped cold drinks

from paper cups and hurled the expected insults or encouragements at the players. June was coming on with her usual hot breath and moist hands, making spring a fond memory. Sun poured onto the field and drenched it in heat and humidity.

Steam from the concession stand pumped out as Seth passed it to clamber up the stands.

He spotted Junior Crawford, a billed cap shielding his bald head and wrinkled gnome face, with a boy of no more than three perched on his bony knee.

"Hey there, Seth." Junior scooted his skinny ass over an inch in invitation. "How come you ain't down there on the field?"

"Came back too late for the draft." He scanned the field first and noted Aubrey was on deck as the current batter took ball three. Then he winked at the little boy. "Who's this guy?"

"This here's Bart." Junior gave the boy a bounce. "My great-grandson."

"Great-grandson?"

"Yup, got us eight grands now, and this one." Junior's attention swung back to the field at the crack of the bat. "Gone foul," he muttered. "Straighten out that bat, Jed Wilson!" he shouted. "Chrissake."

"Jed Wilson? Is that Mrs. Wilson's grandson?"

"The same. Affable enough boy, right enough, but can't bat worth shit."

"Worth shit," Bart said happily.

"Now, boy." Chuckling, Junior wagged his finger at Bart. "You know you're gonna get me in the doghouse again if you go saying that in front of your mama."

"Worth shit! Pappy!" Bart bubbled out a laugh, then

poked his mangled hot dog toward Seth. "Bite?"

"Sure." Grateful for the distraction, Seth leaned down and pretended to take a huge bite.

When ball four was called, the crowd erupted, and Junior let out a whoop. "Walked him. By God. You're in for it now, you stinking Rockfish."

"Stinking Rockfish," Bart echoed joyfully.

"We're gonna see some action now, goddamn it! Now we'll see what's what."

The Blue Crab fans began to croon "Aub-*rey*! Aub-*rey*!" as she swaggered to the plate.

"Knock one out, Aub! That girl can do it," Junior said with such wild enthusiasm Seth wondered he didn't have a stroke on the spot. "You watch!" He stabbed Seth with the razor point of his elbow. "You just watch her slam that bastard."

"Slam that bastard!" Bart shouted, waving his mushed hot dog and dripping mustard.

For both their sakes, Seth nipped the boy from Junior's knee and set him on his own.

She was a pleasure to watch, Seth thought. No question about it. That compact, athletic build. The undeniable femaleness of it despite—maybe because of—the mannish baseball jersey.

But that didn't mean he thought about her . . . that way.

She scuffed at the plate. There was a short exchange with the catcher Seth imagined was derisive on both sides. She took a couple of testing swings. Wiggled her butt.

Jesus, why was he looking at her butt?

And took a hard cut at the first pitch.

The crowd surged to their feet on a roar. Aubrey shot toward first like a bullet banged from its gun.

Then the crowd deflated, and she jogged back to the plate as the ball curved foul.

The crowd began to chant her name again as she picked up the bat and went through the same routine. Two swings, wiggle the bat, wiggle the butt and set for the pitch.

She took it, checking her swing. And when the ump called strike two, she rounded on him. Seth could see her lips move, could hear the bite of her words in his head.

Strike, my ass. Any more outside, that pitch would have been in Virginia. Just how big a strike zone you want to give this guy?

Don't refer to the dubious sexual practices of his mother, Seth warned her mentally. Don't go there and get tossed.

Whether she'd learned some control in the last couple years or his warning got through, Aubrey skinned the ump with one baleful look, then stepped back in the batter's box.

The chant rose again, feet began to stomp on wood until the bleachers vibrated. In Seth's lap, little Bart squeezed what was left of the dog and bun to pulp and shouted, "Slam the bastard."

And she did.

Seth knew the minute the ball met her bat that it was gone. So, obviously, did Aubrey because she held her position—shoulders front, hips cocked, front leg poised like a dancer—as she watched the ball sail high and long.

The crowd was on their feet, an eruption of sound as she tossed her bat aside and jogged around the bases.

"Goddamn fricking grand slam." Junior sounded as if he was about to weep. "That girl is a fricking peach."

"Fricking peach," Bart agreed and leaned over from Seth's arms to plant a sloppy kiss on Junior's cheek.

* * *

THE Rockfish went scoreless in the seventh, shut down on a strikeout, and a spiffy double play started by Aubrey at short. Seth wandered down toward the dugout as the fans began to drift toward home. He saw Aubrey standing, glugging Gatorade straight from the jug.

"Nice game, Slugger."

"Hey." She tossed the jug to one of her teammates and sauntered over to Seth. "I didn't know you were here."

"Came in bottom of the sixth, just in time to see you kick Rockfish ass."

"Fast ball. Low and away. He should've known better. I thought you were painting the flower girl today."

"Yeah, well, we had a sitting."

She cocked a brow, then rubbed at her nose as Seth stared at her. "What? So, I've got dirt on my face."

"No, it's not that. Listen, I need to talk to you."

"Okay, talk."

"No, not here." He hunched his shoulders. They were surrounded, he thought. Players, spectators, kids. Dozens of familiar faces. People who knew both of them. My God, did other people think he and Aubrey . . . ?

"It's, ah, you know. Private."

"Look, if something's wrong—"

"I didn't say anything was wrong."

She huffed out a breath. "Your face does. I rode in with Joe and Alice. Let me tell them I'm catching a lift home with you."

"Good. Great. I'll meet you at the car."

He shifted the blanket and painting to the backseat. Leaned on the hood. Paced around the car. When Aubrey walked toward him, a mitt in her hand, a bat over her shoulder, he tried to look at her the way he would if he'd never met her before.

But it just wouldn't work.

"You're starting to get me worried, Seth," she said.

"Don't. Here, let me put those in the trunk. I've got my stuff in the back."

She shrugged, passed off her ball gear, then peered into the backseat. "Wow." Transfixed, she yanked open the door for a better look at the watercolor. "No wonder you've been so hot to paint her. This is wonderful. Jeez, Seth, I never get used to it."

"It's not finished."

"I can see that," she said dryly. "It's sexy, but it's soft. And intimate." She glanced up at him, those pretty green eyes meeting his.

He tried to gauge if he felt any sort of a sexual jolt, the way he did when Dru's darker ones leveled on his face.

It was almost too embarrassing to think about.

"Is that what you're after?"

"What?" Appalled, he gaped at her. "Is what what I'm after?"

"You know, soft, sexy, intimate."

"Ah . . ."

"With the painting," she finished, feeling totally confused.

"The painting." The terror in his belly churned into faint nausea. "Yeah, that's it."

Now her face registered mild surprise when he opened the car door for her. "We in a hurry?"

"Just because you hit grand slams doesn't mean a guy shouldn't open the door for you." He bit the words off as he rounded the car, slammed in the other side. "If Will doesn't treat you with some respect, you ought to ditch him."

"Hold on, hold on. Will treats me just fine. What are you in such a lather about?"

"I don't want to talk about it yet." He pulled out, started to drive.

She let him have silence. She knew him well enough to understand that when he had something in his craw, he went quiet. Went inside Seth to a place even she wasn't permitted.

When he was ready, he'd talk.

He pulled into the lot of the boatyard, sat tapping his hands on the steering wheel for a moment. "Let's walk around to the dock, okay?"

"Sure."

But when he got out, she continued to sit until he came around and wrenched the door open. "What're you doing?"

"Merely waiting for you to treat me with the proper respect." She fluttered her lashes and slid out of the car. Then, laughing at him, pulled a pack of Juicy Fruit from her back pocket, offered it.

"No, thanks."

"What's up, Seth?" she asked as she unwrapped a stick of gum.

"I need to ask you for a favor."

She folded the gum into her mouth. "What do you need?"

He stepped onto the dock, stared out at the water, and at the osprey resting on a post before he turned back to her. "I need to kiss you."

She lifted her palms. "That's it? God, I was wondering if you had six months to live or something. Okay. Jeez, Seth, you've kissed me hundreds of times. What's the big deal?"

"No." He crossed his arms over his chest, then ran his

hands over his hips and finally stuck them in his pockets. "I mean, I need to *kiss* you."

"Huh?" Shock registered on her face.

"I need to settle something, so I need to kiss you. Like a regular guy would."

"Seth." She patted his arm. "This is weird. Did you get hit on the head or something?"

"I know it's weird," he shot back. "Do you think I don't know it's weird? Imagine how I feel bringing it up in the first place."

"How come you brought it up in the first place?"

He stalked down the dock, back again. "Dru has this idea that I—that we—Christ. That I'm attracted to you in a guy way. And possibly vice versa. Probably."

Aubrey blinked twice, slow as an owl. "She thinks I've got the hots for you?"

"Oh, Jesus, Aub."

"She thinks there's something like that between you and me, so she gave you the boot."

"More or less," he muttered.

"So you want to plant one on me because of her?"

"Yes. No. I fucking don't know." Could it be any worse? he wondered. Could he be more embarrassed, more itchy, more stupid?

"She put this damn idea in my head. I can't work it back out again. What if she's right?"

"What if she's right?" There was a laugh burbling in her throat, but she managed to swallow it. "What if you've got some suppressed fantasy going about us? Get real, Seth."

"Look, look." Impassioned in a way that made her blink again, he took her by the shoulders. "It's not going to kill you to kiss me."

"Okay, okay. Go ahead."

"Okay." He blew out a breath, started to lower his head, then straightened again. "I can't remember my moves. Give me a minute."

He stepped back, turned away and tried to clear his head. "Let's try this." He turned back, laid his hands on her hips to draw her against him. Seconds passed. "You could put your arms around me or something."

"Oh, sorry." She reached up, threaded her fingers together behind his head. "How's this?"

"Fine. That's fine. Come up a little," he suggested, so she rose on her toes. He bent his head. His mouth was a breath from hers when she snorted out a laugh.

"Oh Christ."

"Sorry. Sorry." The fit of giggles forced her to move back and hold her stomach. He stood, scowling, until she controlled herself. "I balked, that's all. Here we go." She started to put her arms around him again. "Shit, wait." Conscientiously, she took the gum out of her mouth, folded it into the old wrapper in her pocket. "If we're going to do this, let's do it right. Right?"

"If you can control the pig snorts."

"Free lesson, sport: When you're about to tangle tongues with a woman, you don't mention pork or swine."

She put her arms around him again, took a good strong hold this time and moved in herself before either of them could think about it.

They stayed locked, the breeze off the water fluttering over them. There was a hum as a car drove by on the road behind them, and the sudden desperate barking of a dog as it chased along behind the fence until the car disappeared.

Their lips separated, their eyes met. The silence between them held for several long seconds.

Then they began to laugh.

Still holding each other, they rocked in a kind of whooping hilarity that would have put either one of them on the ground without the support. He lowered his forehead to hers on a relieved breath.

"So." She gave his butt a friendly pinch. "You want me, don't you?"

"Shut up, Aubrey."

He gave her, his sister, a fierce hug before he eased back. "Thanks."

"No problem. Anyway, you're good at it."

"You too." He rubbed his knuckles over her cheek. "And we're never going to do that again."

"That's a deal."

He started to swing an arm around her shoulders, then stopped as an appalling thought struck. "You're not going to tell anybody about this, right? Like your mom, or Will. Anybody."

"Are you kidding?" Even the idea of it had her shuddering. "You either. Promise." She spat into her palm, held it out.

Seth grimaced down at her hand. "I should never have taught you that one." But resigned, and respectful of the pledge, he spat into his own, then solemnly shook hands.

HE was too restless to go home. And, he admitted, he needed a little more time before he faced his family with the kiss incident still fresh in his mind.

He had half a mind to go back to Dru's and let her know

just how off the mark, how insulting, how *wrong* she'd been.

But the other half of his mind, the smarter half, warned him he wasn't in the mood to have a rational conversation with her yet.

She'd made him doubt himself, and it stung. He'd worked hard to reach and maintain his level of confidence, in himself, in his work, in his family. No woman was allowed to shake it.

So they'd just move back a step before things went any further. He'd paint her because he couldn't do otherwise. But that would be all.

He didn't need to be involved with a woman who was that complicated, that unpredictable and that damn opinionated.

It was time to slow down, to concentrate on work and family. To solve his own problems before he took on anyone else's.

He parked at his studio, carted his equipment and the painting up the steps. He used his new cell phone to call home and let Anna know he wouldn't be back for dinner.

He turned on music, then set up to work on the watercolor from memory.

As with sailing, worries, annoyances, problems faded away when he painted. As a child, he'd escaped into drawing. Sometimes it had been as dramatic as survival, others as simple as warding off boredom. It had always been a pleasure for him, a quiet and personal one or a soaring celebration.

In his late teens he'd harbored tremendous guilt and doubt because he'd never suffered for his art, never felt the drama of emotional conflict over it.

When he'd confessed all that to Cam, his brother had

stared at him. "What, are you stupid?" Cam had demanded.

It had been exactly the right response to snap Seth out of a self-involved funk.

There were times when a painting pulled away from him and he was left baffled and frustrated by the image in his mind that refused to be put on canvas.

But there were times when it flew for him, beyond any height he'd imagined he could achieve.

When the light dimmed through the windows and he was forced to hit the overheads, he stepped back from the canvas, stared at what he'd done. And realized this was one of the times it had flown.

There was a vibrancy to the colors—the green of the grass and leaves, the sunstruck amber of the water, the shock of red from the blanket and the milky white of her skin against it. The garden of flowers on her skirt was bold, a contrast to the delicate way the filmy material draped high on her thigh.

There was the curve of her shoulder, the angle of her arm, the square edge of the blanket. And the way the diffused fingers of light fell over the dreamy expression on her face.

He couldn't explain how he'd done it. Any more than he'd been able to tell Dru what he thought about when painting. The technical aspects of the work were just that. Technicalities. Necessary, essential, but as unconsciously accomplished when he worked as breathing.

But how it was that a painting would sometimes draw out the heart of the artist, the core of the subject and allow it to breathe, he couldn't say.

Nor did he question it. He simply picked up his brush and went back to work.

And later when, still fully dressed, he tumbled into bed,

he dropped straight into sleep with the image of Drusilla sleeping beside him.

"WHAT are you calling it?" Stella asked him.

They were standing in front of the painting, studying it in the glare of his studio lights. "I don't know. I haven't thought about it."

"*Beauty Sleeps,*" Stella suggested. "That's what I'd call it."

She was wearing an oversized chambray shirt and baggy jeans with flat canvas shoes that looked as though they'd walked a lot of miles. And when she tucked her arm through Seth's he could smell hints of lemon from her shampoo and soap.

"We're proud of you, Seth. Not for the talent so much. That's God-given. But for being true to it. Being true to what you have and what you are, that's what makes the difference."

She stepped back and looked around. "Wouldn't hurt you to clean up this place some. Being an artist doesn't mean you have to be a slob."

"I'll take care of it in the morning."

She sent him a wry look. "Now where have I heard that one before? That one there." Stella jerked her head toward the painting. "She's neat as a pin. Maybe too neat—which sure as hell isn't your problem. Worries about letting anything shift out of place. Untidiness confuses her, especially when it comes to her own emotions. You've got to figure they're pretty messy where you're concerned already."

He lifted a shoulder in a way that made Stella smile. "I'm putting the brakes on there. She's too much damn work."

"Uh-huh." She twinkled at him. "You keep telling yourself that, boy."

He wanted to leave that area alone. He didn't mind messy emotions, but his own were in such a state he couldn't be sure he'd ever manage to tidy them up again.

"Cam said I should ask you about the zucchini bread."

"He did, did he? Maybe he thinks I've forgotten. Well, you can tell him I may be dead, but I've still got my wits. I wasn't much of a cook. Ray handled that end for the most part. But now and again I stuck my oar in. One day in the fall I got a yen for zucchini bread. We'd planted the stuff, and Christ knows we had more than we could eat in six years. Especially since Ethan wouldn't touch a morsel. So I got out the cookbook and tried my hand at baking some zucchini bread. Four loaves, from scratch, and I set them on a rack to cool. I was damn proud of that bread, too."

She paused a moment, tipped her head up as if looking at the memory. "About a half hour later, I walked back into the kitchen. Instead of four loaves, there were just three. My first thought was, well, those boys have been in here and helped themselves. Felt pretty smug about that one. Until I looked out the kitchen window. What do you think I saw?"

"I've got no clue." But he was sure he was going to enjoy it.

"I'll tell you what I saw," she said with a jut of her chin. "My boys, and my loving husband, out there in the yard using the zucchini bread I'd made from scratch as a goddamn football. Whooping and hollering and tossing that thing around like it was the Super Bowl. I was out that door like a shot, gonna skin the lot of them. About that time, Phil heaved that loaf high and hard, and Ethan loped over to receive. And Cam—he always was quick as a snake—he streaked over the grass, leaped up to intercept. Misjudged, though. The loaf caught him right about here."

She tapped just over her eyebrow. "Knocked him flat on his ass, too. Damn thing was hard as a brick."

She laughed, rocking back and forth on her heels as if her humor had weight. "Ethan snapped up the bread, stepped right over Cam as he sat there with his eyes rolling back in his head, and made the touchdown. By the time I got out to Cam to check him out and give them a piece of my mind, he'd shaken it off and the four of them were howling like loons. They called it the Bread Bowl. Last time I ever baked bread, I'll tell you that. I miss those days. I sure do miss them."

"I wish I'd had time with you. I wish I'd had time with you and Ray."

She moved to him, brushed at the stray tendrils of hair that had fallen over his forehead. The gesture was so tender it made his heart ache.

"Is it okay if I call you Grandma?"

"Of course it is. Sweet boy," Stella murmured. "She couldn't cut that sweet heart out of you, no matter how hard she tried. She couldn't understand it either, that's why hurting you's always been so easy for her."

They weren't talking about Dru now, he thought. But about Gloria. "I don't want to think about her. She can't hurt me anymore."

"Can't she? Trouble's coming. Trouble always does. You be strong, you be smart, and you be true. You hear me? You're not alone, Seth. You'll never be alone."

"Don't go."

"You're not alone," she repeated.

But when he woke with the early sunlight just sliding through his windows, it seemed he was.

Worse, he saw the folded note under the door. He forced himself to get up, to walk over and pick it up.

Lucy's Diner, next to the By-Way Hotel on Route 13.
Eleven o'clock tonight.
Make sure it's in cash.

Trouble's coming. Seth thought he heard the echo of a voice. *Trouble always does.*

TEN

$\smile$

AUBREY STEWED ABOUT it, picked it apart and put it together again. And the more she fumed and fiddled, the madder she got. Temper made it very clear in her mind that Drusilla Whitcomb Banks needed a come-to-Jesus talk, and Aubrey Quinn was just the one to give it to her.

Since she and Seth had made a pact, she couldn't vent to her mother, her father. She couldn't go by Sybill's and ask for some sort of psychological evaluation of the thing. And she couldn't go to Anna just to spew out her annoyance and resentment.

So it built, layer by layer, until she'd worked up quite a head of steam by the time she left the boatyard at five o'clock.

She practiced what she intended to say as she drove into town. The cool, the controlled, the keen-edged slice of words that would cut Little Miss Perfect down to size.

No one got away with making Seth unhappy.

Mess with one Quinn, she thought as she scooted her pickup into a space at the curb, mess with them all.

In her work boots, dirty T-shirt and well-sprung jeans, she marched into Bud and Bloom.

Yeah, she was perfect, all right, Aubrey thought, and bit down on her ire while Dru wrapped a bunch of daisies for Carla Wiggins. Just perfect in her pink silk blouse and wood-nymph hair. The slacks were stone gray and fluid. Probably silk, too, Aubrey thought, annoyed with herself for admiring the classy, casual look.

Dru's gaze shifted up and over as the door opened. What might have been polite warmth chilled into caution when Aubrey glared at her.

At least that was something.

Carla, bouncy and glowing, turned. "Hi, Aubrey. That was some game yesterday. Everybody's talking about your home run. Bases loaded," she said to Dru. "Aub knocked those Rockfish out of the water."

"Really?" Dru had heard the same, a half dozen times, already that day. "Congratulations."

"I swing to score."

"I about had a heart attack when that ball flew." Carla patted her tidy little breasts to demonstrate. "Jed's still flying. He got walked," she said to Dru, "to load the bases before Aubrey came to bat. Anyway, I'm cooking dinner for his parents tonight—talk about the wedding plans some more—and there I was running around straightening the place up—I took a half day off work—and it hit me I didn't have any flowers for a centerpiece. It's going to be spaghetti and meatballs. That's Jed's favorite. Just fun and cheerful, you know. So Dru said daisies would be nice in that red vase I've got. What do you think?"

Aubrey looked at the flowers, moved her shoulder.

"They're pretty. Friendly, I guess. Kind of simple and sweet."

"That's it. That's just exactly right." Carla fussed with her fine blond hair. "I don't know why I get so nervous. I've known Jed's folks all my life. It's just different now that we're getting married in December. I told Dru my colors are going to be midnight blue and silver. I didn't want to go with the red and green, you know, but wanted to keep it Christmassy and festive. Do you really think those colors will work?" Carla chewed on her lip as she looked back at Dru. "For the flowers and all."

"Beautifully." The warmth came back into Dru's face. "Festive, as you say, and romantic, too. I'm going to put some ideas together, then you and your mother and I will go over everything. Don't worry about a thing."

"Oh, I can't help it. I'll drive everyone crazy before December. I've got to run." She scooped up the flowers. "They'll be coming along in an hour."

"Have a nice evening," Dru said.

"Thanks. See you later, Aubrey."

"Yeah. Hi to Jed."

The door closed behind Carla, and as the bells on it stopped ringing, the cheer that had filled the shop faded.

"I don't think you're in the market for flowers." Dru folded her hands. "What can I do for you?"

"You can stop screwing with Seth's brain and putting me in the role of the other woman."

"Actually, I was worried that was my role, and I didn't care for it."

All the cool, controlled, keen-edged words Aubrey had practiced flew out of her head. "What the hell's wrong with you? Do you think Seth would be poking at you if he were interested in someone else?"

" 'Poking at'?"

Aubrey hunched her shoulders. "Family phrase," she muttered. "What do you take him for? He'd never move on you if he was moving on someone else. He's not like that, and if you don't already know it, you're just stupid."

"Calling me stupid is going to end this conversation before it gets started."

"So is punching you in the nose."

Dru lifted her chin—Aubrey gave her points for it, and for the derisive tone. "Is that how you solve your disagreements?"

"Sometimes. It's quick." Aubrey showed her teeth. "And I owe it to you for the 'buxom blonde in black' remark."

Dru winced, but she kept her voice even. "A stupid comment doesn't make me stupid. But it was uncalled for and ill advised. I apologize for it. I suppose you've never had something pop out of your mouth that you've instantly regretted."

"All the time," Aubrey said, cheerful now. "Apology accepted. But that doesn't cover the bases regarding Seth. You messed with his head and you made him unhappy. That's worth a hell of a lot more than a punch in the nose, from where I stand."

"It wasn't my intention to do either." And she felt a flare of guilt. She'd had no trouble making him mad, but she'd never meant to make him unhappy. Still, she'd done what she thought right for everyone.

"I won't be a game piece to a man, even if he doesn't realize that's what he's making me. I've seen the two of you together. I saw the way you looked at me yesterday when I came into the boatyard. I'm standing here right now with you jumping down my throat because of what you are to each other."

"You want to know what we are to each other?" Riled up

again, Aubrey leaned on the counter. "We're family. And if you don't know family loves each other and sticks up for each other and worries when one of them looks to be getting in deep where he doesn't belong, then I'm sorry for you. And if the way I look at you makes you unhappy, too bad. I'm going to keep right on looking at you, because I'm not sure you're good for him."

"Neither am I," Dru said calmly and stopped Aubrey in her tracks. "There we have a point of agreement."

"I just don't get you," Aubrey admitted. "But I get Seth. He already cares about you. I've known him . . . I don't remember ever not knowing him, and I can see it when he's gone soft on someone. You hurt him yesterday, and I can't stand to see him hurting."

Dru looked down, saw that her hands were gripping the counter. Deliberately, she relaxed them. "Let me ask you something. If you found yourself getting involved with a man—at a point in your life where it's really the last thing you want, but it's happening anyway—and you see that man has a relationship with another woman—a really attractive, vibrant, interesting woman—that you can't define—all you can see is that it's special and it's intimate and beyond your scope—how would you feel?"

Aubrey opened her mouth, shut it again. She had to take another moment before she answered. "I don't know. Damn it. Damn it, Dru, I love him. I love him so much that when he was in Europe it was like a piece of me was missing. But it's not sexual or romantic or anything like that. He's my best friend. He's my brother. He's my Seth."

"I never had a best friend, or a brother. My family doesn't have the . . . vitality of yours. Maybe that's why it's hard for me to understand."

"You'd have gotten a clue if you'd seen the two of us cracking up after kissing yesterday." Aubrey's lips twitched. "That's Seth for you. You planted that seed and so he worries over it, picks at it. 'Gee, am I screwing around with her, am I messing up people I care about? How can I fix it?' So he tracks me down and gives me the big picture, tells me he needs to kiss me—a real guy-girl smackeroo—so we can make sure there's nothing going on in that direction."

"Oh God." Dru closed her eyes. "And he didn't see that was insulting to you?"

"Nope." Surprised, and rather pleased Dru had seen that angle, Aubrey leaned more companionably on the counter. "I didn't let it bother me that way because he was so stupid about the whole thing, so worried and flustered. So we had our little experiment. He gets major points in the lip-lock department. He knows how to kiss."

"Yes, he does."

"There was relief all around because the earth did not move. It didn't even tremble. Then we laughed ourselves silly, and we're fine. I wasn't going to tell you that part," Aubrey added. "I thought letting it hang would make you suffer more. But since you said I was attractive and vibrant and interesting, I'm cutting you a break."

"Thanks. And I'm sorry. It was beginning to . . ." Dru trailed off, shook her head. "Never mind."

"We've come this far, don't hold back now."

She started to shake her head again, then realized that was one of her flaws. She held back. "All right. What's happening between Seth and me was beginning to worry me a little. I had someone I cared about, very much, cheat on me. I started to see myself as that woman, with some sympathy for her position. I didn't want to have any sympathy for her. I prefer despising her."

"Well, sure." Nothing could have been clearer to Aubrey's way of thinking. "You can relax. The field's all yours. Are we square on that?"

"Yes. Yes, we are. I appreciate your coming in to talk to me, and not punching me."

"Punching you would've pissed off Seth, not to mention my parents, so it's just as well. I guess I'd better get going."

"Aubrey." It was always a terrifying thing for Dru to go with impulse. "I don't make friends easily. It's not one of my skills. I'm terrific at making acquaintances, at social small talk and casual conversation. But I don't have many friends."

She took a long breath. "I'm going to close a little early today. It'll take me a few minutes to close out and lock up. Are you in a hurry, or would you like to go have a drink?"

Seth was a goner, Aubrey realized. He'd never hold out against those hints of vulnerability and need hiding under the polish. "Got any good wine at your place?"

"Yes." Dru's lips curved. "I do."

"I'll swing by home, grab a shower. Meet you there."

FROM his studio window, Seth watched Aubrey stride back out to her truck. He'd seen her stride in nearly a half hour before. And though he hadn't been able to see her face, he'd read her body language clearly.

She'd been ready to brawl.

He hadn't gone down. Until he'd seen Gloria, and locked that entire business back in his mental vault, he was keeping a distance from his family.

But he'd listened for the sounds of shouts or breaking

glass. If it had come to that, he'd have run down to pull them apart.

But it hadn't come to that, he noted as Aubrey jumped nimbly into the cab of her truck and zipped off without any indication of temper.

One less worry, he supposed, as he walked into the kitchen to look at the clock on the stove. A little more than five hours left to obsess, he thought. Then he'd meet Gloria, give her the cash he'd withdrawn from his account.

And get back to his life.

DRU had barely walked through the door when Aubrey pulled into the drive. It gave her no time to fuss with the crackers and cheese she'd planned to set out, or to wash the fat purple grapes she'd picked up on the way home.

However casual the invitation, she was accustomed to entertaining a certain way. That certain way wasn't having her guest walk in, push a brown bag into her hand, then look around and whistle.

"Cool. Front page, *House & Garden*." She sent Dru a cheeky grin. "That wasn't really a dig. Man, my mother would love this. She's been itching to get a look at the inside. You got a cleaning service?" Aubrey asked and smoothed a finger over a tabletop. No dust.

"No. It's just me, and I don't—"

"Ought to. Working woman and blah, blah. Mom can give you the whole pitch. Big place." Aubrey began to wander without invitation as Dru stood holding the bag. "I want a big one when I get out on my own. Rattle around a bit, you know? Change from living with what feels like a million people sometimes. Then I'll be lonely and miss them and spend half my time at the house anyway."

She looked up. "High ceilings," she commented. "Must cost you some to heat this place in the winter."

"Would you like to see the bills?" Dru said dryly and made her laugh.

"Maybe later. I'd rather have wine. Oh, those are cookies in the bag. Mom baked some yesterday. Double chocolate chip. Awesome. Kitchen this way?"

"Yes." Dru sighed, then followed, decided to try to go with the flow.

"Nancy Neat, aren't you?" Aubrey said after one glance, then opened the back door. "Man, this is great! It's like your own little island. Do you ever get spooked out here all alone, city girl?"

"No. I thought I might," Dru said as she set the bag on the counter and got out a bottle of Pinot Grigio. "But I don't. I like listening to the water, and the birds and the wind. I like being here. I don't want the city. And I realized the first morning I woke up here, in the quiet, with the sun coming in the windows, I never did. Other people wanted it for me."

She poured the wine. "Do you want to sit out on the patio?"

"That'd be good. I'll bring the cookies."

So they had tart white wine and fat-filled cookies while the sun slid slowly down behind the trees.

"Oh." Aubrey swallowed a mouthful. "I should tell you, Seth and I made a pact not to tell anybody about the big experiment."

"The . . . oh."

"I don't figure you count, since it was your idea. Sort of. But since I spilled it, I've either got to kill you, or you have to swear not to tell anybody."

"Does this oath involve my blood in any way?"

"I usually do it with spit."

Dru thought about it for about two seconds. "I'd rather not involve any bodily fluids. Is my word good enough?"

"Yeah." Aubrey picked up another cookie. "People like you keep their word."

"People like me?"

"Yeah. Breeding," she said with a broad wave of a hand. "You're a fucking purebred."

"I'll assume that's a compliment of some sort."

"Sure. You've got this 'I'm much too cultured and well-bred to make an issue of it' air. You always look perfect. I admire that even when I hate it. It's not like you're all fussy and girly and stuff. You just always look good."

Aubrey stopped, mouth full. Then swallowed fast. "Oh hey, listen, I'm not coming on to you or anything. I like guys."

"Oh, I see. Then I suppose there's no point in us having a big experiment of our own." After two long beats, Dru's laughter burst out. She had to lean back, hold her sides as they ached from the force of it. "Your face. Priceless. It's the first time I've ever seen you speechless."

"That was good." Nodding approval, Aubrey picked up her wine. "That was damn good. I might just like you after all. So, are you going to talk Seth out of the watercolor portrait when he's finished?"

"I don't know." Would he finish it? she wondered. Or was he too angry with her to *see* her as he had? No, he'd finish, she decided. The artist would have no choice.

"If it were me, I'd wheedle it out of him."

"I think I'd feel strange having a painting of myself hanging on the wall. Besides, I haven't seen it. He was too angry to let me."

"Yeah, he gets all tight-assed when he's mad. Okay,

here's a tip." Watching Dru, Aubrey rested her elbows on the table. "You don't want to cry. What you want to do is bravely battle back tears. You know, so your eyes get all shiny and wet and your lip quivers a little. Hold on."

She leaned back again, closed her eyes, took a couple of deep breaths. Then she opened them again, stared at Dru with a kind of wide-eyed, pitiful expression as tears swam into her eyes.

"My God," Dru murmured in admiration. "That's really good. In fact, it's brilliant."

"Tell me." Aubrey sniffled. "You can let one spill over if you have to, but that's it." A single tear dripped down her cheek. Then she giggled. "You start to flood, and he's all about patting your head and stuffing a paint rag or whatever in your hand before he goes into full retreat. Then you've lost him. But you give him the shimmery-eyes, quivery-lip deal, and he'll do anything. It *destroys* him."

"How did you learn to do that?"

"Hey, I work with guys." Aubrey swiped the single tear off her cheek. "You develop your weapons. You can bite the tip of your tongue to get started if you have to. Me, I can turn it on and off. Speaking of guys, why don't you tell me about that creep you were engaged to, then we can trash him."

"Jonah? Assistant communications director. West Wing staff, a man with the president's ear. Brilliant mind, smooth style, gorgeous face and a body made for Armani."

"This isn't making me hate him. Get to the dirt."

"It's not far under the surface. Washington social circles—my grandfather remains a strong force in Washington, and my family is influential. Socially active. We met at a cocktail party, and things moved from there. Smoothly and at a reasonable pace. We enjoyed each other, and we liked each other. Had interests and people and philosophies in common. Then, I thought we loved each other."

It was never anger she felt when she thought of that. But sadness.

"Maybe we did. We became lovers—"

"How was he? In the sack?"

Dru hesitated, then poured more wine. She didn't discuss this sort of thing. Then again, she realized, she'd never had anyone who made her feel able to discuss this sort of thing.

Aubrey made it seem easy.

"What the hell. He was good. I thought we were good—but then again, lovers fall into the same category as friends with me. I don't make them easily."

"That'd make it hurt more when it gets messed up," Aubrey offered.

"Yeah, I guess it does. But I thought Jonah and I were good together, in bed and out of it. I was ready when he asked me to marry him. We'd been moving in that direction, and I was prepared. I'd thought it through."

Curious now, Aubrey tilted her head. "If you had to think it through, maybe you weren't in love with him."

"Maybe not." Dru looked away, watched the fluttering flight of a butterfly, listened to the quiet hum of a boat motor as someone cruised by on the river. "But I need to think things through. The bigger the step, the longer and more carefully I think. I wasn't sure I wanted to be married. My parents' marriage—well, it's not like your parents' marriage. But I felt, with Jonah, it would be different. We never quarreled."

"Never?" Pure shock covered Aubrey's face. "You never had a good shouting fight?"

"No." She smiled a little now as she realized how dull that would seem to anyone named Quinn. "When we disagreed, we discussed."

"Oh yeah, that's how we handle things in my family. We discuss our disagreements. We just do it at the top of our lungs. So you and this guy were good in bed, you didn't fight and you had a lot in common. What happened?"

"We got engaged, we had a round of parties and began making plans for a wedding set for the following summer. July because that was most convenient for our schedules. He was busy with work, and I was busy letting my mother drag me around to bridal shows. We house-hunted—Jonah and me, my mother and me, my father and me."

"That's a lot of hunting."

"You have no idea. Then one night, we were at his apartment. We went to bed. While we were making love, I kept feeling something scrape at the small of my back. Eventually I had to stop. It was funny, really, I made a joke out of it. Then we turned on the lights and I went over the sheets. And came up with another woman's earring."

"Oh." Aubrey's face filled with sympathy. "Ouch."

"I even recognized it. I'd seen her wearing them at some event or other. I'd admired them, commented on them. Which is probably why she made sure to leave it there, where I'd find it at the worst possible moment."

"Bitch."

"Oh yes." Dru lifted her glass in a half toast. "Oh yes indeed. But she loved him, and that was a discreet and surefire way to get me out of the picture."

"No excuses." Aubrey wagged a finger. "She was trespassing on another woman's man, even if the man wasn't worth jack shit. She was as sneaky as he was, and just as guilty."

"You're right. No excuses. They deserve each other."

"Damn straight. So, did you tie his dick in a knot? What?"

Dru let out a long sigh. "God, I wish I could be you. I wish I could, even for one single day. No, I got up, and I got dressed, while he started making excuses. He loved me. This other thing was just physical, it didn't mean anything."

"Christ." Disgust was ripe in her voice. "Can't they ever come up with something original?"

"Not in my experience." The instant, unqualified sympathy and support eased some of the rawness she still carried over it all. "He had needs, sexual needs that I was just too restrained to meet. He'd just wanted to get it out of his system before settling down. Basically, he said that if I'd been hotter, more responsive or creative in bed, he wouldn't have had to look elsewhere for that kind of satisfaction."

"And yet he lives," Aubrey murmured. "You let him turn the thing around on you instead of cutting off his balls and hanging them on his ears."

"I wasn't a complete doormat," Dru objected, and told her about the systematic destruction of Jonah's prized possessions.

"Nuked his CDs. That's a good one. I feel better now. Just as a suggestion, instead of cutting up his cashmere coat? I'd have filled the pockets with, oh, I don't know, say a nice mixture of raw eggs, motor oil, a little flour to thicken it up, maybe a hint of garlic. All easily accessed household items. Then, I'd've folded it up really neat, with the pockets to the inside. Wouldn't he have been surprised when he pulled it out of the box?"

"I'll keep that in mind, should the occasion ever come up again."

"Okay. But I really like the CDs, and the bit with the

shoes. If the guy was anything like Phil about his shoes, that one really hurt. What do you say we take a walk, work off some of these cookies? Then we can order some Chinese."

It wasn't, Dru realized, so hard to make a friend after all. "That sounds terrific."

THE diner was lit like a runway, and business wasn't exactly booming. Seth sat on the sun-faded red vinyl of the booth in the very back. Gloria wasn't there. She would be late.

She always came late. It was, he knew, just another way for her to show she had the upper hand.

He ordered coffee, knowing he wouldn't drink it. But he needed the prop. The ten thousand in cash was in an old canvas bag on the seat beside him.

There was a man with shoulders wide as Montana sitting on a stool at the counter. His neck was red from the sun, and his hair shaved so sharp and close it looked as if it could slice bread. He was wearing jeans, and the tin of tobacco he must have carried habitually in his pocket had worn a white circle in the fading denim.

He ate apple pie à la mode with the concentration of a surgeon performing a tricky operation.

The Waylon Jennings tune crooning out of a corner juke suited him right down to the ground.

Behind the counter, the waitress wore candy pink with her name stitched in white over the right breast. She picked up a pot of coffee from the warmer, breezed up to the pie eater, and stood, hip cocked, as she topped off his cup.

Seth's fingers itched for his sketch pad.

Instead he drew in his head to pass the time. The counter

scene—done in bright, primary colors. And the couple midway down the line of booths who looked as if they'd been traveling all day and were now worn to nubs. They ate without conversation. But at one point the woman passed the man the salt, and he gave her hand a quick squeeze.

He'd call it *Roadside*, he thought. Or maybe *Off Route 13*. It relaxed him considerably to pull it all together in his mind.

Then Gloria walked in, and the painting faded away.

She'd gone beyond thin. He could see the sharp bones pressing against the skin at the sides of her throat, the whip-edge blades of her hips jutting against the tight red pants. She wore open-toed, backless heels that flipped and clicked against her feet and the aged linoleum.

Her hair was bleached a blond that was nearly white, cut short and spiky, and only accented how thin her face had become. The lines had dug deep around her mouth, around her eyes. The makeup she'd applied couldn't hide them.

He imagined that upset and infuriated her when she looked in the mirror.

She hadn't yet hit fifty, he calculated, but looked as though she'd been dragged face first over it some time before.

She slid in across from him. He caught a drift of her perfume—something strong and floral. It either hid the smell of whiskey, or she'd held off on her drinking before the meeting.

"Your hair was longer last time," she said, then shifted to flash her teeth at the waitress. "What kind of pie you got tonight?"

"Apple, cherry, lemon meringue."

"I'll have a slice of cherry, with vanilla ice cream. How about you, Seth honey?"

Her voice, just her voice, set his teeth on edge. "No."

"Suit yourself. You got any chocolate sauce?" she asked the waitress.

"Sure. You want that, too?"

"You just dump it over the ice cream. I'll have coffee, too. Well now." She leaned back, slung one arm over the back of the booth. Skinny as she was, he noted, the skin there was starting to sag. "I figured you'd stay over in Europe, keep playing with the Italians. Guess you got homesick. And how are all the happy Quinns these days? How's my dear sister, Sybill?"

Seth lifted the bag from the seat beside him, watched her focus in on it as he laid it on the tabletop. But when she reached out, he closed his fist around it.

"You take it, and you go. You make a move toward anyone in my family, you'll pay. You'll pay a hell of a lot more than what's in this bag."

"That's a hell of a way to talk to your mother."

His tone never changed. "You're not my mother. You never were."

"Carried you around inside me for nine months, didn't I? I brought you into the world. You owe me."

He unzipped the bag, tilted it so she could see the contents. The satisfaction on her face dragged at his belly. "There's your payment. You stay away from me and mine."

"You and yours, you and yours. Like you got something with those assholes I give two shits about. Think you're a big shot now, don't you? Think you're something special. You're nothing."

Her voice rose enough to have the man at the counter take notice and the waitress give them a wary look. Seth rose, took ten dollars out of his wallet and tossed it on the table.

"Maybe I am, but I'm still better than you."

Her hand curled into a claw, but she fisted it, laid it on the table as he walked out. She snatched the bag, tucked it against her hip on the seat.

Down payment, she mused. Enough to tide her over for a few weeks while she worked out the rest.

She wasn't done with Seth. Not by a long shot.

ELEVEN

HE BURROWED IN his studio. He used painting as an escape, an excuse, and as a channel for his frustration.

He knew his family was worried about him. He'd barely seen them, or anyone else for that matter, for three days. He hadn't been able to go back to them after leaving Gloria.

He wouldn't take any part of her into their homes, their lives. She was the monkey on his back, and he'd do whatever it took to stop her from leaping onto theirs.

Money was a small price to pay to get rid of her. She'd be back. She always came back. But if ten thousand bought a space of peace, it was a bargain.

So, he'd work through his anger until he found that peace.

He'd hauled the big canvas up from storage, and he'd painted what he felt. The messy mix of emotions and images took shape and color and, as they did, emptied out of him.

He ate when he was hungry, slept when his vision blurred. And painted as if his life depended on it.

That's what Dru thought as she stood in the doorway. It was a battle between life and death, between sanity and despair waged with a brush.

He had one in his hand, stabbed at the canvas, sliced at it. Another was clamped between his teeth like a weapon in reserve. Music boomed, a violent guitar riff that was like a battle cry. Paint was splattered on his shirt, his jeans, his shoes. Her floor.

A kind of blood loss, she thought and gripped the vase she carried.

He hadn't heard her knock over the blasting music, but looking at him now, she realized he wouldn't have heard her if the room had been silent and she'd screamed his name.

He wasn't in the room. He was in the painting.

She told herself to back up and close the door, that she was trespassing on his privacy and his work. But she couldn't.

To see him like this was compelling, intimate, oddly erotic. He seduced her with a passion that wasn't simply beyond anything she understood, but was as distant from her world as the moon.

So she watched as he switched one brush for the other, as he swiped and swirled at the paint, then whipped at the canvas. Bold, almost vicious strokes, then delicate ones that seemed to hold a kind of contained fury.

Despite the breeze spilling in through the windows, she could see the dark line of sweat riding up the center back of his shirt, the damp gleam on the flesh of his arms and throat.

This was labor, she thought, and not all for love.

He'd told her he'd never suffered for art, but he'd been wrong, Dru realized. Anything that consumed so utterly came with pain.

When he stepped back from the canvas, she thought he stared at it as if it had appeared out of thin air. The hand that held the brush fell to his side. He took the one he'd clamped between his teeth, set it aside. Then rubbed, almost absently, at the muscles of his right arm, flexed his fingers.

She started to ease back now, but he turned, peered at her like a man coming out of a trance. He appeared to be exhausted, a little shell-shocked and painfully vulnerable.

Since she'd missed her chance to leave unnoticed, she did the only thing she could think of. She walked in, crossed over to his stereo and turned the music down.

"I'm sorry. You didn't hear me knock." She didn't look at the painting. She was almost afraid to. So she looked at him. "I've interrupted your work."

"No." He shoved away the stray strands of hair that fell over his forehead. "I think it's finished."

He hoped to Christ it was, because he didn't have any more to give it. It had, finally, blessedly, emptied him.

He shifted to his workbench to clean his brushes. "What do you think?" he asked with a nod of his head toward the canvas.

It was a storm at sea. Brutal, savage, and somehow alive. The colors were dark and fearful—blues, greens, blacks, vicious yellows that combined like painful bruises.

She could hear the wind screaming, feel the terror of the man who fought a desperate battle to keep his boat from being swallowed by towering walls of waves.

The water lashed, lightning speared out of the turbulent sky. She saw faces—just ghostly hints of them—in the feral clouds that spewed a sharp and angry rain. More, she realized as she was drawn to it, more faces in the sea.

They seemed hungry to her.

The single boat, the single man, were alone in the primal war.

And in the distance, there was land, and light. There, that small piece of the sky was clear and steady blue. There was home.

He was fighting his way home.

"It's powerful," she managed. "And it's painful. You don't show his face, so I wonder, would I see despair or determination, excitement or fear? And that's the point, isn't it? You don't show his face so we look and we see what we'd feel if we were the one fighting our demons alone."

"Don't you wonder if he'll win?"

"I know he will because he has to get home. They're waiting for him." She looked over at him. He was still caught up in the painting, and rubbing his right hand with his left.

"Are you all right?"

"What?" He glanced at her, then down at his hands. "Oh. Yeah. They cramp sometimes when I've been at it too long."

"How long have you been working on this?"

"I don't know. What day is it?"

"That long. Then I imagine you want to get home and get some rest." She picked up the vase of flowers she'd set beside his stereo. "I put this together before I closed tonight." She held it out. "A peace offering."

It was a mix of blooms and shapes in a squat blue vase. "Thanks. It's nice."

"I don't know whether to be disappointed or relieved

that you haven't been up here the last few days stewing over our disagreement."

He gave the flowers a quick sniff. Something in the bouquet smelled a little like vanilla. "Is that what we had?"

"Well, we weren't in agreement. I was wrong. I very rarely am."

"Is that so?"

"Very rarely," she acknowledged. "So it's always a shock when I am, and when I am, I like to admit it, apologize and move on as quickly as possible."

"Okay. Why don't you tell me which portion of the disagreement you were wrong about?"

"About you and Aubrey. Not only wrong about the aspect of your relationship, but wrong to make an issue out of something that's your personal business."

"Huh. So you were wrong twice."

"No. That equals one mistake with two parts. I was wrong once. And I am sorry."

He set the flowers down, then rolled his shoulders to try to ease some of the stiffness. "How do you know you were wrong?"

Well, she thought, if she'd expected him to let it go with an apology, she should have known better. "She stopped by the shop the other day and explained things to me very clearly. Then we had some wine and Chinese at my place."

"Back up. I explained things to you, and you kick me out—"

"I never—"

"Metaphorically. Aub explains things to you, and everything's peachy?"

"Peachy?" She chuckled, shrugged. "Yes."

"You just took her word for it, then ate spring rolls?"

"That's right." It pleased her to think of it. The entire evening with Aubrey pleased her. "Since she wasn't trying to get me into bed, she didn't have any incentive, that I could see, to lie about it. And if she had been interested in you in a romantic or sexual way, she'd have no motive for clearing the path where I was concerned. Which means I was wrong, and I apologize."

"I don't know why," he said after a moment. "I can't put my finger on it, but that pisses me off again. I want a beer. Do you want a beer?"

"Does that mean you accept my apology?"

"I'm thinking about it," he called back from the kitchen. "Go back to that 'clearing the path' part. I think that might turn the tide."

She accepted the bottle he handed her when he came back in. "I don't know you, not very well," she said.

"Sugar, I'm an open book."

"No, you're not. And neither am I. But it seems I'd like to get to know you better."

"How about pizza?"

"Excuse me?"

"How about we order some pizza because I'm starving. And I'd like to spend some time with you. You hungry?"

"Well, I—"

"Good. Where the hell's that phone?" He shoved at things on his workbench, rattled items on his shelves, then finally dug the phone out from under a pillow on the bed. "Speed dial," he told her after he pushed some buttons. "I keep all vital numbers— Hi, it's Seth Quinn. Yeah, I'm good. How about you? You bet. I want a large, loaded."

"No," Dru said and had him frowning over at her.

"Hold it a minute," he said into the phone. "No, what?"

"No toppings."

"No toppings?" He gaped at her. "*None?* What are you, sick?"

"No toppings," she repeated, primly now. "If I want a salad, I have a salad. If I want meat, I have meat. If I want pizza, I have pizza."

"Man." He huffed out a breath, rubbed his chin in a way she'd seen Ethan do. "Okay, make that half totally boring and half loaded. Yeah, you got it. At my place over the flower shop. Thanks."

He disconnected, then tossed the phone back on the bed. "Won't take long. Look, I need to clean up." He dug into a packing box and came out with what might have been fresh jeans. "I'm going to grab a shower. Just, you know, hang. I'll be right back."

"Can I look at some of your other paintings?"

"Sure." He waved a hand as he carried his beer into the little bathroom. "Go ahead."

And just like that, she realized, they were back on even ground. Or as even as it ever had been. Just hang, he'd said, as if they were friends.

Wasn't it a wonder that she felt they were. Friends. Whatever else happened, or didn't happen between them, they were friends.

Still, she waited until the door was shut and she heard the shower running before she moved over to the painting propped on the easel by the front windows.

The breath caught in her throat. She supposed it was a typical reaction for someone seeing themselves as a painting. That moment of surprise and wonder, the simple fascination with self, as seen through another's eyes.

She wouldn't see herself this way, she realized. Not as romantic and relaxed and sexy all at once. Made bold by the colors, made dreamy by the light, and sexy by the pose with her leg bare and the bright skirt carelessly draped.

Made, somehow, powerful even at rest.

He'd finished it. Surely it was finished, because it was perfect. Perfectly beautiful.

He'd made her beautiful, she thought. Desirable, she supposed, and still aloof because it was so clear she was alone—that she wished to be alone.

She'd told him she didn't know him well. Now more than ever she understood how true that was. And how could anyone really know him? How could anyone understand a man who had so much inside him, who was capable of creating something so lovely and dreamy in one painting, and something so passionate and fierce in another?

Yet with every step she took with him, she wanted to know more.

She wandered to the stacks of canvases, sat on the floor, set her beer aside and began to learn.

Sun-washed scenes of Florence with red-tiled roofs, golden buildings, crooked, cobbled streets. Another exploding with color and movement—Venice, she realized— all a blur with the crowds.

An empty road winding through luminous green fields. A nude, her eyes dark and slumberous, her hair in untamed splendor around her face and shoulders, and the glory of Rome through the window at her back.

A field of sunflowers baking in the heat that was almost palpable—and the laughing face of a young girl running through them trailing a red balloon behind her.

She saw joy and romance, sorrow and whimsy, desire and despair.

He saw, she corrected. He saw everything.

When he came back in, she was sitting on the floor, a painting in her lap. The beer sat untouched beside her.

He crossed over, picked up the bottle. "How about wine instead?"

"It doesn't matter." She couldn't take her attention away from the painting.

It was another watercolor, one he'd done from memory on a rainy day in Italy. He'd been homesick and restless.

So he'd painted the marsh he'd explored as a boy with its tangle of gum and oak trees, with its wigeongrass and cattails, with its luminous light trapped in dawn.

"That spot's not far from the house," he told her. "You can follow that path back to it." He supposed that's what he'd been doing in his head when he'd painted it. Following the path back.

"Will you sell it to me?"

"You keep coming up here, I'm not going to need an agent." He crouched down beside her. "Why this one?"

"I want to walk there, through that mist. Watch it rise over the water while the sun comes up. It makes me feel . . ."

She trailed off as she tipped her face up to look at him.

He hadn't put on a shirt, and there were still a few stray beads of water gleaming on his chest. His jeans rode low, and he hadn't fastened the top button.

She imagined sliding her finger there, just over that line of denim. Just under it.

"Feel what?" he prompted.

Needy, she thought. Itchy. Brainless.

"Um." With some effort, she shifted to admire the painting again. "A little lonely, I suppose. But not in a sad way. Because it's beautiful there, and the path means you're only alone if you want to be."

He leaned in, closer to the painting. She smelled the shower on him—soap and water—and her stomach muscles tightened even as those in her thighs went loose. "Where would you put it?"

If this was desire, Dru realized, if this was lust, she'd never felt its like before.

"Ah, in my office at home. So when I'm tired of working on the books, I can look at it. And take a quiet walk."

She eased away from him, propped the painting up again. "So, can I buy it?"

"Probably." He straightened as she did, and their bodies brushed. From the glint in his eye she decided he was perfectly aware of her reaction to him. "Did you see your portrait?"

"Yes." It gave her an excuse to put a little distance between them when she walked to it. "It's lovely."

"But you don't want to buy it?"

"It's not for me. What will you call it?"

"Beauty Sleeps," he said, then frowned as the dream he'd forgotten came back to him. "Zucchini football," he muttered.

"Excuse me?"

"Nothing. Just a weird flash. Pizza," he said at the brisk knock on the door.

He snatched his wallet off the workbench and, still shirtless and barefoot, went to the door. "Hey, Mike, how's it going?"

"Hanging loose."

The skinny, pimply-faced teenager handed Seth the pizza box. Then his gaze shifted, and he caught sight of Dru. The way his Adam's apple bobbed, the way surprise, interest and envy sped over his young, bumpy face, warned Dru there would be fresh fruit on the grapevine, and it would have her and Seth clustered together.

"Um, hi. Um. Grandma sent you a bunch of napkins and stuff." He shoved the paper bag into Seth's hands as well.

"Great. Tell her thanks. Here you go, Mike. Keep the change."

"Yeah. Well. Um. See you."

"Looks like Mike's got a little crush on you," Seth commented as he booted the door closed.

"I'd say Mike's double-timing it back to Village Pizza so he can spread the word that the artist and the florist are having hot pizza and hot sex."

"I hope he's right. If we're going to make the first part come true, we'd better dig into this." He dropped the box on the bed. "You need a plate?"

Her heart had given a little lurch, but she nodded. "Yes, I need a plate."

"Now, now, don't get twitchy. I'll get you a glass of very nice Chianti instead of the beer."

"I can drink the beer."

"You could," he commented as he headed into the kitchen again. "But you'd rather have the wine. I'll drink the beer. And, sugar, if you don't like people talking about you, you shouldn't live in a tight-knit little community."

"I don't mind people talking about me so much." Not the way they did here, she thought, that was different, so much less bitchy than the way they gossiped in Washington. "I just don't care for them talking about me doing something before I have a chance to do it."

"Would that be the pizza or the sex?" he asked as he came back with paper plates.

"I haven't decided." She pushed through the clothes in his packing box until she found a denim work shirt. "Put this on."

"Yes 'm. Can you handle sitting on the bed to eat if I promise not to jump you?"

She sat and, using one of the white plastic forks Mike's grandmother had put into the bag, worked a slice free. She plopped it on her plate, then using the same method, lifted a piece of his half.

"You know, we've been dating for a while now—"

"We are not dating. This is not a date. This is a pizza."

"Right. Anyway." He sat down, cross-legged, his shirt carelessly unbuttoned.

It was worse, she realized than no shirt at all.

"We haven't asked some of the essential questions to make sure this relationship has a chance."

"Such as?"

"Vacation weekend. The mountains or the shore?"

"Mountains. We live at the shore."

"Agreed." He bit into the pizza. "Favorite guitar player. Eric Clapton or Chet Atkins?"

"Chet who?"

He actually went pale. "Oh God." With a wince, he rubbed his heart. "Let's skip that one. It's too painful. Scariest movie ever—classic category, *Psycho* or *Jaws*?"

"Neither. *The Exorcist.*"

"Good one. Who would you trust, with your life, against the forces of evil? Superman or Batman?"

"Buffy—the vampire slayer."

"Get out." He swigged beer. "Superman. It *has* to be Superman."

"One whiff of kryptonite and he's down for the count. Besides"—she polished off her slice and went for another—"Buffy has a much more interesting wardrobe."

He shook his head in disgust. "Let's move on. Shower or bath?"

"It would depend on—"

"No, no, no." He snagged more pizza. "No depends. Pick."

"Bath." She licked sauce off her finger. "Long, hot and full of bubbles."

"Just as I suspected. Dog or cat."

"Cat."

He set the slice down. "That is just so wrong."

"I work all day. Cats are self-reliant, and they don't chew your shoes."

He shook his head in deep regret. "This might be the end of things between us. Can this relationship be saved? Quick. French fries or caviar?"

"Really, that's ridiculous. French fries, of course."

"Do you mean it?" As if hope had sprung giddily into his heart, he grabbed her hand in a tight grip. "You're not just saying that to string me along so you can have your way with me?"

"Caviar is fine on occasion, but it's hardly an essential element of life."

"Thank God." He gave her hand a loud kiss, then went back to eating. "Other than a woeful ignorance of music and poor judgment over pets, you did really well. I'll sleep with you."

"I don't know what to say. I'm so touched. Tell me about the woman in the painting—the brunette sitting in front of the window in Rome."

"Bella? Want some more wine?"

She lifted that eyebrow in the way that stirred his blood. "Are you stalling?"

"Yeah, but do you want some more wine anyway?"

"All right."

He got up to get the bottle, topped off Dru's glass before sitting down again. "You want to know if I slept with her?"

"Amazing. I'm transparent as glass to you." She took another bite of pizza. "You could tell me it's none of my business."

"I could. Or I could lie to you. She's a tour guide. I'd see her now and then when I was out and around. We got to know each other. I liked her. I painted her, and I slept with her. We enjoyed each other. It never got any deeper or more complicated than that. I don't sleep with every woman who models for me. And I don't paint every woman I sleep with."

"I wondered. And I wondered if you'd lie to me. That's a habit of mine, assuming someone will give the handy lie instead of the more complicated truth. You're not the kind of man I'm used to."

"Drusilla—" He broke off with a muttered oath when his cell phone rang.

"Go ahead. I'll put this away for you."

She eased from the bed, gathered the pizza box, the plates, while he flipped on the phone. "Yeah? No, I'm okay. I was distracted. Anna, I'm fine. I finished the painting I was working on. As I matter of fact I'm not starving myself to death. I just had pizza with Dru. Uh-huh. Sure. I'll be home tomorrow. Absolutely. I love you, too."

He hung up as Dru came back in. "Anna."

"Yes, I heard." She picked up the phone, set it on a nearby table. "Do you know you have beer, wine, a month's supply of soft drinks and now leftover pizza as the total contents of your refrigerator?"

"There used to be half a meatball sub, but I ate it."

"Oh, well then." She walked to the door. Locked it. The sound of that turning lock might have echoed in her head, but it wasn't going to stop her.

She crossed to him.

"The last time I went to bed with a man it was a humiliating experience for me. That's been nearly two years ago now. I haven't particularly missed sex. It's very possible, on some level, I'm using you to take back something I feel someone else took from me."

Since he was still sitting cross-legged on the bed, she slid onto his lap, hooked her legs around his hips, her arms around his neck. "Do you mind?"

"I can't say I do." He ran his hands up her back. "But here's the thing. You may get more than you bargained for."

"Calculated risk," she murmured and brought her mouth to his.

TWELVE

~

HIS HANDS GLIDED over her skin, and nerves sparked under it. She wanted this, wanted him. The decision to come to his bed had been her own. But she knew the pounding of her heart was as much from panic as from desire.

And so, she realized as those wonderful hands rubbed up and down her back, did he.

"Relax." He whispered it as his lips trailed over her cheek. "It's not brain surgery."

"I don't think I want to relax." Those nerves were a separate kind of thrill, running fast along the tingle of needs. "I don't think I can."

"Okay." And still he stroked, easy hands, easy lips. "Then just be sure."

"I'm sure. I am sure." She eased back. She wanted to see his face. "I never seem to do anything unless I am." She brushed at the strands of hair that fell over his forehead. "It's just . . . been a while."

How could she tell him she'd lost her confidence in this area? If she told him, she'd never be sure that whatever happened between them now was as much her doing as his.

"So we'll take it slow."

She steadied herself. Intimacy, she'd always believed, took courage as well as desire. She'd taken the step. She'd locked the door. She'd come to his bed. Now she'd take another.

"Maybe." Watching him, she unbuttoned her shirt, saw his gaze drift down. Saw the blue of his eyes deepen as she parted the cotton, let it fall off her shoulders. "Maybe not."

He trailed his fingertips along the swell of her breasts, the soft flesh above the fancy white lace of her bra.

"You know one of the really great things about women?" he said conversationally as his fingers danced down over lace and back again. "Not just that they have breasts—which can't be over-appreciated—but all the cool things they put them in."

It made her laugh even as her skin began to shiver. "Like lingerie, do you?"

"Oh yeah." He toyed with the right strap, then nudged it off her shoulder. "On women, that is. I used to swipe Anna's Victoria's Secret catalogues so I could . . . Well." He nudged the left strap. "Probably shouldn't get into that at such a moment. You wearing panty things that match this?"

A quickening of power began to throb under the nerves. "I guess you'll just have to find out for yourself."

"I just bet you are." He leaned in to rub his lips over her shoulder. "You're a coordinated sort of woman. You know what other part—anatomically speaking—I really like about you?"

His lips were gliding along her throat now, rousing and soothing at the same time. "I hesitate to ask."

"This right here." His fingers stroked the nape of her neck. "Drives me crazy. I'll warn you I'm going to have to bite it in just a little while, so don't be alarmed."

"I appreciate you . . . mmmm." His teeth scraped along her jaw, closing lightly over her chin before they nipped at her bottom lip.

"You were starting to relax," he whispered when her breath caught. "Can't have that."

This time his mouth took hers, hot, hard, in a proprietary kiss that was almost a branding. The leap from playful to possessive was so fast, so high she could do nothing but cling while he ravaged.

Steady, she thought as her mind reeled. Had she believed she'd needed to be steady and sure? Oh no, this breathless race was better. So much better.

Her legs tightened around his waist, her body strained. On a jolt of need she answered the demand of the kiss with demands of her own.

No, this wasn't just want, she realized. This was craving. She shoved at his shirt, pushing it off his shoulders so that her fingers could dig into flesh, could mold muscle.

Her scent was everywhere, as if she'd bathed in wildflowers. The delicacy of it, the silky texture of that fragrant skin misted his mind. The quiet, throaty moans she made when he touched, when he tasted, sprinted through his blood.

The light was changing, softening toward evening. He wanted to see that gentle sunlight glow over her, watch it catch in the green and gold of her eyes.

Her breath trembled out, and she arched back when he

feasted on the long line of her throat. Flowed back, as if boneless, when his tongue slid toward her breast.

Struggling not to rush, he lifted his head to look down at her. "Flexible, aren't you?"

"I take"—she shuddered, bowed—"yoga. Twice a week."

"Mother of God," was all he could manage as the long, lean length of her stretched back with her legs still locked around his waist.

Almost reverently now, his hands moved over her, exploring the slope of shoulder, curve of breast, the line of torso. He flipped open the button at her waist and eased the zipper down. Slowly.

"I was right." He tortured them both by slipping his fingers just under the elastic of white lace panties. "Coordinated. In more ways than one."

Tucking his hands under her hips, he lifted them. And nuzzled at her belly. He felt the muscles quiver under his lips, then jerk when he pressed his mouth to the lace between the V of cotton.

The thrill coiled inside her, tight as a fist, then spread, fingers of pleasure that stroked toward an aching. When her legs trembled, he nudged them down, then drew the trim, tailored slacks away.

"I need to work my way up to the nape of your neck." His lips and fingers played over her legs. "It may take a while."

"That's okay." Her breath caught, then released on a sigh. "Take your time."

He didn't rush. As the aches built she fisted her hands in the sheets to stop herself from begging. She wanted to comb her fingers through his hair, to run them over his body, but was afraid if she released her anchor, even for an instant, she would fly out of this pool of swirling pleasures.

She wanted to drown in it.

He nipped lightly at her thigh and had her turning her face into the mattress, choking back a moan. His tongue slipped and slid along the edge of lace, turned moan into sob. Then stroked under it so sob became quick, gasping cries.

Her need was his need, and still his hands were easy as he rolled the lace down, as he brushed his palm over the heat. Watching her rise up, seeing her eyes go shocked, go blind as he urged her up, was glorious.

When she went limp, he moved up her body with lazy kisses. He wanted her to tremble, to call out his name, to clamp around him as if life depended on it.

And she would, he promised himself as he suckled her breast through the lace. Before they were done, she would.

Her heart was thudding under his mouth, and its beat kicked higher when he pulled the lace away and took flesh.

Her fingers tangled in his hair, pressed him closer, then streaked down his back.

"Let me." Her voice was thick and dreamy as she tugged at his jeans. "Let me."

The music was a low, pumping, primal beat, as urgent as her pulse. She rolled as she dragged denim away, pressed her body along the length of his. Found his mouth in a desperate kiss.

She needed, needed to fill herself with him, and took her lips on a wild journey over his face, his throat, his chest.

God, so hard, so lean, so male.

She wanted, wanted him to fill her, to know that shock, that wonder of being invaded, of being joined. But when she would have straddled him, have taken him into her, he reared up.

"Not yet." And flipped her over on her stomach.

"I want—"

"So do I. Christ, so do I."

When he closed his teeth over the nape of her neck, the erotic shock had her crying out. Her hands closed over the iron rungs of the headboard, but there was no anchor this time.

She went wild.

She bucked under him, felt herself hurtling toward something like madness. "God. Oh God. Now."

His hand shot under her, and those clever fingers plunged into her, into the heat and the wet. She came on a violent leap that left her helpless and shuddering.

When her hands unclasped the rungs, he pushed her to her back. "Now," he said, and crushed his mouth to hers, swallowing her scream as he drove into her.

She closed around him, arched to him. A fast rise and fall, flesh pounding damply against flesh. Each time her breath would catch, his blood beat.

So he watched her as the last glints of sunlight glowed on her face, caught in the green and gold of her eyes as they hazed with tears.

She lifted a hand to his cheek, and there was a kind of wonder in her voice when she said, "Seth."

The beauty of it all but drowned him.

He watched her still as everything inside them shattered.

THE next best thing to making love, in Seth's opinion, was floating along on the warm river of satisfaction after making love. There was something incredibly soft and lovely about a woman's body after completion that made it the perfect resting place.

They'd lost sunset and were drifting toward dusk. Somewhere along the way, he realized, his last CD had finished playing. Now there was only the sound of wind rising up and Drusilla's breathing.

Rain was coming. He could smell it—could sense the storm dancing on the air.

He'd have to shut the windows. Eventually.

He lifted a hand to stroke it along the side of her breast. "I guess you're relaxed now," he murmured. "Whether you like it or not."

"I guess I am."

He certainly was, she thought. That was a good sign. Wasn't it? She hated herself for being stupid. Hated knowing that now that her mind was clearing again, the doubts were creeping in.

She could hardly ask if it had been good for him without sounding like a ridiculous cliché.

But it didn't stop her from wanting to know.

"Thirsty?" he asked her.

"A bit."

"Hmm." He nuzzled in. "I'll get us something, when I can move again."

She combed her fingers through his hair. He had such soft hair, so straight, so full of lights. "Ah . . . you're all right?"

"Uh-huh. Rain's coming in."

She glanced toward the windows. "No, it isn't."

"I mean rain's coming." He turned his head to look out at the sky. "Storm's blowing in. Your car windows up?"

Why the hell was he asking about her car windows when she'd just had a life-altering experience? "Yes."

"Good."

She stared at the ceiling. "I should go, before it rains."

"Uh-uh." He wrapped her close, then rolled over with her. "You should stay, and we'll listen to the rain when we make love again."

"Again?"

"Mmm. Did you know you have this little dimple right at the base of your spine?" He skimmed his finger there as he opened his eyes, and saw her face. "Something wrong?"

"I don't know. Is there?"

He caught her head in his hands, and considered. "I know that face. You're mildly peeved and working toward seriously pissed. What's wrong? Was I too rough?"

"No."

"Not rough enough, what? Hey." He gave her head a little shake. "Tell me what's wrong, Dru."

"Nothing. Nothing. You're an incredible lover. I've never been with anyone as thorough or exciting."

"Then what is it?" he demanded as she pulled away and sat up.

"I said it's nothing." She could hear the testiness of her own voice. God, she thought, she'd whine in a minute. The first threatening rumble of thunder seemed the perfect accent to her mood. "You might say *something* about me. Even the standard, 'Oh baby, that was amazing.'"

"Oh baby, that was amazing." He might have laughed, but he saw the glint in her eye wasn't just temper. "Hold on." He had to move fast to grab her before she could scoot off the bed. And to avoid a tussle, just rolled on top of her again to keep her in place. "Just what happened between you and that guy you were engaged to?"

"That's hardly relevant now."

"It is when you've just plopped him down in bed with us."

She opened her mouth, prepared to strike out with a sharp, damning reply. And sighed instead. "You're right. You're absolutely right. And I'm absolutely stupid. Let me up. I can't carry on any sort of conversation this way."

He eased back so she could shift. And said nothing when she tugged the sheet up over her breasts, though he recognized the gesture as a lifting of the shield.

She tried to gather her thoughts as thunder rolled again and lightning shuddered through the dark. "He cheated on me, and as he claimed to love me, his reason was the fact that I was unimaginative in bed."

"Were you taking yoga back then?" When she merely stared, coolly, Seth shook his head. "Sugar, if you bought that line, you are stupid."

"I was going to *marry* him. We'd ordered the invitations. I'd had my first fitting for the wedding dress. Then I find out he's been romping between the sheets—ones I bought, for your information—with a *lawyer*."

Wind blew in a gust through the windows, and lightning slashed behind it. But he didn't look away from her. He didn't rush over to shut the windows against the oncoming rain.

"And he expected me to understand his reasoning," she went on. "He expected me to go through with the wedding because it was just sex, which was something I wasn't particularly skilled at."

Prick, Seth thought. The kind of prick that gave regular guys a bad name. "And do you figure a guy who'd go shopping for wedding invitations with one woman and sneak around with another is worth one minute of your time?"

"Hardly, or I wouldn't have walked out on him, causing myself and my family considerable embarrassment. I'm not thinking of him. I'm thinking of me."

She was wrong about that, but he let it go. "Do you want me to tell you what it was like being with you? It was magic." He leaned forward to touch his lips to hers. "Magic."

When he took her hand, she looked down at the way they joined. Then sighing, looked toward the windows. "It's raining," she said softly.

"Stay with me awhile." He brought their joined hands to his lips. "We'll listen to it."

IT was still raining when she rose. The soft, steady patter after the storm turned the room into a cozy nest, one she wished she could wallow in.

"Stay the night. I'll even run out early and hunt up something decent for breakfast."

"I can't." It seemed so intimate, so romantic to talk to him in the dark that her first reaction was disappointment when he turned on the light. The second was shock as she realized she was in full view of the windows. "For heaven sake." She scrambled with her underwear toward the bathroom.

"Yeah, like there's anyone out there at this time of night, in the rain." Unconcerned with modesty, he got up and, comfortably naked, followed her. He managed to stop the door from slamming in his face. "Look at it this way, you'll only have to walk downstairs to go to work in the morning."

"I don't have any clothes. Any fresh clothes," she added

when he gestured to the shirt still in a heap on the bedroom floor. "Only a man could suggest I go to work in the morning wearing the same thing I wore yesterday. Would you mind getting that shirt for me?"

He obliged her, but that didn't mean he couldn't stall. "Bring extra clothes tomorrow. I'll pick up some supplies. We'll have dinner. I can cook," he claimed when she lifted an eyebrow. "Adequately. Or we could hang at your place, and you could fix dinner."

"I don't cook, even adequately."

"We can go out, then come back here. Or your place," he added, easing his arms around her. "I don't care where. A planned date, instead of our usual impromptu."

"This wasn't a date." She wiggled away to button her shirt. "This was sex."

"Excuse me. We had food, alcoholic beverages, conversation and sex. That, baby, is a date."

She could feel her lips quiver into a smile. "Damn. You got me."

"Exactly." He caught her around the waist again when she moved by him, drew her back against him. "Have dinner with me, go to bed with me, wake up with me."

"All right, but we'll have to eat after eight. I have a yoga class tomorrow."

"You're just saying that to torment me. But since we're on the subject, can you actually hook your heel behind your head?"

She laughed and pulled away. "I've got to go. It's after midnight. I'll come back here around eight. I'll risk your cooking."

"Great. Hey, do you want me to frame the watercolor for you?"

She beamed at him. "I can have it?"

"That depends. I'm willing to trade a painting for a painting."

"You've already finished the one of me."

"I want another."

She put on her shoes. "You've done two."

"One day, when I'm a dead, famous artist whose work is studied, and the prices of which are ridiculously jacked up, they'll call this my Drusilla period."

"Interesting. If that's what you want as payment, I'll pose again."

"Sunday."

"Yes, fine. Do you know what you're looking for with this one? What you want me to wear?"

"I know exactly what I'm looking for." He walked over, laid his hands on her shoulders and kissed her. "And you'll be wearing rose petals."

"I beg your pardon?"

"Red rose petals. Seeing as you're a florist, you should be able to get me a supply."

"If you think I'm going to pose wearing nothing but . . . No."

"You want the watercolor?"

"Not enough to be blackmailed."

She turned away, but he only caught her hand, spun her back. "You admire my work enough to want to own it."

"I admire your work very much, but you're not painting me naked."

"Okay, I'll wear clothes, but you're wearing rose petals. Ssh." He tapped a finger on her lips before she could speak again. "Obviously I'm not having you pose nude so I can get you into bed because I've already gotten you into bed. And for the record, I don't use art that way. I've had this image in my head since the first time I saw you. I have to paint it."

He took her hands. "I need to paint it. But I'll make you a deal."

"What's the deal?"

"I won't show it to anyone. When it's finished, you'll decide what to do with it."

He recognized the look on her face—one of mulling and consideration.

And knew he had her.

"I decide?"

"I'll trust you to be honest about it. You have to trust me to paint what I see, what I feel. Deal?"

"Red rose petals." She angled her head. "I'm going to order a lot of them."

SETH walked whistling into the boatyard the next morning. He carried a box of doughnuts, fresh from the bakery.

Cam was already at work, drilling turnbuckles into a hull.

"She's a beauty," Seth called out as he strolled up to the prettily proportioned yawl. "You guys must've busted tail to get her this close to finished so soon."

"Yeah. She's done except for a little brightwork, some details in the cabin. Client wants to pick her up Sunday."

"Sorry I didn't give you a hand the last couple days."

"We managed."

There wasn't a sting in the tone, but there was the implication of one. "Where's everybody?"

"Phil's upstairs. Ethan and Aubrey are checking crab pots this morning. I've got Kevin coming in after school. Another week or so he'll be sprung, put in more time."

"Sprung? School'll be over already? What the hell day is it?"

"You'd keep up better if you checked in at home once in a while."

"I've been busy, Cam."

"Yeah." Cam set another turnbuckle. "So I hear."

"What're you pissed off about?" Seth tossed the bakery box onto the deck. "I'm here, aren't I?"

"You sashay in and sashay out as the mood strikes you. Decide to come swaggering in today because you finally got lucky last night?"

"What's it to you?"

"What's it to me?" Cam set the drill aside, vaulted down to the floor—a quick blur of aggravated male. "You want to know what it is to me, you asshole? It's a hell of a lot to me when you up and disappear for the best part of a week. You go around with some damn black cloud over your head, then hole up in your studio. It's a hell of a lot to me when I have to watch Anna worrying because you can't be bothered to tell us what the fuck's going on. You think you can just walk back in here feeling fine because you finally got Dru's skirt over her head?"

Guilt, which had begun to shimmer, exploded into a red flash of fury. Seth moved before he thought, shoving Cam back against the hull. "Don't talk about her like that. She's not some easy lay I used to scratch an itch. Don't you ever talk about her like that."

Cam knocked Seth back a full step. They were squared off now, nose to nose. Boxers who didn't give a damn about the bell. "You don't treat your family like this. Like a goddamn convenience."

Temper was a vicious dog that snapped at both their throats.

"You want to go a round with me?" Cam invited as fists bunched.

"Hold it, hold it. Jesus Christ, hold it!" Phillip all but leaped between them, pushed them apart. "What the hell's going on here? I could hear the two of you all the way upstairs."

"Kid thinks he can take me," Cam replied hotly. "I'm about to let him try."

"Hell you are. You two want to pound on each other, you take it outside. As a matter of fact, Seth, you go. Cool off." Phillip pointed toward the cargo doors and the dock beyond them. "You've been scarce enough around here lately, another few minutes isn't going to matter."

"This is between me and Cam."

"This is a place of business," Phillip corrected. "Our business, so that brings me into it. Keep it up, and the first one to take a punch at you may be me. I've had enough aggravation from you."

"What the hell are you talking about?"

"I'm talking about keeping promises, remembering your responsibilities. I'm talking about having a client who expects a completed design, which you agreed to do. Where the hell is it, Seth?"

He opened his mouth, closed it. Drusilla's sloop. He'd forgotten it. Just, he remembered, as he'd forgotten he'd told Anna he'd pick up the mulch she wanted for a new flower bed. And the ride he'd promised Bram in his new car.

As his anger turned inward, he stalked out of the cargo doors.

"Pissant," Cam grumbled. "Needs a kick in the ass."

"Why don't you get off his back?"

Baffled, still steaming, Cam rounded on Phillip. "Well,

fuck you. You're the one who just finished stomping on him."

"I've been as worried and annoyed as you have," he shot back. "But that's enough. He's old enough to come and go as he pleases. When you were his age, you were racing around Europe and getting your hand up as many skirts as you could manage."

"I never broke my word."

"No." Calmer now, Phillip looked out to where Seth stood on the end of the dock. "And from the look of him, he didn't intend to break his either. How long are you going to let him stand out there feeling like shit?"

"A week or two ought to be enough."

At Phillip's steady stare, Cam hissed out a breath, and felt most of the temper expel with it. "Damn it. I must be getting old. I hate that. I'll go deal with it."

Seth heard the footsteps on the dock. He turned. Braced. "Go ahead and take a shot. But you only get the first one free."

"Kid, I'll only need one."

"Christ, I'm sorry," Seth blurted out. "I'm sorry I let you down. I'll do whatever grunt work you need. I'll get the design finished today. I'll make it up to you."

"Oh hell." This time Cam raked his fingers through his hair. Who felt like shit now? he asked himself. "You didn't let me down. You worried me, you pissed me off, but you didn't let me down. Nobody expects you to give all your time to this place. Or to be at home every spare minute. Damn it, first Anna's nagging at me because you're home too much and she doesn't think it's good for you. Then she's ragging because you're not home at all. How the hell did I get caught in the middle?"

"Just lucky, I guess. I had some things I had to take care

of. That's all. And I was working. I got caught up in it and forgot the rest. The family's not a convenience for me, Cam. You can't believe that. It's a miracle. If it wasn't for you—"

"Stop right there. This isn't about old business, it's about now."

"I wouldn't have a now without you."

"You wouldn't have one without Ray. None of us would. Leave it at that." He jammed his hands in his pockets, looked out over the water.

Jesus, he thought. It didn't matter how old a kid got. They were still yours.

"So, you're serious about the sexy florist?"

Unconsciously Seth mirrored Cam's stance, and now they looked over the water together. "It appears that way."

"Maybe now that you've scratched that itch we'll get some work out of you."

"I seem to have some energy to spare this morning," Seth replied.

"Yeah, it always worked that way for me, too. What kind of doughnuts did you pick up?"

They were okay, Seth thought. Somehow, no matter what went on, they came back to being okay. "Variety pack. I got dibs on the Bavarian cream."

"I'm a jelly man myself. Let's go before Phil finds them."

They started back in together, then Seth stopped short. "Zucchini football."

Color drained out of Cam's cheeks. "What the hell did you say?"

"The Bread Bowl. The zucchini bread. She baked bread and you guys used it as a football. She told me."

"When?" Shaken, Cam gripped Seth's shoulders. "When did you see her?"

"I don't know. I don't. I dreamed it. Felt like I dreamed it," he murmured. His stomach jittered, but it wasn't unease he felt. It was, he realized, a kind of joy.

He'd spoken with Stella, he thought. He had a grandmother who'd shared a story with him.

"That's right, isn't it?" That joy leaped out in his voice, filled his face. "And you—you tried to intercept a pass and got hit above the eye. Knocked you down, nearly out. That's right, isn't it?"

"Yeah." Cam had to steady himself. It was a good memory. There were so many good ones. "She came running out the back door, shouting at us just as I was making the jump. I turned, and bam. Fucking galaxy of stars. That bread was like a goddamn brick. She was a hell of a doctor, but she never could cook worth a damn."

"Yeah, she told me."

"So, she bent down, looked at my pupils or whatever, held up fingers for me to count. Said it was just as well I got beaned. Saved her the trouble. Then we all started laughing—me and Dad, Phil and Ethan. Bunch of lunatics. Mom stood there, staring at us, with her hands on her hips. I can still see it. See her."

He let out a long breath. "Then she went back in and got another loaf so we could keep playing. She tell you that part?"

"No." Seth laid a hand on Cam's shoulder as they turned toward the cargo doors. "I guess she wanted you to tell me."

THIRTEEN

⁓

WHEN THE DOUGHNUTS were devoured, and Seth was hunkered down in a corner refining Ethan's basic design for Dru's sloop, Dru stepped outside her shop to snip off any faded blossoms in the whiskey barrel tub of verbena and heliotrope beside the front door.

The night's storm had cooled the air, swept away the dragging humidity and left the morning fresh and bell-clear.

The Bay was rich blue, still kicking a bit from the turbulence of the night. Boats were already rolling over it. The watermen in their workboats, the vacationers in their rented skiffs or motorboats shared the waters. The summer people who moored their boats and stole time to use them were out early. Why waste a minute of a perfect day? Dru mused.

In a few months, she'd be able to spend a pretty morning working on rigging, washing down the deck, polishing the brightwork of her own boat. Owning a boat meant a great deal more than casting off, hoisting sails and riding the wind. It meant pouring time, money, energy into maintenance. But that, she thought, was part of the pleasure. Or would be for her.

She liked to work. It had been one of the many small self-realizations that had come to her over the years. She liked working, producing and the satisfaction of standing back and seeing what she'd managed to do on her own.

She enjoyed the *business* end of running a business. The bookkeeping, the supplies, filling orders, calculating profit. It suited her sense of order just as the nature of her business suited her love of beauty for the sake of beauty.

The boat, when it was finished, would be her personal reward for making it all come together.

And Seth . . . She wasn't entirely sure what Seth was. The night she'd spent with him had been glorious. But like a boat, a relationship with him would never be all smooth sailing, and there was bound to be maintenance.

Just where would they be, she wondered, if the wind that had carried them to this point stalled on them? What would they do if they ran into a serious storm, or ran aground, or simply—as so many did—found the excitement draining from the ride?

And she wished she could do no more than enjoy the moment without looking ahead for problems.

He intrigued her and challenged her. He aroused her and amused her. He stirred up feelings in her no one had— not even, she was forced to admit, the man she'd nearly married.

She was drawn to his solid sense of self, his honesty and his ease. And she was fascinated by the hints of the turbulence and passions she saw bubbling just under the surface of that ease.

He was, she believed, the most compelling man she'd ever met. He made her happy. Now they were lovers, and she was already looking for the trouble ahead.

Because if you didn't look ahead, she reminded herself, you rammed straight into those problems and sank.

She carried the little shears back inside, into the storeroom, where she put it on its place on the shelf. She wished she could talk to someone, another woman, about the thrill and anxiety running so fast inside her. She wanted to be able to sit down with a friend and have a silly conversation where she could ramble on about everything she was feeling.

About how her heart started to flop around when he smiled at her. How it raced when he touched her. How scary and wonderful it was to be with someone who liked and accepted her for who she needed to be.

She wanted to tell someone that she was falling in love.

None of the women in her previous social circle would understand. Not the way she *needed* to be understood. They would be interested, certainly, even supportive. But she couldn't imagine telling any of them how he'd bitten the nape of her neck, then have them groan and sigh in envy.

And *that's* what she wanted.

She couldn't call her mother and tell her she'd had the most incredible sex of her life with a man she was stumbling into love with.

It just wasn't the kind of conversation either of them would be comfortable having.

Though her instincts told her there was nothing she

could say to shock Aubrey, and she was dead certain she'd get the exact reaction she was looking for from her new friend, Aubrey's connection to Seth made that possibility just a bit too sticky.

So she was on her own, Dru supposed. Which was exactly where she'd wanted to be in the first place. But now that she had something to share, now that she felt her life shifting under her feet, there was no one to reach out to.

It was her own doing, she admitted. She could either live with it, or begin to change it. Opening up meant more than taking a lover. It meant more than dipping a toe into the waters of a new friendship.

It meant work. So she'd work.

The bells on the front door jingled, signaling her first customer of the day. Dru squared her shoulders. She'd proven she could remake her life once. She could do it again.

Prepared to be more than the polite and efficient florist, she stepped out of the storeroom with a warm smile.

"Good morning. How can I help you?"

"Oh, I'm not sure. I'm just going to look around."

"Help yourself. It's a gorgeous day, isn't it?" Dru walked over to prop open the front door. "Too gorgeous to be closed in. Are you visiting Saint Chris?"

"That's right," Gloria said. "Taking a nice little vacation."

"You picked a perfect time." Dru ignored a frisson of unease at the way she was being studied. "Are you here with your family?"

"No, just me." Gloria flicked fingers over the petals of an arrangement, and kept her eyes on Dru. "Sometimes a girl just has to get away on her own. You know?"

"Yes, I do." She didn't look like the type to spend time

or money on flowers, Dru thought. She looked . . . hard, edgy—and cheap. Her shorts were too tight, too brief, and her top too snug. When she caught what she thought was a whiff of whiskey along with the woman's florid perfume, she wondered if she was about to be robbed.

Then she dismissed the thought. Nobody robbed florists, certainly not in St. Chris. And if the woman had any sort of weapon it would have to be very, very tiny to be concealed under that outfit.

And to judge someone because she didn't care for the style of her dress wasn't the way to begin the new phase of becoming more personable with her customers.

"If you're looking for something to cheer up your hotel room while you're here, I have carnations on special this week. They have a nice fragrance and they're very low maintenance."

"That might work. You know, you look familiar, and you don't sound like a local. Maybe I've met you before. Do you spend much time in D.C.?"

Dru relaxed again. "I grew up there."

"That's got to be it. The minute I saw you, I thought . . . Wait a minute! You're Katherine's daughter. Prucilla—no, no, Drusilla."

Dru tried to imagine her mother having any sort of acquaintance with the thin, badly dressed woman who smelled of cheap perfume and whiskey. Then cursed herself for being a snob.

"That's right."

"Well, I'll be damned." Gloria planted her hands on her hips, made her smile large and friendly. She'd done her research. "What the hell are you doing down here?"

"I live here now. So you know my mother?"

"Sure, sure. I worked on several committees with Kathy.

Haven't run into her in a while. I guess it's been three or four years. Last time, I think it was a fund-raiser for literacy. Book and author dinner at the Shoreham."

The event had been written up in the *Washington Post,* with enough detail in the archives Gloria had looked up on-line to make her claim smooth. "How is she, and your father?"

No, Dru thought, she wasn't a snob. She was simply a good judge of character. But she spoke evenly. "They're both very well, thank you. I'm sorry, I didn't get your name."

"It's Glo. Glo Harrow," she said, using her mother's maiden name. "Hell of a small world, huh? Seems to me the last time I talked to Kath, you were engaged. She was over the moon about that. Guess it didn't work out."

"No, it didn't."

"Well, men are like buses. Another one always comes along. You know, my mother's friendly with your grandfather." And that was true enough, though "acquainted" would have been more accurate. "The senator, he just keeps trucking along. A regular institution."

"He's an amazing man." Dru spoke coolly now.

"Gotta admire him. A man his age still active the way he is. Then you figure with the family money, he never had to work a day in his life, much less dedicate himself to politics. Tough arena, even for a young man, the way people like to sling mud these days."

"People have always slung mud. My family's never believed that financial advantage means letting someone else do the work."

"Gotta admire that, like I said."

When a man walked in, Dru bit down on her rising irritation and turned toward him. "Good morning."

"Hi. Hey, don't mind me, just finish what you're doing. I'm not in a rush."

"Would you like to look around some more, Ms. Harrow?"

"No." She'd spent more than enough time on this visit. "Why don't I take a dozen of those . . . what was on special?"

"Carnations." Dru gestured to the holding vase where she'd arranged samples in every color. "Would you like any specific color or combination?"

"No, no, just mix them up."

Gloria read the sign under the display and calculated it was a cheap enough price to pay for the up-close look. She took out cash, laid it on the counter.

Now that the contact had been made, Gloria wanted to be gone. She didn't care for the way the guy who'd come in was watching her and trying to pretend he wasn't watching her.

"I hope you enjoy them."

"I already am. Give my best to your mom when you talk to her," Gloria added as she started out.

"Oh, I will." Dru turned to her new customer. Some of the temper that had begun to simmer leaked out on her face.

"Bad time?"

"No, of course not." She readjusted her thoughts. "How can I help you?"

"First, I'm Will. Will McLean." He offered a hand.

"Oh, you're Aubrey's friend." Seriously cute, Aubrey had said. And with perfect accuracy, Dru decided as they shook hands. "It's nice to meet you."

"You, too. I just got off shift, figured on swinging by to see Aub—maybe catch up with Seth, before I go home and crash in a dark room for a few hours. Those flowers Seth got my girl a few weeks back were a really big hit. Can't let him get an edge on me. What've you got that'll knock her out, and make up for me working doubles most of the week?"

"How's your budget?"

"Just got paid." He patted his back pocket. "Sky's the limit."

"In that case, wait right here." She paused, reconsidered. The morning jolt wasn't going to spoil her plans for a more open Drusilla. "Better yet, come on back. If you like what I have in mind, you can sit down, get off your feet for a few minutes while I put them together for you."

"I look that bad?"

"You look exhausted." She gestured him back. "Go ahead, have a seat," she told him while she went to a refrigerated unit. "Delivered fresh this morning," she said as she took out a single long-stemmed rose in cotton-candy pink. "A dozen of these are guaranteed to knock her out."

He sniffed it when she held it out. "Smells great. Maybe I should make it two dozen. I've had to cancel two dates in the last ten days."

"Two dozen will put her in a coma."

"Perfect. Can you put them in one of those fancy boxes?"

"Absolutely." She moved to the work counter. "You and your brother are becoming my best customers. He bought me out of yellow roses about a week ago."

"He got himself engaged."

"Yes, I know. He was floating along about six inches above ground. You and your brother and Seth have been friends a long time."

"Since we were kids," Will concurred. "I can't believe

he's been back a month and I haven't been able to catch up with him. Dan says Seth's been pretty tied up himself between his work, the boatyard and you. Whoops." The crooked smile flashed as he rubbed his eyes. "Sorry. Tongue gets loose when I'm brain-dead."

"That's all right. I don't imagine it's a secret Seth and I are . . ." What? "Seeing each other," she decided.

Will did his best to stifle a yawn. "Well, if we ever get our schedules aligned, maybe the six of us can do something."

"I'd like that." Dru laid the roses and baby's breath in the tissue-lined box. "I'd like that a lot."

"Good. Ah, can I ask you something? That woman who was in here before? Was she hassling you?"

"Why do you ask?"

"I don't know, just a feeling. Plus there was something about her. I think I know her from somewhere. Can't put my finger on it, but it doesn't feel right. Do you know what I mean?"

"I know exactly what you mean." She glanced over at him. He was a friend of Aubrey's, of Seth's. The new, more open Dru was going to consider him a friend as well.

"She claimed to know my mother, but she didn't." No one, Dru thought, absolutely no one referred to her mother as Kathy. It was Katherine, and on rare occasions, Kate. But never Kathy, never Kath. "I don't know what she was after, but I'm glad you came in when you did."

"You want me to stick around awhile, in case she comes back?"

"No, but thanks. She doesn't worry me."

"You called her Harrow?" Will shook his head. "Doesn't ring any bells. But I know her from somewhere. When I come up with it, I'll let you know."

"I appreciate it."

* * *

IT was a mistake to call her mother. Dru realized it immediately. But she hadn't been able to get the morning customer out of her mind. The only way to check out the story was to ask.

Her mother had breezily told her she knew no one named Glo Harrow, though she did know a Laura Harrow, and a former Barbara Harrow. Dru was lulled by her mother's cheerful mood, and the news that she and Dru's father were reconciled.

For the moment, at least.

But the conversation had soon shot down its usual paths. Why didn't she come home for the weekend—better, for the summer? Why didn't they all go spend a few days at the family enclave in North Hampton?

Reasons were brushed aside, excuses ignored, until when they hung up, Dru had no doubt her mother was just as irritated and unhappy as she herself was.

It reminded her to leave bad enough alone.

But she discovered even that was too little, too late, when her mother walked into the shop ten minutes before closing.

"Sweetheart!" Katherine threw out her arms as she rushed to the counter, then wrapped them like ropes around Dru. "I'm so happy to see you. Just so happy."

"Mom." Dru patted Katherine's back and hated herself for the desire to pull away. "What are you doing here?"

"As soon as we hung up, I realized I just couldn't wait to see you. I miss my baby. Just let me look at you." Katherine eased back, stroked a hand over Dru's hair. "When are you going to grow this back? You have such beautiful hair, and here you go around with it chopped off like a boy. You're so thin! You're losing weight."

"I'm not losing weight."

"I worry about you not eating properly. If you'd hire some household staff—"

"Mom, I don't want household staff. I'm eating very well. I haven't lost an ounce since I saw you last month. You look wonderful."

It was invariably true. She wore a beautifully cut pink jacket over pearl gray trousers, both perfectly draped over a figure she maintained with scrupulous diet and exercise.

"Oh, I feel like a hag these days." Katherine waved a hand in dismissal.

Dru softened. "No, you don't, because you have very keen vision and any number of mirrors."

"You're so sweet."

"Did you drive down alone?"

"Henry," she said, referring to her chauffeur. "I told him to take half an hour, walk around a bit. It's a charming little town, really, for a holiday."

"Yes, it is." Dru kept her voice pleasant. "Those of us who live here are very grateful tourists find it as charming as we do."

"But what do you find to do? Oh, don't get angry. Don't get angry." Katherine waved a hand again as she wandered to the front window. "You're so far away from the city. Everything it offers, everything you're used to. Darling, you could live *anywhere*. Though God knows, I'd go mad if you moved away any farther than you have. But seeing you bury yourself here just hurts my heart."

"I'm not buried. And Saint Christopher isn't the end of the earth. If I wanted whatever the city had to offer, I could be there in an hour's drive."

"I'm not speaking geographically, Dru, but culturally, socially. This area's very picturesque, but you've cut yourself off from your life, your family, your friends. My goodness, darling, when's the last time you had a date with an eligible man?"

"Actually, I had one just last night."

"Really?" Katherine arched her brow much as Dru herself was prone to do. "What did you do?"

She didn't bother to bite her tongue. "We had pizza, and sex."

Katherine's mouth opened into a shocked *O*. "Well, my God, Drusilla."

"But that's hardly the issue. I wasn't satisfied with my life, so I changed it. Now I am satisfied. I wish you could be happy for me."

"This is all Jonah's fault. I could just strangle him."

"No, he's only one minor pebble in the bowl. I don't want to go over and over this again with you, Mom. I'm sorry we don't understand each other."

"I only want the best for you. You're my whole life."

Dru's head began to throb. "I don't want to be your whole life. I shouldn't be your whole life. Dad—"

"Well, of course, your father. God knows why I put up with the man half the time. But we do have twenty-eight years invested in each other."

"Is that what your marriage is? An investment?"

"How in the world did we get off on such a topic? This isn't at all why I came down."

"Do you love him?" Dru demanded, and watched her mother blink.

"Of course I do. What a question. And however we disagree, we both have one perfect point of agreement. You are the most precious thing in our lives. Now." She leaned over, kissed Dru on both cheeks. "I have a wonderful surprise for you." She gripped Dru's hand. "We'll run over to your little house right now so you can get your passport, pack a few essentials. No need for much, we'll take care of the wardrobe when we get there."

"Get where?"

"Paris. It's all arranged. I had this wonderful brainstorm after we talked this morning. I called your father, and he'll be joining us in a day or so. The plane's waiting for us at the airport. We'll spend some time in Aunt Michelle's flat in Paris, shop—oh, and we'll throw a little dinner party. Then we'll drive south and spend a week at the villa. Get out of the heat and crowds."

"Mom—"

"Then I think you and I should run off and have a nice girls' weekend. We never spend any real time together anymore. There's this marvelous spa not far from—"

"Mom. I can't go with you."

"Oh, don't be silly. It's all set. You don't have to worry about a single detail."

"I can't go. I have a business to run."

"Really, Dru. Surely you can close down for a few weeks, or ask someone to take care of it. You can't let this hobby of yours deprive you of every bit of fun."

"It's not a hobby. It deprives me of nothing. And I can't blithely close down so I can trot around France."

"Won't."

"All right, won't."

Tears sprang into Katherine's eyes. "Don't you see how much I need to do this for you? You're my baby, my sweet baby. I worry myself sick thinking about you down here alone."

"I'm not alone. I'm almost twenty-seven years old. I need to make my life. You and Dad need to make yours. Please don't cry."

"I don't know what I've done wrong." Katherine opened her purse, pulled out a tissue. "Why you won't take a little bit of your time to be with me. I feel so abandoned."

"I haven't abandoned you. Please—" When the bells jingled, Dru looked over. "Seth," she said with desperate relief.

"I thought I'd come by before you . . ." He trailed off when he saw the woman sniffling into a tissue. "Sorry. Ah . . . I'll come back."

"No. No." She had to force herself not to leap in front of the door to block his path of retreat. She knew nothing would dry her mother up as quickly as social introductions. "I'm glad you stopped in. I'd like you to meet my mother. Katherine Whitcomb Banks, Seth Quinn."

"Nice to meet you."

"And you." Katherine gave him a watery smile as she offered a hand. "You'll have to forgive me. I've been missing my daughter, and it's made me overly emotional." Now as she dabbed at her eyes, they began to sharpen. "Seth Quinn. The artist?"

"Yes," Dru confirmed, brightly now. "We've admired Seth's work, haven't we, Mom?"

"Very much. Very much. My brother and his wife were in Rome last year and fell in love with your painting of the Spanish Steps. I was very envious of their find. And you grew up here, didn't you?"

"Yes, ma'am. My family's here."

"It's so important to remember family," Katherine said with a sorrowful look at Dru. "How long will you be in the area?"

"I live here."

"Oh, but I thought you lived in Europe."

"I was staying in Europe for a while. I live here. This is home."

"I see. Will you be having a showing in D.C., or Baltimore?"

"Eventually."

"You must be sure to let me know when. I'd love to see more of your work. I'd be delighted to have you to dinner when it's convenient for you. Do you have a card, so I can send you an invitation?"

"A card?" He grinned, quick and bright. He couldn't help it. "No, sorry. But you can let Dru know. She knows how to get ahold of me."

"I see." And now she was beginning to. "We'll do it very soon."

"Mom's leaving for Paris," Dru said quickly. "When you get back," she told her mother, and nudged her toward the door, "we'll see about getting together."

"Bon voyage." Seth lifted a hand in farewell.

"Thank you, but I'm not sure I'll be—"

"Mom. Go to Paris." Dru gave her a firm kiss on the cheek. "Enjoy yourself. Have a wonderful, romantic holiday with Dad. Buy out Chanel. Send me a postcard."

"I don't know. I'll think about it. It was lovely to meet you, Seth. I hope to see you again, very soon."

"That'd be great. Have a good trip."

He waited, tapping his fingers on his thighs as Dru walked her mother out. More like goose-stepped her out, he corrected. He saw, through the window, her loading Katherine into a cream-colored Mercedes sedan, with uniformed driver.

It reminded him of a small point he'd forgotten. Dru's family was loaded. Easy enough to forget it, he mused. She didn't live rich. She lived normal.

When she came back in, she locked the door, then leaned back against it. "I'm sorry."

"For what?"

"For using you to wheedle out of a very uncomfortable situation."

"What are friends for?" He moved to her, tapped her chin with his finger. "Do you want to tell me why she was crying and you looked so miserable?"

"She wanted me to go to Paris. Just like that," Dru added, lifting her hands, then letting them drop. "She'd made all the arrangements without asking me, then drove down here expecting me to leap with joy, rush out and pack a bag and go."

"I guess some people would have."

"Some people don't have a business to run," she snapped. "Some people haven't already been to Paris more times then they can count anyway. And *some* people don't like to have their lives neatly arranged for them as if they were still eight years old."

"Sugar." Because he could feel her vibrating with anger and frustration, he rubbed his hands down her arms. "I didn't say you should have, but that some people would have. Got you wound up, didn't she?"

"She nearly always does. And I know she doesn't actually mean to. She really thinks she's doing it for me. They both do, and that makes it worse. She makes assumptions she shouldn't make, makes decisions for me she no longer has the right to make, then I hurt her feelings when I don't go along."

"If it makes you feel any better, I got reamed by Cam this morning because I haven't been around and forgot to do some stuff I said I'd do."

Dru angled her head. "Did he cry?"

"He might've gotten a little misty. Okay, no," he said, relieved when her mouth curved. "But we were on the verge of punching each other when Phil broke it up."

"Well, I can hardly hit my mother. Did you work it out with your brother?"

"Yeah, we're okay. I need to go by and grovel to Anna for a while, but I thought I'd drop off the boat design." He nodded toward the large folder he'd set on the counter.

"Oh." She pressed her fingers to her temples. "Can I look at it later? I need to close up or I'll be late for my class."

"Yoga. Oh yeah. You shouldn't miss that. We still on for tonight?"

"Do you want to be on for tonight?"

"I've been thinking about you all day. About being with you."

It warmed her. "I suppose I might have given you a passing thought. Though I've been pretty busy in here today."

"So I hear. Will came by the boatyard and nearly gave Aub a heart attack with that forest of roses."

"Did she like them?"

"She got gooey—and it's not easy to make Aubrey gooey. Will, on the other hand, looked dead on his feet. I figure he's got to be seriously stuck on her to come by here, buy flowers, give them to her when he looked like he hadn't slept for a week."

"I liked him, and his brother. You're lucky to have friends that go back to childhood."

"Don't you?"

"Not really. In any case," she went on to avoid the subject, "I had yet another odd visit just before he came in. Some woman," she continued as she cashed out, locked up her cash from the day. "She claimed to know my mother, but once she started talking, I knew she didn't. Not only from what she said, but how she looked. That sounds like snobbery, but it's just logic."

"How did she look?"

"Hard, cheap and not like anyone who's ever worked on a charity committee with my mother. She was pumping me, feeling me out." Dru shrugged. "Not that unusual when you come from an influential family."

There was ice in the pit of his stomach. "What did she say? What did she do?"

"Nothing much. I think she was laying groundwork for something, but then Will came in. She bought some carnations and left. Funny, he said he thought he recognized her from somewhere."

And now a sickness coated his throat. "She tell you her name?"

"Mmm? Yes." Dru took a last glance around, gathered her purse and keys. "Harrow, Glo Harrow. I've really got to get moving."

She stopped short, surprised when his hand clamped down on her arm. "Seth?"

"If she comes in again, I want you to call me."

"Why? She's just some woman hoping to con me out of some money, or an introduction to my grandfather. Believe me, I've handled that sort of thing all my life."

"I want you to promise me. I mean it. If she comes in, you go in the back, pick up the phone and call me."

She started to tell him she didn't need protection, but there was a fire, an urgency in his voice that had her nodding instead. "All right. I promise."

FOURTEEN

H E HAD TO wait until morning, until Dru slipped
downstairs to prepare her daily orders. He'd barely
slept. Though he'd struggled to lock the turmoil aside, he'd
lain awake most of the night.

Even the pleasure of having Dru curled beside him had
been tainted.

But he had to be sure.

Though his gut told him Gloria had tromped on yet another part of his life, he knocked on the McLean brothers'
apartment door. He had to be sure.

Dressed for work, an enormous cup of coffee in his
hand, Dan answered. "Hey, what's up? You just caught me.
I've got an early meeting."

"I need to talk to Will."

"Good luck. He's the dead man in the bedroom down the
hall. Want coffee? He'll probably pull his resurrection act
by noon."

"This can't wait."

"Hey, Seth, really, the guy's wasted." Since Seth was already walking through the debris of the living room, Dan went after him. "No, that's mine." Resigned, Dan jerked a thumb toward a second door. There was a sign tacked to it that advised:

Take two aspirin and go far, far away.

Seth didn't bother to knock, but pushed the door open into the dark. Through the light that spilled in from the hallway, Seth could see blackout drapes were pulled tight over the window. The room itself was barely closet-sized and mostly bed.

Will lay on it, faceup, his arms flung out to the sides as if he'd fallen backward in that position and hadn't moved since. He wore Marvin the Martian boxer shorts and one sock.

He snored.

"Let me get my camera," Dan mumbled. "Listen, Seth, this is his first chance for eight straight in two weeks. He wanted to make up time with Aubrey, so he didn't get in until after two. He was barely conscious when he came in the door."

"It's important."

"Well, shit." Dan walked over to the window. "He'll probably be speaking in tongues." And ruthlessly whipped the drapes back.

The bright morning sun flashed over the bed. Will didn't twitch. Seth leaned over the bed, shook Will by the shoulder. "Wake up."

"Glumph missitop."

"Told ya." Dan moved to the bed. "Here's how it works."

He put his mouth close to Will's ear and shouted, "Code blue! Code blue! Dr. McLean, report to Exam Room Three. Stat!"

"Whazit?" Will sprang into a sitting position as if the top half of his body had been shot from a bow. "Where's the crash cart? Where's . . ." Some part of his brain cleared as he blinked into Seth's face. "Aw fuck." He started to flop back, but Seth grabbed his arm.

"I have to talk to you."

"You bleeding internally?"

"No."

"You will be if you don't get the hell out of here and let me sleep." He grabbed a pillow from behind him, put it over his face to block out the light. "Don't see a guy in years, then you can't get rid of him. Go away, and take the moron who used to be my brother with you."

"You were in Dru's shop yesterday."

"I'm gonna cry in a minute."

"Will." Seth yanked the pillow away. "The woman who was in there when you came in. You said you thought you recognized her."

"Right now I wouldn't recognize my own mother. In fact, who the hell are you and what are you doing in my bedroom? I'm calling the cops."

"Tell me what she looked like."

"If I tell you, will you go away?"

"Yeah. Please."

"Christ, let me think." Yawning hugely, Will scrubbed his hands over his face. He sniffed. Sniffed again. "Coffee." His eyes began to track until they landed on Dan's cup. "I want that coffee."

"This is mine, jerkwad."

"Give me that goddamn coffee or I'm telling Mom you think that yellow dress makes her ass look fat. Your life won't be worth living."

"Give him the damn coffee," Seth snapped.

Dan handed it over.

Will slurped, gulped. Seth waited for him to just dunk his head in the oversized cup and lap with his tongue. "Okay, what was the question?"

Seth fisted a hand at his side, imagined his rage inside it. Trapped and controlled. "The woman you saw in Dru's shop."

"Yeah, right." Will yawned again, tried to concentrate. "Something about her weirded me out. Dressed like she should've been working a corner in Baltimore. Not that I'd know anything about that," he added with a cherubic smile. "Bleached, bony, blond. What my dad would call shop-worn. Diagnosis from a quick visual would be serious alcohol abuse, along with some recreational chemicals. Bad tone to her skin. Liver damage, probably."

"How old?" Seth demanded.

"Running toward fifty, but hard years. Could've been younger. Serious smoker's rasp, too. She leaves her body to science, we ain't getting much out of it."

"Yeah." Seth sat heavily on the side of the bed.

"Like I told Dru, there was something familiar about her. Couldn't place it. Maybe it was just the type. Hard, edgy, sort of, I dunno, predatory. What? Did she come back and hassle Dru? I'd've hung around if I'd thought . . ."

Then his jaw dropped as the picture fell into place. "Oh shit. Jesus Christ on a crutch. Gloria DeLauter."

Seth pressed the heels of his hands to his forehead. "Fuck me."

"Wait a minute, wait a minute." Dan held up both hands.

"You're saying Gloria DeLauter was in Dru's flower shop? Yesterday? That can't be. She's gone, she's been gone for years."

"It was her," Will stated. "It didn't click until just now. We only saw her that one time," he said to Dan, "but it's a pretty strong memory. Her yelling and trying to get Seth in that car. Sybill knocking her down, Foolish snarling like he was going to take a chunk out of her. She's changed, but not that much."

"No." Seth dropped his hands. "Not that much."

"What the hell's she doing back here?" Will demanded. "You're not a kid now. She can't try to drag you off so she can squeeze your brothers for ransom or some shit. She can't be looking for a sloppy mother-son reunion, so what's the point?"

"Will's a little slow," Dan commented, "especially when it comes to the dark side. Money would be the point, right, Seth? Our pal here's a successful artist, climbing up the shiny ladder of fame and fortune. Whatever hole she's been in, she'd have heard about it. Now she's back wanting her cut of the profits."

"That covers most of it," Seth grumbled.

"I still don't get it." Will shoved at his hair. "You don't owe her a damn thing. She's got nothing on you."

"I've been paying her for years."

"Aw hell, Seth."

"She just kept popping up. I gave her money so she'd go away again. Stupid, but I couldn't see what else to do to keep her from hassling my family. They'd gotten the business off the ground, and the kids were coming along. I didn't want her making trouble for them."

"They don't know?" Will asked.

"No, I never told anybody." He'd put it inside, in the

place he tried to keep locked away from what his life had become. "She tracked me down in Rome a few months ago. That's when I figured there wasn't any point in me being three thousand miles away. I wanted to come home. She hit me up again about a week ago. Usually she backs off for longer. A year or two. I thought I'd bought some time. But if she went into Dru's shop, it wasn't because she wanted to buy some fucking daisies."

"What do you want us to do?" Dan asked him.

"Nothing you can do. Just keep a lid on this until I figure it out. Meanwhile, I'll wait. See what she does next."

BUT he couldn't just wait. He spent hours driving to hotels, motels, B and B's trying to find her, without a clue what he'd do if and when he did.

He started the search with more fury than plan, thinking only that he needed to confront her, to drive her off by whatever means necessary. But as he drove to and from hotels, he began to cool off. He began to think as she thought. Coldly.

If she thought Dru mattered to him, she would be used. Tool, weapon, victim. Very likely all three. If and when he found her, he would need to take care to paint his relationship with Dru as a casual one. Even a callous one.

If there was one thing Gloria understood, even respected, it was using someone else. Using anyone else for your own purposes.

As long as she thought he was using Dru for sex and studio space, Dru would be safe.

Then at least one person he cared about wouldn't be smeared with Gloria's brush.

He was forty miles outside of St. Christopher before he found an answer.

The motel boasted a pool, cable TV and family suites. The desk clerk was young and perky enough to make Seth decide she'd been hired as summer help.

He leaned on the counter, spoke in a friendly manner. "Hi. How's it going?"

"Just fine, thanks. Will you be checking in?"

"No, I'm here to see a friend. Gloria DeLauter?"

"DeLauter. One moment, please." She caught her bottom lip between her teeth as she began to tap her keyboard. "Um, could you spell the last name?"

"Sure."

When he had, she tapped again, then looked up apologetically. "I'm sorry. There's no DeLauter registered."

"Huh. Oh, you know what, she might've registered under Harrow. That's the name she uses for business."

"Gloria Harrow?" She went back to the keyboard, then frowned. "I'm afraid Miss Harrow checked out."

"She checked out?" Seth straightened, did everything he could to keep his tone mild. "When?"

"Just this morning. I checked her out myself."

"That's weird. Blond? Thin? About this tall." He held up a hand to estimate.

"Yes, that's right."

"Well, hell, I must've messed up the dates. Thanks." He started out, then turned back casually. "She didn't mention heading down to Saint Christopher, did she?"

"No. Seems to me she headed out the other way. Gosh, I hope nothing's wrong."

"Just a mix-up," he said and let himself feel a cautious trickle of relief. "Thanks for your help."

* * *

HE told himself she was gone. She'd taken the ten thousand and split. She'd checked out Dru, and that was worrying, but Seth imagined Gloria had, once she'd met her, dismissed the idea of him and Dru having any sort of serious relationship she could exploit.

The fact was, he was far from sure where he stood with Dru himself.

She wasn't the type who wore her heart on her sleeve, he thought. Or anywhere else he could get a good look at it. And wasn't part of his fascination with her the very fact that she was so contained?

At least it had been; interest and attraction had melded into something a great deal stronger.

Now he wanted more.

One way he used to see into people was by painting them.

He knew she was far from sold on the idea of posing for him again—particularly in the way he had in mind. But he set up his studio on Sunday morning as if she were in enthusiastic agreement.

"Why won't you just take money for the painting?"

"I don't want money." He arranged the sheets on the bed, ones he'd borrowed from Phil after a raid on his brother's linen closet.

The material was soft, would drape fluidly. And their color, the palest honeysuckle, would be perfect against the bold red of the rose petals and the delicate white of Dru's skin.

He wanted that mix of tones and moods—warm, hot, cool—because she was all of them.

"That's the point of selling your work, isn't it?" She

clutched her robe closed at the throat and cast uneasy glances at the bed. "To make money?"

"I don't paint for money. That's a handy by-product, and I leave it to my rep."

"I'm not a model."

"I don't want a model either." Dissatisfied, he shoved, dragged, pushed, until he'd changed the angle and position of the bed. "Professionals can give you a terrific study. But I find using regular people gives me more. Besides, I can't use anyone but you for this work."

"Why?"

"Because it's you."

She hissed between her teeth as he opened the first bag of petals. "What does that *mean*?"

"I see you." He tossed petals on the sheets in seemingly random patterns. "Just relax and leave it to me."

"I can't possibly relax when I'm lying naked on a bed strewn with rose petals and you're staring at me."

"Sure you can." He added more petals, stepped back, considered.

"We made love on that bed a few hours ago."

"Exactly." Now he looked at her, smiled. "It'd help if you thought about that when I'm working."

"Oh, did you have sex with me to put me in the right mood?"

"No, I had sex with you because I can't seem to get enough of you. But the mood's another handy by-product."

"Let me tell you where you can put your handy by-product."

He only laughed, then grabbed her before she could stride into the bathroom. "I'm crazy about you."

"Stop it." She seethed as he nibbled on her earlobe. "I mean it, Seth."

"Absolutely crazy. You're so beautiful. Don't be shy."

"You can't get me to strip with flattery or cajolery."

"Cajolery. Very cool word. How about appealing to your appreciation of art? Just try." He skimmed his lips down to hers. "Give me one hour. If you're still uncomfortable, we'll rethink this. The human body's natural."

"So's cotton underwear."

"It sure is, the way you wear it."

And of course, he made her laugh. "One hour?" She eased back. "And I get the painting?"

"Deal. Now is this music okay with you, or do you want me to put on something to strip by."

"Oh, you're very funny."

"Let's just take this off." He untied the robe, eased it gently from her shoulders. "I love looking at you. I love the shape of you." He spoke softly, easing her toward the bed. "The way your skin looks in the light. I want to show you how you look to me."

"How is seducing me supposed to help me relax?"

"Lie down. Don't think about anything yet. I want you turned on your side, facing me. Your arm like this." He lifted it, draped it low over her breasts.

She did her best to ignore the sensation along her skin where his fingertips, his knuckles brushed. "I feel . . . exposed."

"Revealed," he corrected. "It's different. Slide this knee up. Keep this arm angled down. Palm up, open. Good. Comfortable?"

"I can't believe I'm doing this. This is not me."

"Yes, it is." He reached into the bag, scattered petals over her, letting some drift into her open palm before he placed some more deliberately on her hair, on the slope of her breasts, over her arm, along the line of hip and leg.

"Try to hold that for me." He stepped back, ran his gaze over her in a way that made her skin flush.

"Seth."

"Just try not to move too much. I need your body first. I'm not too worried about the head and face just yet. Talk to me." He retreated behind the canvas.

"About what? How ridiculous I feel?"

"Why don't we go for a sail this evening? We'll bum dinner off of Anna and go out after."

"I can't think about dinner, and I certainly don't want to think about your sister-in-law when I'm . . . People are going to see this, see *me*. Naked."

"People are going to see a painting of a striking woman."

"My mother," Dru said in sudden horror.

"How is she? She and your father still back together?"

"As far as I know. They went to Paris, but they're not happy with me."

"Hard to make everybody happy all the time." He sketched the curve of her shoulder, the stem of her neck, the slender line of torso. "When's the last time you were in Paris?"

"About three years ago. My aunt's wedding. She lives there now—outside of Paris, actually, but they keep a flat in the city."

So he talked to her of Paris, satisfied when he saw the tension draining out of her body. Then he began to paint.

The contrast of the red against white skin, the glint of light, the delicacy of the sheets with their deeper shadows in the soft folds. He wanted the elegance of her open hand and the strong muscles in her calf.

She shifted slightly, but he said nothing to correct her pose. The conversation he carried on to keep her relaxed was in a different part of his mind. The rest was steeped in the image he created with paint and brush.

Here was his faerie queen again, but now she was awake. Now she was aware.

She stopped thinking about the pose, her modesty. It was an incredible thrill to watch him work. An exhilaration. Did he realize, she wondered, how the intensity came over him? The way his eyes changed, took on a certain fierceness of effort that was in direct opposition to the casual flow of his words.

Did he see himself? Surely he must. He had to know the fluidity and focus that were so much a part of his technique. The sexuality of it. And the beauty, the power, that made the subject he took along with him feel beautiful, feel powerful.

She forgot the time limit they'd set. Whatever fantasy he'd created in his mind, she'd become too much a part of it to break the spell.

Did the subject always fall in love with the artist? she wondered. Was it just the nature of things for her to feel this outrageous intimacy with him, and this stupefying need for him?

How had he become the first man, the only man, she wanted to give to? To give anything he asked. It was frightening to know it, to understand that love could mean giving up so much of self.

What would be left of her if she yielded to it?

When his gaze moved over her, as if absorbing what she was, she shivered.

"Are you cold?" His voice was impatient. Then, as if he turned a knob, he spoke more easily. "Sorry, are you cold?"

"No. Yes. Maybe a bit. A little stiff."

He frowned, then glanced down at his wrist for the

watch he'd once again forgotten to put on. "Probably hit the hour."

"At least." She worked up a smile.

"You need a break. You want some water? Juice? Did I buy juice?"

"Water's fine. Can I sit up now?"

"Sure, sure." He wasn't looking at her now in any case, but at the work.

"And can I see what you've done so far?"

"Uh-huh." He set down his brush, picked up a rag. And never took his eyes off the canvas.

Dru slipped out of bed, picked up the robe and, wrapping herself into it, walked to him.

The bed was the center of the canvas, with much of the outer space still white and unpainted. She was the center of the bed.

He'd yet to paint her face, so she was only a body—long limbs adorned with rose petals. Her arm covered her breasts, but it wasn't a gesture of modesty. One of flirtation, she thought. Of invitation. Of knowledge.

Only a fraction done, she realized, and already brilliant. Did she ever look and see light and shadow playing so beautifully?

He'd chosen the bed well. The slim iron bars offered simplicity and a timelessness. The delicate tone of the sheets warmed her skin and was yet another contrast to all the rich, bold strokes.

"It's beautiful."

"It will be," he agreed. "This is a good start."

"You knew I wouldn't stop you once I'd seen what you'd done."

"If you'd looked and hadn't seen what I wanted you to see, I'd have failed. Drusilla."

She studied him. Her pulse scrambled when she saw that same narrowed intensity on his face, the strength of focus, of purpose. The need that vibrated around him when he worked.

But now, it was for her.

"I've never wanted anyone like this," she managed. "I don't know what it means."

"I don't give a damn." He pulled her against him, captured her mouth.

He was already yanking off her robe as he dragged her toward the bed.

A part of her—that had been born and bred in luxury, in grace—was shocked at the treatment. Shocked more by her response to it. And the part that responded triumphed.

She tore at his shirt even as they tumbled onto sheets strewn with rose petals.

"Touch me. Oh, touch me." She clawed her way over him. "The way I imagine you touching me when you're painting me."

His hands streaked over her, rough and needy, stroking the flames that had simmered as she'd lain naked for him. It energized her, sparked in her blood until she felt herself become a quivering mass of raw need tangled with reckless greed.

Her mouth warred with his in a frantic battle to give.

He was lost in her, trapped in the maze of emotions she'd wound through him. Steeped in the flood of sensations she aroused by every caress, every taste, every word.

Hunger for more stumbled against a rocky ledge of love.

When he drew her close, held—held tight—he fell over.

Some change, some tenderness eked through the urgency. It swamped her, and she went pliant against him.

Now mouths met, a long, sumptuous kiss. Now hands

brushed skin delicately. The air thickened, filled with the scents of roses, of paint, of turpentine, all stirred by the breeze off the water.

She rose over him, and looked down at love.

Her throat ached. Her heart swelled. Unbearably moved, she lowered her lips to his until her throat ached from the sweetness.

This, she knew, was more than pleasure, beyond desire and need. This, if only she could let it, was everything.

If it was consuming, then she would be consumed. And she took him inside her, gave herself over to the everything.

Slow and silky, deep and intent, they moved together. Trembled as they climbed, sighed as they floated. It seemed to her colors, the rich bold tones he'd used in the painting, spread inside her.

He lifted to her, finding her mouth with his again as his arms enfolded her. Wrapped tight, they surrendered.

For a time they didn't speak. She kept her head on his shoulder, looked at the light through the window.

He'd opened a window, she realized. One she'd been so certain needed to remain shut. Now the light, the air was streaming through.

How could she ever close it again?

"I've never made love on rose petals before," she said quietly. "I liked it."

"Me too."

She plucked one from his back. "But now look what we've done." She held it out to him. "The artist is going to be very annoyed with us."

"He should be, but he's not. Besides"—joy, pure joy, was running inside him in long, loose strides—"the artist is very inventive."

"I can verify that."

"Give me another hour."

She leaned back to stare at him. "You're going to paint again? Now?"

"Trust me. It's important, really important. Just—here." She was still gaping at him when he shifted her and gave her a light shove back onto the bed. "Do you remember the pose, or do you need me to set you?"

"Do I . . . oh, for heaven sake." More than a little miffed, she rolled to her side, flopped her arm over her breasts.

"Okay, I'll set you." Cheerful, energized, he moved her, redistributed rose petals, stepped back, then forward again to make more adjustments.

"It's okay to pout now, but turn your head toward me."

"I'm not pouting. I'm entirely too mature to pout."

"Whatever." He grabbed his jeans, tugged them on. "I need the angle of your head . . . chin up. Whoa, not that far, sugar. That's better," he said, grabbing the brush he needed. "Tilt your head, just a . . . Ah, yeah, that's it. You're amazing, you're perfect. You're the best."

"You're full of shit."

"Now, that's mature." He went to work. "And a little crude coming from you."

"I can be crude when the occasion calls for it." As far as she was concerned, having a man more interested in his work than in holding her when she'd just fallen in love was the perfect occasion.

"Okay, shut up. Just look at me now, listen to the music."

"Fine. I've nothing to say to you anyway."

Maybe not, he thought, but her face had a great deal to say. And he wanted it all. He painted the arrogant angle of it, the strong chin with that lovely shadow in the center, the sculpted cheekbones, the gorgeous shape of her eyes, eyebrows, the straight patrician line of her nose.

But for the rest, for her mouth, for the look *in* her eyes, he needed something more.

"Don't move," he ordered as he came back to the bed. "I want you to think about how much I want you."

"I beg your pardon?"

"Think about how powerful you are, the way you look. As if you're just waking up and you see me looking at you. Craving you. You've got all the power here."

"Is that so?"

"I'm desperate for you." He leaned down, his lips a whisper from hers. "You know it. All you have to do is crook a finger. All you have to do is smile." He laid his lips on hers, took the kiss slow and deep, gave her a taste of his yearning. "And I'm a slave."

He backed up, his eyes on hers as he eased around the canvas. "It's you, Drusilla. You."

Her lips curved, a kind of knowing. In her eyes an invitation shimmered that was both luminous and languid.

He saw everything he wanted in that one moment, the awareness, the confidence, the desire and the promise.

"Don't change."

He saw nothing but her, felt nothing but her to the point where he was almost unaware of his own hand moving. Of mixing the paint, dabbing it, stroking it, all but breathing it onto the paper so that her face bloomed for him.

He caught what he could, knew he would see that light on her face forever. It would be there when he needed to complete the work.

It would be there, in his mind and heart, whenever he was alone. Whenever he was lonely.

"I can do it," he said, and laid aside his brush. "When I do, it'll be the most important thing I've ever done. Do you know why?"

She couldn't speak now, could barely breathe over the tumult of her heart. She could only shake her head.

"Because this is what you are to me. What I knew, somehow, you'd be to me from the first moment. Drusilla." He stepped toward the bed. "I love you."

Her breath shuddered out. "I know." She pressed a hand to her heart, in wonder that it didn't simply burst free in one mad leap of joy. "I know. I'm terrified. Oh God, Seth, I'm terrified, because I love you, too."

She sprang up, scattering rose petals, and leaped into his arms.

FIFTEEN

H URRICANE ANNA SWEPT through the house and had her men ducking for cover. She blew through the living room, snatching socks, shoes, ball caps, empty glasses. Those who didn't move fast enough to evacuate were forced to catch hurled items, or get beaned.

By the time she reached the kitchen, the survivors had made themselves scarce. Even the dog had gone into hiding.

From what he hoped was a safe distance, Seth cleared his throat. "Um, Anna, it's just dinner."

She rounded on him. He figured he outweighed her by a good forty pounds, and still his belly contracted in something like fear at the kill lights in her dark eyes. "Just dinner?" she repeated. "And I suppose you think food just makes itself?"

"No. But whatever we were having is fine. Is great," he amended. "Dru's not fussy or anything."

"Oh, Dru's not fussy or anything," Anna tossed back as

she yanked open cupboards, pulled out ingredients, slammed them shut again. "So it's just fine to give me an hour's notice that we're having company for dinner."

"It's not company, exactly. I thought we'd just grab something, then—"

"Oh, you thought you'd just grab something." She walked toward him with the slow, deliberate steps that struck terror into the very center of his heart. "Maybe we'll just order pizza and have her pick it up on the way."

Cam, hoping her skewering Seth like a bug would keep her attention diverted, tried to sidle in to sneak a beer out of the fridge. He should've known better.

"And you." She bared her teeth at Cam. "You think you can march into my kitchen in your dirty shoes? Don't you even think about plopping your butt down in the living room, sucking on that beer. You're not king around here."

He had the beer, and whipped it behind his back just in case she got any ideas. "Hey, I'm an innocent bystander."

"There are no innocents in this house. Stay!" she ordered when Seth tried to slip out of the room. "I'm not finished with you."

"Okay, okay. Look, what's the big deal? Somebody's always dropping by for dinner. Kevin had that freak friend of his over just the other night."

"He's not a freak," Kevin called out from the safety of the living room.

"Hey, he had a nose ring and kept quoting Dylan Thomas."

"Oh, Marcus. He's a freak. I thought you meant Jerry."

"See?" Seth lifted his hands. "We've got so many people in and out of here we can't even keep them straight."

"This is different." Since Anna had just pulled a large

chef's knife out of the block, and Cam, the coward, had deserted the field, Seth decided not to argue.

"Okay. I'm sorry. I'll help."

"Damn right you will. Red potatoes." She stabbed the knife toward the pantry. "Scrub."

"Yes 'm."

"Quinn!"

"What?" Voice aggrieved, Cam eased back into the doorway but kept the beer out of sight. "I didn't do anything."

"Exactly. Shower. Do *not* throw your towel on the floor. Shave."

"Shave?" He rubbed a hand over his chin and looked harassed. "It's not morning."

"Shave," she repeated and began to mince garlic with such violent enthusiasm, Seth tucked his fingers safely in his pockets, just in case.

"Jesus Christ." Cam curled his lip at Seth and stalked away.

"Jake! Pick up your crap on the floor of the den. Kevin! Run the vacuum."

"Why do you want them to hate me?" Seth pleaded.

Anna's only answer was a steely look. "When you've scrubbed those potatoes, I want them cut into chunks. About this size," she said, holding up her thumb and forefinger. "When you finish that, put out the guest soap and towels in the downstairs bath. The first one I catch using the guest soaps or leaving handprints on the towels gets their fingers chopped off," she called out.

She dumped ingredients into a bowl and whisked.

"It's not all my crap on the den floor, I want you to know." Jake stomped in, shot Seth a sneer. "Lots of other people throw crap around this place, too."

"What do you think you're doing?" Anna demanded as Jake pulled open the refrigerator.

"I was just going to get a—"

"No, you're not. I want you to set the table—"

"It's Kev's night to set and clear. I'm on dish duty."

"Tonight you set and wash."

"How come I have to set and wash? I didn't invite some dopey girl to dinner."

"Because I said so. Set the table in the dining room. Use the good dishes."

"How come we're eating in there? It's not Thanksgiving."

"And the linen napkins," she added. "The ones with roses on them. Six place settings. Wash your hands first."

"Jeez. She's just a girl. You'd think the Queen of England or somebody was coming over."

He stalked to the sink, ran water while he curled his lip, exactly as his father had done. "I'm *never* bringing a girl over here."

"I'll remind you of that in a couple of years." Because the idea of her little boy bringing a girl home to dinner made her eyes sting, Anna sniffed and poured marinade over chicken breasts.

"I'll think twice about it myself," Seth muttered under his breath.

"I beg your pardon?"

He winced. "Nothing. It's just, well hell, Anna, I've brought girls over before. Dru even ate here before and you didn't go into a fit over it."

"That's different. She dropped by unexpectedly, and you barely knew her."

"Yeah, but—"

"And you may have brought girls here before, but you

never invited the woman you're in love with to dinner before. Men don't understand anything. They understand nothing at all, and I don't know why I've been plagued by a herd of them."

"Don't cry. Oh man. Oh God. Please, don't do that."

"I'll cry if I want to. You just try to stop me."

"Nice going," Jake muttered and fled to the dining room.

"I'll make the chicken." Desperate, Seth abandoned his potatoes and rushed over to stroke Anna's hair. "You just tell me what you want me to do with it. And the rest of it, too. And I'll do the dishes after, and . . ." He stepped back. "I never said I was in love with Dru."

"What, now I'm blind and stupid?" She grabbed the olive oil and Dijon to mix up her special sauce for the potatoes. "Get me the damn Worcestershire sauce."

Instead, he took her hands, then ran his up her arms. "I barely finished telling her. How come you know this stuff?"

"Because, you stupid idiot, I love you. Get away from me. I'm busy."

He laid his cheek on hers, and sighed.

"Damn it." She threw her arms around him. "I want you to be happy. I want you to be so happy."

"I am." He pressed his face into her hair. "A little spooked along with it."

"It's not real if you're not a little spooked." She held tight another moment, then let go. "Now get out of here. Guest soaps, towels. Toilet seats down. And find a pair of jeans that doesn't have holes."

"I'm not sure I have any. And thanks, Anna."

"You're welcome. But you're still doing the dishes."

From the dining room came Jake's enthusiastic *woo-hoo*.

* * *

"I appreciate your letting me impose this way. Again."

Anna chose a dark blue vase for the cheerful black-eyed Susans Dru had brought her. "We're happy to have you. It's no trouble at all."

"I can't imagine a last-minute dinner guest, after you've worked all day, is no trouble at all."

"Oh, it's just chicken. Nothing fussy." Anna smiled thinly as Jake rolled his eyes dramatically behind Dru's back. "Is there something you want, Jake?"

"Just wondering when we're going to eat."

"You'll be the first to know." She set the flowers on the kitchen table. "Go tell Seth to come open this lovely wine Dru brought for us. We'll have a glass before dinner."

"People could starve around here," Jake complained—in a whisper—as he trooped out of the kitchen.

"Is there anything I can do to help?" Dru asked. The kitchen smelled fantastic. Something, she assumed it was the chicken, was simmering in a covered skillet.

"We're under control, thanks." With a deft hand, Anna lifted the lid on the skillet, shook it lightly by the handle, poked with a kitchen fork, then set the lid back. "Do you cook?"

"Not like this. I've gotten very adept at boiling pasta, nuking up jarred sauce and mixing it together."

"Oh. My heart," Anna said, and laughed. "Raw clay. I love molding raw clay. One of these days I'll show you how to make a nice, basic red sauce, and see where we can go from there. Seth." Anna beamed at him when he came in. "Open the wine, will you? Pour Dru a glass. You can take her out and show her how my perennials are coming along while I finish putting dinner together."

"I'm glad to help," Dru protested. "I may not cook, but I follow instructions well."

"Next time. Just go out with Seth, enjoy your wine. We'll be ready in ten minutes."

Anna shooed them out, then, delighted with herself, rubbed her hands together before diving into the rest of the preparations.

In fifteen minutes, they were seated in the rarely used dining room, a half dozen tea lights flickering. The dog, Dru noted, had been banished.

"These are beautiful dishes," Dru commented.

"I love them. Cam and I bought them in Italy, on our honeymoon."

"If you break one," Jake put in as he attacked his chicken, "you get shackled in the basement so the rats can eat your ears."

"Jake!" With a baffled laugh, Anna passed the potatoes to her left. "What a thing to say. We don't even have a basement."

"That's what Dad said you'd do, even if you had to dig a basement. Right, Dad?"

"I don't know what you're talking about. Eat some asparagus."

"Do I have to?"

"If I have to, you have to."

"Neither of you have to." Anna prayed for patience.

"Cool, more for me." Kevin reached enthusiastically for the platter before he caught his mother's warning look. "What? I like it."

"Then ask for it, Mr. Smooth, instead of diving across the table. We don't let them out of the kennel very often," Cam told Dru.

"I always wanted brothers."

"What for?" Jake asked her. "They mostly just pound on you."

"Well, you do look pretty well battered," she considered. "I always thought it would be fun to have someone to talk to—and to pound on. Someone to take some of the heat when my parents were annoyed or irritated. When you're an only child, there's no one to diffuse the focus, if you know what I mean. And no one to eat the asparagus when you don't want it."

"Yeah, but Kev swiped half the good Halloween candy last year."

"Jeez, get over it."

Jake eyed his brother. "I never forget. All data is stored in my memory banks. And one day, candy pig, you will pay."

"You're such a geek."

"Thesbo."

"That's Jake's latest insult." Seth gestured with his wineglass. "A play on thespian, since Kev's into that."

"Rhymes with lesbo," Jake explained helpfully while Anna stifled a groan. "It's a slick way of calling him a girl."

"Clever. I enjoyed your school play last month," she said to Kevin. "I thought it was wonderfully done. Are you thinking of going on to study theater in college?"

"Yeah. I really like it. Plays are cool, but I like movies even better. The guys and I have made some really awesome videos. The last one we did, *Slashed*, was the best. It's about this one-armed psycho killer who stalks these hunters through the woods. Carves them up, one by one, in revenge because one of them shot off his arm in this freak hunting accident. It has flashbacks and everything. Want to see it?"

"Sure."

"I didn't know you went to Kevin's play."

Dru shifted her attention to Seth. "I like to keep up with community events. And I love little theater."

"We could've gone together."

She picked up her wine, smiled at him over it in a way that made Anna's heart swell. "Like a date?"

"Dru has a philosophical objection to dating," Seth said, with his eyes on hers. "Why is that?"

"Because it often involves men who don't interest me. But primarily I haven't had time for that sort of socializing since I moved here. Starting up, then running the shop have been priorities."

"What made you decide to be a florist?" Anna asked her.

"I had to ask myself what I could do—then out of that, what I'd enjoy the most. I enjoyed flowers. I took some courses, and discovered I had a talent with them."

"It takes a lot of courage to start a business, and to come to a new place to do it."

"I'd have withered if I'd stayed in Washington. That sounds dramatic. I needed a new place. My own place. Everything I considered doing, everywhere I considered going, kept circling back around to Saint Christopher and a flower shop. A flower shop puts you right in the deep end of the pool."

"How is that?" Cam wondered.

"You become instantly intimate with the community. When you sell flowers, you know who's having a birthday, an anniversary. You know who's died, who's had a baby. Who's in love, or making up from a fight, who got a promotion, who's ill. And in a small town, like this one, you invariably get details along with it."

She thought for a moment, then spoke in a lazy Shore

accent. "Old Mrs. Wilcox died—would've been eighty-nine come September. Came home from the market and had a stroke right there in the kitchen while she was putting away her canned goods. Too bad she didn't make things up with her sister before it was too late. They haven't spoke word one to each other in twelve years."

"That's good." Amused, Cam propped his chin on his hand. More than looks and brains, he thought. There was warmth and humor in there, too. Once you tickled it out of her.

Seth was toast.

"And I thought it was just pushing posies," he added.

"Oh, it's a great deal more than that. When a man comes in, frantic because he just remembered his wedding anniversary, it's my job not to simply put the right flowers into his hands, but to remain discreet."

"Like a priest," Cam put in and made her laugh.

"Not so far from that. You'd be amazed at the confessions I hear. It's all in a day's work."

"You love it," Anna murmured.

"I do. I really do. I love the business itself, and I love being part of something. In Washington . . ." She caught herself, a bit amazed at how easily she'd rambled. "Things were different," she said at length. "This is what I was looking for."

HE followed her home, where they sat on her porch steps in the warm summer night, watching fireflies dance in the dark.

"You had a good time?"

"I had a wonderful time. The dinner, getting to know your family a little better. The sail."

"Good." He brought her hand to his lips. "Because Anna's going to pass the word, and you'll be expected to repeat the performance at Grace's, and at Sybill's."

"Oh." She hadn't thought of that. "I'll need to reciprocate. I'll need to have everyone over for . . ."

She'd have to have it catered, of course. And she'd have to determine how best to keep a number of teenagers entertained.

"I'm out of my league," she admitted. "The kind of dinner party I'm used to hosting isn't what's called for here."

"You want to have everyone over?" The idea delighted him. "We'll get a grill and cook out. We'll toss on some steaks and corn on the cob. Keep it simple."

We, she thought. Somehow they'd slid from individuals into *we*. She wasn't quite sure how she felt about it.

"I've been meaning to ask you something." He leaned back on the step so he could study her profile. "What's it like to grow up filthy rich?"

That eyebrow winged, the way he loved. "We preferred the term 'lavishly wealthy' to 'filthy rich.' And obviously, it has its points."

"I bet. We sort of established why the lavishly wealthy society chick is running a flower shop on the waterfront, but how come she doesn't have household help, or a staff of employees?"

"I have Mr. G, who's worked out perfectly. He's flexible, dependable, and he knows and loves flowers. And I plan on hiring someone else, to work part-time in the shop. I needed to make certain there'd be enough business to justify it first. I'm going to start looking very soon."

"But you do the books."

"I like doing the books."

"And the ordering, and the inventory, whatever."

"I like—"

"Yeah, got that. Don't get defensive." It amused him when her shoulders stiffened. "You like manning the rudder. Nothing wrong with that."

"Speaking of rudders, I like the sloop design. I like it very much. I'm going to contact Phillip and have him draw up the contract."

"Good, but you're evading the subject. How come you don't have a housekeeper?"

"If this is a plug for Grace's service, Aubrey's already nagging me about it. I'm going to talk to her."

"It wasn't, but that's a good idea." He ran his fingers down her leg, an unconscious gesture of intimacy. "Spread the wealth, and free up your time. A twofer."

"You're awfully interested in wealth all of a sudden."

"In you," he corrected. "Sybill's the only person I know, really know, who came from money. And I get the drift that her family's pretty small potatoes compared to yours. Your mother comes down to see you, driven by a uniformed chauffeur. Snazzy stuff. You don't even have somebody coming in to scrub the john. So I ask myself how come that is. Does she *like* scrubbing johns?"

"It was a childhood dream of mine," she said dryly.

"Anytime you want to fulfill the dream in the studio bathroom, feel free."

"That's very generous of you."

"Well, I love you. I do what I can."

She nearly sighed. He loved her. And he wanted to understand her. "Money," she began, "great amounts of money solve a lot of problems. And create others. But one way or the other, rich or poor, if you stub your toe, your toe hurts. It can also insulate you, so that you don't meet or develop friendships with people outside that charmed circle.

You gain a great deal, you miss a great deal. Certainly you miss a great deal when your parents feel so strongly about shielding you from a variety of things out of that circle."

She turned to look at him now. "That's not 'poor little rich girl' talk. It's just fact. I had a privileged upbringing. I never wanted for a single material thing, and will never have to. I had an exceptional education, was allowed to travel extensively. And if I'd stayed in that charmed circle, I think I'd have died by inches."

She shook her head. "There's that drama again."

"I don't think it's dramatic. There are all kinds of hunger. If you don't get fed, you starve."

"Then I guess we could say I needed a different menu. In the Washington house, my mother runs a staff of sixteen. It's a beautiful home, perfectly presented. This is the first place I've had alone. When I moved to my own place in Georgetown, they—despite my telling them I didn't want or need live-in help—hired a housekeeper for me as a housewarming gift. So, I was stuck."

"You could have refused."

Dru only shook her head. "Not as easy as you think, and it would have created more conflict when I'd just gone through the battle of moving out on my own. In any case, it wasn't the housekeeper's fault. She was a perfectly nice, absolutely efficient and completely pleasant woman. But I didn't want her there. I kept her because my parents were frantic enough at the idea of me no longer living at home, and kept on me about how worried they were about me, how much better they felt knowing I had someone reliable living with me. And I was just tired of the hammering."

"Nobody pushes buttons better than family."

"Not in my experience," she agreed. "It seems ridiculous to complain about having someone who'll cook, clean, run errands and so on. But you give up your privacy in exchange for the convenience and leisure. You are never, never alone. And no matter how pleasant, how loyal, how discreet a household staff may be, they know things about you. They know when you've had an argument with your parents, or your lover. They know what you eat, or don't eat. When you sleep, or don't sleep. They know if you've had sex, or haven't had sex. Every mood, every move, and if they're with you long enough, every thought you have is shared with them.

"I won't have that here." She let out a breath. "Besides, I like taking care of myself. Seeing to my own details. I like knowing I'm good at it. But I'm not sure how good I'll be at putting together a dinner party for the Quinn horde."

"If it makes you feel any better, Anna was a maniac for the hour before you got there tonight."

"Really?" The idea warmed her. "It does make me feel better. She always seems so completely in charge."

"She is. She scares us boneless."

"You worship her. Every one of you. It's fascinating. This is very new territory for me, Seth."

"For me, too."

"No." She turned her head. "It's not. Family gatherings, whether they're casual or traditional, impromptu or planned, are very old territory for you. You don't need a map. You're very lucky to have them."

"I know it." He thought of where he'd come from. He thought of Gloria. "I know it."

"Yes, it shows. You're all so *full* of each other. They made room for me because you asked them to. You care for me, so they'll care for me. It won't be like that with my family. If and when you meet them, you'll be very carefully questioned, studied, analyzed and judged."

"So, they're looking out for you."

"No, not so much for me as themselves. The family name—names," she corrected. "The position. Discreet inquiries will be made as to your financial stability, to ensure you're not after my money. While my mother will be, initially, thrilled that I'm involved with someone with your panache in art circles—"

"Panache. You do use those cool words."

"It's shallow."

"Oh, give her a break." He ruffled her hair as he might have a ten-year-old boy's. "I'm not going to be insulted because someone's impressed with my reputation as an artist."

"You may be insulted when your background is quietly and thoroughly investigated, when the credit line on Boats by Quinn is checked."

The idea of the background check had his blood chilling. "Well, for Christ's sake."

"You need to know. This is standard operating procedure in my family. Jonah passed with high marks, and his political connections were a bonus. Which is why no one was particularly pleased with me for calling off the wedding. I'm sorry. I know I'm spoiling the mood of the evening, but I realized with the way things seem to be moving between us you needed to know this sooner rather than later."

"Okay. Tell me this sooner rather than later." He took her hand, toyed with her fingers. "If they don't like what they find, do things stop moving between us?"

"I pulled myself away from there, from them, because I couldn't live that way." And curled her fingers into his. "I make up my own mind, and heart."

"Then let's not worry about it." He drew her into his arms. "I love you. I don't care what anyone else thinks."

* * *

HE wanted it to be just that simple.

He'd learned that love was the single most powerful force. It could overcome and overset greed, pettiness, hate, envy. It changed lives.

God knew it had changed his.

He believed in the untapped power of love, whether it showed itself in passion or selflessness, in fury or in tenderness.

But love was rarely simple. It was its facets, its complexities that made it such a strong force.

So, loving Dru, he faced the fact that he would have to tell her everything. He wasn't born at the age of ten. She had a right to know where he'd come from, and how. He had to find the way to tell her of his childhood. Of Gloria.

Eventually.

He told himself he deserved the time to just be with her, to enjoy the freshness of their feelings for each other. He made excuses.

He wanted her to get to know and become more comfortable with his family. He needed to finish the painting. He wanted to put his time and effort into building her boat, so that when it was done it would somehow belong to both of them.

There was no time limit, after all. No need to rush everything. Days passed into weeks and Gloria made no contact. It was easy to convince himself she'd gone again. Maybe this time she'd stay gone.

He bargained with himself. He wouldn't think about any of it until after the July Fourth celebrations. Every year, the Quinns held a huge come-one, come-all picnic. Family, friends, neighbors gathered at the house, as they had since Ray and Stella's day, to eat, drink, gossip, swim in the cool water of the inlet and watch the fireworks.

But before the beer and crab, they were due for champagne and caviar. With obvious reluctance, and after considerable nagging by both her parents, Dru had agreed to attend one of the Washington galas with Seth as her escort.

"Shit, look at you." Cam stood in the bedroom doorway and whistled at Seth in his tux. "All slicked up in your monkey suit."

"You only wish you could look this good." Seth shot his cuffs. "I get the feeling I'm going to be the artist on display at this little soiree. I nearly bought a cape and beret instead of a tux. But I restrained myself."

He began to fuss with the tie. "This rig was Phil's pick. Classic, according to him, but not dated."

"He oughta know. Stop messing with that. Jesus." Cam straightened from the doorjamb and crossed over to fuss with Seth's tie himself. "You've got more nerves than a virgin on prom night."

"Yeah, maybe. I'll be swimming in a lot of blue blood this evening. I don't want to drown in it."

Cam's eyes shifted up, met his. "Money don't mean jack. You're as good as any of them and better than most. Quinns don't take second place to anyone."

"I want to marry her, Cam."

There was a little clutch in his belly. The trip from boy to man, he thought, never took as long as you thought it should. "Yeah, I got that."

"When you marry someone you take on their family, their baggage, the whole shot."

"That's right."

"I deal with hers, she has to deal with mine. I get through tonight in one piece, she makes it though the insanity around here on the Fourth, then . . . I have to tell her about before. About Gloria, a lot more than I have. I have to tell her about . . . all of it."

"If you're thinking she'll run, then she's not the one for you. And knowing women, and I do, she's not the running type."

"I'm not thinking she'll run. I don't know what she'll do. What I'll do. But I have to lay it out for her and give her the chance to decide where she wants to go from there. I've put it off too long already."

"It's history. But it's your history so you have to tell her. Then put it away again." Cam stepped back. "Real slick." He gave Seth's biceps a squeeze, knowing it would ease the trouble on his face. "Oooh, you've been lifting."

"Cram it."

Seth was laughing when he left the house, grinning when he opened his car door. And the panic slammed into his throat like a fist when he saw the note on the front seat.

> *Tomorrow night, ten o'clock.*
> *Miller's Bar, St. Michael's.*
> *We'll talk.*

She'd come here, he thought as he balled the paper in his hand. To his home. Within feet of his family.

Yeah, they'd talk. Damn right they'd talk.

SIXTEEN

H E   R E M E M B E R E D   T O tell her she looked
beautiful. She did, in the stoplight-red dress that
skimmed down her body and left her back bare but for a
crisscross of skinny, glittering straps.

He remembered to smile, to make conversation on the
drive to Washington. He ordered himself to relax. He
would deal with Gloria as he always dealt with her.

He told himself she could take nothing from him but
money.

And he knew it was a lie.

Wasn't that what Stella had intimated in the dream? he
thought now. It wasn't just money Gloria wanted. She
wanted to gouge at his heart until every bit of happiness
bled out of it.

She hated him for being whole. On some level, he'd always known that.

"I appreciate your going to all this trouble tonight."

He glanced over, brushed a hand over hers. "Come on.

It's not every day I get to mix with the movers and shakers at some spiffy party. Very swank," he added.

"I'd rather be at home, sitting on the porch swing."

"You don't have a porch swing."

"I keep meaning to buy one. I'd like to be sitting on my imaginary porch swing, having a nice glass of wine while the sun sets." And so, she thought, would he.

Whatever he said, something was wrong. She knew his face so well now—well enough that she could close her eyes and paint it, feature by feature, in her mind. There was definitely trouble lurking behind his eyes.

"Two hours," she said. "We'll stay two hours, then we're gone."

"This is your deal, Dru. We'll stay as long as you like."

"I wouldn't be going at all if I could've avoided it. My parents double-teamed me on this one. I wonder if we ever really get beyond the point where a parent can emotionally blackmail us into doing something we don't want to do."

Her words made him think of Gloria, and dread curled in his stomach. "It's just a party, sugar."

"Oh, if only. A party's where you go to have fun, to relax and enjoy the company of people you have something in common with. I don't have anything in common with these people anymore. Maybe I never did. My mother wants to show you off, and I'm going to let her because she wore me down."

"Well, you've got to admit, I look terrific tonight."

"Can't argue with that. And you're trying to cheer me up. So thanks. I'll promise to do the same on the way home when you're glazed and incoherent from being interrogated."

"Does it matter to you, what they think of me?"

"Of course." Amused with herself, she took out her lipstick and missed the way his jaw tightened. "I want all those people who gave me that sticky sympathy over my breakup with Jonah, all the ones who brought it up to my face hoping I'd say or do something they could dine out on the following evening, to take one look at you. I want them to think, Well, well, Dru certainly landed on her feet, didn't she? She bagged herself *il maestro giovane*."

Tension settled on the back of his neck, too weighty to be shrugged off. "So, I'm a status symbol now," he said, and tried to keep it light.

She freshened her lipstick, capped the tube. "Better than a Harry Winston diamond necklace. It's mean, it's petty, it's pitifully female. But I don't care. It's a revelation to realize I've just that much of my mother in me that I want to show you off, too."

"There's no escaping where we come from. No matter how far we run."

"Now that's depressing. If I believed that, I'd jump off a cliff. Believe me, I am *not* going to end up chairing committees and giving ladies' teas on Wednesday afternoons."

Something in the quality of his silence had her reaching over to touch his arm. "Two hours, Seth. Maximum."

"It'll be fine," he told her.

SETH got his first real taste of Dru's previous life minutes after they entered the ballroom.

Groups of people mixed and mingled to the muted background music of a twelve-piece orchestra. The decor was a patriotic red, white and blue echoed in flowers, table linens, balloons and bunting.

A huge ice sculpture of the American flag had been carved as if it were waving in a breeze.

There was a great deal of white on the female guests as well, which took its form in diamonds and pearls. Dress was conservative, traditional and very, very rich.

Part political rally, he supposed. Part social event, part gossip mill.

He'd do it in acrylics, he thought. All sharp colors and shapes with bright crystal light.

"Drusilla." Katherine swept up, resplendent in military blue. "Don't you look lovely? But I thought we said you'd wear the white Valentino." She kissed Dru's cheek and, with an indulgent *tsk-tsk,* brushed her fingers over Dru's hair.

"And Seth." She held out a hand to him. "How wonderful to see you again. I was afraid you must be stuck in traffic. I was so hoping you and Dru would come stay with us for the weekend so you wouldn't have that terrible drive."

It was the first he'd heard of it, but he rose to the occasion. "I appreciate the invitation, but I couldn't get away. I hope you'll forgive me and save me a dance. That way I'll be able to say I danced with the two most beautiful women in the room."

"Aren't you charming?" She pinked up prettily. "And you can be certain I'll do just that. Come now, I must introduce you. So many people are looking forward to meeting you."

Before she could turn, Drusilla's father strode up. He was a striking man with silver-streaked black hair and hooded eyes of dense brown. "There's my princess." He caught Dru in a fierce and possessive embrace. "You're so late, you had me worried."

"We're not late."

"For heaven's sake, let the girl breathe," Katherine demanded, and tugged at Proctor's arm.

In an instant, Seth had the image of Witless trying to wedge his way in between Anna and anyone who tried to hug her when he was nearby.

"Proctor, this is Drusilla's escort, Seth Quinn."

"Good to meet you. Finally." Proctor took Seth's hand in a firm grip. Those dark eyes focused on Seth's face. Studied.

"It's good to meet you." Just when Seth began to wonder if he was about to be challenged to Indian-wrestle, Proctor released his hand.

"It's a pity you couldn't make time to come down for the weekend."

"Yes, I'm sorry about that."

"Dad, it's not Seth's fault. I told you—both of you—that I couldn't manage it. If I—"

"Dru's shop is terrific, isn't it?" Seth interrupted, his tone cheerful as he took champagne from a tray offered by a waiter, passed flutes to Katherine, to Dru, to Proctor before taking one for himself. "I'm sure the business aspects are complicated and challenging, but I'm speaking aesthetically. The use of space and light, the evolving blend of color and texture. One artist's eye admiring another," he said easily. "You must be incredibly proud of her."

"Of course we are." Proctor's smile was sharp, lethally so. *She's my girl*, it said as clearly as Katherine's tugging had done. "Drusilla is our most cherished treasure."

"How could she be anything but?" Seth replied.

"There's Granddad, Seth." Dru reached down, gripped Seth's hand. "I really should introduce you."

"Sure." He shot a beaming smile at her parents. "Excuse us a minute."

"You're very good at this," Dru told him.

"The tact and diplomacy department. Probably get that from Phil. You might've mentioned the weekend invite."

"Yes, I'm sorry. I should have. I thought I was saving us both, and instead I put you in the hot seat."

They were stopped a half dozen times on the way to the table where Senator Whitcomb was holding court. Each time, Dru exchanged a light kiss or handshake, made introductions, then eased away.

"You're good at it, too," Seth commented.

"Bred in the bone. Hello, Granddad." She bent down to kiss the handsome, solidly built man.

He had a rough and cagey look about him, Seth thought. Like a boxer who dominated in the ring as much with wit as with muscle. His hair was a dense pewter, and his eyes the same brilliant green as his granddaughter's.

He got to his feet to catch her face in two big hands. His smile was magnetic. "Here's my best girl."

"You say that to all your granddaughters."

"And I mean it, every time. Where's that painter your mother's been burning my ears about? This one here." Keeping one hand on Dru's shoulder, he sized Seth up. "Well, you don't look like an idiot, boy."

"I try not to be."

"Granddad."

"Quiet. You got sense enough to be making time with this pretty thing?"

Seth grinned. "Yes, sir."

"Senator Whitcomb, Seth Quinn. Don't embarrass me, Granddad."

"It's an old man's privilege to embarrass his grand-daughters. I like your work well enough," he said to Seth.

"Thank you, Senator. I like yours well enough, too."

Whitcomb's lips pursed for a moment, then curved up. "Seems to have a backbone. We'll see about this. My sources tell me you're making a decent living off your painting."

"Quiet," Seth told Dru when she opened her mouth. "I'm lucky to be able to make a living doing something I love. As your record indicates you're a strong patron of the arts, you obviously understand and appreciate art for art's sake. Financial rewards are secondary."

"Build boats, too, don't you?"

"Yes, sir. When I can. My brothers are the finest designers and builders of wooden sailing vessels in the East. If you visit Saint Chris again, you should come by and see for yourself."

"I might just do that. Your grandfather was a teacher. Is that right?"

"Yes," Seth said evenly. "He was."

"The most honorable of professions. I met him once at a political rally at the college. He was an interesting and exceptional man. Adopted three sons, didn't he?"

"Yes, sir."

"But you come from his daughter."

"In a manner of speaking. I wasn't fortunate enough to have my grandfather for the whole of my life, as Dru's been fortunate enough to have you. But his impact on me, his import to me, is every bit as deep. I hope he'd be half as proud of me as I am of him."

Dru laid a hand on Seth's arm, felt the tension. "If you've finished prying for the moment, I'd like to dance. Seth?"

"Sure. Excuse me, Senator."

"I'm sorry." Dru turned into Seth's arms on the dance floor. "I'm so sorry."

"Don't be."

"I am. It's his nature to demand answers, however personal."

"He didn't seem to want to roast me over an open fire, like your father."

"No. He's not as possessive, and he's more open to letting me make my own decisions, trust my own instincts."

"I liked him." That, Seth thought, was part of the problem. He'd seen a shrewd and intelligent man who loved his grandchild, and expected the best for her. Who obviously concluded that she'd expect the best for herself.

And the best was unlikely to be a stray with a father he'd never met and a mother with a fondness for blackmail.

"He's usually more subtle than that," she said. "And more reasonable. The situation with Jonah infuriated him. Now, I suppose, he'll be overprotective where I'm concerned for a while. Why don't we just go?"

"Running away doesn't work. Believe me, I've tried it."

"You're right, and that's very annoying."

She eased back when the music stopped, and saw Jonah over his shoulder. "If it's not one thing," she said quietly, "it's two more. How's your tact and diplomacy holding up?"

"So far, so good."

"Lend me some," she said, then let her lips curve into a cool and aloof smile.

"Hello, Jonah. And Angela, isn't it?"

"Dru." Jonah started to lean in, as if to kiss her cheek. He stopped short at the warning that flickered in her eyes, but his transition to a polite handshake was silky smooth. "You look wonderful, as always. Jonah Stuben," he said to Seth and offered a hand.

"Quinn, Seth Quinn."

"Yes, the artist. I've heard of you. My fiancée, Angela Downey."

"Congratulations." Well aware dozens of eyes were on her, Dru kept her expression bland. "And best wishes," she said to Angela.

"Thank you." Angela kept her hand tucked tight through Jonah's arm. "I saw two of your paintings at a showing of contemporary artists at the Smithsonian last year. One seemed a very personal study in oil, with an old white house, shady trees, people gathered around a big picnic table, and dogs in the yard. It was lovely, and so serene."

"Thanks." *Home*, Seth thought. One he'd done from memory and his rep had shipped back for the gallery.

"And how's your little business, Dru?" Jonah asked her. "And life in the slow lane?"

"Both are very rewarding. I'm enjoying living and working among people who don't slide into pretense every morning along with their wing tips."

"Really?" Jonah's smile went edgy. "I got the impression from your parents that you were moving back shortly."

"You're mistaken. And so are they. Seth, I'd love a little fresh air."

"Fine. Oh, Jonah, I want to thank you for being such a complete asshole." Seth smiled cheerfully at Angela. "I hope you're very happy together."

"That was neither tactful nor diplomatic," Dru admonished.

"I guess I get the calling an asshole an asshole from Cam. The restraint for not busting his balls for calling your shop 'your little business' is probably Ethan's influence. Want to go out on the terrace?"

"Yes. But . . . give me a minute, will you? I'd like to go out alone, settle down. Then we can make the rest of the rounds and get the hell out of here."

"Sounds good to me."

He watched her go, but before he could find someplace to hide, Katherine swooped down on him.

Outside, Dru took two steadying breaths, then a sip from the champagne she'd taken before stepping onto the terrace.

This town, she thought, looking out at the lights and the landmarks, smothered her. Was it any wonder she'd bolted to a place where the air was clear?

She wanted to sit on her porch, to feel that quiet satisfaction after a long day's work. She wanted to know Seth was beside her, or would be.

How strange it was that she could see that image so clearly, could see it spinning on, day after day. Year after year. And she could barely make out the shape and texture of the life she'd led before. All she knew was the weight of it at moments like this.

"Drusilla?"

She glanced over her shoulder, managed to suppress the sigh—and the oath—when Angela stepped up to her. "Let's not pretend we have something to say to each other, Angela. We played for the crowd."

"I have something to say to you. Something I've wanted to say for a long time. I owe you an apology."

Dru lifted an eyebrow. "For?"

"This isn't easy for me. I was jealous of you. I resented you for having what I wanted. And I used that to justify sleeping with the man you were going to marry. I loved him, I wanted him, so I took what was available."

"And now you have him." Dru lifted a hand, palm up. "Problem solved."

"I didn't like being the other woman. Sneaking around, taking whatever scraps he had left over. I convinced myself it was your fault, that was the only way I could live with it. All I had to do was get you out of the way and Jonah and I could be together."

"You did do it on purpose." Dru turned, leaned back against the railing. "I wondered."

"Yes, I did it on purpose. It was impulse, and one I've regretted even though . . . well, even though. You didn't deserve to find out that way. You hadn't done anything. You were the injured party, and I played a large role in hurting you. I'm very sorry for it."

"Are you apologizing because your conscience is bothering you, Angela, or because it'll tidy up the path before you marry Jonah?"

"Both."

Honesty at least, Dru thought, she could respect. "All right, you're absolved. Go forth and sin no more. He wouldn't have had the guts to apologize, to come to me this way, face-to-face, and admit he was wrong. Why are you with someone like that?"

"I love him," Angela said simply. "Strong points, weak points, the whole package."

"Yes, I think you do. Good luck. Sincerely."

"Thank you." She started back in, then stopped. "Jonah's never looked at me the way I saw Seth Quinn look at you. I don't think he ever will. Some of us settle for what we can get."

And some of us, Dru realized, get more than we ever knew we wanted.

* * *

HE was worn out when they got back to Dru's. From the drive, from the tension, from the thoughts circling like vultures in his mind.

"I owe you big."

He turned his head, stared at her blankly. "What?"

"I owe you for tolerating everything. My grandfather's interrogation, my ex-fiancé's smugness, my mother's prancing you around for over an hour like you were a prize stallion at a horse show, for all the questions, the intimations, the speculations. You had to run the gauntlet."

"Yeah, well." He jerked his shoulders, shoved open the car door. "You warned me."

"My father was rude, several times."

"Not especially. He just doesn't like me." Hands in his pockets, Seth walked with her toward the front door. "I get the impression he's not going to like any guy, particularly, who touches his princess."

"I'm not a princess."

"Oh, sugar, when your family's got themselves a couple of business and political empires, you're a princess. You just don't want to live in an ivory tower."

"I'm not what they assume I am. I don't want what they persist in believing I want. I'm never going to please them in the way they continually expect. This is my life now. Will you stay?"

"Tonight?"

"To start."

He stepped inside with her. He didn't know what to do with the despair, with the sudden, urgent fear that he was going to lose everything he'd tried so hard to hold on to.

He pulled her close, as if to prove he could hold on to

this. And could hear the mocking laughter rising in his brain.

"I need . . ." He pressed his face into the curve of her neck. "Goddamn it. I need—"

"What?" Trying to soothe, she stroked her hands over his back. "What do you need?"

Too much, he thought. More, he was sure, than fate would ever let him have. But for now, for tonight, all needs could be one.

"You." He spun her around, shoved her back against the door in a move as sharp and shocking as a whiplash. His mouth cut off her gasp of surprise in a kiss that burned toward the savage.

"I need you." He stared down into her wide, stunned eyes. "I'm not going to treat you like a princess tonight." He dragged her dress up to the waist, and his hand, rough and intimate, pressed between her legs. "You're not going to want me to."

"Seth." She gripped his shoulders, too dazed to push him away.

"Tell me to stop." He stabbed his fingers into her, drove up her hard and fast.

Panic, excitement, burst inside her with the darkest of pleasures. "No." She let herself fly, vowed to take him with her. "No, we won't stop."

"I'll take what I need." He snapped one of the thin jeweled straps so the material slithered down to cling to the tip of her breast. "You may not be ready for what I need tonight."

"I'm not fragile." Her breath clogged in her throat. "I'm not weak." Though she shuddered, her gaze stayed on his. "You might not be ready for what I need tonight."

"We're about to find out." He whipped her around,

pressed her against the door and fixed his teeth on the nape of her neck.

She cried out, her hands fisting against the door as his raced over her.

They had loved urgently, with great tenderness, even with laughter. But she'd never known the kind of desperation he showed her now. A desperation that was ruthless, reckless and rough. She hadn't known she could revel in it, could feel that same whippy violence herself. Or that she could rejoice in the snapping of her own control.

He assaulted her senses, and left her writhing on the wreckage.

He yanked the second strap, broke the elegant jeweled length in half so the dress slid down into a red puddle on the floor.

She wore a strapless bra and a garter of champagne lace, sheer, sheer hose and high silver heels. When he turned her, looked at her, his fingers dug into her shoulders.

She was quivering now, her skin flushed and damp. And that power, that knowledge were in her eyes. "Take me to bed."

"No." He molded her breasts. "I'm going to take you here."

Then his hands were on her hips, lifting her up, bringing her to him. He ravaged her mouth while he took his hands on an impatient journey over lace and flesh and silk. While his blood pounded, he ran the same hot trail with his mouth.

He wanted to eat her alive, to feed on her until this grinding hunger was finally sated. He wanted to lose his mind so he could think of nothing but this driving primal need.

The delicacy of her skin only made him mad to possess it. Her fresh female scent only stirred feral appetites.

When she exploded against him, he knew only a bright and burning triumph.

She dragged at his jacket, her fingers fumbling in her rush, her choked cries muffled against his mouth. Dizzy, desperate, she yanked at his tie.

"Please." She no longer cared that she was reduced to begging. "Please. Hurry."

He was still half dressed when he pulled her to the floor. And she was arching up in demand when he drove himself into her.

Her nails raked over his shirt, under it to dig into flesh gone hot and damp. Racing with him now, she met him thrust for frantic thrust.

Their breath in rags, their hearts slamming to the same primal beat, they surrendered to the frenzy.

Rider and ridden, they plunged off the edge together.

She lay spent, and used, and blissful on the bare, polished floor with the light from her prized Tiffany lamp spreading jewels in the air. As the pounding of blood in her ears faded, she could hear the night sounds coming through her open windows.

The water, the lazy call of an owl, the song of insects.

The heat still pumped from him, and spread through her like a drug. She rubbed her foot indolently against his ankle.

"Seth?"

"Hmm."

"I never thought I'd hear myself say this, but I'm so very glad we went to that tedious, irritating party tonight. In fact, if they put you in this kind of mood, I think we should go to one at least once a week."

He turned his head, saw the bright pool of red on the floor. "I'll pay to have your dress fixed."

"Okay, but it might be awkward to explain the damage to a tailor."

He came from violence, he thought. He knew how to control it, channel it. He recognized the difference between passions and punishments. He knew sex could be mean, just as he knew what had just happened between them was a world away from what he'd known and seen during the first years of his life.

And still . . .

"There's a lot you don't know about me, Dru."

"I imagine there's a lot we don't know about each other yet. We've both been with other people, Seth. We're not children. But I know I've never felt like this about anyone else. And for the first time in my life, I don't seem to need to plan every detail, to know every option. That's . . . liberating for me. I like discovering who you are, who I am. Who we are together."

She stroked her fingers through his hair. "Who we will be together. For me, it's a wonderful part of being in love. The discovery," she said as he lifted his head to look down at her. "The knowing there's time to discover more."

He was afraid time was the problem, and that it was running out.

"You know what I'd like you to do now?" she asked him.

"What would you like me to do now?"

"Carry me up to bed." She hooked her arms around his neck. "Here's something you didn't know about me. I've always, secretly, of course, fantasized about having some strong, gorgeous man carry me up the stairs. It goes against my sense of intellect, but there you are."

"A secret romantic fantasy." Determined to have this one night of peace, he laid his lips lightly on hers. "Very interesting. Let's see if I can fulfill that for you."

He rose, then glanced down at himself. "I'm going to lose the shirt first. It's a pretty silly image, some guy wearing nothing but a tuxedo shirt, carrying a naked woman upstairs."

"Good idea."

He dealt with the studs, the cuff links, then tossed the shirt over by her dress. He reached down for her; she reached up for him.

"How's it going so far?"

"Perfectly," she said, nuzzling his neck as he carried her toward the stairs. "Tell me something I don't know about you."

It broke his stride, but he shifted her and continued up the stairs. "I've been dreaming about my grandfather's wife. I never met her. She died before I came to Saint Chris."

"Really? What kind of dreams?"

"Very detailed, very clear dreams where we have long conversations. I used to listen to the guys talk about her and wish I'd gotten a chance to know her."

"I think that's lovely, and loving."

"The thing is, I don't think they're dreams. I think I'm having these conversations with her."

"You think that when you're dreaming?"

"No." He laid Dru on the bed, stretched out beside her, then drew her against his side. "I think that right now."

"Oh."

"That got you."

"I'm thinking." She shifted until her head rested comfortably in the nook of his neck. "You think they're some sort of visitation? That you're communicating with her spirit?"

"Something like that."

"What do you talk about?"

He hesitated, and evaded. "Family. Just family stuff. She told me things I didn't know, stuff that happened when my brothers were kids. Stuff that turned out to be true."

"Really?" She snuggled against him. "Then I suppose you'd better listen to her."

"THAT'S a smart woman you've got there," Stella commented.

They walked through the moist, heavy night air near the verge of Dru's river. The lamp in the living room window sent pretty colored light against the glass.

"She's got a strong, complicated brain. Everything about her's on the strong and complicated side."

"Strong's sexy," Stella said. "Don't you think she looks to you for the same? Strength of mind, of character, of heart? All the rest is just glands—not that there's anything wrong with glands. Makes the world go round."

"I fell for her so fast. One minute I'm standing up, the next I'm flat on the ground. I never thought it would be the same for her. But it is. Somehow."

"What're you going to do about it?"

"I don't know." He picked up a stone, skipped it out over the ink-black river. "You take somebody on, for the long haul, you take up their baggage, too. My baggage is damn heavy, Grandma. I have a feeling it's about to get a lot heavier."

"You've handcuffed yourself to that baggage, Seth. You've got the key, you always have. Don't you think it's time to use it and pitch that load overboard?"

"She'll never go away and stay away."

"Probably not. What you do about it is what makes the

size of the load. Too damn stubborn to share it. Just like your grandfather."

"Really?" The idea simply warmed his heart. "Do you think I take after him in some ways?"

"You got his eyes." She reached up, touched his hair. "But you know that already. And his stubborn streak. Always figured he could handle things himself. Irritating. Had a calm way about him—until he blew. You're the same. And you've made the same damn mistakes he made with Gloria. You're letting her use your love for your family, and for Dru, as a weapon."

"It's just money, Grandma."

"Hell it is. You know what you have to do, Seth. Now go on and do it. Though being a man, you'll find a way to screw it up some first."

His jaw set. "I'm not dragging Dru through this."

"Hell. That girl doesn't want a martyr." She planted her hands on her hips and scowled at him. "Stubborn to the point of stupid. Just like your grandfather," she muttered.

And was gone.

SEVENTEEN

THE BAR WAS a dive, the sort of place where drinking was a serious, mostly solitary occupation. The blue curtain of smoke, thick enough to part with your hands, turned it all into a poorly produced black-and-white movie scene. The lights were dim, encouraging patrons to mind their own, with the added benefit of hiding the stains when someone decided to mind his neighbor's.

It smelled of last year's cigarettes and last week's beer.

The recreation and socializing area consisted of a stingy strip of space along the side where a pool table had been jammed. A bunch of guys were playing a round of eight ball while a few more stood around sucking beers, the expressions of bored disgust on their faces showing the world what badasses they were.

The air-conditioning unit was framed in a window with a sheet of splintered plywood, and did little more than stir the stink and make noise.

Seth took a seat at the end of the bar and, playing it safe, ordered a Bud in the bottle.

He supposed it was fitting she'd dragged him out to a place like this. She'd dragged him into them often enough when he was a kid—or if she'd had transportation, he'd slept in the car while she'd gone in.

Gloria might have been raised in a solid upper-class environment, but all the benefits and advantages of that upbringing had been wasted on a spirit that continually sought, and found, the lowest level.

He'd stopped wondering what it was inside her that drove her to hate, to despise anything decent. What compelled her to use anyone who'd ever had reason to care for her until she'd sucked them dry or destroyed them.

Her addictions—men, drugs, liquor—didn't cause it. They were only one more form of her absolute self-indulgence.

But it was fitting it would be here, he thought, as he sat and listened to the sharp smack of balls, the rattling whine of the failing AC, and smelled the smells that pulled him back into the nightmare of his childhood.

She'd have come in to pick up a john, he remembered, if she needed cash. Or if she'd had money, to drink herself drunk—unless booze hadn't been her drug of choice for that night. Then she'd have come in to score.

If the john was the target, she'd take him back to whatever hole they were living in. Sex noises and wild laughter in the next room. If it was drink or drugs, and they put her in a good mood, there would've been a stop at some all-night place. He'd have eaten that night.

If the mood had turned nasty, there would have been fists instead of food.

Or so it had been until he'd been big enough, fast enough, mean enough to avoid the punches.

"You gonna drink that beer?" the bartender demanded, "or just look at it all night?"

Seth shifted his gaze, and the cold warning on his face had the bartender easing back a step. Keeping his eyes level, Seth pulled a ten out of his pocket, dropped it on the bar by his untouched beer.

"Problem?" His voice was a soft threat.

The bartender shrugged and got busy elsewhere.

When she walked in, a couple of the pool players looked over, checked her out. Seth imagined Gloria considered their leering smirks a flattering assessment.

She wore denim cutoffs that hugged her bony hips and frayed at the hem just below crotch level. The snug top was hot pink, left several inches of midriff bare. She'd had her belly button pierced and added a tattoo of a dragonfly beside the gold bar. Her nails, fingers and toes were coated in a glitter polish that looked black in the ugly light.

She slid onto a stool, then sent the pool players one long, hot look.

It only took one look at her eyes for Seth to realize at least a portion of the money he'd given her had gone up her nose.

"G and T," she told the bartender. "Easy on the T."

She took out a cigarette, flicked on a silver lighter, then blew a slow stream of smoke at the ceiling. She crossed her legs, and her foot jiggled in triple time.

"Hot enough for you?" she said and laughed.

"You've got five minutes."

"What's your hurry?" She sucked in more smoke, tapped her glittery nails in a rapid tattoo on the bar. "Drink your beer and relax."

"I don't drink with people I don't like. What do you want, Gloria?"

"I want this gin and tonic." She picked up the glass the bartender set in front of her. Drank long and deep. "Maybe a little action." She sent the pool players another look, licked her lips in a way that curdled Seth's stomach. "And just lately I've been thinking I need a nice little place at the beach. Daytona maybe."

She took another drink, left lipstick smeared on the rim. "You, now, you don't want a place of your own, do you? Still living in that same house, crowded in with those kids and dogs. You're in a rut."

"Stay away from my family."

"Or what?" She sent him a smile as glittery and black as her nails. "You'll tell your big brothers on me? You think the Quinns worry me? They've all gone soft and stupid, the way people do when they hang around some dead-ass town their whole fucking, useless lives, breeding noisy kids and sitting around the TV every night like a bunch of goddamn zombies. Only smart thing they did was take you in so they could get the old man's money—just like that asshole married my spineless sister for hers."

She tossed back the rest of her drink, rapped it hard twice on the bar to signal for another. Her body was in constant motion—the jiggling foot, the tapping fingers, the swivel of her head on her neck. "The old man was my blood, not theirs. That money should've been mine."

"You bled him for plenty before he died. But it's never enough, is it?"

"Fucking A." She fired up another cigarette. "You got yourself some smarts, after all these years. Hooked yourself up with a live one, didn't you? Drusilla Whitcomb Banks. Woo-hoo." Gloria threw back her head, let out a hoot. "Fancy stuff. Rich stuff. Bagging her's the only smart thing you ever did. Set yourself up for life."

She snatched the glass the minute the bartender set it down. "'Course you've been doing pretty well for yourself drawing pictures. Better than I realized." She crunched down on ice. "Can't figure why people'd piss away all that money on something to hang on the wall. Takes all kinds."

He laid a hand on her wrist, slowly closed his fingers around it in a grip mean enough to make her jolt. "Understand this: You go near my family or Dru, you go around anyone who matters to me, and you'll find out exactly what I'm capable of. It'll be a hell of a lot worse on you than Sybill knocking you on your ass the way she did years ago."

She leaned her face into his. "You threatening me? *Son?*"

"I'm promising you."

Through the drugs and alcohol, she caught some hint of that promise. And eased back, as the bartender had done. "That your bottom line?" She picked up her drink with her free hand, and her thin, used face went cagey. "You want me to steer clear of your nearest and dearest?"

"That's my bottom line."

"Here's mine." She jerked her hand free, reached for her cigarette. "We've been playing nickel and dime long enough, you and me. You're raking in the dough with your pictures, and you're screwing your way into a big, fat pile of it. I want my cut. One-time deal, lump-sum payment, and I'm gone. That's what you want, right? You want me gone."

"How much?"

Satisfied, she took another deep drag, let the smoke

stream into his face. He'd always been the easiest of marks. "One million."

He didn't even blink. "You want a million dollars."

"I've done my homework, sweetie pie. You get big bucks when the suckers plunk it down for your paintings. You pulled in a pile over there in Europe. Who knows how long you can run that con? Add to that the fancy piece you're busy banging."

She shifted on the stool, recrossed her legs. The mix of drugs and alcohol raging through her system made her feel powerful. Made her feel *alive*.

"She's rolling in it. Lots of money there. Old money, too. The kind of money that doesn't like scandal. Mess things up for you if it got out in the press that the senator's purebred granddaughter was spreading her legs for a mongrel. One that was ripped from his mother's arms when she came to the father she'd never known for help. I can play it all kinds of ways," she added. "You and the Quinns won't come out clean in any of them. And the dirt'll stick to your girlfriend, too. She won't hang around once the shit starts to fly."

She signaled for a third drink, shifted again. "She'll dump you, and fast, and maybe people won't be so willing to shell out for your pictures once they hear my side of things. Oh, I bought him his first little paint kit. Sniff, sniff."

She threw back her head and laughed, the sound so full of malice and glee, the pool players stopped smacking balls to look over. "Press'll lap it up. Fact is, I could sell the story, make a nice little bundle. But I'm giving you a chance to buy it first. You can consider it an investment. You pay me, and I'm out of your life once and for all. You don't, and someone else will."

His face was blank, had stayed blank throughout her rant. He wouldn't give her even his disgust. "Your story's bullshit."

"Sure it is." She laughed and gulped gin. "People can't get enough bullshit, not when it's piling up on somebody else. I'll give you a week to come up with it—cash. But I want a down payment. We'll just call it good-faith money. Ten thousand. You bring it here, tomorrow night. Ten o'clock. You don't show, then I start making some calls."

He got to his feet. "Spend another ten on nose candy, Gloria, you'll be dead in the back room of some dump like this long before you can enjoy any part of that million."

"Just let me worry about me. Pay for the drinks."

He simply turned his back on her and walked toward the door.

HE couldn't go home, not when he intended to sit in the dark and get quietly and thoroughly drunk.

He knew better. He knew it was an escape, self-pity, a one-way trip. Steady, deliberate drinking was a crutch, an illusion, a trapdoor.

He didn't give a damn. So he poured another shot of Jameson and studied its deep amber glow in the single light he'd turned on in his studio.

His brothers had given him his first taste of whiskey on his twenty-first birthday. Just the four of them, Seth remembered, sitting around the kitchen table with the kids and the women gone.

It was one of those solid, rich-toned memories that he knew would never leave him. The sharp scent of the cigar smoke after Ethan had passed them around. The sting of the whiskey on his tongue, down his throat, mellowing out as it reached his belly. The sound of his brothers' voices, their laughter, and the absolute certainty he'd felt of his own belonging.

He hadn't cared much for the taste of the whiskey. Still didn't. But it was what a man reached for when his single intention was oblivion.

He'd long since stopped questioning what Gloria De-Lauter was, and how she became. Part of her was inside him, and he accepted that as he would a birthmark. He didn't believe in the sins of the father—or mother. He didn't believe in tainted blood. Each one of his brothers had come from some sort of horror, and they were the best men he knew.

Whatever there was of Gloria inside him had been drowned out by the decency and pride and compassion given to him by the Quinns.

Maybe that alone was part of the reason she hated him— hated all of them. It didn't matter why. She was part of his life, and he had to deal with her.

One way or the other.

He sat drinking by that single light in a room filled with his paintings and the tools of the work he loved. He'd already made his decision, and he would live with it. But for tonight, he'd cloud his future with Irish whiskey and the throb of the mournful blues he'd chosen as his drinking music.

When his cell phone rang he ignored it. Picked up the bottle, poured another shot.

DRU hung up and paced her living room. She'd tried Seth's number half a dozen times, had worn a path on the floor over the last two hours. Since Aubrey had called, looking for him.

He wasn't with Aubrey, as he'd told Dru he would be that evening. Nor was he with Dru—as he'd told Aubrey and his family he would be.

So where the hell was he?

He'd been off. *Something* had been off, she decided, since the night before. Even before the party, she thought now. Before the drive. There'd been some kind of repressed violence in him—viciously repressed, she realized. It had, eventually, taken its form in rough sex.

And even then, after they'd exhausted each other, she'd sensed an underlying turbulence. She'd let it go, Dru admitted. It wasn't in her nature to pry. She resented the way her parents questioned and picked apart her every mood. Moods, she liked to think, were often private matters.

Now he'd lied to her. That, she felt strongly, was not his nature.

If something was wrong, she needed to help. Wasn't that part of the duty of love?

She checked her watch, barely stopped herself from wringing her hands. It was after midnight. What if he was hurt? What if he'd been in an accident?

And what if he'd simply wanted an evening to himself?

"If he did, he should have said so," she mumbled and marched to the door.

There was one place she imagined he could be. She wasn't going to rest until she checked.

On the drive into town she lectured herself. Her relationship with Seth didn't mean he had to account to her for every minute of his time. They both had lives, interests, obligations of their own. She certainly wasn't the sort of woman who couldn't be content and productive with her own company.

But that didn't give him the right to lie to her about his plans for the evening. If he'd just answer his goddamn phone, she wouldn't be driving into town in the middle of the night to look for him like some clichéd, nagging sitcom wife.

And she was going to ream him inside out for making her feel like one.

She'd worked up a good head of steam by the time she turned toward the rear lot and saw his car parked. The insult of it nearly had her driving right past and back home again. He couldn't have told her, and everyone else, that he'd wanted to work? He couldn't just pick up the phone and . . .

She slammed on the brakes.

What if he couldn't get to the phone? What if he was unable to answer because he was unconscious, or ill?

She whipped the car into the lot, leaped out and charged up the stairs.

The image of him lying helpless on the floor was so strong that when she burst in, saw him sitting on the bed pouring liquor from a bottle into a short glass, it didn't register.

"You're all right." The relief came first, made her knees weak. "Oh, Seth, God! I was so worried."

"What for?" He set the bottle down, studied her out of bleary eyes as he drank.

"Nobody knew where . . ." Realization came next, made her blood boil. "You're drunk."

"Working on it. Got a ways to go yet. What're you doing here?"

"Aubrey called looking for you hours ago. Your stories got crossed. Since you didn't answer your phone, I was foolish enough to worry about you."

He was still much too sober. Sober enough to consider her mood could make it easier on both of them. "If you came running in here hoping to catch me in bed with another woman, I'm sorry to disappoint you."

"It never occurred to me that you would cheat." Nearly as baffled as she was angry, she walked toward the bed, noted the level of whiskey in the bottle. "Then again, it never crossed my mind that you'd need to lie to me either. Or that you'd sit here alone drinking yourself drunk."

"Told you there's a lot you don't know about me, sugar." He jerked a thumb at the bottle. "Want one? Glasses in the kitchen."

"No, thank you. Is there a reason you're worrying your family and having a drinking marathon?"

"I'm a big boy, Dru, and I don't need you crawling up my ass because I want a couple drinks. This is more my style than a couple polite belts of champagne at some boring political gala. You can't deal with it, it's not my problem."

It stung, and had her chin lifting. "I was obliged to go. You weren't. That choice was yours. You want to drown yourself in a whiskey bottle, that's certainly your choice as well. But I won't be lied to. I won't be made a fool of."

He gave a careless shrug and, riding on the whiskey, decided he knew what was best for her. A few more jabs to the pride, he thought, and she'd be gone.

"You know the problem with women? You sleep with them a few times, you tell them what they want to hear. You show them a good time. Right away, they start crowding you. Take a little breather, and they're all over you like lice on a monkey. Jesus, I knew I should never've gone to that deal with you last night. Told myself it'd give you ideas."

"Ideas?" she repeated. She felt her throat fill and burn. *"Ideas?"*

"Can't just let things be, can you?" He shook his head, poured another drink. "Always got to be looking ahead. What's the deal for tomorrow, what's going to happen next week? You're plotting out a future, sugar, and that's just not what I'm about. You're a hell of a lot of fun to be with once you loosen up, but we'd better quit while we're ahead."

"You—you're dumping me?"

"Aw now, don't put it like that, sweetheart. We just need to throttle back some."

Grief rolled up, and numbed her. "All this, all this was just for, what, for sex and art? I don't believe that. I don't."

"Let's not make a big thing out of it." He reached for the bottle again. Poured whiskey onto whiskey. Anything to keep from looking at her, at the tears swimming in her eyes.

"I trusted you, with my body and my heart. I never asked you for anything. You always gave it before I could. I don't deserve to be treated this way, discarded this way, only because I fell in love with you."

He looked at her then, and the combination of pride and sadness on her face destroyed him. "Dru—"

"I love you." She said it calmly, while she could still be calm. "But that's my problem. I'll leave you alone with yours, and your bottle."

"Goddamn it. Goddamn it, don't go," he said when she spun toward the door. "Dru, don't walk out. Please don't." He shoved the glass onto the table, dropped his head in his hands. "I can't do this. I can't let her steal this from me, too."

"You think I'm going to stand here and cry in front of you? Even *speak* to you when you're drunk and insulting?"

"I'm sorry. Christ, I'm sorry."

"You are that. You're very sorry." The hand that gripped the doorknob trembled, and a tear spilled over. The combination infuriated her. "I don't want your pathetic guilty male conscience because you hurt me enough to bring on a few tears. What I really want right now is for you to go straight to hell."

"Please don't walk out the door. I don't think I could stand it." Everything inside him—grief, guilt, loathing and love—clamped his throat like strangling hands. "I thought I should shove you out before you got pulled under. I can't do it. I can't *stand* it. I don't know if it's selfish or if it's right, but I can't let you go. For God's sake, don't walk on me."

She stared at him, at the naked misery on his face. Her heart, already cracked, split in two. "Seth, please tell me what's wrong. Tell me what's hurting you."

"I shouldn't have said those things to you. It was stupid."

"Tell me why you said them. Tell me why you're sitting here alone, drinking yourself sick."

"I was sick before I bought the bottle. I don't know where to start." He raked his hands through his hair. "The beginning, I guess." He pressed his fingers to his lids. "I got about halfway drunk. I'm going to need some coffee."

"I'll make it."

"Dru." He lifted his hands again, then just let them fall. "Everything I said to you since you walked in the door was a lie."

She took a deep breath. For now, she thought, she would tuck the anger and hurt away, and listen. "All right. I'll make you coffee, then you can tell me the truth."

* * *

"IT goes back a long time," he began. "Back before my grandfather. Before Ray Quinn married Stella. Before he met her. Dru, I'm sorry I hurt you."

"Just tell me. We'll deal with that later."

He drank coffee. "Ray met this woman, and they got involved. They had an affair," he corrected. "They were both young and single, so why not? Anyway, he wasn't the type she was looking for. You know, a teacher, one who leaned toward the left while she leaned right. She came from a family like yours. What I mean is—"

"I know what you mean. She had a certain social position, and certain social aspirations."

"Yeah." He let out a breath, drank more coffee. "Thanks. She broke it off, left. She was pregnant, and not too pleased about it from the way I've heard it. She met another guy, one she clicked with. So she decided to go through with the pregnancy, and she married him."

"She never told your grandfather about the child."

"No, she never told him. Little ways down the road, she had a second daughter. She had Sybill."

"Sybill, but . . . oh." Dru let it sift in her mind until it fell into place. "I see. Ray Quinn's daughter, Sybill's half sister. Your mother."

"That cuts through it. She—Gloria. Her name's Gloria. She's not like Sybill. Gloria hated her. I think she must've been born hating everyone. Whatever she had growing up, it never seemed to be enough."

He was pale, and looked so drawn and ill, Dru had to bank down on the urge to simply gather him close and comfort. "For some, nothing is ever enough."

"Yeah. She took off with some guy at some point, got

knocked up. That would be me. Turns out he married her. That's not important. I've never met him. He doesn't come into this."

"Your father—"

"Sperm donor," Seth corrected. "I don't know what happened between them. I don't lose sleep over it. When Gloria ran out of money, she went back home, took me with her. I don't remember any of that. They didn't kill the fatted calf for her. Gloria's got an affection for the bottle, and various chemical enhancements. I think she came and went for a few years. I know when Sybill had a place of her own in New York, she dumped me there. I don't remember much about it. Didn't remember Sybill at all when I first met her again. I was a couple years old. Sybill gave me this stuffed dog. I called it Yours. You know, when I asked whose it was she said . . ."

"Yours," Dru finished, and touched, brushed a hand over his hair. "She was kind to you."

"She was great. Like I said, I don't remember much, except feeling safe when I was with her. She took us in, bought us food, clothes, took care of me when Gloria didn't show up for a few days. And Gloria paid her back by stealing everything she could fence when Sybill was out, and taking off with me."

"You didn't have a choice. Children don't."

"I'm not taking on responsibility for it. I'm just saying. I don't know why she didn't leave me and head out on her own. I can only figure it was because Sybill and I had made a connection, because we . . ."

"Because you'd started to love each other." Dru took his hand, let his fingers grip tight on hers. "And she resented you both, so she couldn't have that."

He closed his eyes a moment. "It helps that you get it."

"You didn't think I would."

"I don't know what I thought. She fucks me up; that's the only excuse I've got."

"Save the excuses. Tell me the rest."

He set the coffee aside. It wasn't doing anything for his headache or queasy stomach but making him more awake and aware of them. "We lived a lot of different places, for short amounts of time. She had a lot of men. I knew about sex before I could write my own name. She'd get drunk or high, so I was on my own a lot. She ran low on money, couldn't get high, she'd take it out on me."

"She hit you."

"Jesus, Dru. However perceptive you are, you don't know that kind of world. Why should you? Why should anybody?" He pulled himself in. "She'd beat the shit out of me if she felt like it. I'd go hungry if she didn't feel like feeding me. And if she paid for drugs with sex, I'd hear them going at it in the next room. There wasn't much I hadn't seen by the time I was six."

It sickened her. It made her want to weep. But if Seth needed anything from her now, it was strength. "Why didn't Social Services do something to help you?"

He just looked at her for a moment, as if she'd spoken in a language he didn't recognize. "We didn't hang around in places where concerned adults call the authorities on junkie mothers and their abused kids. She was mean, but she's never been stupid. I thought about running away, started to save up for it. A nickel here, a quarter there. When I was old enough, she dumped me in school—gave her more time to cruise. I loved it. I loved school. Never admitted it, couldn't be so uncool, but I loved it."

"None of your teachers realized what was going on?"

"It never occurred to me to tell anybody." He shrugged.

"It was life, that's all. And under it, I was just so fucking scared of her. Then . . . I guess I was about seven the first time. One of the men she brought back with her . . ."

He shook his head, pushed to his feet. Even after all the years between, the memories could slick his skin with sweat. "Some of them had a taste for young boys."

Her heart simply stopped, then jolted again to pound in her throat. "No. No."

"I always got away. I was fast, and I was mean. I found places to hide. But I knew what it meant when one of them tried to put his hands on me. I knew what it meant. It was a long time before I could stand anyone touching me. I couldn't stand being touched. I can't get through this if you cry."

She willed back the tears that threatened to overflow. But she rose, crossed to him. Without a word she wrapped her arms around him.

"Poor baby," she crooned, rocking him. "Poor little boy."

Undone, he pressed his face to her shoulder. The smell of her hair, of her skin was so clean. "I didn't want you to know about this."

"Did you think I would love you less?"

"I just didn't want you to know."

"I do know, and I'm so awed by who you are. You think this is beyond my scope, because of my background. But you're wrong." She held tight. "You're wrong. She never broke you, Seth."

"She might have, but for the Quinns. I have to finish." He drew himself away. "Let me finish it."

"Come sit down."

He went with her, sat on the side of the bed again. "During one of her scenes with her mother, Gloria found out about Ray. It gave her someone else to hate, someone else to blame for all the injustices she liked to think were aimed at her. He was teaching at the university here when she found him. This was after Stella had died, after my brothers were adults and had moved out of the house. Cam was in Europe, Phil in Baltimore and Ethan had his own place in Saint Chris. She blackmailed Ray."

"For what? He didn't even know she existed."

"Didn't matter to her. She demanded money; he paid. She wanted more, went to the dean and spun some lie about sexual harassment. Tried to pass me off as Ray's kid. It didn't fly, but it started planting seeds here and there. He made a deal with her. He wanted to get me away from her. He wanted to take care of me."

"He was a good man. Every time I've heard his name mentioned by anyone in Saint Chris, it's with affection and respect."

"He was the best," Seth agreed. "She knew he was a good man. That's the kind of thing she despises, and needs to use. So she sold me to him."

"Well, that was a mistake," Dru said mildly. "And the first decent thing she ever did for you."

"Yeah." He let out a long breath. "You get it. I didn't know who he was. All I knew was that this big old man treated me . . . decent, and I wanted to stay in that house on the water. When he made promises, he kept them, and he never hurt me. He made me toe the line, but, hell, you wanted to when it was Ray's line. He had a puppy, and I never had to go hungry. Most of all, I was away from her, for the first time away from her. I was never going back. He said I'd never have to, and I believed him. But she came back."

"Realized her mistake."

"Realized she'd sold off cheap. She wanted more money or she was taking me. He gave her more, kept giving it. One day, he had an accident on the way back from paying her. It was bad. They called Cam back from Europe. I still remember the first time I saw him, the first time I saw the three of them together, standing around Ray's hospital bed. Ray made them promise to take care of me, to keep me with them. He didn't tell them about Gloria or the connection. Maybe he wasn't thinking about that. He was dying, and he knew it, and he just wanted to make sure I was safe. He trusted them to take care of me."

"He knew his sons," Dru said aloud.

"He knew them—better than I did. When he died, I figured they'd ship me off, or I'd have to run off. I never figured they'd keep me around. They didn't know me, so what did they care? But they kept their promise to Ray. They changed their lives around for him, and for me. They made a home—pretty wild one at first with Cam running it."

For the first time since he'd begun, some of the misery lifted. Humor slid into his voice. "He was always blowing something up in the microwave or flooding the kitchen. Guy didn't have a clue. I pushed at them, gave them—Cam mostly—as much grief as I could dish out. And I could dish out plenty. I kept waiting for them to kick me out, or smack me senseless. But they stuck with me. They stood up for me, and when Gloria tried to hose them like she'd done with Ray, they fought for me. Even before we found out I was Ray's grandson, they'd made me one of them."

"They love you, Seth. Anyone can see it's as much for your sake as it is for their father's."

"I know it. There's nothing I wouldn't do for them. Including paying off Gloria, the way I've been doing on and off since I was fourteen."

"She didn't stay away."

"No. She's back now. That's where I was tonight, meeting her to discuss her latest terms. She came into your shop. Guess she wanted to get a close-up look at you while she was figuring her angles on this one."

"The woman." Dru stiffened, rubbed suddenly chilled arms. "Harrow, she said. Glo Harrow."

"It's DeLauter. I think Harrow's a family name. She knows about your family. The money, the connections, the political implications. She's added that to the mix. She'll do her best to hurt you, the way she'll do whatever she can to hurt my family if I don't give her what she's after."

"It's just another form of blackmail. I know something about this kind of blackmail, the kind that uses your feelings to squeeze you dry. She's using your love as a weapon."

A chill danced over his skin at the phrase, and he heard the echo of Stella's voice in his mind. "What did you say?"

"I said she's using your love as a weapon, and you're handing it to her. It has to stop. You have to tell your family. Now."

"Jesus, Dru, I haven't figured out if telling them's the right thing to do. Much less telling them at two in the morning."

"You know very well it's the right thing, the only thing to do. Do you think what time it is matters to them?"

She crossed to the workbench where he'd tossed his phone. "I'd say Anna would be the one to call first, and she can contact the others." She held out the phone. "Do you want to call her and tell her we're on our way, or shall I?"

"You're awful damn bossy all of a sudden."

"Because you need to be bossed just at the moment. Do

you think I'm going to stand by and let her do this to you? Do you think any of us will?"

"The point is, she's the monkey on my back. I don't want her taking swipes at you, my family. I need to protect you from that."

"Protect me? You're lucky I don't knock you senseless with this phone. Your solution was to let me go. Do you think I want some self-sacrificing white knight?"

He nearly smiled. "Would that be the same thing as a martyr?"

"Close enough."

He held out his hand. "Don't hit me. Just give me the phone."

EIGHTEEN

～

THE KITCHEN HAD always been the place for family meetings. Discussions, small celebrations were held there; decisions and plans were made there. Punishments were meted out and praise was given most often at the old kitchen table no one had ever considered replacing.

It was there they gathered now, with coffee on the stove and the lights bright enough to push away the dark. It seemed to Dru there were too many of them to fit in that limited space. But they made room for one another. They made room for her.

They had all come without hesitation, dragging themselves and their sleeping kids out of bed. They had to be alarmed, but no one peppered Seth with questions. She could feel the tension quivering in the sluggish, middle-of-the-night air.

The younger ones were shuffled upstairs and back to any available bed, with Emily in charge. Dru imagined there was quite a bit of whispered speculation going on up there by anyone who'd managed to stay awake.

"I'm sorry about this," Seth began.

"You drag us all out of bed at two in the morning, you've got a reason." Phillip closed his hand over Sybill's. "You kill somebody? Because if we've got to dispose of a body this time of night, we'd better get started."

Grateful for the attempt to lighten the mood, Seth shook his head. "Not this time. Might be easier all around if I had."

"Spit it out, Seth," Cam told him. "The sooner you tell us what's wrong, the sooner we can do something about it."

"I met with Gloria tonight."

There was silence, one long beat. Seth looked at Sybill, understanding she'd be the most upset. "I'm sorry. I was going to try to find a way not to tell you, but there isn't one."

"Why wouldn't you tell us?" There was strain in Sybill's voice, and her hand tightened visibly on Phillip's. "If she's in the area and bothering you, we need to know."

"It's not the first time."

"It's going to be the last." Fury snapped into Cam's voice. "What the hell is this, Seth? She's been back around before and you didn't mention it?"

"I didn't see the point in getting everyone worked up— the way you're going to be worked up now."

"Fuck that. When? When did she start coming back around you?"

"Cam—"

"If you're going to tell me to calm down," he said to Anna, "you're wasting your breath. I asked you a question, Seth."

"Since I was about fourteen."

"Son of a bitch." Cam shoved back from the table. Across from him, Dru jumped. She'd never seen that kind of rage, the kind with a ready violence that threatened to smash everything in its path.

"She's been coming around you all this time, for years, and you don't say a goddamn word?"

"No point yelling at him yet." Ethan leaned on the table, and though his voice was calm, there was something in his eyes that warned Dru his manner of fury would be every bit as lethal as his brother's. "She get money from you?"

Seth started to speak, then just shrugged.

"Now you can yell at him," Ethan muttered.

"You paid her? You've been paying her?" Shock vibrated as Cam stared at Seth. "What the hell's the *matter* with you? We'd've booted her greedy ass to Nebraska if you'd said one goddamn word about it. We took all the legal steps to keep her away from you. Why the hell did you let her bleed you?"

"I'd've done anything to keep her from touching any one of you. It was just money. For Christ's sake, what do I care about that as long as she went away again?"

"But she didn't stay away," Anna said quietly. Quietly because her own temper was simmering under the surface. If it boiled over, it would make Cam's seem like a little boy's tantrum. "Did she?"

"No, but—"

"You should've trusted us. You had to know we'd be there for you."

"Oh God, Anna, I knew that."

"This isn't the way to show it," Cam snapped.

"I gave her money." Seth held out his hands. "Just money. It was all I knew how to do, to protect you. I needed to do *something*, anything I could to pay you back."

"Pay us back? For what?"

"You *saved* me." Emotions swelled in Seth's voice and the almost desperate flood of them silenced the room. "You gave me everything I've ever had that was decent, that was clean, that was fucking *normal*. You changed your lives for me, and you did it when I was nothing to you. You made me family. Goddamn it. Goddamn it, Cam, you made me."

It took a moment before he could speak, but when he did Cam's voice was rough, and it was final. "I don't want to hear that kind of crap from you. I don't want to hear about fucking checks and fucking balances."

"That's not what he meant." Struggling with tears, Grace spoke softly. "Sit down now. Sit down now, Cam, and don't slap at him that way. He's right."

"What the hell does that mean?" But Cam dropped back in his chair. "Just what the hell does that mean?"

"He never lets me say it," Seth managed. "None of them ever let me—"

"Hush now," Grace said. "They did save you, and they started it when you were nothing more than a promise to their father, because they loved him. Then they did it for you, because they loved you. All of us loved you. If you weren't grateful for what they did, for what they've never stopped doing, there'd be something wrong with you."

"I wanted to—"

"Wait." Grace only had to lift a finger to stop him. "Love doesn't require payment. Cam's right about that. There are no checks and balances here."

"I needed to give something back. But that wasn't all. She said things about Aubrey." He stared at Grace as the color ran out of her face.

Aubrey, who'd been silently weeping, found her voice. "What? She used me?"

"Just things like wasn't she pretty, and wouldn't it be a shame if anything happened to her. Or her little sister, or her cousins. Christ, I was terrified. I was fucking fourteen. I was scared to death if I said anything to anybody she'd find a way to hurt Aubrey, or one of the kids."

"Of course you were," Anna said. "She counted on that."

"And when she said I owed her for all the trouble I'd caused her, how she needed a few hundred for traveling money, I figured it was the best way to get rid of her. Jesus, Grace was pregnant with Deke, and Kevin and Bram were just babies. I just wanted her gone and away from them."

"She knew that." Sybill let out a sigh, rose to go to the coffeepot. "She knew how much your family mattered to you, so that's what she used. She was always good at finding just the right button to push. She pushed mine often enough when I was a lot older than fourteen." She laid a hand on his shoulder, squeezed as she topped off mugs. "Ray was a grown man, but he paid her."

"She'd go away, months at a time," Seth continued. "Even years. But she came back. I had money. My share from the boatyard, what you gave me from Ray, then from some paintings. She hit me twice when I was in college, then came back for a third. I'd figured out she wasn't going anywhere, not for long. I knew it was stupid to keep paying her. I had the chance to go to Europe to study, to work. I took it. Wasn't any point in her coming around here if I was gone."

"Seth." Anna waited until he looked at her. "Did you go to Europe to get away from her? To get her away from us?"

The look he sent her was so fierce, so full of love it made Dru's throat hurt. "I wanted to go. I needed to find out what I could do with my work, on my own. That was just another door you opened up for me. But in the back of my mind . . . Well, it weighed in, that's all."

"Okay." Ethan turned his mug in slow circles. "You did what you thought you had to do then. What about now?"

"About four months ago, she showed up on my doorstep in Rome. She had some guy with her she was stringing along. She'd heard about me—read stuff—and figured the pot was a whole lot richer now. She said she'd go to the press, to the galleries, and give them the whole story. Her story," he amended. "The way she'd twisted it around. Dragging Ray's name through the dirt again. I paid her off, and I came home. I wanted to come home. But it turns out I brought her back with me."

"You never brought her anywhere," Phillip corrected. "Get that through your thick head."

"Okay, she came back. Only this time the money didn't send her off again. She's been staying around, somewhere. She came into Dru's shop."

"Did she threaten you?" Temper fired into Cam's face again. "Did she try to hurt you?"

"No." Dru shook her head. "She knows Seth and I are involved. So she's added me to the mix, using me as another weapon to hurt him. I don't know her, but from everything I've heard, everything I'm hearing, she wants that as much as she wants money. To hurt him. To hurt all of you. I don't agree with what Seth did, but I understand why he did it."

Her gaze traveled around the table, from face to face. "I shouldn't be sitting here at this table while you talk about this. This is family business, and as personal as it gets. But no one questioned my being here."

"You're Seth's," Phillip said simply.

"You can't know how special you are. All of you. This . . . unit. Whether Seth's trying to protect that unit was right or wrong, smart or stupid doesn't much matter at this point. The point is he loved you all too much to do otherwise—and she knew it. Now it has to stop."

"There's a woman with brains," Cam said. "Did you pay her tonight, kid?"

"No, she set new terms. She'll go to the press, tell her story. Blah blah." He shrugged, and realized a great deal of the weight on his shoulders had already lifted. "But she's got a new spin, pulling Dru into it. Senator's granddaughter in sex scandal. It's bull, but if she does it, it's going to pull everybody in. Reporters hounding her at the flower shop, hounding all of you, turning her family upside down. All of us, too."

"Screw her," Aubrey said, very clearly.

"Another girl with brains." Cam winked at Aubrey. "How much she want this time?"

"A million."

Cam choked on the coffee he'd just sipped. "A million— a million fucking dollars?"

"She won't get a penny." Face grim, Anna patted Cam on the back. "Not a penny this time, or ever again. Is that right, Seth?"

"I knew when I sat with her in that dive she had me meet her in, that I had to cut it off. She'll have to do whatever she's going to do."

"We won't be sitting on our hands," Phillip promised. "When are you supposed to meet her again?"

"Tomorrow night, with a ten-thousand-dollar down payment."

"Where?"

"This redneck bar in Saint Michael's."

"Phil's thinking." Cam grinned a wide, wide grin. "I love when that happens."

"Yeah, I'm thinking."

"Why don't I start some breakfast." Grace got to her feet. "And you can tell us all what you're thinking."

DRU listened to the ideas, the arguments and, incredibly from her point of view, the laughter and casual insults as a plan took shape.

Bacon sizzled, eggs were scrambled and coffee was brewed. She wondered if the lack of sleep had made her dull-witted, or if it was just impossible for an outsider to keep up with the dynamics.

When she started to get up, to help set the table, Anna laid a hand on her shoulder, rubbed. "Just sit, honey. You look exhausted."

"I'm all right. It's just I don't think I really understand. I suppose Gloria hasn't committed an actual crime, but it just seems as if you should talk to the police or a lawyer instead of trying to deal with it all yourselves."

Conversation snapped off. For a few seconds there was no sound but the gurgle of the coffeepot and the snap of frying meat.

"Well now," Ethan said in his thoughtful way, "that would be one option. Except you have to figure the cops would just tell Seth how he was a moron to give her money in the first place. Seems we've already covered that part here."

"She *blackmailed* him."

"In a manner of speaking," Ethan agreed. "They're not going to arrest her for it, are they?"

"No, but—"

"And I guess a lawyer might write a whole bunch of papers and letters and what-all about it. Maybe we could sue her or something. You can sue anybody for any damn thing, it seems to me. Maybe it goes to court. Then it gets ugly and it drags out."

"It isn't enough to stop the extortion," Dru insisted. "She should pay for what she's done. You work in the system," she said to Anna.

"I do. And I believe in it. I also know its flaws. As much as I want this woman to pay for every moment of pain and worry and unhappiness she's brought Seth, I know she won't. We can only deal with now."

"We deal with our own." Cam spoke in a tone of flat finality. "Family stands up. That's all there is."

Dru leaned toward him. "And you're thinking I won't stand up."

Cam leaned right back. "Dru, you're as pretty as they come, but you're not sitting at this table for decoration. You'll stand up. Quinn men don't fall for a woman unless she's got a spine."

She kept her eyes on his. "Is that a compliment?"

He grinned at her. "That was two compliments."

She eased back, nodded. "All right. So you handle it your way. The Quinn way," she added. "But I think it might be helpful to find out if, considering her lifestyle and habits, she has any outstanding warrants. A call to my grandfather ought to get us that information before tomorrow night. It wouldn't hurt for her to realize we play hard, too."

"I like her," Cam said to Seth.

"Me too." But Seth took Dru's hand. "I don't want to drag your family into this."

"Not wanting to drag yours into it or me into it is why we're sitting here at four in the morning." She took the platter of eggs Aubrey passed, scooped some onto her plate. "Your bright idea was to get drunk and dump me. How'd that work out for you?"

He took the platter, tried a smile. "Better than expected."

"No thanks to you. I wouldn't advise you going down that path again. Pass the salt."

While his family looked on, he reached over, took her face in his hands and kissed her. Hard and long. "Dru," he said. "I love you."

"Good. I love you, too." She took his wrist, squeezed lightly. "Now pass the salt."

HE didn't think he would sleep, but he dropped off like a stone for four hours. When he woke in his old room, disoriented and soft-brained, his first clear thought was that she wasn't beside him.

He stumbled out of the room and downstairs to find Cam alone in the kitchen. "Where's Dru?"

"She went into work, about an hour ago. Borrowed your car."

"She went in? Jesus." Seth rubbed his hands over his face, tried to get his brain to engage after too much whiskey, too much coffee, too little sleep. "Why didn't she just close for the day? She couldn't have gotten very much sleep."

"She looked like she handled it a lot better than you did, pal."

"Yeah, well, she didn't down half a bottle of Jameson first."

"You play, you pay."

"Yeah." He opened a cupboard to search for the kitchen aspirin. "Tell me."

Cam poured a glass of water, handed it to Seth. "Down those, then let's take a walk."

"I need to clean up, get into town. Maybe I can give Dru a hand in the shop. Something."

"She'll hold for a few minutes." Cam opened the kitchen door. "Let's take it outside."

"If you're planning on kicking my ass, it won't take much this morning."

"Thought about it. But I think it's been kicked enough for now."

"Look, I know I fucked up—"

"Just shut up." Cam gave Seth a shove out the door. "I've got some things to say."

He headed for the dock, as Seth had expected. The sun was strong and hot. It was barely nine in the morning, and already the air had a mean, threatening weight that promised to gain more muscle before it was done.

"You pissed me off," Cam began. "I'm mostly over it. But I want something made clear—and I'm speaking for Ethan and Phil. Get that?"

"Yeah, I get it."

"We didn't give up a goddamn thing for you. Shut up, Seth," he snapped out when Seth opened his mouth. "Just shut the hell up and listen." He let out a breath. "Ha. Looks like I'm still pissed off after all. Grace has some points, and I'm not going to argue about them. But none of us gave up jack."

"You wanted to race—"

"And I raced," Cam snapped out. "I told you to shut up. Now shut the fuck up until I'm done. You were ten years old, and we did what we were supposed to do. Nobody wants a fucking obligation from you, nobody wants payment from you, and it's a goddamn insult for you to think otherwise."

"It's not like that."

Cam stepped closer. "Do you want me to tie your tongue in a knot or are you going to shut up?"

Because he *felt* ten again, Seth shrugged.

"Things changed for you the way they were supposed to change. Things changed for us, too. Ever stop to think that if I hadn't been stuck with some smart-assed, skinny, pain-in-the-ass kid I might not have met Anna? I might have had to live my whole life without her—and without Kevin and Jake. Phil and Sybill, same deal. They found each other because you were in the middle. I figure Ethan and Grace might be getting around to dating just about now, almost twenty years after the fact, if you being part of things hadn't nudged them along."

He waited a beat. "So, how much do we owe you for our wives and children? For pulling us back home, for giving us a reason to start the business?"

"I'm sorry."

Pure frustration had Cam dragging at his own hair. "I don't want you to be sorry, for sweet Christ's sake! I want you to wake up."

"I'm awake. I don't feel much like George Bailey, but I'm awake. *It's a Wonderful Life*," Seth added. "Grandma—Stella told me I ought to think about it."

"Yeah. She loved old movies. I should've figured if anybody could put a chip in that rock head of yours, it would be Mom."

"I guess I didn't listen to her either. I think she's pissed off at me, too. I should've told you right along."

"You didn't, and that's done. So we start with now. We'll deal with her tonight."

"I'm looking forward to it." Seth turned with a slow smile. "I never thought I'd say it, but I'm looking forward to meeting her tonight. It's been a long time coming. So . . . you want to kick my ass, or slap me around?"

"Get a grip on yourself. Just wanted to clear the air." Cam slung a friendly arm around Seth's shoulder. Then shoved him into the water. "I don't know why," Cam said when Seth surfaced, "but doing that always makes me feel better."

"Glad I could help," Seth sputtered and let himself sink.

"YOU'RE staying here. That's the end of it."

"And when did we come to the point where you dictate where I go and what I do? Play it back for me, I must have missed it the first time around."

"I'm not going to argue about this."

"Oh yes," Dru said, almost sweetly, "you are."

"She's not getting near you again. That's number one. The place I'm meeting her is a dive, and you don't belong there. That's two."

"Oh, I see. Now you decide where I belong. That's a tune I've been hearing all my life. I don't care for it."

"Dru." Seth paused, then paced to the back door of the family kitchen, back again. "This is hard enough without me going in there worrying about some asshole hassling you. The place is one step up from a pit."

"I don't know why you think I can't handle assholes. I've been handling you, haven't I?"

"That's real funny, and I'll bust into hilarity over it later.

I want this done and over. I want it behind me. Behind us. Please." He changed tack, laid his hand gently on her shoulder. "Stay here and let me do what I have to do."

It was turmoil in his eyes now rather than temper. And she responded to it. "Well, since you ask so nicely."

His shoulders relaxed as he laid his forehead on hers. "Okay, good. Maybe you should stretch out for a little while. You didn't get much sleep last night."

"Don't push it, Seth."

"Right. I should go."

"You know who you are." She turned her head to brush her lips over his. "And so do I. She doesn't. She never could."

SHE let him go, and stood on the front porch with the other Quinn women as the two cars drove away.

Anna lowered the hand she'd lifted in a wave. "There go our strong, brave men, off to battle. And we womenfolk stay behind, tucked up safe."

"Put on the aprons," Aubrey mumbled. "Make potato salad for tomorrow's picnic."

Dru glanced around, saw the same look in her companions' eyes she knew was in her own. "I don't think so."

"So." Sybill rolled her shoulders, glanced at her watch. "How much lead time do we give them?"

"Fifteen minutes ought to be about right," Anna decided.

Grace nodded. "We'll take my van."

SETH sat at the bar, brooding into his untouched beer. He figured the dread in the pit of his stomach was natural.

She'd always put it there. The venue, he supposed, was the perfect place for this showdown with her, with his early childhood, with his own ghosts and demons.

He intended to walk out of it when he was finished, and leave all of that misery behind, just another smear on the dirty air.

He needed to feel clean again, complete again. He wondered if Ray would have understood this nasty tug-of-war between fury and grief.

He liked to think so. Just as he liked to think some part of Ray was sitting beside him in the bar.

But when she walked in, there was only the two of them. The drinkers, the pool players, the bartender, even that nebulous connection with the man who'd been his grandfather faded away.

It was just Seth, and his mother.

She relaxed onto a stool, crossed her legs and sent the bartender a wink.

"You look a little rough around the edges," she said to Seth. "Tough night?"

"You look the same. You know, I've been sitting here thinking. You had a pretty good deal growing up."

"Shit." She snagged the gin and tonic the bartender put in front of her. "Lot you know about it."

"Big house, plenty of money, good education."

"Fuck that." She drank deep. "Bunch of jerks and assholes."

"You hated them."

"My mother's a cold fish, stepfather's pussy-whipped. And there's Sybill, the perfect daughter. I couldn't wait to get the hell out and live."

"I don't know about your parents. They don't have anything to do with me either. But Sybill never hurt you. She took you in, took both of us in when you landed on her doorstep, broke and with nowhere else to go."

"So she could lord it over me. Goddamn superior bitch."

"Is that why you stole from her when we were in New York? Cleaned her out and took off after she'd given you a place to stay?"

"I take what I need. That's how you get ahead in life. Had to support you, didn't I?"

"Let's not bullshit. You never gave a damn about me. The only reason you didn't take off without me, dump me on Sybill, was because you knew she cared about me. So you took me away, you stole her things because you hated her. You stole so you could buy drugs."

"Oh yeah, she'd've loved it if I'd left you behind. She could've gone around feeling righteous, telling everybody how worthless I was. Fuck her. Whatever I took out of her place, I was entitled to. Gotta look out for number one in this life. Never could teach you that."

"You taught me plenty." When Gloria rattled the ice in her glass, he signaled the bartender for another drink. "Ray didn't even know about you, but you hated him. When he found out, when he tried to help you, you only hated him more."

"He owed me. Bastard doesn't keep his dick zipped, knocks up some idiot coed, he oughta pay."

"And he paid you. He didn't know Barbara was pregnant with you, he never knew you existed. But when you told him, he paid you. And it wasn't enough. You tried to ruin him with lies. Then you used his decency against him and sold me to him like I was a puppy you were tired of."

"Fucking A I was tired of you. Kept you around for ten

years, cramping my style. Old man Quinn owed me for giving him a grandson. And it all worked out pretty well for you, didn't it?"

"I guess I owe you for that one." He lifted his beer in a toast, sipped. "But it worked out pretty well for you, at least when he was alive. You just kept hitting him up for more money, using me as the bait."

"Hey, he could've tossed you back anytime. You were nothing to him, just like I was nothing."

"Yeah, some people are just stupid, weak, natural marks, believing a promise made to a ten-year-old boy needs to be kept. The same type who think that same kid deserves a shot at a decent life, a home, a family. He'd have given you the same, if you'd wanted it."

"You think I wanted to be stuck in some backwater bum-fuck town, paying homage to an old man who picks up strays?" She gulped her gin. "That's your scene, not mine. And you got it, so what're you bitching about? And if you want to keep it, you'll pay. Just like you've always paid. You got the down payment?"

"How much you figure you've gotten from me over the years, Gloria? Between what you bled out of Ray, what you've been bleeding out of me? Must be a couple hundred thousand, at least. Of course, you never got anything out of my brothers. You tried—the usual lies, threats, intimidation—but they didn't bleed so easy. You do better with old men and kids."

She smirked. "They'd've paid if I'd wanted them to pay. I had better things to do. Bigger fish to fry. You wanna fry your own fish now, keep that fancy art career you've got going from getting screwed up, wanna keep sticking it to the senator's granddaughter, you pay for it."

"So you said. Let me get the terms clear. I pay you, one million dollars starting with the ten-thousand-dollar down payment tonight—"

"In cash."

"Right, in cash, or you'll go to the press, to Dru's family, and spin another web of lies about how you were used and abused by the Quinns, starting with Ray. You'll smear them and me and Dru along with it. The poor, desperate woman, girl really, struggling to raise a child on her own, begging for help only to be forced to give up the child."

"Has a nice ring. Lifetime Movie of the Week."

"No mention in there of the tricks you turned while that child was in the next room—or the men you let touch him. No mention of the drugs, the booze, the beatings."

"Bring out the violins." She leaned in, very close. "You were a pain in the ass. You're lucky I kept you around as long as I did." And lowered her voice. "You're lucky I didn't sell you to one of my johns. Some would've paid top dollar."

"You would have, sooner or later."

She shrugged. "Had to get something out of you, didn't I?"

"You've been tapping me for money since I was fourteen. I've paid you to protect my family, myself. Mostly I've paid you because the peace of mind was worth a hell of a lot more than the money. I've let you blackmail me."

"I want what's due me." She snatched the third drink. "I'm making you a deal here. One lump-sum payment and you keep your nice, boring life. Screw with me, and you'll lose it all."

"A million dollars or you'll do whatever you can to hurt my family, ruin my career and destroy my relationship with Dru."

"In a nutshell. Pay up."

He nudged his beer aside, met her eyes. "Not now, not ever again."

She grabbed his shirt in her fist, yanked his face close to hers. "You don't want to fuck with me."

"Oh yeah, I do. I have." He reached in his pocket, pulled out a mini recorder. "Everything we've said is on here. Might be a problem in court, if I decide to go to the cops."

When she grabbed for it, he cuffed her wrist with his hand. "Speaking of cops, they'll be interested to know you jumped bail down in Fort Worth. Solicitation and possession. You go public and some hard-ass skip tracer is going to be really happy to scoop you up and haul you back to Texas."

"You son of a bitch."

"Truer words," he said mildly. "But you go right ahead and try to sell your version of things. I figure anybody who wants to write a story about all this will be really interested in this informal interview."

"I want my money." She shrieked it, tossed what was left in her glass in his face.

The quartet playing pool looked over. The biggest of them tapped his cue against his palm as he sized Seth up.

She leaped off the stool, and fury had her practically in tears. "He stole my money."

The four men started forward. Seth rose from the stool.

And his brothers walked in, ranged themselves beside him.

"That seems to even things up." Cam tucked his thumbs in his front pockets and gave Gloria a fierce grimace. "Been a while."

"You bastards. You're all fucking bastards. I want what's mine."

"We've got nothing of yours." Ethan spoke quietly. "We never did."

"I take anything from her?" Seth asked the bartender.

"Nope." He continued to wipe the bar. "You want trouble, take it outside."

Phillip scanned the faces of the four men. "You want trouble?"

The big man tapped his cue twice more. "Bob says he didn't take nothing, he didn't take nothing. None of my never mind."

"How about you, Gloria? You want trouble?" Phillip asked her.

Before she could speak, the door opened. The women came in.

"Goddamn it," Cam muttered under his breath. "Should've figured it."

Dru walked directly to Seth, slid her hand into his. "Hello again, Gloria. It's funny, my mother doesn't remember you at all. She isn't the least bit interested in you. But my grandfather is." She took a piece of paper out of her pocket. "This is the number to his office on the Hill. He'll be happy to speak to you if you'd like to call him."

Gloria slapped the paper from Dru's fingers, then retreated quickly when Seth stepped forward.

"I'll make you sorry for this." She shoved through them, pausing briefly to snarl at Sybill.

"You shouldn't have come back, Gloria," Sybill told her. "You should've cut your losses."

"Bitch. I'll make you sorry. I'll make you all sorry." With one last bitter glance, she shoved through the door.

"You were supposed to stay home," Seth told her.

"No, I wasn't." Dru touched his cheek.

NINETEEN

⌒

THE HOUSE AND the yard were crowded with people. Crabs were steaming, and a half dozen picnic tables were loaded with food.

The Quinns' annual Fourth of July celebration was well under way.

Seth pulled a beer from the keg, grabbed some shade, and took a break from the conversations to sketch.

His world, he thought. Friends, family, slow Shore voices and squealing kids. The smells of spiced crabs, of beer, of talcum powder and grass. Of the water.

A couple of kids were out in a Sunfish with a bright yellow sail. Ethan's dog was splashing in the shallows with Aubrey—old times.

He heard Anna's laugh and the cheerful clink of horseshoes.

Independence Day, he thought. He would remember this one for the rest of his life.

"We've been doing this here since before you were born," Stella said from beside him.

The pencil squirted out of Seth's fingers. No dream this time, he thought in a kind of breathless wonder. He was sitting in the warm, dappled shade, surrounded by people and noise.

And talking to a ghost.

"I wasn't sure you were speaking to me."

"Nearly made a mess of it, and that ticked me off. But you figured things out in the end."

She was wearing the old khaki hat, a red shirt and baggy blue shorts. Without any real thought, Seth picked up the pencil, turned the page in his book and began to draw her as she looked, sitting contentedly in the shade.

"Part of me was always scared of her, no matter what. But that's gone now."

"Good. Stay that way, because she'll always cause trouble. My God, look at Crawford. How'd he get so old? Time just goes by, no matter what the hell you do. Some things you let go. Some things are worth repeating. Like this party, year after year after year."

He continued to sketch, but his throat had tightened. "You're not coming back again, are you?"

"No, honey. I'm not coming back again."

She touched him, and he would never forget the sensation of her hand on his knee. "Time to look forward, Seth. You don't want to ever forget what's behind you, but you've got to look ahead. Look at my boys." She let out a long sigh as she gazed over at Cam, and Ethan, and Phillip. "All grown up, with families of their own. I'm glad I told them that I loved them, that I was proud of them, while I was still breathing."

She smiled now, patted Seth's knee. "Glad I got a chance to tell you I love you. And I'm proud of you."

"Grandma—"

"Make a good life for yourself or I'm going to be ticked off at you again. Here comes your girl," she said, and was gone.

His heart wrenched in his chest. And Dru sat down beside him. "Want company?" she asked.

"As long as it's you."

"So many people." She leaned back on her elbows. "It makes me think Saint Chris must look like a ghost town right now."

"Just about everyone swings by, at least for a while. It whittles down by nightfall, and the rest of us stay here and watch the fireworks."

Some things you let go, he remembered. Some are worth repeating.

"I love you, Drusilla. Just thought that was worth repeating."

She angled her head, studied the odd little smile on his face. "You can repeat it whenever you like. And if you come home with me afterward, we can make our own fireworks."

"That's a date."

She sat up again, examined his drawing. "That's wonderful. Such a strong face—and a friendly one." She glanced around for the model. "Where is she? I don't remember seeing her."

"She's not here anymore." He took a last look at the sketch, then gently closed the book. "Wanna go for a swim?"

"It's hot enough, but I didn't think to bring a suit."

"Really?" Grinning, he stood up, pulled her to her feet. "But you can swim, right?"

"Of course I can swim." As soon as the words were out, she recognized the gleam in his eye. "Don't even think about it."

"Too late." He scooped her up.

"Don't—" She wiggled, shoved, then began to panic as he jogged toward the dock. "This isn't funny."

"It will be. Don't forget to hold your breath."

He ran straight down the dock and off the end.

"IT'S a Quinn thing," Anna said as she handed Dru a dry shirt. "I can't explain it. They're always doing that."

"I lost a shoe."

"They'll probably find it."

Dru sat on the bed. "Men are so strange."

"We just have to remember that in some areas, they're really just five years old. These sandals ought to fit you well enough." She offered them.

"Thanks. Oh, they're fabulous."

"I love shoes. I lust for shoes."

"With me it's earrings. I have no power against them."

"I like you very much."

Dru stopped admiring the sandals and looked up. "Thank you. I like you very much, too."

"It's a bonus. I would have made room for any woman Seth loved. All of us would. So you're a very nice bonus. I wanted to tell you."

"I . . . I don't have experience with families like yours."

"Who does?" With a laugh, Anna sat on the bed beside her.

"Mine isn't generous. I'm going to try to talk to my parents again. Seeing what Seth's been through, what he faced down last night, made me realize I have to try. But whatever understanding we reach, we'll never be like yours. They won't welcome him the way you're welcoming me."

"Don't be so sure." She wrapped an arm around Dru's shoulders. "He has a way of winning people over."

"Certainly worked with me. I love him." She pressed a hand to her stomach. "It's terrifying how much."

"I know the feeling. It'll be dark soon." Anna gave Dru a quick squeeze. "Let's go get a glass of wine and get a good spot to watch the show."

When she stepped outside, Seth met her with one very soggy canvas slide and a sheepish grin. "Found it."

She snatched it, set it beside the back door where she'd put its mate. "You're a baboon."

"Mrs. Monroe brought homemade peach ice cream." He brought his hand out, with a double-scoop cone in it, from behind his back.

"Hmm." She sniffed, but she took the cone.

"Want to sit on the grass with me and watch fireworks?"

She took a long lick. "Maybe."

"Gonna let me kiss you when nobody's looking?"

"Maybe."

"Gonna share that ice cream?"

"Absolutely not."

WHILE Seth was trying to cadge his share of a peach ice cream cone, and excited children were bouncing in anticipation of that first explosion of light and color in the night sky, Gloria DeLauter pulled into the parking lot of Boats by Quinn.

She jerked to a halt and sat stewing in the messy juices of her fury laced with a pint of gin.

They'd pay. All of them would pay. Bastards. Thought they could scare her off, gang up on her the way they had and go back to their stupid house and laugh about it.

They'd see who laughed when she was finished with them.

They *owed* her. She beat the heel of her hand on the steering wheel as rage choked her.

She was going to make that son of a bitch she'd given birth to sorry. She'd make all of them sorry.

She shoved out of the car, stumbling as the gin spun in her head. She weaved her way to the trunk. *God!* She loved being high. People who went through life sober and straight were the assholes. World was fucking full of assholes, she thought as she stabbed her key at the trunk lock.

You need to get into a program, Gloria.

That's what they told her. Her worthless mother, her spineless stepfather, her tight-assed sister. The sainted sucker Ray Quinn had tried that with her, too.

It was all bullshit.

On the fourth try, she managed to get the key in the lock. She lifted the trunk, then hooted with delight as she dragged out the two cans of gasoline.

"We're gonna have some motherfucking fireworks, all right."

She stumbled again, stepped right out of one of her shoes but was too drunk to notice. Limping now, she carted the cans to the door, then straightened up, caught her breath.

It took her a while to uncap the first can, and as she fought with it she cursed the gawky kid at the gas station who'd filled them for her.

Just another asshole in a world of assholes.

But her good humor returned when she splashed gasoline on the doors and the sharp, dangerous smell of it stung the air.

"Stick your wood boats up your ass. Fucking Quinns."

She splashed it on the brick, on glass, on the pretty barberry bushes Anna had planted along the foundation. When one can was empty, she started on the second.

It was a thrill to heave it, still half full, through the front window. She danced in the dark to the sound of breaking glass.

Then she hobbled back to the trunk and retrieved the two bottles she'd filled with gas earlier and plugged with rags. "Molotov cocktail." She giggled, swayed. "I got a double for you bastards."

She fumbled out her lighter and flicked. And was smiling when she set the flame to the rag.

It caught faster than she'd expected, burned the tips of her fingers. On a little shriek, she heaved it toward the window, shattered it on brick.

"Shit!" Flames leaped along the bushes, ate down to the ground and crept toward the doors. But she wanted more.

She edged closer and, with the heat soaking her face, lit the second rag. Her aim was better this time, and she heard the boom of glass and flame as the bottle crashed on the floor inside the building.

"Kiss my ass!" She screamed it and gave herself the pleasure of watching the fire sprint before she ran to her car.

THE rocket exploded across the sky in a fountain of gold against black. With Dru nestled between his legs, his arms around her waist, Seth felt almost stupidly content.

"I really missed this when I was overseas," he told her.

"Sitting in the backyard on the Fourth of July and watching the sky go crazy." He turned his lips to the nape of her neck. "Do I still get the fireworks later?"

"Probably. In fact, if you play your cards right, I might let you . . ."

She trailed off, glancing over as Seth did at the sound of raised voices. He was on his feet, pulling Dru to hers even as Cam raced toward them.

"Boatyard's on fire."

THE fire department was already fighting the blaze. The doors and windows were gone, and the brick around them blackened. Seth stood, hands fisted, as water pumped through the openings and smoke billowed out.

He thought of the work inside that old brick barn. The sweat and the blood that went into it, the sheer determination and family pride.

Then he bent down and picked up the high-heeled backless shoe at his feet. "It's hers. Stay with Anna and the rest," he told Dru, and went to his brothers.

"COUPLE of kids heard the explosion and saw the car drive away." Cam rubbed his hands over eyes that stung from smoke. "Not much doubt it was arson since she left the gas cans behind. They got the make and model of her car, and a description. She won't get far."

"She'll see this as payback," Seth said. "Fuck with me, I'll fuck with you more."

"Yeah, well, she's got a surprise coming. This time she's going to jail."

"She messed us up real good first."

"We're insured." Cam stared at the blackened brick, the trampled bushes, the stream of smoke still belching out of the broken door.

The pain in his heart was a physical stab. "We put this place together once, we can do it again. And if you're planning on taking any guilt trips—"

"No." Seth shook his head. "That's done." He held out his hand as Aubrey walked to them.

"We're okay." She squeezed his fingers. "That's what counts." But the tears on her cheeks weren't all from smoke.

"Hell of a mess," Phillip said as he walked up. His face was smeared with soot, his clothes filthy with it. "But it's out. Those kids who called nine-one-one saved our asses. Fire department responded in minutes."

"You got their names?" Cam asked him.

"Yeah." He let out a breath. "Ethan's over talking with the fire marshal. He'll let us know when we're clear to go in. It's gonna be a while with the arson investigation on top of it."

"Which one of us is going to talk the women into taking the kids home?"

Phillip stuck his hand in his pocket, pulled out a coin. "Flip you for it. Heads it's your headache, tails it's mine."

"Deal. But I flip. Your fingers are a little too sticky to suit me."

"You saying I'd cheat?"

"Over this? Damn right."

"That's cold," Phillip complained, but handed over the coin.

"Damn it." Cam hissed through his teeth when he flipped heads.

"Don't even think about saying two out of three."

Scowling, Cam tossed Phillip the coin, then stalked over to argue with the women.

"Well." Phillip folded his arms and studied the building. "We could say screw it, move to Tahiti and open a tiki bar. Spend our days fishing until we're brown as monkeys and our nights having jungle sex with our women."

"Nah. Live on an island, you end up drinking rum. Never had a taste for it."

Phillip slapped a hand on Seth's shoulder. "Then I guess we stick. Want to break it to Ethan?" He nodded toward his brother as Ethan crossed the muddy lawn.

"He'll be okay. He doesn't like rum either." But the optimism Seth was fighting to hold on to wavered when he saw Ethan's face.

"They picked her up." Ethan swiped a forearm over his sweaty brow. "Sitting in a bar not five miles out of town. You all right with that?" he asked Seth.

"I'm fine with that."

"Okay then. Maybe you ought to go talk your girl into going on home. It's going to be a long night here."

I T was a long night, and a long day after. It would be, Seth thought, some long weeks before Boats by Quinn was back in full operation.

He'd tromped through the wreckage and the stink of the building, mourned with his brothers and Aubrey the loss of the pretty, half-built hull of a skiff that was now no more than scraps of blackened teak.

He grieved over the sketches he'd drawn from childhood on, which were nothing but ashes. He could, and would, reproduce them. But he couldn't replace them, nor the joy each one had given him.

When there was no more to do, he went home, cleaned up and slept until he could do more.

· It was nearly dusk the next evening when he drove to Dru's. He was tired down to the bone, but as clearheaded as he'd been in his life. He hauled the porch swing he'd bought out of the bed of the truck he'd borrowed from Cam, got his tools.

When she stepped out, he was drilling in the first hook.

"You said you wanted one. This seemed like the place for it."

"It's the perfect place." She walked over, touched his shoulder. "Talk to me."

"I will. That's why I'm here. Sorry I didn't get in touch today."

"I know you've been busy. Half the town's been in and out of my shop, just like half the town was there at the fire last night."

"We got more help than we could handle. Fire didn't spread to the second level."

She knew. Word spread every bit as quickly as flame. But she let him talk.

"Main level's a wreck. Between the fire, the smoke, the water, we'll have to gut it. Lost most of the tools, toasted a hull. Insurance adjuster was out today. We'll be okay."

"Yes, you'll be okay."

He stepped over to drill for the second hook. "They arrested Gloria. Kids made her car, and the kid who sold her the gas ID'd her. Plus she left her fingerprints all over the gas can she dumped outside the building. When they picked her up for questioning, she was still wearing one shoe. Losing shoes seems to be going around."

"I'm so sorry, Seth."

"Me too. I'm not taking it on," he added. "I know it's not

my fault. All she managed to do was mess up a building. She didn't hurt us. She can't. We've built something she can't touch."

He looped the chain, hooked a link. Tugged to test it. "Not that she'll stop trying."

He walked around, looped the other chain. "She'll go to jail." He spoke conversationally, and she wondered if he thought she couldn't see the fatigue on his face. "But she won't change. She won't change because she can't see herself. And when she gets out, it's a pretty sure bet she'll come back this way, sooner or later, make another play for money. She's in my life, and I can deal with that."

He gave the swing a little nudge, sent it swaying. "It's a lot to ask someone else to take on."

"Yes, it is. I plan on having a long heart-to-heart with my parents. But I don't think it'll change anything. They're overly possessive, discontent people who will, most likely, continue to use me as a weapon against each other, or an excuse not to face their own marriage on its own terms. They're in my life, and I can deal with that."

She paused, tilted her head. "It's a lot to ask someone else to take on."

"Guess it is. Want to try this out?"

"I do."

They sat, swung gently as dusk thickened and the water lapped the shore. "Does it work for you?" he asked her.

"It certainly does. This is exactly where I would've hung it."

"Dru?"

"Hmmm?"

"Are you going to marry me?"

Her lips tipped up at the corners. "That's my plan."

"It's a good plan." He took her hand, lifted it to his lips. "Are you going to have children with me?"

Her eyes stung, but she kept them closed and continued to swing gently. "Yes. That's the second stage of the plan. You know how I feel about stages."

He turned her hand over, kissed her palm. "Grow old with me, here, in the house by the water."

She opened her eyes now, let the first tear spill down her cheek. "You knew that would make me cry."

"But just a little. Here." He drew a ring out of his pocket, a simple gold band with a small round ruby. "It's pretty plain, but it was Stella's—it was my grandmother's." Slipped it on her finger. "The guys thought she'd like me to have it."

"Oh-oh."

"What?"

Her fingers tightened on his as she pulled his hand to her cheek. "It may not be just a little after all. It's the most beautiful thing you could have given me."

He laid his lips on hers, drawing her in as she wrapped her arms around him. "Somebody really smart told me you've got to look ahead. You can't forget what's behind you, but you got to move forward. It starts now. For us, it starts now."

"Right now."

She laid her head on his shoulder, held his hand tight in hers. They rocked on the swing in the heavy night air while the water turned dark with night, and the fireflies began to dance.

Can't get enough of Nora Roberts?
Try the #1 *New York Times* bestselling
In Death series, by Nora Roberts
writing as J. D. Robb.

Turn the page to see where it all began . . .

NAKED IN DEATH

S HE WOKE IN the dark. Through the slats on the window shades, the first murky hint of dawn slipped, slanting shadowy bars over the bed. It was like waking in a cell.

For a moment she simply lay there, shuddering, imprisoned, while the dream faded. After ten years on the force, Eve still had dreams.

Six hours before, she'd killed a man, had watched death creep into his eyes. It wasn't the first time she'd exercised maximum force, or dreamed. She'd learned to accept the action and the consequences.

But it was the child that haunted her. The child she hadn't been in time to save. The child whose screams had echoed in the dreams with her own.

All the blood, Eve thought, scrubbing sweat from her face with her hands. Such a small little girl to have had so much blood in her. And she knew it was vital that she push it aside.

Standard departmental procedure meant that she would spend the morning in Testing. Any officer whose discharge of weapon resulted in termination of life was required to undergo emotional and psychiatric clearance before resuming duty. Eve considered the tests a mild pain in the ass.

She would beat them, as she'd beaten them before.

When she rose, the overheads went automatically to low setting, lighting her way into the bath. She winced once at her reflection. Her eyes were swollen from lack of sleep, her skin nearly as pale as the corpses she'd delegated to the ME.

Rather than dwell on it, she stepped into the shower, yawning.

"Give me one oh one degrees, full force," she said and shifted so that the shower spray hit her straight in the face.

She let it steam, lathered listlessly while she played through the events of the night before. She wasn't due in Testing until nine, and would use the next three hours to settle and let the dream fade away completely.

Small doubts and little regrets were often detected and could mean a second and more intense round with the machines and the owl-eyed technicians who ran them.

Eve didn't intend to be off the streets longer than twenty-four hours.

After pulling on a robe, she walked into the kitchen and programmed her AutoChef for coffee, black; toast, light. Through her window she could hear the heavy hum of air traffic carrying early commuters to offices, late ones home. She'd chosen the apartment years before because it was in a heavy ground and air pattern, and she liked the noise and crowds. On another yawn, she glanced out the window, followed the rattling journey of an aging airbus hauling laborers not fortunate enough to work in the city or by home 'links.

She brought the *New York Times* up on her monitor and scanned the headlines while the faux caffeine bolstered her system. The AutoChef had burned her toast again, but she ate it anyway, with a vague thought of springing for a replacement unit.

She was frowning over an article on a mass recall of droid cocker spaniels when her telelink blipped. Eve shifted to communications and watched her commanding officer flash onto the screen.

"Commander."

"Lieutenant." He gave her a brisk nod, noted the still-wet hair and sleepy eyes. "Incident at Twenty-seven West Broadway, eighteenth floor. You're primary."

Eve lifted a brow. "I'm on Testing. Subject terminated at twenty-two thirty-five."

"We have override," he said, without inflection. "Pick up your shield and weapon on the way to the incident. Code Five, Lieutenant."

"Yes, sir." His face flashed off even as she pushed back from the screen. Code Five meant she would report directly to her commander, and there would be no unsealed interdepartmental reports and no cooperation with the press.

In essence, it meant she was on her own.

BROADWAY was noisy and crowded, a party that rowdy guests never left. Street, pedestrian, and sky traffic were miserable, choking the air with bodies and vehicles.

In her old days in uniform she remembered it as a hot spot for wrecks and crushed tourists who were too busy gaping at the show to get out of the way.

Even at this hour steam was rising from the stationary and portable food stands that offered everything from rice noodles to soy dogs for the teeming crowds. She had to swerve to avoid an eager merchant on his smoking Glida-Grill, and took his flipped middle finger as a matter of course.

Eve double-parked and, skirting a man who smelled worse than his bottle of brew, stepped onto the sidewalk. She scanned the building first, fifty floors of gleaming metal that knifed into the sky from a hilt of concrete. She was propositioned twice before she reached the door.

Since this five-block area of West Broadway was affectionately termed Prostitute's Walk, she wasn't surprised. She flashed her badge for the uniform guarding the entrance.

"Lieutenant Dallas."

"Yes, sir." He skimmed his official CompuSeal over the door to keep out the curious, then led the way to the bank of elevators. "Eighteenth floor," he said when the doors swished shut behind them.

"Fill me in, Officer." Eve switched on her recorder and waited.

"I wasn't first on the scene, Lieutenant. Whatever happened upstairs is being kept upstairs. There's a badge inside waiting for you. We have a homicide, and a Code Five in number eighteen-oh-three."

"Who called it in?"

"I don't have that information."

He stayed where he was when the elevator opened. Eve stepped out and was alone in a narrow hallway. Security cameras tilted down at her, and her feet were almost soundless on the worn nap of the carpet as she approached 1803. Ignoring the hand plate, she announced herself, holding her badge up to eye level for the peep cam until the door opened.

"Dallas."

"Feeney." She smiled, pleased to see a familiar face. Ryan Feeney was an old friend and former partner who'd traded the street for a desk and a top-level position in the Electronics Detection Division. "So, they're sending computer pluckers these days."

"They wanted brass, and the best." His lips curved in his wide, rumpled face, but his eyes remained sober. He was a small, stubby man with small, stubby hands and rust-colored hair. "You look beat."

"Rough night."

"So I heard." He offered her one of the sugared nuts from the bag he habitually carried, studying her, and measuring if she was up to what was waiting in the bedroom beyond.

She was young for her rank, barely thirty, with wide brown eyes that had never had a chance to be naive. Her doe-brown hair was cropped short, for convenience rather than style, but suited her triangular face with its razor-edge cheekbones and slight dent in the chin.

She was tall, rangy, with a tendency to look thin, but Feeney knew there were solid muscles beneath the leather jacket. But Eve had more—there was also a brain, and a heart.

"This one's going to be touchy, Dallas."

"I picked that up already. Who's the victim?"

"Sharon DeBlass, granddaughter of Senator DeBlass."

Neither meant anything to her. "Politics isn't my forte, Feeney."

"The gentleman from Virginia, extreme right, old money. The granddaughter took a sharp left a few years back, moved to New York and became a licensed companion."

"She was a hooker." Dallas glanced around the apartment. It was furnished in obsessive modern—glass and thin chrome, signed holograms on the walls, recessed bar in bold red. The wide mood screen behind the bar bled with mixing and merging shapes and colors in cool pastels.

Neat as a virgin, Eve mused, and cold as a whore. "No surprise, given her choice of real estate."

"Politics makes it delicate. Victim was twenty-four, Caucasian female. She bought it in bed."

Eve only lifted a brow. "Seems poetic, since she'd been bought there. How'd she die?"

"That's the next problem. I want you to see for yourself."

As they crossed the room, each took out a slim container, sprayed their hands front and back to seal in oils and fingerprints. At the doorway, Eve sprayed the bottom of her boots to slicken them so that she would pick up no fibers, stray hairs, or skin.

Eve was already wary. Under normal circumstances there would have been two other investigators on a homicide scene, with recorders for sound and pictures. Forensics would have been waiting with their usual snarly impatience to sweep the scene.

The fact that only Feeney had been assigned with her meant that there were a lot of eggshells to be walked over.

"Security cameras in the lobby, elevator, and hallways," Eve commented.

"I've already tagged the discs." Feeney opened the bedroom door and let her enter first.

It wasn't pretty. Death rarely was a peaceful, religious experience to Eve's mind. It was the nasty end, indifferent to saint and sinner. But this was shocking, like a stage deliberately set to offend.

The bed was huge, slicked with what appeared to be genuine satin sheets the color of ripe peaches. Small, soft-focused spotlights were trained on its center where the naked woman was cupped in the gentle dip of the floating mattress.

The mattress moved with obscenely graceful undulations to the rhythm of programmed music slipping through the headboard.

She was beautiful still, a cameo face with a tumbling waterfall of flaming red hair, emerald eyes that stared glassily at the mirrored ceiling, long, milk-white limbs that called to mind visions of *Swan Lake* as the motion of the bed gently rocked them.

They weren't artistically arranged now, but spread lewdly so that the dead woman formed a final X dead-center of the bed.

There was a hole in her forehead, one in her chest, another horribly gaping between the open thighs. Blood had splattered on the glossy sheets, pooled, dripped, and stained.

There were splashes of it on the lacquered walls, like lethal paintings scrawled by an evil child.

So much blood was a rare thing, and she had seen much too much of it the night before to take the scene as calmly as she would have preferred.

She had to swallow once, hard, and force herself to block out the image of a small child.

"You got the scene on record?"

"Yep."

"Then turn that damn thing off." She let out a breath after Feeney located the controls that silenced the music. The bed flowed to stillness. "The wounds," Eve murmured, stepping closer to examine them. "Too neat for a knife. Too messy for a laser." A flash came to her—old training films, old videos, old viciousness.

"Christ, Feeney, these look like bullet wounds."

Feeney reached into his pocket and drew out a sealed bag. "Whoever did it left a souvenir." He passed the bag to Eve. "An antique like this has to go for eight, ten thousand for a legal collection, twice that on the black market."

Fascinated, Eve turned the sealed revolver over in her hand. "It's heavy," she said half to herself. "Bulky."

"Thirty-eight caliber," he told her. "First one I've seen outside of a museum. This one's a Smith and Wesson, Model Ten, blue steel." He looked at it with some affection. "Real classic piece, used to be standard police issue up until the latter part of the twentieth. They stopped making them in about twenty-two, twenty-three, when the gun ban was passed."

"You're the history buff." Which explained why he was with her. "Looks new." She sniffed through the bag, caught the scent of oil and burning. "Somebody took good care of this. Steel fired into flesh," she mused as she passed the bag back to Feeney. "Ugly way to die, and the first I've seen it in my ten years with the department."

"Second for me. About fifteen years ago, Lower East Side, party got out of hand. Guy shot five people with a twenty-two before he realized it wasn't a toy. Hell of a mess."

"Fun and games," Eve murmured. "We'll scan the collectors, see how many we can locate who own one like this. Somebody might have reported a robbery."

"Might have."

"It's more likely it came through the black market." Eve glanced back at the body. "If she's been in the business for a few years, she'd have discs, records of her clients, her trick books." She frowned. "With Code Five, I'll have to do the door-to-door myself. Not a simple sex crime," she said with a sigh. "Whoever did it set it up. The antique weapon, the wounds themselves, almost ruler-straight down the body, the lights, the pose. Who called it in, Feeney?"

"The killer." He waited until her eyes came back to him. "From right here. Called the station. See how the bedside unit's aimed at her face? That's what came in. Video, no audio."

"He's into showmanship." Eve let out a breath. "Clever bastard, arrogant, cocky. He had sex with her first. I'd bet my badge on it. Then he gets up and does it." She lifted her arm, aiming, lowering it as she counted off, "One, two, three."

"That's cold," murmured Feeney.

"He's cold. He smooths down the sheets after. See how neat they are? He arranges her, spreads her open so nobody can have any doubts as to how she made her living. He does it carefully, practically measuring, so that she's perfectly aligned. Center of the bed, arms and legs equally apart. Doesn't turn off the bed 'cause it's part of the show. He leaves the gun because he wants us to know right away he's no ordinary man. He's got an ego. He doesn't want to waste time letting the body be discovered eventually. He wants it now. That instant gratification."

"She was licensed for men and women," Feeney pointed out, but Eve shook her head.

"It's not a woman. A woman wouldn't have left her looking both beautiful and obscene. No, I don't think it's a woman. Let's see what we can find. Have you gone into her computer yet?"

"No. It's your case, Dallas. I'm only authorized to assist."

"See if you can access her client files." Eve went to the dresser and began to carefully search drawers.

Expensive taste, Eve reflected. There were several items of real silk, the kind no simulation could match. The bottle of scent on the dresser was exclusive, and smelled, after a quick sniff, like expensive sex.

The contents of the drawers were meticulously ordered, lingerie folded precisely, sweaters arranged according to color and material. The closet was the same.

Obviously the victim had a love affair with clothes and a taste for the best and took scrupulous care of what she owned.

And she'd died naked.

"Kept good records," Feeney called out. "It's all here. Her client list, appointments—including her required monthly health exam and her weekly trip to the beauty salon. She used the Trident Clinic for the first and Paradise for the second."

"Both top-of-the-line. I've got a friend who saved for a year so she could have one day for the works at Paradise. Takes all kinds."

"My wife's sister went for it for her twenty-fifth anniversary. Cost damn near as much as my kid's wedding. Hello, we've got her personal address book."

"Good. Copy all of it, will you, Feeney?" At his low whistle, she looked over her shoulder, glimpsed the small gold-edged palm computer in his hand. "What?"

"We've got a lot of high-powered names in here. Politics, entertainment, money, money, money. Interesting, our girl has Roarke's private number."

"Roarke who?"

"Just Roarke, as far as I know. Big money there. Kind of guy that touches shit and turns it into gold bricks. You've got to start reading more than the sports page, Dallas."

"Hey, I read the headlines. Did you hear about the cocker spaniel recall?"

"Roarke's always big news," Feeney said patiently. "He's got one of the finest art collections in the world. Arts and antiques," he continued, noting when Eve clicked in and turned to him. "He's a licensed gun collector. Rumor is he knows how to use them."

"I'll pay him a visit."

"You'll be lucky to get within a mile of him."

"I'm feeling lucky." Eve crossed over to the body to slip her hands under the sheets.

"The man's got powerful friends, Dallas. You can't afford to so much as whisper he's linked to this until you've got something solid."

"Feeney, you know it's a mistake to tell me that." But even as she started to smile, her fingers brushed against something between cold flesh and bloody sheets. "There's something under her." Carefully, Eve lifted the shoulder, eased her fingers over.

"Paper," she murmured. "Sealed." With her protected thumb, she wiped at a smear of blood until she could read the protected sheet.

ONE OF SIX

"It looks hand-printed," she said to Feeney and held it out. "Our boy's more than clever, more than arrogant. And he isn't finished."

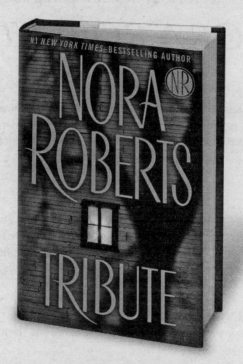

A stunning trilogy from
#1 *New York Times* bestselling author

NORA ROBERTS

DARING TO DREAM

Margo, Kate, and Laura were brought up like sisters amidst the peerless grandeur of Templeton House. But it was Margo, the housekeeper's daughter, whose dreams first took her far away, on a magnificent journey full of risk and reward.

HOLDING THE DREAM

Although Kate lacked Margo's beauty and Laura's elegance, she knew she had something they would never possess—a shrewd head for business. But now, faced with professional impropriety, Kate is forced to look deep within herself...

FINDING THE DREAM

Margo seemed to have it all—until fate took away the man she thought she loved...

M69AS0907